David Munro was born in Edinburgh and lived there until the age of twenty-seven. Employed by a major brewer, he relocated to Aberdeen and then to Glasgow. He attended University and College to attain Chartered Professional status in the Arts. His experience of different cultures and environments, plus being educated in an artistic discipline, lends itself well to his creative literature.

# THE TIME JIGSAW

This book is dedicated to
my mother and father.

David Munro

# The Time Jigsaw

AUSTIN MACAULEY
PUBLISHERS LTD.

A CIP catalogue record for this title is available from the British Library.

ISBN 978 184963 374 1

www.austinmacauley.com

First Published (2013)
Austin Macauley Publishers Ltd.
25 Canada Square
Canary Wharf
London
E14 5LB

Printed and Bound in Great Britain

## Acknowledgments

To a particular group of former colleagues; thanks for the memories.

# Chapter 1

*The Mystery Lady*

I came to Nice with a renewed optimism. After a number of enjoyable years in Aberdeen, the clutches of ambition and restlessness took hold. They urged me to move further south and sample a warmer foreign environment. Those severe winters I endured in my West End granite tenement flat and hazardous journeys on snow-ridden roads ensured my eventual departure. The decade drew to a close.

Since I learned about French history and culture in my youth, there had been an ambition to experience this particular European country. I chose Nice to become my ultimate destination. Initial investigation had revealed this as a popular city within the southern region of France. Nice had built up a reputation for commerce, tourism, excellent cuisine and a sociable climate. The city consisted of a population larger than Aberdeen but smaller than Edinburgh, whom it twinned with in 1958. Like Edinburgh, Nice emerged as a place to attract many visitors. Only Paris had a busier airport within France. The luxurious sandy beach, Art Deco shop façades, museums and art galleries together with an assortment of trading markets cemented the appeal. Nice also consisted of an old and new identity which enhanced its character. The ancient part had narrow streets and was part pedestrianised to supplement the shopping experience. Being located within close proximity to the Alps, accentuated the tourist potential and desirability.

Upon my arrival in late July, I noticed similarities with Aberdeen. Both cities had a long and wide main street of comparable size. Nice also possessed a prominent established beach and seaside promenade located within a short distance from the city centre. A fishing port and reputable University completed the uncanny resemblance. However, at a certain time of the year my previous residence did not possess a warm and dry climate.

The accommodation I obtained comprised of a first floor balcony in a three-apartment property. It had a characteristic ceiling cornice in each of the trim rooms. The lounge had a pale blue colour scheme, whereas the rest of the rooms consisted of plain white. All of the windows throughout the property had a set of shutters – necessary for stifling the heat from the glorious sunshine. Located a short distance from central Nice, the apartment appeared ideal for commuting. An initial task would be to purchase some items of furniture to enhance my basic property.

When in the city centre, a building caught my eye; a blue and yellow façade of a restaurant. The establishment had an enticing aroma of food which captivated my taste buds, and it was an easy decision to enter and sample the cuisine. Many customers had also been captivated, but I spotted an empty table next to a window. The light bright interior and wooden furniture contrasted well. A waiter soon appeared, welcomed me and took my order. Whilst at my table, I could not help noticing a lady who made discreet glances in my direction. The waiter soon arrived with my order. The same lady called him over, paid her bill and departed. During my meal, I sat and observed people outside in summer clothes pass me by. They all wore genuine smiles. I finished my delicious steak and paid the waiter.

"Do you have regular customers?"

"Yes we do, monsieur. The lady who sat across from you dines here every Monday and Thursday evening. Most of our regulars visit at the weekend."

I walked back to my apartment through the narrow sun-kissed streets of the old town. I speculated on whether the same lady would be at the restaurant on Thursday. She had looked my way several times. Maybe she recognised me from somewhere, or could it be due to my unusually pale skin? I *did* look like a stranger who had just arrived in the city. It was worth seeing what would transpire, and perhaps by then I may have purchased certain items of furniture.

I had been fortunate to secure a speedy position of employment. My previous business expertise and academic qualifications had proved beneficial in order to join an advertising firm. To experience a new environment and communicate in a different language could be traumatic! However, my knowledge of French carried me through with only minor mishaps. I recollected my arrival in Aberdeen from Edinburgh – it also took a while to master the native dialogue.

The twenty members of staff comprised of men and women within the twenty-five to forty-five age group. This particular agency had their premises on the second floor of a modern office block in central Nice. They had a client base whose businesses focused on the local and regional areas. My colleagues and I would liaise with them to enhance their profile, products and services in order to obtain higher sales. Aberdeen and Nice portrayed different cultures but similar in terms of business philosophy. 'For a business to succeed, it must have a stipulated turnover of units and profit or it will fail. Customer awareness through marketing techniques remains essential for a business to compete and survive.' Astute people!

A busy day ensued on this particular Thursday. The office personnel started to depart for home at six o'clock. I did not manage to read my edition of the local *Nice Matin* newspaper. After seven o'clock, I departed the building and made the short journey to my 'adopted' restaurant. When I entered, only two customers occupied the establishment. Work colleagues had told me that prior to eight o'clock, local people did not frequent restaurants. I sat at my usual window table and the waiter took my order. By thirty minutes past eight, a few more people had arrived; a handful of middle-aged gentlemen dressed in smart, light-coloured suits. All of them had a clean-shaven appearance. As time progressed and wine flowed, their infectious laughter got louder. I finished my meal and paid the bill.

"It is good to see you again, monsieur," said the waiter.

"See you later." No lady with a discreet 'look' this evening!

"Take care, monsieur."

I took a walk to savour the atmosphere of the city's old town district. I proceeded to stumble across an uncharacteristic type of French bar. Tables and chairs did not feature outside the establishment. All of the restaurants, bars and cafés I had seen adhered to a certain protocol. I entered and then discovered what resembled a 1970s British cocktail bar; it consisted of black leather upholstery, matching bar stools, chrome aplenty and mirrored walls. The bright silver floor sparkled and contrasted well with my shiny black shoes. I sat on one of the stools and gazed at the décor. The ceiling had small spotlights, which dazzled my eyes. It reminded me of a bygone age and did they also have a list of promiscuous cocktail drinks? I looked around the bar but no such list existed. In fact, the same could be said for bar staff, customers and music! In the next instant, 'Bad Girls' by Donna Summer burst through the speakers. Three slender and stylish young ladies appeared behind the bar. They wore silver tops and black skirts. Two of them had short blonde hair, whilst the tallest of the three had long dark hair down to her waist.

She stepped forward. "What would you like to drink, monsieur?"

"A bottle of lager please."

"What type of lager? As you can see, we have an assortment!"

"That one with the gold label." I pointed to it.

"This one?" She pointed to another bottle.

"No, the bottle next to it."

As a certain Scottish lager did not appear in stock, I settled for a local French beer. The contents got poured into a glass and I took a drink. It had a bitter taste, but quenched my thirst. Then I heard music from artists such as David Bowie, T-Rex and Roxy Music. Due to the warm, dry evening I ordered another beer. It soon got consumed and I paid the bar lady.

She took the money and smiled. "Thank you, monsieur, see you later."

"Yes, you shall."

As I left the uncharacteristic establishment, 'One of Those Nights' by The Eagles started to play. Interesting!

I tried to head in the direction of my apartment but could not remember the exact route. Most of the narrow streets all looked similar. A frustrated and misguided thirty minutes followed. I wandered into another street and found myself confronted by three strangers. With their mean expressions and untidy appearance, to say I sensed danger would be accurate. They looked as hard as nails!

The tallest one moved towards me. "Do you have any money on you?"

"No, why? Do you have some?" *Give me a break!*

"You are English?" said a second man.

"No, I come from Scotland. What nationality are you?"

He looked at the other two men.

"Hand over what money you have," said the third man.

"Sorry, no money, I'm skint!" I pulled out my trouser pockets. I took off one shoe and offered it to him.

He looked at the other two. "Allez."

I put my shoe back on. Just as well I keep cash in my back pocket!

I got back to my apartment with an enforced belief that humour and a steady nerve can deflate a tricky situation. One of those nights indeed!


Nice had been different in terms of culture and climate. However some events remain the same, even in France! The month of August heralded the start of a new football season. I had to participate in one of my main interests. A short distance from Nice lay the Principality of Monaco. Their team, AS Monaco, had received rave previews from the media ahead of the new season. I therefore elected to attend their initial home fixture with Montpellier at the Louis II stadium.

I boarded a regular train to Monaco and arrived at the trim double platform station twenty-five minutes later. I went down the hilly streets of the Principality to their football stadium. It epitomised wealth and sophistication through rich exterior architectural design, a comfortable panoramic viewpoint seating, plush restaurants and computerised ticketing facilities to eliminate entry queues. Yes, a football ground in 1989. Those primitive conditions I have endured over the years!

I sat and watched Monaco claim a narrow victory in a slow, methodical and uneventful game. Their star striker squandered four blatant chances to score. His face at the final whistle matched his team's red football strip! Still, I heard no angry expletives aimed at the player from this affluent 'audience' of supporters. I reminisced on the fierce and fiery passionate competitive duels filled with controversy witnessed in Scotland. Perhaps positives about Scottish football exist, but we fail to appreciate them!

I reached the Monaco-Monte Carlo railway station in time for the last connection to Nice. At the station, I noticed someone look my way on the same platform. A similarity existed to a certain lady from the restaurant which I had visited on a recent occasion. The train arrived and I observed she boarded the same carriage. Only a few spare seats remained. I managed to get one and found myself in close proximity to this lady. For the twenty-five minute journey, I speculated on why she would be in the area. I came to the conclusion she had been to meet a friend or visit a relative. I did not get the impression she had gone to the football game – not her style! She would have found a more refined form of amusement.

As the train entered Nice, we both stood up. She looked at me in a tantalising manner. When we got off, I noticed an object fall out her jacket pocket. I picked it up – a handkerchief! I tried to catch up with her but she got into a taxi, which sped away.

Several weeks had gone by when I sat in my regular eating establishment on a sunny September evening. With a cordial atmosphere, plus delicious food, I tended to look on this place as essential to my well-being.

A lady walked past my customary window table and sat a short distance away. My heart skipped a beat. I recognised the blonde shoulder length hair, slim build and smart stylish appearance as that of the person who boarded the train at Monaco-Monte Carlo railway station. She did not order a meal but settled for a beverage. After I finished my delightful main course, the waiter came over and removed my empty plate. I contemplated whether to have dessert or pay the bill and leave. I did not do either, as the lady came across to my table.

"I would like to introduce myself. My name is Michelle Duvallier."

I stood up. "I am James Carsell-Brown. Please have a seat." *What a pleasant surprise!*

She sat down. "Do you come from England?"

"I speak English, but Scotland is where I come from," I smiled.

"Oh, forgive me!"

"There is no need to apologise. Most people presume I am English."

"You look familiar."

"I do?" *That was a coincidence!*

"Have we met on a previous occasion?"

"I don't believe so. I would have remembered if our paths had crossed. I have only just arrived in France."

Her use of the English language impressed me. I started to speculate on her background; perhaps she was a linguist by profession.

"If we had met, then it would have been in Scotland. I have spent most of my life there."

"What about vacations? Have you ever visited any other country apart from France?"

"I have a fondness for Scotland – no other place can compare."

"*Formidable*, how patriotic!"

"At times the weather can be unpredictable and the winters as cold as ice!"

She had a nice smile.

"Why did you come to Nice?"

"To work and enjoy a warmer, drier climate."

She liked to smile.

A couple of hours soon passed. Daylight started to diminish, and customers started to depart the restaurant.

She looked at her watch. "Oh my goodness, is that the time? I have to go – I start work at eight!"

"Me also, allez!"

We finished our drinks, paid the bill and then left. The waiter smiled and bid us goodnight. After a walk through the vibrant city centre, we arrived at her apartment block. We arranged to meet on Friday evening at the local Ramaz Bistro.

Michelle Duvallier had assured me I would be impressed with the Ramaz. How could I refuse? We settled on a time around eight – also the number of the day in September.

I arrived ten minutes early, and sat down at a table within view of the entrance. A waiter came forward. I ordered a local beer to quench my thirst on this warm evening. Whilst waiting for him to return, I surveyed the establishment. Situated in a street near the city centre, it had a mixed clientele of stylish couples and singles. A variety of music could be heard and played at a comfortable noise level. I looked at my watch and it showed fifteen minutes past eight. Why couldn't ladies be on time? At that moment, she materialised

"My apologies for being late. I hope you have not been here too long?"

"I have just this minute got here."

The waiter appeared with my drink and I ordered one for her. He returned a short time later with a glass of her favoured white wine. In my conversation with Michelle Duvallier, I got the impression she had been well educated. Knowledgeable, communicative and polite. I also observed when I talked about Scotland, she became attentive. My curious nature had surfaced. I asked if she had any connection with Scotland.

"There had been talk of a link to our family but no person could be traced."

I noticed a particular act of behaviour that intrigued me. When she discussed or got asked about a sensitive matter, she would pull on her hair. Also when a man entered the bistro, she would become distracted. When a sturdy grim-faced male entered, the clock on the wall showed just after eleven. He pulled a stool forward and sat at the bar. As she glanced his way, an agitated and nervous expression appeared on her face.

"Do you know that person?"

"Can we go now? I will explain later."

I paid the waiter for the drinks and we departed. The man at the bar sat motionless with a glass in his hand.

As we made our way back to her apartment, she had a look of relief. When inside, she still had not mentioned the stranger.

"Have a seat."

"Thanks." I had to ask, "Have you been in any kind of trouble?"

"No. I have not committed any crime but I do have an ex-partner who has tried to find me. We split up a few months ago."

"When that man appeared, why did you become nervous?"

"He is an acquaintance of my partner."

"How do you feel now?"

She moved closer. "I will be fine, but could you stay a while longer?"

"Yes, of course."


The following morning, I returned to my apartment block around ten o'clock. I entered the upstairs landing and noticed the door to my accommodation ajar. With apprehension, I pushed the door wide open and entered. My bedroom and study appeared the main focus of the intruder. All the drawers had been opened and their contents emptied onto the floor. I checked if any items had been taken. Everything seemed intact. Valuables and money stored in a bedroom cabinet had not been taken. Why the intrusion? I examined my entrance door. No damage had been sustained. The intruder must have been experienced in the art of unauthorised entry! I consulted people who resided in my block, but nobody could recollect anything suspicious.

Being a recent arrival in a foreign country, and with no items stolen, I did not inform the authorities of the incident.

Could Michelle Duvallier's anxiety on the previous evening and my apartment being broken into be linked? It crossed my mind. I called her to make sure she had not encountered any trouble. Her phone kept on ringing. Perhaps she had gone out for a stroll or to do some shopping. Later I called again, but still no answer. I now became anxious. I went to her apartment block and pressed the intercom buzzer. No response. I waited for a few minutes then tried again. I hung around for a short while, hoping she would appear. I concluded to try again the following morning.

At a slow pace, the next day arrived. I called her number but still no answer. In the evening, I went to the bistro which we had frequented two days earlier. The waiter who served us looked my way. He acknowledged me in a polite manner, and I ordered a coffee. When he returned, I asked if the lady with me last Friday evening had been back.

"No monsieur, not on my shift. I will check with my colleague."

"Merci bien." I sipped my coffee.

"Sorry monsieur. Nobody has seen her."

I went back to my apartment and contemplated what to do next.

On Monday, I tried to concentrate on my work. Cerice, the perceptive and persistent department administrator, came over to my desk.

"Did you have an enjoyable weekend, James?"

"Yes."

"Did you go anywhere special?"

"Yes."

"Meet any nice ladies?"

I nodded.

It would not have been difficult for her to realise I had something on my mind! Tuesday and Wednesday did not bring any relief. Therefore, after three endless days, I called Michelle from my office, but still no answer. When work finished I went to her apartment block. I pressed the intercom button – no response. I went home to ponder my next move. I concluded to alert the authorities of a person I believe may be in danger.

I walked to the city's Police Headquarters, entered the tall building and observed a police officer behind the reception desk. He sat with his head buried in a document. As I walked towards him my footsteps echoed on the marble surface.

He raised his head. "Oui, monsieur?"

I leaned over the desk. "I would like to report a possible missing person."

"Male or female?"

"Female – a young woman."

The officer reached for a blank sheet of paper and pen. "Her name?"

"Michelle Duvallier." He was a quick writer.

"Can you describe her?"

"About one and three quarter metres tall, late twenties, slim and blonde hair."

"Short or long hair?"

"Shoulder length."

"How long has she been missing?"

"Since last Saturday." Apart from her name and a description, she remained a mystery. I had become so engrossed in what she wanted to know about me that we did not discuss her.

"We will investigate and contact you if any developments arise. Please fill in this form." He handed it to me.

I wrote down my contact details.

He took the form and examined it. "Thank you monsieur, we will be in touch."


Six days later, two uniformed police officers came to my apartment at seven in the evening. They had a manner of officialdom about them.

An officer stated, "Our visit relates to the disappearance of Michelle Duvallier "

*Good, they had found her.*

"A young woman's body has been found. It has been washed ashore at the nearby beach. It is presumed she has drowned."

"When did this happen?"

*Not Michelle.*

"We understand the body had been in the water for about eight to ten days. We would like you to accompany us to Police Headquarters."

"Am I a suspect?"

"No, monsieur – it is routine. A senior officer wants to speak with you about the case. Also, bring your passport."

"Give me a few minutes."

I searched for my passport. Trust me to get involved in a fatal death inquiry! *Ah, here was the passport.*

They took me to Police HQ and then into a room with only a table and four chairs. A plain-clothes officer entered the room, accompanied by another uniformed office. They sat opposite to me across the table.

"I am Sergeant Perez," said the non-uniformed police officer. "Please tell me how you met Michelle Duvallier."

I spoke of seeing her for the first time in a local restaurant, and then at the Monaco-Monte Carlo railway station, when she had later approached me in the same restaurant and the occasion on which we had last met. I also recalled that she had become nervous at the appearance of a man in the bistro.

"Can you describe him?"

"Shaven head, around two metres tall, well-built and about fifty years of age."

"Did he have any distinctive features?"

"No, not that I can remember. I should add that my apartment got broken into on the same evening."

"At what time did this happened?"

"After I left my apartment and until I returned home. Between seven thirty in the evening and ten o'clock the next morning."

"Why did you not report the intrusion?"

"No items had been stolen and no damage occurred."

"D'accord monsieur. You can go. Please leave your passport."

"My passport?"

"Just a routine practice, monsieur. Someone shall be in touch."

The uniformed officer took me to the exit door of the building and thanked me for my time. I went to a nearby café for a strong cup of coffee.

When I got back to my apartment, I made up my mind to contact Cerice the next day and explain I needed to take a few days leave. She would no doubt ask why but after what had happened, I wanted to gather my thoughts. I had been shocked but also experienced a tinge of sadness. I would not see this lady again. Our last encounter had been an enjoyable one.

I received a call from Sergeant Perez. He wished to see me at my earliest convenience.

I left my apartment and arrived at Police HQ within the hour. I met with Sergeant Perez and he stated I had to attend the local morgue. I was being taken to identify the body of Michelle Duvallier.

"Why me? Is there no one else who can make the identification?"

"We cannot trace any family or friends."

On my way to the morgue, my stress level started to increase. I had only just met this lady yet had to identify her dead body – it beggared belief!

I got taken inside the grey building and into a room. On a table lay a body covered by a white sheet.

"Ready?" A morgue representative in a white coat looked at me and nodded. He then pulled back the sheet to reveal a woman's head and neck.

My hand gripped a corner of the table.

"Are you okay?" said Sergeant Perez.

"Yes. I'll be fine." I turned to him. "Now you have a dilemma."

"Pardon, monsieur?"

"This isn't the lady I met."

"Are you sure?"

"Positive! What led you to believe this body is Michelle Duvallier?"

"Personal documents in her possession. These led us to believe the deceased could only be Michelle Duvallier."

Whom had I met on that particular Friday evening?

The doctor replaced the sheet.

We left the morgue, and Sergeant Perez gave me a lift back to the centre of Nice. This had now become a mystery in more ways than one.

"Sergeant, has the man whose description I gave been traced?"

"Not yet, monsieur, but our enquiries are on-going."

"Did you check the address of the property I visited?"

"We investigated the location, but the apartment had been vacated. However, we have taken hair samples from a rug, plus fingerprints. They will be analysed for clues to the occupant."

After yet another eventful day, I went back to my apartment for some sanctuary. Who had I met, and how or why had she vanished? Could the person who intimidated her be connected to the disappearance? All questions but no answers. As I hung up my jacket, the phone rang.

I picked up the receiver. "Yes?"

"Monsieur Carsell-Brown?"

"It is he."

"My name is Detective Laurant. My call concerns the sample analysis carried out."

"Oh, yes."

"The hair and fingerprints did not match those of the dead woman."

"Whom did they belong to?" I asked. Indeed a mystery!

"We have still to identify the body and possible whereabouts of a certain Madame Duvallier."

"What about the apartment?"

"The apartment had been vacant for about two weeks. Nobody in the building noticed anything unusual. I will advise you of any developments, monsieur."

"Thank you, Detective." I replaced the receiver into the cradle.

I now enthused about my return to work. My usual routine would be a welcome distraction from recent events.

Three days passed, and when I got home from a frustrated Monday, a voicemail message awaited my attention. I listened to it but the background interference made it difficult to comprehend. The person who spoke sounded familiar. I replayed the message again and again. There was a nervousness apparent in her voice.

"James, I have to speak with you! I will explain everything."

She gave directions for a bar called Dutrecs, located on the outskirts of Nice. I had to be there at eight o'clock.

As the bar stood just on the outskirts of Nice, I took a taxi. The steep road through the countryside also endured an assortment of sharp bends. To the right lay the sea, and on the opposite side, large villas were scattered across the landscape. I found this view picturesque and exhilarating.

"You like the view, monsieur?" said the taxi driver.

"I suppose the residents must have paid dearly for it."

He laughed. "You bet!"

"How much further?"

"Just round the next bend, monsieur. Here we are."

"Splendid." I paid the fare.

He gave me a business card. I looked at it.

"Give me a call when you want a lift back. I can be here in less than fifteen minutes."

I put the card in my shirt pocket. "Will do."

He drove off. Located off the main road, the solitary building looked desolate and run-down. It had no doubt been put there to cater for passers-by on the main road. Their impression and mine must be compatible. Surrounded by the countryside, I could see the justification why Michelle would want to meet here – seclusion!

When I entered the bar, I observed only a barman and a single customer. I approached the counter and ordered a beer. I sat down close to a window and gazed around the bar. The nicotine-stained ceiling, scraped tables and a damaged floor did not endear me to this place. I then looked at my watch – twelve minutes past the stipulated time. I recalled poor timekeeping for our previous arrangement. Here we went again – so much for an urgent meeting!

Two men entered and stood at the bar. They looked as tough as old boots. A few moments later, I went to the washroom. Similar to the bar, it had seen better days. The dingy grey walls suffered from severe dampness and the hand basin had a distinctive crack. The smell of the room ensured a quick departure. I dried my hands on the last paper towel and turned towards the exit door.

"Hands in the air!" A man pointed a gun at my stomach.

"What's this all about?" I raised my hands.

"Outside! Do as I say and you won't be killed."

"I'm meeting someone."

"You'll meet your maker if you don't move!"

A second man approached and searched me. "Get into the car!"

I sat in the back seat of the black saloon. "Where are you taking me?"

I received no reply. *Oh well, don't speak then.*

We followed the main road and turned off to a large villa. It had a cream exterior, complete with swimming pool. A car had already parked outside the villa. Our car pulled up alongside.

The driver got out and opened the rear door. "Out of the car."

His companion led me into a furnished room. "Wait here." He walked out and closed the door.

A few minutes later, a distinguished middle-aged man entered the room. Then another man followed. He looked familiar.

"Allow me to introduce myself. My name is Mr Diaz and this is Mr Guerrin. Both of you attended the Ramaz one Friday evening not so long ago."

"I have an appointment with a business colleague. Why have you brought me here?"

"The reason why we have brought you here? You know only too well. Mr Guerrin and I are impatient men. Do not pretend you don't know."

"The taxi driver who drove me to Dutrecs will return to collect me at a certain time. I owe him a fare. He expects me to turn up."

Guerrin held up my taxi card. "We contacted the firm to say you will make an alternative way home."

I touched my shirt pocket – no card. When I had been searched, they must have taken it.

Diaz walked to a wall cabinet and opened the small wooden doors. "As you come from Scotland, perhaps you would like a whisky?"

"How do you know I come from Scotland?" My accent is not distinctive.

"Documents in your room," said Guerrin.

That explains the break-in. Diaz poured a full glass.

"I can't drink that!"

"Oh, but I insist!"

The two men who brought me came into the room and stood on each side, their grim expressions still in place.

"This is no way to treat a guest, Diaz."

No reaction.

"I will now leave you in the capable hands of Mr Guerrin and these gentlemen. As we will not meet again, I bid you farewell, Mr Carsell-Brown." He left the room and shut the door.

Guerrin moved towards me. "We can do this the easy way or the hard way. Take a seat."

I sat down. He leaned over.

"Do you and Michelle Duvallier work for the same outfit?"

"Outfit! What do you mean? We are friends, not colleagues."

"Cut the pretence! What did she tell you?"

"I don't understand what you're talking about."

"Oh, yes, you do."

"You've got the wrong person, Guerrin." I sensed the atmosphere becoming tenser.

"Drink this – it will loosen you up."

He shoved the full glass of whisky into my hand. It had a vile smell.

"Drink it now – or else!" Guerrin glared down at me.

They had taken me to an outhouse and dumped me in a corner. My amateur dramatic skills came in handy. Overplaying a drunken state of behaviour must have fooled them. I checked the door, and found it had not been locked. I opened it with care and looked around the vicinity. I could not detect anyone in sight. I exited the outhouse and searched for a way to escape. I observed the two saloon cars parked outside. As I got closer, one car still had a key in the ignition. I crept alongside, opened the driver's door of the blue Peugeot and eased into the seat. I took a deep breath and turned the ignition. I drove off and could see Guerrin in the mirror run out of the house. *Explain that to your boss!* I steered onto the main road towards Nice.

As the car went down the steep road, it soon gathered speed. I approached a sharp bend and put my foot on the brake – it made no difference! The car gained momentum. I tried to slow down by applying the handbrake – this also did not work! The car swayed out of control. Another bend approached. I kept close to the centre of the road, but just missed an oncoming car. Tyres screeched and I attempted to keep the car straight. I looked for a fence to collide with and slow down the car. On my left was the coastline. I spotted a protective barrier at the next bend and drove towards it. The car smashed through the barrier and I found myself hurtling towards the sea. I wound down the window. The car plunged into the water. As it sank, I got out through the open window. I swam to the shore and staggered to the road. Water dripped from my clothes. Thank goodness the sea was calm and warm. I stopped a car and explained that there had been an accident. The gracious driver gave me a blanket from the boot of his car. I wrapped it around myself and the motorist went for police assistance. They appeared on the scene within the hour. After the ordeal, I did my best to act sober but the experience had helped to revive me. I explained to the officers on the scene what had happened. They took me to Nice Police HQ where an overnight stay beckoned. Given my current predicament, I just longed for some dry clothes and a bed in which to rest.

By morning, I had a hangover placed high in my all-time top ten. Not since a Licensed Trade 'reunion' at the Caledonian Hotel in Stornoway had I drank as much and lived to tell the tale! After a period of painful recovery and discomfort, the time approached for an appointment with a Detective Laurant. An officer took me from a dull, compact cell to a bright spacious office. He told me to take a seat, walked out and closed the door. The room had a large desk complete with a black leather chair, bookcase and two filing cabinets. I got up and looked out the window. The park with many trees and landscaped gardens made for a wonderful view. A choir of birds could be heard in harmony. The door opened and in strolled a man of average height and a dark, receding hairline. He was in his mid-forties and clearly enjoyed his food.

"Do you like the view, Monsieur Carsell-Brown?"

"Yes, terrific. The leaves will soon fall off the trees."

He held out his hand. "I am Detective Claude Laurant."

I shook his hand.

He sat down behind his desk. "How do you feel, given your exploits of yesterday?"

"Terrible!" I sat down. My dejected profile told him. "Have you any more painkillers?"

"Sorry, monsieur." He gave me a wry smile. "Perhaps some water with your whisky in future?"

He proceeded to ask questions about my recent 'adventure', and quizzed me about a certain Mr Diaz and his gang.

"Diaz?"

"I am surprised he had you brought to the house and let you leave!"

"I wasn't supposed to survive my departure."

"Guerrin is the person who intimidated Madame Duvallier when you last met her?"

"Yes, him – no question about it."

I referred to the call received from a lady to meet at Dutrecs, outside the city. The place where my abduction occurred.

"Who called you?"

"The voice sounded similar to Michelle Duvallier's. I did not get the chance to ask any questions."

"Why not?"

"The message had been left on my answering machine."

"Pity." He sat back on his chair. "This morning, two of my officers visited the house you described, but it was unoccupied."

"Diaz gave me the impression he had to be somewhere soon – perhaps to leave the country."

"My officers will do all they can to find Diaz and his gang. I suggest you go home and get some rest."

"They may come back for me to finish the job!"

"They will presume you could not have survived your ordeal." He gave me a card. "Contact me if you have any more concerns."

"Detective, have you discovered the true identity of the dead woman?"

"Not yet. We will also attempt to trace Madame Duvallier." He got up out of his chair and smiled. "Do not bother to return the set of clothes we gave you."

"Thanks."

"I'll see you out, monsieur. One of our officers will give you a lift home."

*Thank goodness, I was shattered!*

"Au revoir, monsieur." He shook my hand.

I arrived home, a relieved but fatigued individual. I went straight for the medicine cabinet. Where were those aspirins? *Ah, I got them.* I then headed for the bedroom and my own nice, comfortable, cosy bed.

I awoke a short time later and got up to have a drink of water. After the exertions of yesterday, my appetite had now started to return. I hadn't even bothered to check my phone messages. I picked up the handset – a solitary message had been left. Given my previous message, I hesitated but then played it. The voice belonged to Cerice. She advised me about a work-related problem, which concerned a client. I sighed. Being alert to the client could wait – I would deal with the problem later.

At the office on Friday, Detective Laurant called. He informed me they had identified the dead woman as none other than a Monique Duvallier.

"Are they related?"

"We believe they are, monsieur."

"Has there been any news about Michelle Duvallier?"

"We have made progress and questions shall shortly be answered! Can you call into Police HQ tonight – say around seven?"

"Sure."

After work I took the familiar route to meet with Detective Laurant. This situation had not just taken over my life but almost ended it! When I arrived at reception, an officer took me along the corridor to a private room. As I entered, Detective Laurant stood behind a table and gave one of his characteristic smiles.

"Now we have some answers, Monsieur Carsell-Brown, please have a seat." He sat down.

*What an uncomfortable chair.* I fidgeted.

"Are you okay?"

"Fine."

He explained that Monique Duvallier was the younger sister of Michelle Duvallier. She lived in Montpellier and had come to visit her sister in Nice. A short time ago, Michelle Duvallier had arranged to meet her sister in Monaco but Monique failed to appear.

"Michelle Duvallier looked tense that evening."

"The next day, Monique contacted her sister and they made a new arrangement. She planned to arrive at Michelle's apartment in Nice at a later date. When you visited the Ramaz bistro and Guerrin walked in, she panicked."

"Why?"

"All shall be revealed, monsieur."

He told me that not long after I had departed from her apartment, she also left but failed to notify her sister. Monique intended to arrive in the afternoon. She had passkeys and let herself into the apartment. She assumed that Michelle had gone shopping and waited for her to return. After several hours, we presume Monique visited a nearby establishment and had something to eat.

"What is it called?"

"Nicos. The location is close to the beach. We believe she left there and went for a walk along the promenade."

"What happened next?" The light-hearted Detective's voice changed from being informative to one of sorrow.

"Two of Guerrin's accomplices spied on the apartment building. When they spotted Monique depart, they assumed it must be Michelle. They have a similar appearance. The two men would then have followed Monique and confronted her at an opportune place."

"Would she not have tried to convince them they had the wrong person?"

"Monique had letters in her possession addressed to her sister. If they had met earlier, she would have given them to Michelle. When the two men searched her bag and found the letters, Monique Duvallier's fate was sealed. They killed her and disposed of the body."

"Did anyone witness the incident?"

"The attack would have taken place at the secluded part of the beach.

"Thugs!"

"She did not suffer. Her death resulted in a single fatal bullet. The attack had been carried out in a discreet and professional manner."

"Professionals indeed!" I wanted to know what sort of plot I had got involved in and why the need to take a life. This could not be about some break-up with an ex-partner!

"Someone wants to see you, monsieur." He went to the door and opened it.

Michelle Duvallier walked into the room. I got to my feet.

"James, my apologies. I should not have got you involved. It must have been traumatic for you."

A bit! But she had lost her sister in a horrific act of violence.

Detective Laurant said, "As you no doubt have much to discuss, please excuse me." He closed the door.

We both sat down. I wanted to know more about her sister. Michelle told me of their inseparable childhood and a happy life with parents who adored them. When they were young teenage girls, they had lost both of their parents in a car accident. This had a traumatic effect. I could relate to those circumstances.

"Who took care of you?"

"Our aunt – my father's sister. A warm, considerate person who tended to spoil us! She died of a severe illness two years ago. This left Monique as my sole family member."

I could see the pain in her expression, and how she had suffered another family bereavement.

She revealed information about the letters Monique had in her possession. An ex-boyfriend had sent them – someone from her time at university.

"Why send the letters to Monique's address?"

"Before I moved to Nice, Monique and I shared her apartment in Montpellier. I should have stayed."

"It is not your fault this tragedy happened."

I had a lot of questions which started to circulate around my head. The evening at the Ramaz, the frantic phone call, and why would anyone try to kill her? She must have read my mind.

"James, you must have more questions to ask and I will attempt to answer them."

"A voicemail message had been left for me, but I could not make out the caller."

"I left the message. I made the call from a busy bar. I just wanted to explain everything."

"Tell me about Monique."

"She loved sport and often attended games which involved her favourite team, hence the reason why we agreed to meet in Monaco that evening. When she did not appear, I became concerned and was unable to contact her."

Michelle started to pull her hair in that same gentle motion. "What about the person known as Guerrin?"

"That will shortly be explained to you."

Detective Laurant knocked and then re-entered the room with an authoritative gentleman. He was in his late fifties, over two metres in height, bald and regimental. He struck me as a type not to compromise – his way or else!

"Monsieur Carsell-Brown, may I present Colonel Jacques Fontaine of the French Secret Service."

I stood up. "Pleased to meet you, Colonel." He had a strong forceful handshake.

"You must be a lucky person, Monsieur Carsell-Brown. You should work for us!"

"Only if the price is right."

The Colonel laughed. "Please, sit down."

He admitted that Diaz had become a target for constant surveillance. He had links to a country that wanted to obtain knowledge about a new French military device. It embraced well-advanced technology and a blueprint of the design would command a high price. The severity of the situation had resulted in Monique Duvallier's death.

I had a question on my mind. "When I turned up to meet Michelle, two of Diaz's men appeared at the agreed time and location. How did they know?"

"The intruders who entered your apartment would have then monitored your movements. Whenever you left the apartment, someone would follow close by." The Colonel looked at Michelle. "This lady remains one of our top operatives in the region. She had infiltrated Diaz's organisation and recovered the documents he stole from the government. However, Diaz did not have them long enough to do any damage." The Colonel put his hand on my shoulder. "We have devised a plan to capture Diaz, Guerrin and their accomplices, but we need your assistance monsieur."

"I will assist in any way possible." My lust for adventure made me an ideal participant!

Colonel Fontaine twirled his grey moustache. "I shall be in touch."

Detective Laurant opened the door, and the Colonel walked out.

"I will be in touch, monsieur." He closed the door behind him.

Michelle moved her chair closer. "After you left that Saturday, I received a call from Colonel Fontaine to vacate my apartment. He believed my cover had been jeopardised."

"Why did you get involved with espionage?"

She smiled. "As with you, James, I also enjoy a sense of adventure!"

# Chapter 2

*Retribution*

On Monday, I attended to my 'day job', and chatty Cerice enquired if Nice had lived up to my expectations.

"Most definitely, and more!"

"Oh!" She raised her head for a moment then continued with her paperwork.

I reflected on recent events which had infringed on my short spell in the Cote d'Azur. I had almost been killed whilst I attempted to drive a car with severed brakes down a notorious road. The brutal murder of innocent Monique Duvallier and an imminent participation in a plot to capture Zoren Diaz. If I did assist Colonel Jacques Fontaine, then that period in my life would become not just an adventure, but a deadly liaison! However, should any contribution I made help capture Diaz, then it would also serve justice to avenge a cruel death.

When work ended for the day, I did not go home, but took a stroll down to the older part of the city. The weather remained pleasant and I needed the exercise. Most of the shops remained open in the evening, and I grabbed the opportunity for some retail therapy.

In the market I came across a place which would reveal your future. I stood and read a description notice of the various forms of service provided. A frilly white sheet covered the entrance. Then a petite lady appeared from within. She had long jet-black hair, a pale complexion and wore an ankle-length purple dress with jewellery to match.

"Can I be of assistance, monsieur?"

"Can you read my palm?"

"Yes. This way if you please." She led me into a small dark room.

It consisted of a white table and two white chairs. An array of lighted candles gave it a mystical ambience. I could smell a jasmine fragrance.

"Please sit down." She pointed to a seat.

"Thanks."

She sat opposite. "You do not come from here. You are a foreigner?"

"That is correct."

"What country do you come from?"

"Scotland."

She took my hand and held it gently, and then she studied my palm and smiled.

*Please only give me good news!*

"You will go on a journey. This will be beneficial not just for yourself, but also others with a connection."

"When do I go on this journey?"

"In the near future. You will have experiences nobody else can. The gift you are to receive, embrace it with wisdom."

"I shall." I gave her the fee.

"Thank you." She led me to the tent exit and bowed her head.

I still remained a sceptic!

It did not take long to walk home. As I entered my apartment, the phone started to ring. I shut the door and rushed to pick up the receiver.

"Monsieur Carsell-Brown, how are you?"

"I am fine, Detective."

"I would like you to come and visit my office tomorrow at six o'clock."

"Why the urgency?"

"When you arrive, all will be explained."

"Detective, I trust that is six in the evening?

He laughed. "But of course, monsieur!"

"See you then." I replaced the receiver into the cradle.


At Police Headquarters, I could see Detective Laurant and the Colonel in discussion along the main corridor. Detective Laurant spotted me.

He walked over. "Come this way, monsieur. Ca va?"

"Oui, ca va." I walked into his office.

Colonel Fontaine stood beside a filing cabinet. "How do feel today, Monsieur Carsell-Brown?"

"Ready to go, Colonel."

The Colonel took off his uniform cap. "We have discovered Diaz does plan to leave the country. Therefore, any action must be taken right away. We believe he has been involved in the theft of other classified government documents plus Monique Duvallier's death but we need to catch him red-handed! Every Tuesday evening; Diaz frequents the Hotel de Paris in Monte Carlo to play black jack."

"A gambler in more ways than one!" I said.

The plan allowed me to confront and inform Diaz that in the time Michelle Duvallier and I spent together, she did discuss certain aspects of a 'delicate' nature.

"Will he believe me, Colonel?"

"As he plays for high stakes, Diaz cannot afford to take any chances you may be bluffing. If an opportunity exists for him to get the documents which Michelle stole, he will not pass this up. He is a desperate man."

No doubt, given the fate of Monique Devallier.

The Colonel straightened his tie. "The game of black jack takes place in the Salle des Ameriques casino suite within the luxurious Hotel de Paris. The game commences at nine o'clock and finishes around four in the morning. I hope you will have left the establishment by then."

"You want me to do this tonight?"

"Do not look too concerned, monsieur. Detective Laurant and I shall brief you. Bon chance!" The Colonel put on his cap and departed.

Detective Laurant smiled. "You will be fine, monsieur."

"I have to start work at eight o'clock tomorrow morning. I will be exhausted at midnight, let alone four in the morning!"

"Leave that to me. Give me your Company Director's name."

I scribbled it on a piece of paper.

After my lift home, I had a bite to eat and changed into my formal evening attire. An unmarked police car and driver would take me to the Hotel de Paris. Detective Laurent accompanied me on the journey and confirmed a development.

"I spoke to your Company Director about this situation."

"And the outcome?"

"When I stressed it involved the security of our country, he said to take all the time off you need, within reason."

"Splendid. I shall keep that in mind!"

I had a miniature microphone placed inside my suit in order to monitor conversations between Diaz and myself.

"Will I not be searched by members of hotel security?"

Detective Laurant turned to me and gave one of his smiles. "The Head of Security works for us, and he has been informed of the situation. I also have men inside the hotel to assist if a problem arises."

Just before ten o'clock, we arrived at the Hotel de Paris in Monte Carlo. The lights, which surrounded the building, glittered in the dark to give a magical effect.

"Good luck, monsieur." Detective Laurant handed me a pass card for the casino suite.

"Thanks." I got out of the rear seat and closed the car door. Only dark attire could be worn in the hotel casino, and therefore I would at least look the part in my black evening suit!

I entered the hotel and approached reception.

An elegant lady smiled. "The casino suite is straight along the corridor, monsieur."

The exclusive hallway consisted of a marble domed ceiling, a large gold chandelier and plush, deep red carpets. I reached the casino suite and two uniformed security guards stood at the doorway. As I approached, one stepped forward and gave me a security check. He looked at me and nodded. I started to walk into the suite, but the second security guard stopped me.

"Pardon, monsieur."

"Yes? What now?"

"You have dropped your game pass." He handed it to me. "Have a good evening, monsieur."

"Merci bien." Phew!

I looked around the dozen or so green baize tables for Diaz. Not much noise could be heard. No doubt the card players concentrated on their game. As Guerrin would have told his boss about my fatal car accident, Diaz would be in for a surprise! I spotted him, along with three other players. They appeared Middle Eastern. I walked over to their table and stopped. Guerrin appeared from nowhere, turned, and stared with an expression of disbelief. He bent down and whispered in Diaz's ear.

He glanced sideways and got up from his chair. "Mr Carsell-Brown will not do anything stupid."

"Correct."

Diaz excused himself from the table and confronted me. "You must either be lucky or have friends in high places to still be alive."

"Again, you are correct, Diaz – a bit of both!"

"I have a game to finish, Mr Carsell-Brown. What do you want?"

"I know you had Madame Duvallier killed."

Guerrin moved closer toward me. "You know nothing!"

"Let us discuss this with a little more privacy." Diaz ushered me to a small lounge next to the suite. It had a strong smell of cigars.

"It concerns my conversation with Madame Duvallier. After several glasses of wine, she started to talk about a matter of national security."

Diaz gave me a blank stare. "What has all this got to do with me, Mr Carsell-Brown?"

"I have the blueprint you lost. Madame Duvallier put them in a locker at Nice railway station. I managed to get hold of the key and retrieve it. I now have what you want, Diaz."

Guerrin glared but Diaz kept calm. "What do you want?"

"One million francs, payable in cash – tomorrow evening."

Guerrin laughed. "Are you serious?"

I smiled. "Yes, I am."

"Very well, Mr Carsell-Brown – you have a deal."

"Good. Tomorrow evening?"

He nodded. "Tomorrow evening."

I gave him a card. "Contact me at this number around three o'clock. Only call if you have the money. Tell me, Diaz, did you have to kill Madame Duvallier?"

"It is the consequence of what happens to someone who interferes in my affairs, Mr Carsell-Brown!"

His stare was as cold as ice.

I left the casino suite and went to the hotel exit. I got into an arranged car driven by one of the Colonel's men. We drove to a nearby location where Colonel Fontaine and Detective Laurant waited for me to join them. I got out the car and the driver took me into a large detached house.

"This way, monsieur." He led me into a room.

"Well, you survived!" Colonel Fontaine smiled.

"Yes, no problem."

"How did Diaz react, monsieur?" Detective Laurant pulled his moustache.

"Just the way you said he would. Is it advisable for me to return home?"

Detective Laurant laughed. "Until the blueprint can be retrieved, they will not harm you in any way!"

That was a comfort.

Colonel Fontaine put on his cap. "The situation should come to a conclusion tomorrow, with Zoren Diaz and his gang put into custody!"

"Do not worry about a return to your apartment monsieur. My men have been on surveillance duty for some time! One of my officers will give you a lift home."

I met with Detective Laurant on Wednesday afternoon. Another tense evening ensued. Upon my arrival I got taken to his office and asked to wait.

"He will not be long, monsieur," said an Officer.

I gazed out the window and watched children at play in the park. How uncomplicated my life had once been! Detective Laurant appeared and made an apology.

"Today has been busy. Not enough hours in the day – quelle vie!" He sat down behind his desk.

"C'est la vie, Detective!"

He laughed. "Are you prepared for this evening, Monsieur Carsell-Brown?"

"Yes, I am." *Hopefully!*

"It could get unpleasant tonight. These villains can be callous. Look what happened to Monique Duvallier."

"Without doubt a good enough reason for me to carry on and conclude this matter."

"Bravo, monsieur."

"Do not worry, Detective, I shall be fine." He tried to gauge my fortitude for the imminent duel.

"At what time will Diaz contact you?"

"Three o'clock." I looked at my watch – two minutes past three. "Is there any chance he can trace the call to here?" That would put a spanner in the works!

"No, monsieur – it is an independent number which we have set up."

The telephone started to ring. Detective Laurant and I looked at each other. I had that tense feeling once more.

"You had better answer it, monsieur."

I picked up the receiver and held it tight in my hand. "Yes?"

"I will meet you at the Boulevard in Nice. There is a small area of waste ground under a railway viaduct. I shall see you at nine o'clock sharp. Do you understand?"

"Do you have the one million francs in cash?"

"Yes, Mr Carsell-Brown. It will be in a black leather case. Come alone. Do you understand?"

"I understand. I will see you at nine." I slowly put the receiver back in its cradle.

"Do not worry, monsieur. The Colonel and his men shall be close by."

"Bon." How I missed my normal day job!

The Colonel arrived and, as usual, breezed in with a superior air of confidence. He took off his cap and positioned himself in the centre of the room.

He twirled his moustache. "Tonight, Monsieur Carsell-Brown, we can celebrate the demise of Zoren Diaz and his gang with a bottle of whisky from your native land."

I nodded. *Oh no, not whisky again!*

"You are about to undertake a mission of vital importance for the security of the nation." He put his hand on my shoulder. "Detective Laurant and I will ensure your safety."

"What about a microphone to monitor the situation?"

Detective Laurant rose from his chair. "You will be searched by one of Diaz's men. If they find a microphone on you then the exchange would be in jeopardy, along with your life. Do not worry – we shall be close at hand."

At the agreed location, I waited with anticipation. I tapped my finger on the car dashboard. I observed the barren waste ground and the grey viaduct above. Unoccupied boarded-up premises surrounded the area. A grim landscape would be an accurate description. Colonel Fontaine had assigned Lucas, one of his men, to act as a driver.

"Do not be concerned, monsieur. The operation should go to plan."

*Should!* "I hope so."

"Do you get nervous?"

"Not usually, but this evening is a bit different!"

"Colonel Fontaine and a number of his men shall be hidden around the vicinity." Lucas handed me a gun.

I looked at it and then him. "A gun!"

"Do you know how to use this?"

"I have never used one and would rather keep it that way." I gave the gun back to him.

"D'accord, monsieur." He put the gun inside a compartment next to the steering wheel.

I glanced at my watch. Three minutes to nine.

A silver BMW then came into sight and stopped almost thirty metres from our Renault. Both cars faced each other in a confrontational manner. I counted four people in the shiny BMW. Diaz and his gang had arrived. We stood outnumbered if a problem arose. Diaz got out of the car and walked a few short paces. He looked around our rendezvous spot. I got out of the Renault, walked towards him and halted.

"You have the blueprint, Mr Carsell-Brown?"

"Do you have my money, Diaz?"

"I see you have not come alone."

"I see you did not come alone either. He is the driver of a local taxi firm."

"I want him out of the car, where my men can see him."

"Okay, if you insist."

I asked Lucas to step out of the car. Diaz and I both had black leather briefcases. We walked towards each other. As he approached, I put down my case.

"I want to see the one million francs."

He snapped his fingers.

One of his men got out of the car. He approached, and frisked me up and down. He also searched inside my jacket.

"He is clean, boss." The man returned to the BMW.

"I do not take any chances, Mr Carsell-Brown." Diaz opened his case.

I checked the notes.

"It is all there. The blueprint document now, if you please."

I opened my briefcase and gave him a file.

"Wait here." Diaz opened the file and browsed through it. He walked at a slow pace to his car.

Then two cars screeched to a halt alongside us. Colonel Fontaine, Detective Laurant and a number of agents got out of the two vehicles. Their guns pointed at the occupants of the BMW.

The Colonel pointed a gun at Diaz. "Hands in the air, Diaz, and I will take the file." He grabbed it.

Guerrin and the other two men got out of the BMW. Surrounded by Detective Laurant and other agents, they put their hands in the air.

"You won't sneak out of this, Diaz. We also have conclusive evidence on the murder of Madame Duvallier."

The four villains were handcuffed and hustled into the navy blue cars. Diaz and Guerrin in one, and the two accomplices in the other.

Colonel Fontaine walked towards me and shook my hand. "Bravo, monsieur, bravo!"

"Je vous en prie, Colonel!" I gave him the case full of money.

He then got into the front car, where Diaz and Guerrin perched in the rear seat. The window wound down and the Colonel clenched his fist. The car sped off into the distance. Lucas and I got into our car.

"Perfect timing by the Colonel and his men."

"Monsieur." Lucas grinned and pulled out of his jacket pocket a small device the size of a credit card.

I stared. "What's that?" It had a screen and a control panel which looked futuristic.

He pointed. "I pressed this button and the Colonel received a pre-scripted message sent to his similar device. The message simply read 'go!'"

"Go?"

"This stated you had made the exchange."

"*Formidable*!" I studied the device.

"This is the prototype I use."

"How long have you had this?"

"Since the end of 1988 – almost ten months. Soon this device will become a standard issue for every agent. It can also be used to converse, exchange identity profiles and access criminal intelligence data. Our scientists are continuing to work on a more advanced model."

"There could be a commercial market for this type of technology."

"Diaz thought so! To your apartment, monsieur?"

I nodded.

Two days passed and I started to become relaxed and enjoy the pleasantries of Nice once again. When I returned to work, I had a chat with the Company Director, who quizzed me on my 'seconded' role. His philosophy was that variety is the spice of life!

On Friday evening I attended a work presentation and headed home the worse for wear. I let my hair down, since it had been a while. However, when Saturday morning came, I suffered. Then the telephone started to ring. I did not want to lift the receiver.

"Monsieur Carsell-Brown, it is Detective Laurant. We have just received word that Guerrin has escaped from custody!"

"Guerrin?" I croaked.

"He may attempt to flee the country, but also to seek his own retribution."

"How did he manage to escape?"

"He complained of extreme stomach pains and got taken to the local infirmary. He eluded his guards and got out of the building."

*Just my luck!*

"I will send two of my officers to patrol your area. As a precaution, they will keep a constant watch."

"Thank you, Detective."

I replaced the receiver into the cradle. Guerrin had already entered my apartment, and therefore I would not be surprised if he tried again. Even two police officers may not have been enough to stop him. Quelle vie!

As I had a social life to consider, I could not remain a prisoner in my apartment. On Saturday evening, I ventured to a place called Raddisson Rouge. The small and busy city centre venue played live music from eight until late. It had become one of my favourite nightspots in Nice. As the façade and interior walls had been decorated in red, the name sounded appropriate. The bar got so busy that staff had little time to draw breath. Before eight o'clock, if a customer did not get a seat, their feet could have a sore night ahead.

Around eleven, I made haste for home. As I exited the venue, my ears started to ring! At least I could breathe fresh air! Whilst on my way home I checked for my door keys. Where were they? I searched in all of my pockets. When at the bar to pay my bill, the keys must have dropped out. I turned around to retrace my steps. A man confronted me, unshaven and untidy.

"Have you by any chance lost these?" He dangled my keys.

*Guerrin!* "How did you find me?"

"Easy when you know how!" He pointed a gun at my chest and ordered me into a nearby disused and littered alley.

I stood inside the alley facing the street.

"You shall regret getting involved in other peoples' business!"

"You won't escape a second time."

I spotted three men walk past the entrance to the alley and then turn back. One of them picked up a piece of wood from the ground. He tiptoed towards Guerrin.

"Guerrin, there is a man behind you with a club!"

"Surely you do not expect me to fall for that?"

Then came a loud thud and Guerrin dropped straight to the ground. He lay sprawled out and motionless.

I stared at the three 'saviours' with relief and gratitude! I recognised them as the trio who had demanded money from me!

"My grandfather is also Scottish!" said the tallest of the three. He threw down the 'instrument of faith'.

A second man searched Guerrin. He handed me the gun and a knife concealed in his jacket. "Keep these – they will protect you until further help comes along."

"Thank you for your help."

"Monsieur, de rien!" confessed the third man.

I bade them farewell and asked a passer-by to telephone for police assistance. Detective Laurant and his men arrived within thirty minutes. He looked at me with a gun pointed at the dazed Guerrin.

"Monsieur Carsell-Brown, you never fail to surprise me. There must be a guardian angel who watches over you!"

"Detective, not one but three!" I passed the gun and knife to him.

"Merci, monsieur."

An officer handcuffed Guerrin and led him to a waiting police car.

"That man has a commendable quality."

"Commendable?"

"Oui, monsieur. His loyalty to Diaz. He sought his own retribution for your assistance in the capture of his boss."

"Indeed!" As I left the scene, looked upwards to the starry sky. *Merci bien.*

# Chapter 3

## *Docharnea*

Since my liaison with the French Secret Service to catch villains, Nice could only become less dramatic. Thank goodness for the sanity of reverting from dangerous operative to office executive. To deal with client's business solutions and my frequent browse through the *Nice Matin* at lunchtime would be adequate. In fact, over the next decade, life developed into a normal routine. One noticeable change did occur. The '70s bar transformed into an Elvis-themed venue – the wonder of him!

Life became a comfortable, relaxed and prestigious existence in the Cote d'Azur. However, I would often recall my past life and times in Scotland. The longer I had been away, the more I reflected about Edinburgh and its character; the Royal Mile and many historical buildings, haunted closes and infamous public houses. Aberdeen, with its endless falls of snow and burst pipes in winter. However, both cities held special good memories.

"James, James!" said Cerice.

I raised my head.

"Have you completed your expense form for last month?"

"You startled me." My nostalgic memories were disrupted. I opened my desk drawer and handed the form to her.

"Thank you."

"Don't mention it!"

After an ordinary day at the office, I got home around seven o'clock and found a pile of letters in the mailbox. I looked through them. My attention focused on one letter with a Scottish postmark. I laid the rest on a glass reception table and went into the lounge. I did not bother to take off my grey raincoat. I opened the well-sealed envelope and read the letter. A firm of solicitors from Ardrishaig, Scotland, had written to me. They represented a relative of mine, a lady called Olivia Carsell-Brown who had passed away and I had now become the beneficiary of her property. Why me? I did not recollect the name. The contents of the letter stated, the three-acre property had a name – Docharnea. It lay in a small hamlet called Dochar close to Loch Fyne. I did recall a visit with my mother and father many years ago, that being the time I met my great-aunt Ann. I observed buildings surrounded by tall trees and large grassy gardens. This had proved ideal for me because I had ample space to kick my ball. I also remember a loch and being allowed to sail my toy boat at the shallow water's edge; happy memories of the visit in 1967. Mind you, the long and tiresome journey from Edinburgh and back took an eternity! But I did not recall the name Olivia.

I put the letter on an arm of the cream couch and sat down. I suspected another crossroads had arrived in my life – whether to leave a career in this desirable location or venture to a picturesque area of Scotland. I elected to ponder over dinner and beyond. After all, que sera, sera!

Over the next few days, I made my decision. I would return to Scotland. A new millennium had begun, and therefore a poignant time for change had come. I finalised arrangements for the trip to Scotland.

Waiting in the airport departure lounge, I recalled various instances of my stay in Nice. The enigmatic Michelle Duvallier who worked undercover for the French Secret Service. After the Diaz case, the government reassigned her to another country. Due to mistaken identity, her sister, Monique, had been murdered. A cruel end to a young woman's life. The likeable Detective Claude Laurant who got promoted and moved to Marseilles. After the case, our paths did not cross again. Colonel Jacques Fontaine retired in 1995 and, less than a year later, passed away. I had sought adventure and it had come in those early months. Maybe the ownership of a substantial property would make me adopt a more stable outlook on life. I heard an announcement for Glasgow and looked up at the departure screen. Ah good, time to board.

As my flight left Nice, I remembered what Cerice had said to me a few days earlier. She maintained certain individuals have a destiny in life. *No matter what path they take,* she said, *it shall be fulfilled.* Then she'd smiled.

I looked out of the window and reminisced about my time spent in Scotland, and my childhood in the northern scenic part of Edinburgh. On a clear summer day you could observe the landmarks of neighbouring Fife across the River Forth. The harbour at Granton was filled with an array of small boats – trawlers lined the quay and a flotilla of yachts paraded in splendour out at sea, their white sails in contrast to the deep blue colour of the water. The sunshine and blue skies of my childhood stayed in place for each summer season. Edinburgh emerged from the austere period, which followed the Second World War. The city became a place worthy of capital status, attributed to an abundance of historic architecture, cultural venues and amenities; the Castle, International Festival and Fringe, sporting activities and facilities, museums, libraries, theatres, cinemas and sophisticated restaurants gave the city a wide appeal. Also, those dance halls, which played a higher tempo of music introduced for older teenagers and younger adults. The Palais ballroom at Fountainbridge had been responsible for many a match made in heaven – at least until the couples fell out! Shoppers had prestigious department stores in and around Princes Street; Binns at the West End and Patrick Thomson's on North Bridge provided consumers with a range of quality products and an exclusive shopping experience. And that included children like me at Christmas. I will not forget the festive picture of the city centre with bright lights, snow, winter clothes and harassed parents.

A blue uniformed stewardess approached. "A drink, sir?"

"White coffee please, no sugar."

She handed me a well-filled, white, plastic cup.

I hoped that there would be no imminent turbulence. I took a sip – the coffee tasted strong.

Visiting locations in and around Edinburgh had become a popular and frequent leisure pursuit. Families took advantage of an increase in quality time at their disposal. The amount of hours people worked decreased, and fathers began to smile a lot more. To travel on a train which hurtled through the landscape resulted in a treat to enjoy and savour. Somehow, a bus journey to the same location appeared ordinary. It lacked the speed, escapism and excitement of the powerful train. That short train journey from Granton to Princes Street could be interpreted as an adventure rather than a short excursion. Oh, Dr Beeching, the clouds of disappointment and despair still poured down on us enthusiasts.

Those favourite subject areas at school which made going there worthwhile were history, social and cultural studies. Historical events, which had happened in the past, shaped our futures. I learned about the Victorian period and up to the First World War – a prosperous and prestigious era for Great Britain. Due to the amount of armoury and territory, its position of being a major world power was undeniable. After the First World War, people grew weary of conflicts and their perceptions changed from glory to despondency. Great Britain had been a victor, but war, this costs money, lives and heartache. In the decades which followed, the vast majority of British citizens endured perpetual hardship and misery. How a country's fortune can change.

Social and cultural pursuits brought the study of particular societies to my attention. All those early finishes at school in order to carry out phantom research! Still, my football skills improved.

A stewardess leaned over. "I'll take that empty cup, sir."

"Thanks."

Skills of the Victorian engineers who developed and enabled progress to flourish; the monumental Forth Railway Bridge structure which increased trade through Fife to northern Scotland. The creation of this railway line altered the landscape, but enhanced towns and cities along the route. This became a positive aspect of Victorian Britain, but a negative side also existed. A great deal of social depravation engulfed parts of the country. Many rural citizens had to emigrate and thus escape starvation. The majority of the working class had low incomes, poor conditions and endless health issues to contend with. A notable change in this period resulted from a shift in power from the aristocracy to the middle class then recognition of the working class. By the end of 1900, social depravation had become highlighted and was earmarked for action.

My schooldays and subsequent studies at university – I must have studied well! The time I joined an advertising company in Aberdeen; an opportunity to experience a different type of culture and increase my bank balance with a regular income. Aberdeen had thrown off the old unfashionable image of being portrayed as a northern fishing port. In fact, it had been transformed into the new focal point in commerce and affluence for the nation. The dramatic change in identity came because of that most precious commodity – oil – which was a valuable asset for the local area in terms of employment. With their beneficial oil-driven economy in full swing, I still found many citizens of the Aberdeen business fraternity cautious.

"All's well at present but circumstances can change!"

How prophetic! A recession hit the industry in 1986. Memories – what would I do without them? It was time for a quick nap.

"Excuse me, sir – sir!"

I awoke and turned my head towards the stewardess.

"Please fasten your seat belt, sir. We will soon arrive in Glasgow."

That was a quick flight!

I checked out of Glasgow Airport late in the afternoon. The grey sky and cold temperature confirmed I had arrived in Scotland. I hoped I had made the correct decision! Where did I pack my coat?

I hailed a black cab and got in. "Glasgow city centre, please."

"Just got back from holiday, sir?" said the driver.

"Yes, I have – almost eleven years!"

He laughed. "I take it you had an enjoyable stay then, sir?"

"Yes, I did thanks." Now for the next stage of the journey. "How do I get to a place called Dochar?"

He looked at me in his mirror. "Where, sir?"

"Dochar. I believe it lies close to Ardrishaig."

"Ardrishaig? Where's that?"

"On the way to the Mull of Kintyre." My journey to Dochar could be another adventure. Ah, the city centre.

"Where do you want to be dropped off, sir?"

"The Tourist Information Office."

"Be there soon, sir. There it is." He pointed.

"Thanks." I paid the fare, plus the tip, and got out of the taxi.

"Good luck, sir!"

I entered the building located on George Square. The rain had started, and therefore I appreciated the refuge! Four ladies each sat at a customer point and dealt with enquiries from people no doubt in a similar situation to myself. A vacancy appeared.

A lady moved her head forward. "Yes, sir? Can I help you?"

"How can I get to Dochar?"

"Can you please spell the name, sir?"

"D-O-C-H-A-R. I believe it could be in close proximity to Ardrishaig."

The lady studied her computer screen and also a pamphlet. "Let's see. You have to take the Ardrishaig bus. Dochar is about one mile from there."

"Any train service?"

"Sorry, no train goes there."

"When does the next bus depart?"

She looked at the clock on the wall, "I'm sorry – the last one today departed over an hour ago! Here is a timetable for your information and a list of hotels for an overnight stay."

"Thanks."

On this day, Glasgow lacked a particular quality Nice had in abundance – continuous sunny days! The recent rainfall took me by surprise. I could smell the rain. However, the humour reigned supreme.

A small elderly woman toddled towards me. "Did you enjoy your holiday, son?"

I smiled. "Yes thanks."

"You don't half make me look peely-wally, so you do!" She walked on, trailing a bag in each hand.

A car stopped at the pedestrian crossing. I waited for the signal to walk. The car window zipped down.

"How do I get to the beach?" said the driver.

"Take a flight to Nice!"

He laughed.

I crossed the road and went into a coffee shop. I ordered a white coffee and looked through the list of hotels. One close to George Square seemed appropriate. I finished my coffee and walked the short distance to the establishment.

I managed to get a room and had a nap, and then dinner in the restaurant. After a delicious steak, I went into the bar. I found it a contrast to most trim, dim bars with wooden furniture in Nice. This had bright décor, sophisticated lighting and comfortable leather seats. The bar person poured a long cool pint of Scottish lager, complete with froth. How I had missed my favourite brew on draught! As all the seats had been taken, I stood at the bar. The background music consisted of swing, rhythm and soul. Not only did the beer satisfy my taste buds, but the music became pleasant on my ears.

I walked to Buchanan bus station and got the morning service to Ardrishaig. When aboard, I asked the driver if he could drop me off at a place called Dochar.

"No problem, sir. Before we arrive, I'll give you a shout."

I had arranged to meet a member of the firm who handled my late relative's affairs. The name Olivia still remained a mystery, but no doubt I would soon be enlightened.

On the journey, I sat back to admire the landscapes of the Argyll countryside. Picturesque lochs, woodland and valleys covered this region of Scotland. My window seat was ideal to consume the scenic views. When we passed the banks of Loch Lomond, a small boat sailed through the water and left white waves behind it. With lush green hills in the background, it was a sight to behold, and soon I was reunited with another. The coach went through a valley, veered down a hill and around a bend. It then continued on a route parallel to the shore of Loch Fyne. I couldn't sail my toy boat at the water's edge this time!

"Soon be there, sir," the driver shouted. "Just a few miles to Dochar."

"Splendid."

Even though another few miles beckoned, I could not wait to get off the bus. I had travelled for three hours and fidgeted on my seat for the last hour. However, the journey with my parents from Edinburgh had taken over four hours – perhaps the reason why we only visited on a single occasion.

"Here we are, sir." He applied the handbrake, got off the bus, and retrieved my suitcase from the storage compartment.

"Thanks."

"You're welcome, sir."


As the bus departed, I stood alone at the side of the road. I gazed around the beautiful and tranquil part of Argyll. A small number of large villas all lay on the side of the road, and therefore they enjoyed an unimpaired view of Loch Fyne. I took a deep breath. I felt a light breeze on my face. This place endeared itself to me.

I could hear a car in the distance, breaking the silence of the countryside. It sped along the rural road and came to a halt close to where I stood.

A light grey-suited gentleman got out of the small white sports car. "You've found it, then? Have you been here long?"

"No, I've just arrived."

"I am John Macmillan, the youngest partner in the firm."

I shook his hand. "Pleased to meet you." I looked towards the loch. "What a superb view."

He also looked across the loch. "Yes fantastic. I don't suppose you would sell the property?"

I gave a contented smile and shook my head.

The property which I inherited lay about fifty yards from where the bus stopped. We walked towards it and then up the driveway. This had grass verges and mature trees on either side. John Macmillan unlocked the large double doors and took me inside.

"Built in 1896. This is the reception area."

My bedroom in Nice was the same size!

"This way." He led me to the hall.

He showed me four public rooms that consisted of high ceilings and attractive well-sculptured cornice. A utility room and two bathrooms completed the ground floor. Upstairs had five bedrooms and two bathrooms.

"You may have to hire a cleaner, Mr Carsell-Brown."

I looked out from one of the red, wooden-floored bedrooms. "And also an able gardener!"

"Let me show you the coach house. You will be fascinated by this."

We went downstairs and exited the property from the utility room. In view, a traditional Victorian coach house in total splendour. I recalled my great Aunt taking me on a tour of this building many years ago. The coach house did not match the size of the main house. The white walls, dark pointed slated roof and shiny black doors gave the coach house a distinctive appearance. It had a downstairs and upstairs with two separate rooms on each floor. Downstairs contained the stable where the horses had once been kept, and the other larger room accommodated the coach. Another door located between both downstairs entrances gave stairway access to the floor above, and this consisted of the hayloft and coachman's quarters. The hayloft's use related to the storage of hay to feed the horses. Across this landing lay a room the coachman used. It had confined space, yet was adequate for him to maintain a humble but comfortable existence. The quarters comprised of a washroom, sleeping area, cupboard, elevated storage compartments and a piece of equipment used for cooking and warmth. As an added bonus, his quarters had a superb view over Loch Fyne.

"The original family who built Docharnea must have been proud of what they accomplished."

I had to agree. The main building had elegant furniture, tasteful décor and affluent designs to capture the imagination.

However, an aura surrounded the coach house. I had sensed that thirty-three years ago.

"What became of Ann Carsell-Brown?"

"Never heard of Ann Carsell-Brown. My father should have an idea – ask him tomorrow."

I did not take ownership of Docharnea for another twenty-four hours. John Macmillan took me into Ardrishaig, where a room had been reserved at the Grey Gull Inn.

"It's a well-known establishment which dated back to the nineteenth century. Similar to your property!"

He made the short journey in a matter of minutes. If his sports car had not got stuck behind a tractor, it would have been quicker. He stopped outside the inn.

"Our office is just at the end of this street. We'll see you tomorrow morning at ten o'clock." He gave me a business card.

I got out of the cramped car and closed the door. He waved and drove off. I entered the inn.


Later, I went through to the bar for a beer. It had a dark red carpet to match the upholstery – both were in need of being upgraded.

The barman leaned forward. "Yes, sir, what can I get you?"

I observed the various beer fonts on the bar. "A pint of lager, please."

"Sorry sir, no draught beer available. The next delivery doesn't arrive for two days. The owner's fault – 'e forgot to submit the beer order."

"Have you any French beer?"

"No, but we do have bottled lager sir."

"Splendid."

The barman opened a bottle and poured the beer into a glass.

As I chatted to him, I noticed a well-worn, elderly chap sitting by himself in a corner of the bar. He kept looking in my direction.

He shouted, "The house is haunted!"

The chap must have overheard my conversation with the barman. "Well, the ghosts shall have to pay rent," I said.

"Don't worry about old Angus sir," said the barman. "'e's been tellin' us that tale all his life!"

The chap finished his drink and approached the bar. "I'm seventy-four years old and my grandfather told me the property's haunted. After the first family moved in, strange goings on started to 'appen."

I asked, "In what way?"

"You'll soon find out!" He then stormed out of the door and into the cold windy night.

"Don't pay any attention, sir. His grandfather worked as a gardener at Docharnea but got dismissed. His family still hold a grudge against the Carsell-Browns to this day."

Given the current state of the grounds, had the vacant position ever been filled? I bid the barman goodnight and retired to my room. I envisaged tomorrow might be another day of interest.


I struggled to traverse along the blustery main street which led to the solicitor's office and noticed several shops boarded up. Not the ideal impression to give visitors! I stopped and stood for a moment to look at the nearby canal, a landmark I remember from my first visit here due to the array of small boats moored around it. Today they would no doubt be well secured.

Alistair Macmillan and his predecessors had acted for each of the Carsell-Brown families in Ardrishaig. After what had been said the previous evening by a stranger, would any other controversy about the property be revealed?

When I entered the office of Macmillan-Mackay, the lady receptionist greeted me in a polite manner.

"Good morning, Mr Carsell-Brown. Mr Macmillan will be with you shortly. Please have a seat."

I took a seat and received a warm cup of coffee, and accepted it with gratitude given the current inclement weather.

The receptionist said, "The weather tends to fluctuate here in the early months of the year."

"I've noticed!"

She smiled. "No doubt different from the south of France."

I nodded and sipped my warm coffee. The cup kept my hands warm.

Ten minutes later, a tall thin gentleman in a charcoal three-piece suit came into the reception area and greeted me.

"How do you do, Mr Carsell-Brown? I am Alistair Macmillan." He shook my hand. "Please, come this way." He led me into a bright compact office. "Please, have a seat. Would you like something to drink, perhaps a whisky?" He went to a table and held a bottle of whisky in his hand.

"Oh no!"

"You look a bit pale Mr Carsell-Brown."

"I'll pass – it's a bit too early in the day."

"You don't mind if I do?"

I shook my head. "Not at all."

He poured himself a glass and sat behind his wooden desk. "Good health." He took a sip and laid the glass within easy reach.

"Yes, good health."

"James, you have been left Docharnea by Olivia Carsell-Brown, this being her wish."

"Can I ask a question?"

"Of course."

"Who is this lady, and why has she left Docharnea to me in her will?

"I'll explain. I must also tell you about Docharnea's history. Olivia wanted me to inform you."

"Why?"

"She stipulated this in her will. No doubt there is a good reason – of what, I am not sure."

Intriguing. Why inform me of Docharnea's history?

"I'll begin. Charles and Mary Carsell-Brown built the property. After just a few months, a tragedy occurred. In those days, affluent families travelled by coach and horses. On a particular journey, one of the wheels shattered and the coach went out of control and down an embankment. Mr Carsell-Brown and the coachman met their death, but Mrs Carsell-

Brown survived. She took a long time to recover and stayed at the property for a number of years." He took a sip of whisky. "Ill health and the size of the estate proved too much for her."

"A tragedy indeed."

"The property then passed to your namesake, James Carsell-Brown."

"What became of him?"

He took another sip of his whisky. "He then got married, but the couple did not have any dependants. His wife died five years later."

"How did she die?"

"Details are conflicted, but I believe a fatal accident. Mr Carsell-Brown went on to suffer from constant depression. He got weaker and passed away within a year of his wife's death. He died of a broken heart."

Docharnea could be perceived as a poisoned chalice, then.

Mr Macmillan turned the page of his notes. "A cousin from Ayrshire, Philip Carsell-Brown, became the next owner of the property. He got married to a lady called Charlotte. They had two sons, William and Geoffrey. After the start of the Second World War, both sons were killed."

"It must have been devastating for the parents."

"The solitary consolation was that one of them distinguished himself in action."

"What about the other brother?"

"He got killed prior to leaving for France in 1940. I am not aware of how he died. Both parents remained active into their eighties, and then went into care. The wife of the eldest son became the last owner of Docharnea."

"Olivia Carsell-Brown."

"William and Olivia had only been married for eighteen months. She did not remarry, but lived at the property for the last thirty-seven years, until she died."

I became emotional. "Then she is the lady my parents and I visited all those years ago?"

"Yes, James."

"But I can recall my mother and father referring to her as Ann!"

"Yes, known as Ann within the family – her middle name."

"My goodness!"

Then came a knock on the door. Mr Macmillan hid his half full glass of whisky behind a black filing tray.

He straightened his light blue tie. "Come in."

A well-groomed lady walked into the room and looked at Mr Macmillan. "I'm not disturbing you?"

"James, this is our first female partner to join the practice. May I present Jane Mackay."

I got to my feet and shook her hand. It had a soft, gentle touch. I could smell the sweet scent of her perfume. A sense of familiarity came over me.

Mr Macmillan looked at me. "Do you have any plans for this afternoon, James?"

"No, nothing at all."

"Then allow Jane to entertain you. She can advise on any matters connected to the property or this area. You may require a gardener."

I smiled.

We left the office and Jane Mackay drove to an establishment known as the Argyll Arms Hotel, where a table had been reserved. We entered the hotel, which was in an idyllic location, surrounded by trees.

"As this is a popular place to meet, it can be busy at lunchtime. Most people in the village like to socialise at this time of the day."

I looked around the lounge diner. It had a Scottish theme with clan carpet and regalia on each wall. "I can believe that – there are no spare tables!"

She gave a polite smile.

A waitress approached. "Do you have a reservation?"

"Yes – Mackay."

The black outfitted waitress checked a list. "This way, please." She took us to a window table. "I'll be right back to take your orders."

I looked at a menu then around the room. "I notice the majority of people are of retirement age."

"Ardrishaig has a reputation for being a nice place to stay. The scenery can be fantastic. People come here to live and savour their retirement."

"There could also be business opportunities."

She smiled. "The vacant retail units?"

I nodded.

"One of them, the tailor's shop, had been in existence for generations. The main street needs a spark – some sort of revitalisation. Most businesses are close to ruin." She read her menu.

"Can the banks not help?"

"There is a malaise about the main street at present. The banks take the view their investment would be wasted. They have lost money in the past."

"A depressed situation."

"I agree."

As the sea air had given me a healthy appetite, I looked forward to my lunch. Over the next hour, I told her about why I left Edinburgh following my graduation at university to live and work in Aberdeen.

"What subject area did you study?"

"Marketing."

She looked at me with a broad smile. "You do not remember me? We attended Edinburgh University and you stayed close to the Royal Mile!"

"That's right – for four years. I can't recall a Jane Mackay."

"How about Jane Sutherland, with long dark hair and a slimmer waistline!"

My goodness – the hair! She now had short, blonde hair. I now remembered an end-of-term party in my flat. She stayed over. Would she recall that infamous night?

"After one of your parties, I didn't go home 'til the next day."

"Because you consumed too much red wine!" I smiled. "But I gave you my room and I slept on the living room couch."

She nodded.

"Why did you come here to practice law?"

"My husband got offered an excellent position with a local bank. His family comes from Inveraray. One of his relatives recommended me to Mr Macmillan, and I joined the firm. Three years later, I became a partner."

"Splendid. Then it has all worked out well for you?"

"Yes. We have two boys, and both enjoy the area." She looked at me with an impish grin. "Have you not managed to settle down yet?"

"Not yet."

"You appear too much of an adventurer, James!"

I nodded! Time to change the subject. "Olivia Carsell-Brown."

"After a beautiful church service, Olivia was laid to rest in the local cemetery. Many people attended her funeral to pay their last respects."

"I would like to visit the cemetery. Is it far from here?"

"No, after lunch I will take you there." Jane looked up. "At last – here comes the waitress."

We stopped at a local flower shop to get flowers. At the cemetery, Jane took me to Olivia's grave. She left me and returned to her car. After a short while, an elderly man came towards me. He looked similar to the person from the Grey Gull Inn – the same grim expression.

"I know why you're here," he said. "You've come back to haunt me!"

"I'm not a ghost, and I'm also not here to haunt you – or any other person!"

"You don't fool me!" He stormed off.

I walked back to her car and got into the passenger seat.

"A problem, James?"

"He believes I am a ghost."

"Angus took his father's death hard and remains bitter towards most people. He comes here to visit his father's grave most days. Mr Macmillan just called me – he requires your signature for another legal document."

"Fine – we may as well complete all the legalities today."

We arrived back at the firm's premises and Jane knocked on the door. She entered Mr Macmillan's office and nodded to me. I entered.

"James, sorry to bring you back. Another document requires your signature."

"No problem."

On his desk he placed the document in front of me. I put pen to paper.

"Did you enjoy your lunch?"

"Yes, excellent. Jane and I had an interesting conversation!"

He smiled. "Good show."

"What do you intend to do with regard to your profession?"

"To start a consultancy. Assist local firms market their products and services."

"A local hotel holds meetings of the Rotary Club. I am a member, and this would be a good opportunity to introduce yourself. It will make the local business fraternity aware of who you are."

"I agree."

"As Jane has to visit a client in Inveraray, she will take you to Docharnea."

"Splendid."

We left the office and reached Jane's car. The black, immaculate Mondeo hatchback sparkled on that sunny day. Then again, she always had a smart appearance.

She clicked in her seat belt, started the car and drove off. "Do you intend to buy a car?"

"When in France, I had a hair-raising experience. I'm still trying to get over it."

She smiled. "A local service exists, but if you need a car, get in touch. One of our clients has a local garage and can give you a good deal. Ah, here we are."

"That was quick!"

"Minutes from Ardrishaig in a car, James."

"Depends on the driver!"

The car pulled into a gatepost entrance and continued up the grey-pebbled driveway. Jane parked her car outside the front door of the villa.

She reached for her handbag. "James, you will require the services of a gardener."

I looked around the immediate vicinity. "It's a priority."

She handed me the keys for the property. "These are for the main house, and those for the coach house. As you can see, they all have tabs to avoid confusion. Incidentally, those three keys for the coach house are the originals."

"I can believe it!" Their size was twice that of normal keys. I got out of the car.

She lowered her car window and leaned out. "Any problems, phone myself or Mr Macmillan."

Her car ventured down the driveway, onto the road and made haste for Inveraray.

When I stood outside the main building, an eerie sensation came over me. I held a tabbed key in my hand for the main door. Let us hope this key fits in the lock. The burgundy painted double door opened, to reveal a mustard coloured reception room with a dark wooden table and two compatible chairs. On the table lay an envelope. I picked it up and opened it. Inside was a card. "Welcome – Macmillan and Mackay."

What a kind gesture. A business card had been attached, with a local gardener's contact details. Thanks, but he could wait for tomorrow to arrive!

I wandered in and out of the various ground floor rooms. They all appeared to have been well maintained. I went up the beige-carpeted staircase to look around the first floor. I opened a front bedroom window, poked my head out and admired the view of Loch Fyne. I could stay like this for hours – when the warmer spring weather appeared. I wandered downstairs, exited the back door and walked across the courtyard to the coach house. I examined the exterior and then went inside. The building needed a makeover. My initial enthusiasm must have concealed realism. Shabby stained walls, rotted wood, missing slates and a damaged chimney would need immediate restoration. This, plus three acres of overgrown weeds, lawns and many hedges, ensured I would hit the ground running. Tomorrow would be a day to organise work details, and therefore it was an early night for me.

I awoke suddenly. My bedside clock showed just before two. After the events of the previous day, I thought I would sleep like a log! From my bedroom, I could hear the sound of scraping. I pinpointed the noise to the courtyard. As my chosen upstairs bedroom window faced onto it, I peeked out. Through the darkness I could not detect any odd goings-on. I got back into my nice warm bed. Then I heard the creak of a door being opened and closed. Drat! I got up, put on some clothes, and went outside into the courtyard. I waited for a few minutes, but could not hear any further noises. I checked the various doors of the coach house. They were still locked. I therefore wandered back into the house and returned to my bed.

When dawn broke, the loud piercing ring of a doorbell startled me. I hauled myself up from the bed, organised myself and wandered downstairs to reception. I checked my appearance in the wall mirror and opened the door.

"Mr Carsell-Brown?"

I tried to look awake.

"Jane said you needed the services of a gardener."

Jane? "Oh, Mrs Mackay?"

"Yes, sir – she asked me to contact you. My name is Alex Ross."

"Can you start today, Mr Ross?"

"Yes, no problem, sir."

I escorted him around the grounds of Docharnea and highlighted the various sections that required urgent attention.

"It'll take a lot of 'ard work to 'ave the place up to scratch, Mr Carsell-Brown!"

"I agree! Do what is necessary." Poor chap.

A few hours passed and Mr Ross told me he would have to return the next day with an assistant. The magnitude of the task had been underestimated!

Throughout the day I looked around Docharnea with more scrutiny. Although the exterior grounds needed attention, the interior had received this in Olivia's time. At least that task could be erased from my agenda.

Instead of retiring for the night at my usual time, I held off a bit longer. Would I hear any strange noises from or near the coach house? Perhaps my imagination had gone into overdrive. I read a book in the downstairs study. I later glanced at the clock on the wall. It showed ten minutes past one. No weird noises this time! I laid down my book and headed upstairs. The only noise I heard came from the ticking of the clock.

A local firm of painters arrived early April to redecorate a particular part of the property. As the coach house looked tired and weary after decades of neglect, it required a facelift. The seasonal spring weather turned out warm for the time of year and, much appreciated given the climate, I left.

I went into my office to catch up on several business matters and correspondence. At present there were not enough hours in the day! Then I heard a knock on the rear door.

"Mr Carsell-Brown, can you give us a key to open an upstairs closet?"

"Can you show me this closet?"

"Yes sir, this way."

The painter took me to the coachman's quarters on the upstairs landing of the coach house. Sure enough, there was a locked closet there.

I turned to the painter. "This is news to me. I do not have a key."

"Don't you worry, Mr Carsell-Brown – one of our lads has a knack of being able to open locked doors."

Eddie the painter got to it. About ten minutes later, he pushed open the closet door. In front of us hung a dark hat and a red coat. On the floor lay a pair of black boots. These garments appeared to be originals of the attire worn by a resident coachman at Docharnea in the late nineteenth and early twentieth centuries. I put the items aside and let the painters continue their work.

Spring had indeed sprung. The fine weather made Docharnea look full of splendour in the sunshine, and was complimented by leaves on bare trees, trimmed hedges and lawns cut to precision. Rows of yellow daffodils accentuated the scene.

I thought it prudent to put spare house keys in a safe but discreet place out with the property, just in case I lost my set and couldn't gain entry. Once bitten, twice shy! I looked around and spotted a disused water well within the courtyard. I could hide the keys underneath a gap at its concrete base. I lifted it up. To my surprise, a key already lay there; I picked it up and put my house keys in its place. I then went into the coach house and upstairs to the coachman's quarters. I walked to the closet, inserted the key into the lock and turned it. The door locked and unlocked. I returned to the house and put my 'acquired' key in a kitchen drawer. I now had a set of four keys for the coach house.

As dusk fell that evening, I looked out of my panoramic lounge window. Across Loch Fyne, lights glittered along the coastline; a peaceful sight to behold. The Carsell-Browns who built Docharnea deserve great credit for such vision. Since I remained wide-awake, I read for a while. Then I heard an unfamiliar noise. It came from the courtyard. I had become used to the regular sounds of birds and animals within my vicinity. I put down my book and went to the rear entrance door. I stood behind it. There, I heard footsteps, irregular movements on the small pebbles. I went into a nearby cupboard to get my torch and checked to make sure it worked. I opened the rear door with care and apprehension. When I stepped outside, movements could be heard. I peered in the direction of the darkened courtyard. I spotted someone at the main coach house door. I switched on the torchlight and rushed forward.

"Stay where you are and do not move!"

As he turned my way, I recognised the person. He ran off over a lawn and in the direction of the road. I alerted the local Police Constabulary of my intruder. Within the hour, they had captured Angus.

"Did he admit attempting to break into the coach house, officer?"

"Yes, but he would not elaborate on the matter."

"An unauthorised person may have been in the grounds on a recent occasion."

"Angus did tell us he had not been here on any other occasion, sir."

"Maybe I did imagine it."

"If you have any further problems, sir, do not hesitate to contact us."

The two police officers left and I had a look around the coach house. Before I went into the house I gazed at the sky full of stars. What next?

As I wandered upstairs to the bedroom, I recalled that Angus had said the property was haunted. I did hear something in the vicinity of the coach house on my first night. However I did not experience fear or feel threatened. If a ghost did exist, then perhaps it was an amiable spirit.

# Chapter 4

## *Turning Back Time*

The next day I went over to the coach house, with a view of determining options for usage. This historic building, full of character, had potential.

I unlocked a door which led to the first floor, climbed the stairs and entered the coachman's room. Since the renovation, it looked as good as new. Magnolia walls, white ceiling doors and windows plus a sanded wooden floor. The smell of paint lingered. I opened the double window which looked onto the garden and Loch Fyne. The coachman of more than a century ago must have enjoyed his way of life. Plenty of fresh air, driving a fashionable coach and being part of a prestigious household. He was also supplied with an appropriate outfit in order to adhere with a code of dress protocol. I walked over to the closet. I wanted to have another look at the outfit which had been discovered. A pair of authentic coachman's boots, hat and coat. Would the coat fit? It appeared about my size, and perhaps I had found a new item of fashion. I tried on the coat for size. A near perfect fit! I put on the hat – I looked taller. I took off my shoes and managed to squeeze my legs into the tight knee-length boots. I walked over to a mirror situated above the fireplace. I stood up straight – not bad! My white shirt and black trousers matched the dark hat, red coat and black boots.

Then the room started to spin.

I came to, flat on my back with the ceiling in full view. I got up with not too much discomfort. I looked at my watch to discover how much time had passed. It had stopped, no doubt damaged in the fall. Daylight filled the room, but no noise came from the nearby main road. Also, where were my shoes? I walked slowly down the staircase. The boots felt uncomfortable. When I got to the bottom, I found the door locked. Who could have done that, and how? I had the key in my trouser pocket. I unlocked the door and stepped out into the courtyard. The surface was comprised of grass rather than small grey pebbles. The main building appeared smaller – a side extension had disappeared. Also, the door colour had gone from brown to black and someone had closed it. I was glad that I had placed a spare set of house keys outside in a discreet place. I looked under the disused water well's concrete base, and found no keys. In fact, the well appeared operational due to traces of water use. I started to observe other differences. The landscape had altered – there were no trees, bushes or flowers. Properties in close proximity to Docharnea had also been erased. What was going on? I knocked on the door – no answer. Still in my coachman's outfit, I went down to the main road. When I got there, I found yet another contrast. The road to and from Ardrishaig now resembled a rugged and narrower surface. The view across Loch Fyne still portrayed a picturesque scene. At least it remained the same.

I walked eastwards to clear my head and investigate. Soon a car would appear and I could ask the driver what was going on. After a couple of miles, no vehicles had appeared. My feet started to ache in the unfamiliar boots. Then I heard the clip-clop and clatter of something about to come round a bend. Two brown horses and a white cart approached. The driver wore a grey coat with black trousers. He also had knee-length boots, but sported a cap rather than a hat. I could not believe my eyes. As the cart got closer, I moved towards the edge of the road and put out my hand.

The driver pulled on the horse's reigns.

"Excuse me, where can I find Dochar?"

"What is it?" The driver looked puzzled.

"It's a small hamlet."

"There is no place called that around 'ere! I'll take you to Ardrishaig if you want?"

How weird. This was surreal!

"Do you want a lift or not?"

I nodded and got onto the cart. "Thanks."

He made a clicking noise with his mouth and the cart moved off.

"Do you stay around here?"

"I'm the local delivery man. I distribute food, drink, hardware and letters to and from Ardrishaig. I cover most of this area and beyond."

*Admirable.* "Do you work for a company?"

"No sir, I work for meself, but I'm retiring next month. My aunt passed away and left me a small fortune. No need for me to work anymore!"

As to his retirement plans, I became curious. "Any plans?"

"I want to visit Russia. It's such a vast country – might take the rest of my life!"

"Why Russia?"

"I visited part of the country on a previous occasion, but want to see the rest of it."

"Which part?"

"The Crimea – I fought there against the Tsar's army at Balaclava."

I looked at him. "The Charge of the Light Brigade?"

"That's correct sir. I'm one of the survivors. Got wounded but nowt serious, just a bit of shrapnel in my leg."

*What year was this?* Then the cart jerked, I held on tightly.

He looked at me. "You all right, sir?"

"The local authority needs to resurface the road."

"They did sir, thirty years ago!"

"Is the Docharnea estate far from here?" If so, then it was at least 1896.

"Docharnea? A short distance along this road, sir. It has just been built. One of my new customers."

"Are you headed there?"

"Yes, to visit Mr and Mrs Carsell-Brown. They like a tipple!" He nudged me. "I've a case of spirits for them."

"How often do they have a delivery?"

He laughed. "When the case is finished!"

I had somehow been thrown back in time by one hundred and four years! This could not be a hoax.

"Excuse me for askin' sir, but what is that on your wrist?"

My digital wristwatch! I hesitated for a moment. "A present from my aunt. She brought it back from America. A new invention – a clock bracelet!"

"Does it work, sir?"

"Now and again. This is the second time today it has stopped working."

"It looks too advanced, sir. That is why it doesn't work! We get those new fancy inventions but when they break down, nobody knows how to fix 'em."

Interesting theory. However, I removed my watch and concealed it in my trouser pocket. I hope men did have trouser pockets in that era!

"Ah, 'ere we are, Docharnea. My last delivery for Friday." He pulled on the reigns and the horses stopped. He then wrenched back the cart brake lever.

A lady stood at the roadside. "Good day."

The driver got down. "Your delivery, madam." He pulled off a case from the cart.

She looked up at me. "Have you come about the coachman's position?"

"Yes I have." Maybe I could discover what had happened.

"Good show."

I got down and picked up the case. "Let me carry this for you."

The driver handed the lady a receipt.

She gave him a bundle of silver coins.

"Thank you, madam." He got on the cart, pushed forward the brake lever, lifted the horse's reins and moved off.

"Come this way. You have arrived at the perfect time. I have just this minute returned home."

Tall, broad and brash. She wore a long black pleated dress with puffed sleeves and white cuffs. Her grey hair pulled back from her forehead and knotted at the back. The reality now struck me. I could no longer be in the year 2000! No reception room existed in this era. The lady looked at my head. Oops, my hat – I took it off. When entering a house I must remember to remove my hat. I was taken into one of the public rooms, a bold, dark blue coloured 'arena' with large cream plump furniture and a selection of stuffed creatures. The parrot looked real.

"Please sit down." She directed me to a particular chair. "My name is Mary Carsell-Brown." She sat down on a nearby couch.

"My name is James Car… Carlisle."

"Do you have a stutter?"

"No, just a bit nervous."

"I understand; this room can be intimidating."

A close shave – I had to remember that this lady was a distant relative.

"I see you have come dressed for the interview. I like that – authenticity!"

I smiled. No doubt about it, it was accurate timing!

"As a coachman, do you have much experience?"

"I stayed with a family who also had a coach house and carried out various duties."

"Where?"

"Musselburgh, on the outskirts of Edinburgh."

"Why did you leave and come all this way?"

"The family I worked for moved abroad. The new owners already had their own coachman. Also, I wanted to experience more of the Scottish countryside." It sounded plausible.

"Well, you would have covered a large area to get here. Do you like to travel?"

"Yes, it brings a sense of adventure."

"What is the farthest you have travelled?"

"From Edinburgh to Aberdeen. The new railway bridge across the River Forth has made travel to Fife and beyond easier."

"What other interests do you have?"

"I watch vaudeville, attend the theatre, read and go for long walks in the countryside."

She smiled for the first time. "Not many theatres exist out here!"

"Then I can catch up with my books."

"What do you like to read about?"

"Politics, economics, society and technology."

She had a pensive expression. "Technology?"

"It is a new word used for future development."

"I suppose those subjects you read about are connected somehow?"

Correct, in the foreseeable future.

"What major advancements do you envisage will happen in the next century?"

*How the world would change over the next twenty years. Empires would fall and new countries emerge out of the Great War.* "I read that people may one day travel by air to Europe, the United States and beyond."

"If President McKinley of America has his way, then it could be sooner rather than later. The Republicans are proactive."

"There may soon be much faster steam trains which could reduce travel times."

"James, I will settle for a faster horse and carriage."

*That was not too far away either – the motorised version!*

"You spoke of the theatre – do you like Gilbert and Sullivan?"

"Yes, he's a good performer."

She looked puzzled. "He?"

"Oh, both are excellent."

"Which of their plays did you enjoy?"

"The Mikado, which I went to see in Gladstone Theatre, Edinburgh. Also Pirates of Penzance at the Palace Theatre on my visit to Aberdeen." I started to realise the high expectations of a prospective coachman, given the intensity of this interview.

"What is your impression of this new invention called 'cinematography'?"

"All of the music halls could be turned into places where people watch film scenes."

"I disagree – music halls will prevail!"

*Not in the next century, they wouldn't!*

"A final question, James. What level of education have you received?"

All this for the role of a coachman! "I attended Edinburgh University and studied subjects with a creative connection." *Please don't ask about 'creative connection'.*

"That does not surprise me."

The grandfather clock chimed. Then came a knock on the door. A woman came into the room with a similar appearance to my host.

"Madam, would you like afternoon tea served in here or the drawing room?"

"Here is fine, Hannah."

The housekeeper left the room and then returned with a tray. She laid it on a table, poured the tea and departed.

Tea and something to eat – just what I needed.

"You must try one of Hannah's tea cookies."

I lifted one from a plate and had a bite. Delicious! I could taste the vanilla.

"Do have another."

"Thank you." I was famished. I also appreciated the Earl Grey tea with its fruity, citrus aroma.

"James, you appear overeducated for this position, but if you want it, then I shall be delighted."

"And I also, madam."

"Then it is settled."

I sipped my cup of tea. "At present how do you travel to the village?"

"We hire transport, but it can be unreliable and thus inconvenient. The horses and our new coach are in place." She drank her tea. "We had another candidate, but the poor chap could not hear me. When I spoke to him, I had to raise my voice!"

Over tea and cookies, I was informed of my duties. They would include her husband being taken to and from the bank in Ardrishaig where he was employed – this would occur every six days per week – taking Mrs Carsell-Brown to various daily destinations and caring for the horses. I would also clean and maintain the coach, stables and hayloft, plus my quarters, to an acceptable standard. To clean the stables was a task I would not relish. For this I would receive a wage, free accommodation, one meal per day and a free day on Sunday to attend church.

"We can also supply you with another coachman's outfit. It looks similar to the one you have on. Some unused items of furniture exist which you can have to make your quarters more habitable. If you have any problems, let me know."

"There is one problem. I lost my bag, which contained all my clothes. Is there a menswear shop in the village?"

"A charity shop is situated in the main street. It can cater for all your needs." She handed me a set of black keys.

*My goodness, the originals – shiny and new!*

"The smaller one is for a door which leads upstairs to your quarters. This large key is for the stables and the third key relates to the coach room." She then gave me a silver key. "This one is for the closet in your quarters."

*I already knew that.*

"Try not to lose them – however, I have a spare set for emergencies. Come, I will show you around the coach house."

Mrs Carsell-Brown 'introduced' me to both horses, Cole and Char. Appropriate names, I thought. Then she opened one of the large double doors to reveal a coach, which I would estimate was ten feet in length and six feet in width. The black, four-wheeled household vehicle had a forward facing seat, which could accommodate two passengers. It would suffice for short journeys. I got taken upstairs to the quarters and opened the window.

She pointed. "Next door is the hayloft."

*I already knew that too.*

"I'll be back soon."

I looked around my 'new accommodation', which I had been departed from only a matter of hours earlier. How strange to witness the room in its original state. But as I had got the room restored, both appeared similar. The weather in this time period remained warm, and therefore I wouldn't miss my modern central heating system. I took out my watch – it had now started to function. Until I returned to my future, I must have made sure to keep it concealed. When would I be able to return, and how? I heard someone clomp up the staircase.

"James, here is your new coachman's hat and coat. And you will need these." Mrs Carsell-Brown handed me the outfit, plus bed linen. "If you require anything, let me know."

"Thank you."

"Do you like the quarters?"

"Yes, they have been built to last."

"Built to last?"

She had that puzzled look again. "The building looks superb."

"It should be. The tradesmen got paid well for their endeavours."

I smiled.

"Take tomorrow off – it will give you time to settle into your quarters." She left the room.

The workmanship in this construction would stay intact into the twenty-first century. I examined my new coachman's attire – the new black hat, black leather boots and deep, red coat. In fact, it was possibly the same outfit discovered in the locked closet which I was wearing. Due to the passage of time, my coat now looked more of a pale red. I had a spare outfit, but what I would have given for a spare electric razor. I knew that I must somehow adjust to a wet shave.

As my normal day commenced at six, I would have to make sure to adjust my late nights and retire earlier. I put together a makeshift bed and snuggled into it. Then looked at my digital wristwatch in this nineteenth century accommodation – nine forty six. I was glad that I had a sense of adventure, and humour!

The morning before I had met with Mr Carsell-Brown. He was shorter, slimmer and quiet-spoken – most unlike his wife. I got the impression he could be a man of few words and not an open book. I then carried out my initial coachman's duty. A bright April sun shone and made the new black coach gleam. I drove Mr and Mrs Carsell-Brown to Ardrishaig for a Sunday morning church service. Both wore sober black attire and held their own bibles.

When we arrived, the vicinity around the village church had coaches in abundance, this being the era when everyone attended church at least once on Sunday. After I managed to park the coach in a proficient manner, they got out and strolled towards the church. I followed, and when we entered, Charles and his wife made for a particular seat near the pulpit. I got instructed by a church officer to sit in a rear pew along with other coachmen.

On the return journey to Docharnea, my two passengers did not converse with me. I was sure that if my coachman's duties had not been competent, I would have been informed. I could be satisfied with my initial driving performance. Cole and Char kept me on the straight and narrow.

Six o'clock came too soon that Monday morning. I could hardly keep my eyes open for the first hour. At least I got a long lie on a Sunday morning – seven o'clock!

My first duty involved Charles Carsell-Brown being taken to his place of work at the local bank in Ardrishaig. I then returned to Docharnea, collected his wife and returned to the village.

She leaned forward. "James, take a short break. I shall return in an hour from now."

"Fine, madam."

She got out the coach and went into a clothes shop in the main street.

Before a walk along the main street, I secured the coach and horses. After a few minutes in my uncomfortable boots, I came across Macmillan Solicitors. As the office was in the same location, this must have been the Victorian version. I looked through the window with curiosity. Still in the same part of the office stood a reception desk. A lady in a long black dress read a broadsheet newspaper. Some behavioural patterns never change – no matter what century! Similar to Mary Carsell-Brown, the middle-aged lady's hair had been pulled back and knotted.

I continued along the street and noticed a public house named The Highwayman. This outlet did not exist in my future time. I entered the small bar. It had a raw, splintered wooden floor and dark brown painted walls. I could smell pipe tobacco. The bald barman sported a pointed black beard and wore a white apron over a red waistcoat.

He leaned forward with both hands on the bar. "Yes, sir?"

"A glass of lager please."

"Pardon, sir?" He had a bemused expression. "We don't stock it sir – who brews the stuff?"

"A brewery in Glasgow."

"The only beer we sell is ale."

"I'll take a glass."

He poured me a glass and laid it on the bar.

I took a sip, and it tasted terrible; strong was an understatement! Then again, it *was* cask ale. "Barman, could you please add some water?"

"Of course, sir." He took my glass, tipped water into it. "Here you are, sir."

I took a sip. "Better."

A fellow customer gave me a gentle nudge. "He's already added water before the pub opened! Some of us know about his tricks. It's daylight robbery if you ask me!"

I finished my drink and put my empty glass on the wooden counter.

The barman came towards me.

I gave him a shilling. "Will that cover my drink?"

He smiled, nodded and grabbed the coin. "I don't 'ave any change, sir."

Upon my departure from the Victorian establishment, I speculated as to where the barman kept Black Bess.

I next popped into the charity shop for clothes – from one extreme to another. I waited patiently for Mrs Carsell-Brown. She had been kind enough to give me an advance on my wage. I did not enjoy being skint. Pity no money had also been transported back in time. In today's value, it would be worth a small fortune. Whilst perched on my driver's seat, I looked at the clock on a tower. It was time for my passenger to return. She appeared at the side of the coach.

"I hope you haven't been here too long?"

"No, madam. I took a wander along the main street and just got back."

"Good show. Don't use up valuable time sitting around – life is too short!"

As I drove the coach back to Docharnea, she read a newspaper. Perhaps her philosophy could be waste not, want not. I should have taken note.

I slowly adapted to this new way of life. Not just to my role as a coachman, but also to nineteenth century culture. Maybe a keen historical interest for the period was a factor. Whatever – I still focused on a return to the twenty-first century but I wanted to experience this unique opportunity for a bit longer.

Charles Carsell-Brown commenced work at eight thirty each morning from Monday to Saturday. He had a wide dark moustache and pointed beard. His attire for work and church had an uncanny similarity – a top hat, long black frock coat, dark waistcoat and trousers. He always wore a white shirt with the collars turned upwards and a suitable necktie to match. Needless to say, his shoes were also coloured black.

We departed Docharnea at eight o'clock each morning. He would then light his pipe and read a book. Little or no conversation took place on the outward journey. I would collect him around thirty minutes past six in the evening. The resolute Victorian gentlemen put a large amount of hours into their week at work. On the return journey, he would again light his pipe and read a book. On every journey we made apart from Sunday, he buried himself in a book taken from his personal library. However, I did observe each Saturday, he liked to chat and read. On one particular Saturday, he confessed a desire to travel around the world and explore foreign countries. This would allow him to experience their diverse cultures.

I asked, "Which country would you like to visit?"

"Mrs Carsell-Brown and I share an ambition to explore Africa. It has a wide variety of wildlife and primitive civilisations. Before progress removes its infancy, we want to experience this continent while still in a primitive state."

A holiday to Africa would take an eternity by Victorian ships. As he only received two weeks holiday per year; it would take that just to get there. I elected to talk about a topic, which would revolutionise travel within cities.

"I read Glasgow could soon open an underground railway system at the end of this year."

He looked up from his book. "With steam trains?"

"No, only carriages. Cables are used to pull them through the tunnels."

"Extraordinary! The cables must be strong." He returned to his book.

We approached Docharnea. For our next conversation, the possibility of man able to travel towards the moon would be interesting. I awaited with interest the view of a resident Victorian.

When I returned to my quarters, I reflected on the conversation with Charles Carsell-Brown. A gentleman with a steady, rigid and unfashionable job but wanted to explore a distant primitive continent. The zest for adventure must have been a hereditary trait within my family.

On one Tuesday afternoon, Mary Carsell-Brown breezed across the courtyard. I had not yet finished polishing the coach. I hoped there was no imminent task that needed my attention.

"James, I have to visit Ardrishaig. How long will you be?"

"About five minutes, madam." Oh well!

"Good – I'll be right back."

I put away the cleaning materials and got ready for coachman duties. How I hated wearing that hat, especially in nice sunny weather. I waited perched on the coach for my passenger. Here she was.

"Where to, madam?"

"Head for Ardrishaig, James." She got into the coach and closed the door.

We came out the driveway and headed towards the village. What an experience to have exclusive passage on the road.

"Isn't this a lovely view, James?"

I glanced over to the coastline.

"Loch Fyne lives up to its name on a day such as this."

"And with such splendour."

"James, I intend to visit my solicitor about a legal matter."

"Mr Macmillan?"

"Yes, how did you know?"

"Just a hunch, madam. I noticed his office when I last visited Ardrishaig."

"Two other legal firms practice within the area, but he has an excellent reputation for service."

"It always pays dividends."

"Tell me, James, how do you spend your spare time?"

"I still read as much as I can. A Scottish golfer called James Foulis won a tournament in New York last month."

"The American people will sit up and take notice! Any other subject areas of interest?"

"I have just finished a novel written last year by an English author able to travel through time."

"Similar to the fiction that we may somehow fly everywhere one day?"

I smiled.

"Let us talk of another subject. Do you believe women are not recognised in society? All we do is tend to the house and family."

A shot out of the blue! "I believe that in the future, women shall get recognition and representation in most aspects of society. This will ensure a fair and just culture."

"James, you are indeed a smart person!"

It was an advantage to have knowledge of the future.

As we reached the solicitor's office, Mrs Carsell-Brown advised me that she would stay in the village until early evening. She gave me a note of the address to collect her later in the day.

Rather than return to Docharnea, I stayed in the village and visited a tearoom. This warm weather did bring a thirst to my mouth. The outlet had twelve customers and fourteen chairs. The sole waitress spotted me.

"Be there soon, sir."

I removed my hat, nodded, and took a seat.

"Yes, sir?"

"Iced lemon tea, please."

She smiled. "Won't be long."

The room had a light décor, white tables and chairs with red tablecloths. The customers consisted of women who must have felt warm in their long heavy dresses on this warm sunny day. Five of them still had their hats on.

I had my beverage, paid the waitress and walked back along the main street and to the coach. Before collecting Charles Carsell-Brown from the bank, I watered the horses. They nodded their approval.

When I pulled up outside the bank, Mr Carsell-Brown had locked the doors and put the keys inside his waistcoat pocket. He smiled and got into the coach.

"Where is Mrs Carsell-Brown? She mentioned at breakfast about being in the village this afternoon."

"She has arranged to meet some friends, sir. I have to collect her at eight o'clock."

"Not another of those social meetings!" He lit his pipe and started to read a book.

On my way back to Docharnea, I speculated if this could be the inception of women who desired a change in social attitudes. The Suffragette movement had its origins in the late Victorian era; therefore I would watch and listen for evidence of this poignant time.

Before my departure to collect Mrs Carsell-Brown, I had a meal of fish and potatoes. A journey to Ardrishaig would be enhanced by good weather. On the evening drive, the sun shone high in the sky and the calm loch to my right resembled a mirror. Whilst transfixed in this state, it dawned on me that everybody in my future had not yet been born – a unique but strange situation, and the history of my family still to unfold. I perceived this sentiment as one which brought a tinge of solitude. I had to somehow get back to my own era. Was I being missed, or was time stagnant in the future?

I reached the address earlier than expected. The property looked comparable to Docharnea but with mature gardens. The gardener would be kept busy! An elderly, well-dressed gentleman welcomed me at the entrance.

"Come this way." He guided me into the reception area.

Mrs Carsell-Brown emerged from a room. "James, I want you to meet some friends of mine." She led me into a large, elegant and plush room where a group of ladies waited. "This is Lady Lydia Beaumont, Lady Elizabeth Thompson, Dr Flora Murray, Mary Butler and Martha Reid."

I observed their distinguished appearances. Three of them wore a long, dark, bulky gown complete with a high neckline and cuffs. Two of the older ladies, Elizabeth Thompson and Martha Reid, also had a shawl. Mary Butler wore a long black dress similar to Mary Carsell-Brown. All but one wore their hair in a different style, Flora Murray being the exception. Her black hair was loose, curly and short. She had on a sleeveless light-coloured flared dress with frills.

Lady Beaumont gave me a broad smile. "We have heard you are well-read and knowledgeable."

"I like to read and keen to learn about current events – not just in our country, but also further afield. What happens in other countries can affect us."

She turned to her friend. "You were correct, Mary."

Lady Thompson asked, "Have you read any literature on equality in society?"

"No I haven't, Lady Thompson, but I believe that issue could become topical in the future."

Dr Murray said, "What reason would lead you to say that?"

I found myself in a tight corner with five formidable and educated ladies. I had to choose my answers carefully. "As a country develops and prospers, then so should their society and economic structure. We are a powerful nation, therefore to remain in this position, standards must be maintained and raised. Education for all types of class is a step to achieve this. An awareness of equality should ensue through time. Change does come. It may take years, or even decades, but change should occur." The room went silent, with everyone staring in my direction.

"Also a visionary!" said Lady Beaumont.

Mary Carsell-Brown moved towards me. "James, you better take me home. Charles is a stickler for time!"

She excused herself and said goodbye to her friends. At reception the elderly gentleman assisted with putting on her jacket.

As I drove back to Docharnea, I could hear a faint noise. There, I heard it again! The noise came from the front wheel.

"Pity you did not meet Flora Stevenson James. She is a tireless campaigner to give proper education to the extreme poor."

"That would be beneficial to everyone, whether rich or poor!"

She smiled.

"Is the gentleman I met a relative, madam?"

"No, he is the butler. His name is Russell."

When I reached Docharnea, I stopped at the front of the house and allowed Mrs Carsell-Brown to step out. I continued round to the coach house. I parked the coach, got down from my seat and examined the underside. Where had that noise come from? I did not detect any apparent defect. I separated the horses from the coach and took them to the stable.

As I lay in bed, my thought for this day revolved around those ladies I met tonight. Did any of them play a part in society being transformed? To see and experience history unfold is indeed a gift. I will embrace it with wisdom.

Two days later, Charles Carsell-Brown appeared with a small box. I had just finished a sweep of the hayloft.

"James, this is from Lady Beaumont. It got delivered yesterday." He handed the box to me.

"Hold on." I washed my hands at the water tap.

He then gave me the box.

I opened it. I looked down on a ginger cake with icing on the top. I smiled. "Splendid, I shall enjoy this!"

"Incidentally, a chap will start next week to look after the grounds. His name is Angus."

*Where had I heard such a name?*

"In case you see a stranger wandering around." He walked back to the house.

I had not long finished my evening meal, but would manage a piece of cake. This is a welcome treat! I sat down in the courtyard and had a slice. Ginger cake tasted even more delicious in the nineteenth century! However, I then had to collect Mrs Carsell–Brown from another meeting.

I went upstairs to my quarters with the cake and stored it in an appropriate place. I would look forward to the next piece. I changed into my coachman's outfit and departed Docharnea for the estate of Lady Beaumont. I knew I must thank her for the cake.

I arrived promptly and waited in the reception area. Lady Beaumont appeared with a well-dressed dark-haired boy.

"James, this is my son, Edward."

He held out his hand. "How do you do?"

"Very well, thank you." I shook his hand.

Lady Beaumont put both of her hands on Edward's shoulders. "He is keen to learn about the capital city of Scotland."

"It would give me pleasure to enlighten Edward on my home city." Even if my knowledge related to the present rather than the nineteenth century.

We went into a bright public room, sat down on a long couch, and chatted. On occasions it became difficult to try and portray certain features of Victorian Edinburgh, but I managed to improvise. However, some places of interest such as Edinburgh Castle, Holyrood Palace and the Royal Mile remained not too dissimilar over the centuries!

"James, why is it called the Royal Mile?" said Edward.

"Because the street is a mile in length. It has a castle at the top and a palace at the bottom. It is also known as the High Street."

"Do a lot of people stay in the Royal Mile?"

"Yes, people stay in tenement flats up and down the Mile. An acquaintance of mine once stayed there."

"What is a tenement flat?"

"They are properties with a number of rooms where people either live above or below each other."

"Is that not claustrophobic?"

"The acquaintance I knew became convinced."

"How do people enter their properties?"

"Through a doorway called a 'close', and then a stairway."

Edward turned to Lady Beaumont. "It sounds fascinating, mother!"

"Most definitely," said Lady Beaumont.

I then mentioned horses and carriages in the cobbled streets around the centre of Edinburgh, the familiar clip-clop sound of horses, sites of culture in the form of the National Museum of Scotland, and the Scottish Art Gallery, plus Edinburgh University.

"When school finishes, I would like to attend Edinburgh University."

His mother nodded in approval.

I then described Princes Street with its prestigious shops, and the beautiful gardens where brass bands entertained the public on a regular basis. I remembered it well! The castle which overlooked the gardens in Princes Street was a formidable, but picturesque sight.

"James, will you ever return to Edinburgh?"

"Perhaps one day."

I continued to talk of Princes Street and how, at opposite ends of this magnificent street, were Waverley and Caledonian railway stations. They supplied the main lines north, south, east and west of Edinburgh, together with the suburban inner lines. The Forth Railway Bridge, built six years beforehand, created a gateway to the far north of Scotland.

"For so many trains, there must be a large number of people who stay in the city."

This boy was inquisitive. "About two hundred and fifty thousand citizens stay there, and the population will no doubt increase throughout the years. Many people also visit Edinburgh and trains get used to transport coal, iron ore and other materials to assist the welfare of the country."

"Can you travel by boat to Edinburgh?"

"Yes, a route out to sea from Granton Harbour and the port of Leith. Sailors and merchants use the local inns and public houses to socialise and 'barter' in business matters."

"What does 'barter' mean, James?"

"Negotiate to gain an advantage."

Mary Carsell-Brown entered the room. "Has James enlightened you about his birthplace, Edward?"

The twelve year-old nodded his head. "I would very much like to visit the city."

"One day, but it is now time for you to retire," said Lady Beaumont.

"Goodnight," said Edward.

I omitted to tell him of 'haunted closes' in the Royal Mile. That could wait for another day.

I thanked Lady Beaumont for her gift, and then Mary Carsell-Brown and I departed. Another calm, warm evening accompanied us on the journey back to Docharnea.

"Lord Beaumont wants Edward to join the Army. It remains a family tradition."

"I can understand, madam."

"As skirmishes occur on a regular basis with the British Empire, Lady Beaumont prefers a political career."

"I can also understand that view. There are many underdeveloped countries. They may become insecure. This can manifest itself in a period of hostility. History has many examples."

"Correct, James, but when does peace break out?"

"Maybe sometime in the future." Two world wars would bring misery, suffering and carnage.

Just before we reached Docharnea, I heard a faint, unfamiliar sound again and slowed down.

"What is the matter, James?"

"I heard a noise. It came from the front wheel."

"I did not hear any noise."

"I can just hear it."

She leaned forward on her seat. "No, nothing."

"As a precaution madam, I believe the coach should be checked."

"I agree – but only if the noise gets worse."

On the remainder of our journey to Docharnea, I did not hear the noise. However, I sensed something was wrong – even though it was a new coach.

I looked forward to Saturdays. Charles Carsell-Brown would smile on this day of the week. Everyone appeared relaxed. On that particular Saturday afternoon, I tended to the horses and then washed the coach. Mary Carsell-Brown interrupted my relaxed work routine.

"James, have you spotted Angus within the last few days?"

"The new gardener, madam?"

"Yes – since Tuesday he has failed to appear for work!"

"Could he be ill?"

"Well, it must be alcohol poisoning! Charles sent him home for being intoxicated."

I smiled. "Maybe he is still recovering!"

"If he returns, could you monitor his movements?"

I agreed, but I also remembered the situation revealed to me in the twenty-first century. A gardener who worked at Docharnea had been dismissed. Could this be connected to the fateful event where a future relative had held a long-time grudge against the Carsell-Browns?

On that afternoon I sat back to read my book. The sun shone amidst the blue sky. If I had to leave this era, I would miss the superb climate! My book, *The Time Machine* by H.G. Wells, had a certain relevance. I had purchased the book on a visit to Lochgilphead. As I started another chapter, I noticed the gardener cross the lawn and slump onto a bench. He appeared tired – must have been too much hard work! He then got up and staggered towards a nearby outhouse. After forty minutes, he had not come out. I went across to check on his condition. When I entered, he lay fast asleep. I shook his upper arm and he gave me a startled look.

"Sir, I just dozed off!"

"Are you all right?" His breath smelled of alcohol.

"Yes, thank you, sir. My wife has not long given birth to our son. I didn't get any sleep last night!"

He had continued to celebrate the birth. "I would suggest you go home. If Mrs Carsell-Brown catches you in this state, she will not be pleased! I will explain you had to an emergency at home."

"Thank you, sir – I'll go home right away."

Upon meeting her circle of friends, I again collected Mary Carsell-Brown from Lady Beaumont's residence. This must have been the designated place for ladies' discreet discussion!

She got into the coach and sat back. "How have you spent your time today, James?"

I drove off. "I cleaned out the stables and managed to catch up on my book."

"H.G. Wells?"

"Yes madam."

"Did you see Angus today?"

"Yes."

"Did he carry out all of his chores?"

"I believe so – he looked tired!"

"He has worked on the perimeter which surrounds the property. Trees and flowerbeds have been planted."

The work Angus had undertaken would become synonymous with Docharnea. It would add beauty and character for future owners to admire, me being one of them.

"James, a housekeeper has commenced. An excellent cook, so I have been told."

"Splendid." Maybe I would receive larger portions for my meal. I parked the coach and then led both horses into their nice clean stable. I hoped they appreciated my toil and discomfort. I washed some garments in my quarters and then heard footsteps. I opened the door, and there stood a lady with a cheerful expression.

"Hello James, I'm Nancy, the new housekeeper." She held out her hand.

I shook it – ouch! "Please come in." She was about my age, small in height but large in fortitude – deliveries to the house had better be on time! During our chat, I also perceived that she was a warm and genuine person.

She walked to the door and stopped. "James, are you aware the gardener has been dismissed?"

"Dismissed? He is an excellent gardener."

"Well, he has gone!" She continued down the stairs and closed the main door.

I had to speak with Mary to try and rectify the situation. I went across to the house and met with her. Could Angus be given another chance? She would not be aware of his circumstances.

"James, Charles dismissed Angus. His unpunctuality got worse."

"I believe his wife has taken ill and they have a newly-born son to care for."

"I understand, James, but when Charles has made a decision then it is final."

"Does anyone in the area require a gardener?"

"I can contact Lady Beaumont. The grounds which surround her property require urgent attention."

Two days had passed when Mary came across the courtyard. I had just finished cleaning the windows of the coach house.

"The windows in the house could do with a clean, James!"

"Will do, madam"

"I spoke to Lydia. She would welcome someone to tend the grounds of her house."

"Splendid. I will contact Angus."

"Good luck."

I cleaned the windows of the main house and then made my way to Angus' address. But before that, I stopped off at the local coach repair firm in Ardrishaig. A man approached me.

"Yes, sir, can I help you?"

"Would you check the front wheels of the coach? An unusual noise appears now and again."

"I'll examine it right now, sir."

"I have to visit someone. Is this near here?" I showed him a scribbled note of Angus' address.

"Not far, sir."

I got to the address forty minutes later and with two sore feet. Those boots are murder! I found the small house and knocked on the door. The cracked doorstep and window added to a run-down frontage. However, the small compact garden had received professional care. There was no answer, so I tried again. I heard a baby cry, and then the disjointed, squeaky door opened.

"Why have you come here, sir?" Angus looked bedraggled.

"A property requires your skills for garden design and maintenance."

"Me, sir?"

"Yes. Do you want the job?"

"Of course sir, of course."

"It is essential you are always punctual and curtail the consumption of alcohol. In other words, cut out the booze!"

"You have my word sir."

I gave him Lady Beaumont's address, plus a piece of paper. "The latter will inform people of your garden expertise. Take it to the local printer and ask him to make copies. Then distribute them around properties with gardens."

"Distribute, sir?"

"Visit the properties and give the owner a leaflet. This should cover the printing cost." I handed over two half-crowns.

"How can I repay you, sir?"

"Just do your best, and that shall suffice."

He gave me a warm handshake and I departed.

It only took me thirty painful minutes to reach the coach repairers. As I entered the premises, the same man approached.

"Just as well you brought the coach to us, sir!"

"Then there was a problem?"

"Most definitely! The futchel must have got damaged somehow. It connects to the front axle. The wheel would have dislodged from the coach." He stared at the coach. "Unusual for that to 'appen." He turned to me. "I have replaced the part, and it'll be fine now."

A stretch of road three quarters of a mile from Docharnea would be a potential danger spot, with its steep embankments on a sharp bend. If a coach went out of control, then a catastrophe would ensue.

"Here you are, sir." He gave me a bill to pass on to the coach owner.

"Thanks." I got on the coach and drove back to Docharnea.

# Chapter 5

## *The Coachman Returns*

I awoke the next day with a feeling of contentment. Angus had the opportunity to embark on a new career and provide for his family. A possible fatal accident with the coach had been averted. I got ready for my first duty of that fine day. The morning sunshine beamed through the window and lit up my quarters. As usual, I patted my pockets to confirm my keys and watch. Then I looked in the mirror to check my appearance – fine. I started to feel light-headed again.

I gathered my senses. Before passing out, I managed to grab a chair and slump into it. I went into my trouser pocket and took out my watch. I gazed at the time – the watch had stopped. I got up out of the chair and regained my composure. At least this time I did not end up flat on my back. I looked around the room and observed other pieces of furniture. I went over to the closet and opened the door. Unrecognisable garments included a jacket and pair of trousers. Cheekily, I took off my distinctive coachman's outfit and replaced it with those items of clothes. They were a bit on the large side, but would suffice. I hid my uniform in a discreet place.

I went downstairs and unlocked the door. Could I have returned to my own time? I stepped outside and observed the property. I came to the quick conclusion I had not. A number of years had passed, but not one hundred and four! Colourful flowerbeds, precision trimmed hedges, 'bowling green' lawns and tree-lined sections now engulfed and enriched Docharnea. The trees stood just half of a normal height, and therefore I estimated fifteen to twenty years had gone by. The climate had become cooler – surely this couldn't be summertime? The rear door of the main house opened, and a lady walked in my direction. She looked at me with astonishment.

"James, is it you? What happened to you? Where have you been?"

Nancy, the new housekeeper whom I had met in 1896! She looked older, with grey hair and more pounds. "It's complicated. I had to go on a journey."

"Come inside." She led me into the house.

I could smell the peach roses, picked from the garden and now on display in the hall. A freshness flowed throughout the house. It was lighter, brighter and better. Distinctive floral designs, pastel colours and wicker furniture had been introduced. The stuffed creatures and 'plump' furniture had been discarded. Nancy could no doubt sense my amazement.

She smiled. "Elizabeth has changed everything!"

I looked at her. "Elizabeth?"

"She is Mr Carsell-Brown's wife."

"What happened to his first wife, Mary?"

"Come into the kitchen and have a seat. We have a lot to catch up on."

Wooden furniture had altered from dark to light. I sat down. Those hard uncomfortable chairs!

Nancy chopped up a turnip. "Charles and Mary moved to Africa seven years ago, and the property was passed to a James Carsell-Brown."

My namesake.

"Two years later he married Elizabeth. They had been engaged for three years."

"Where are they?"

"James is at work and Elizabeth has gone to visit friends. James is an accountant and based in Lochgilphead."

I had to enquire. "Who is the coachman?"

"His name is Walter. Poor chap, he has a problem with one of his legs. He had a nasty fall from the coach."

"Does he still work?"

Nancy laughed. "Just, and no more! The poor chap is approaching sixty, and it must be a struggle for him to perform everyday duties. You and he share the same taste in clothes!" She smiled.

"How is Angus?"

"Angus?" She looked puzzled.

"Yes, the gardener who once worked here."

"Oh, Angus – that was years ago! He does garden work in and around the village."

I suppose for Nancy it would have been a while, but I spoke with Angus only yesterday! I had the uneasy feeling of being scrutinised.

"James, since we last met, you haven't aged. You seem to have lost weight."

"It is down to an abundance of fresh air and exercise, Nancy." And Walter's larger clothes!

She now looked at me in a serious manner. "Charles and Mary became concerned. They feared something serious had happened to you. They contacted the authorities. When their enquiries proved negative, they did not accept you had just vanished."

My heart sank. "I should have contacted them. Do you have an address?"

Nancy handed me a piece of paper with their details.

"I shall write to them as soon as possible." I realised that travelling in time had a negative impact for people who cared about my well-being. First, I had to find lodgings. "Nancy, can you recommend a local place to stay?"

"A friend of mine has a guest house in the village. She will be delighted to accommodate you. Here is her name and address." She gave me a card.

I put it in my pocket and then realised I had no money. I had left whatever money I had in 1896. I asked Nancy for a loan.

"Take this, James, and pay me back whenever you can."

"Until your cash is returned, I promise not to disappear."

She laughed. "You look as if you need something to eat." She put a bowl of turnip soup on the table and rye bread.

I ignored the smell. It tasted delicious – no doubt because of my hunger.

"Thank you, kind lady."

I finished my light meal, thanked Nancy and left. Whilst on my way to Ardrishaig, I observed a coach headed in the opposite direction. It contained a gentleman and lady passenger. A coachman with a long curled white moustache had the reigns. As the coach passed, he gave me an extended stare. Yes, Walter, I was wearing your jacket and trousers!

I arrived at the guesthouse owned and run by Sophie Syme. I knocked on the pale blue, solid door. A tall, middle-aged lady opened it, dressed in an elegant two-piece ankle-length charcoal suit. She gave me a smile.

"Can I help you?"

"I seek somewhere to stay. Nancy suggested I come here."

"Nancy has excellent taste. Please, come inside." She walked me to a dark wooden reception desk and opened a large black book. "How long do you wish to stay?"

"I'm not sure, but at least one week."

"Do you have any luggage?"

"No, I travel light." I hoped the charity shop still existed in the main street.

"Please sign this guest book. Here is your key. Room eight is located on the second floor."

I signed the register with a fountain pen and glanced at the date – the twenty-fifth of March, 1912. That was why I didn't feel warm – it was not even April! I took the key and proceeded upstairs to the room.

The light green painted walls matched the barren wooden floor. The room had a small single bed, dusty wardrobe, cracked toilet bowl and basic washing facility. The fireplace lay ready if necessary for heat. Paper, wood and coal had been supplied, but no matches, no doubt because most men smoked. Oh, for my twenty-first century comforts, but beggars couldn't be choosers.

I needed to earn money – not just to live on but also reimburse Nancy. I would make an attempt to contact Angus. Perhaps he may require an additional worker? I refreshed myself and went downstairs. Sophie attended to her other guests, and then they left. I enquired if she had heard of Angus, who worked as a gardener in the village.

"He has premises opposite the canal." She gave me a pensive look.

"Splendid." Did Sophie also think I had lost weight? "I'll visit him tomorrow morning."

I left my key at reception, departed the guesthouse and headed for the canal. It remained a prominent feature of the local area. The canal had been created to open up the West Coast, and to improve access to the Western Isles through Ardrishaig and Loch Fyne to Crinan. This avoided the hazardous sailing around the Mull of Kintyre, and also cut a hundred miles off a journey.

After twenty minutes, I came across the premises. I knocked on the door, which was ajar, and pushed it wide open. A young lad in white overalls moulded clay into a shape.

He turned to me. "Yes, sir, can I help you?"

"Does Angus work here?"

"That will be my father, sir. He's out at present. I am Andrew, his son."

The baby son Angus spoke about in 1896 had now developed into a young adult!

"Can I help, sir?"

"It is your father I wanted to speak with."

"Is it about your garden?"

"No, it concerns another matter. I am an old acquaintance." I looked at the shape he had made.

"It's a large ornament for a customer. People now want to enhance their gardens and there's a demand for this type of product." He led me to a collection of completed shapes of birds, gnomes and animals. "If the customer wishes, we also paint these to their specification."

I could detect an entrepreneurial spirit had expanded the business.

"My father and Duncan design and maintain customers' gardens. I make the garden objects and also look after the premises."

A well-run enterprise indeed. I became curious. "Is Duncan a partner in the firm?"

"No, sir, he is an employee. There's a demand for our service right now, and my father wants to take on another helper."

I could hear materials being cut nearby and Andrew spotted my distraction.

"Them's the local boat builder. They fit and repair small boats in the area."

With Loch Fyne and the Crinan Canal close by, they possessed a prime location. "Why not ask your customers if they would like furniture to further excel their gardens?"

He appeared interested. "What kind of furniture?"

"Benches, tables and chairs. Whilst gardens become more attractive, they can be used to entertain guests on warm sunny days. If your father formed an alliance with the boat builder, they could manufacture the furniture and you could sell the items. Both businesses would benefit."

"As well as our customers, sir!"

"Correct." Astute lad. "The warmer weather should be here in a couple of months, and therefore now is the time to prepare."

Andrew nodded.

As I left the premises, he thanked me for my advice. He would pass it on to his father. The sensible teenager portrayed a willingness to listen and learn. Maybe he would evolve the business and initiate an early type of 'garden centre' for the area.

On my way back to the guesthouse, I stumbled across the Grey Gull Inn. As it had opened for business, I entered the establishment. Apart from being repainted, the exterior shape of the building would remain unchanged into the twenty-first century. Interior bare grey walls, sawdust floor, rickety scratched tables and scraped chairs lack appeal. The barman had a non-pointed beard, hair parted in the middle, a brown waistcoat and a clean white apron.

"Can I help you sir?" he said.

"A glass of ale, please."

He poured it with precision and placed it on the bar top.

I paid him for the drink and sat down in a corner beside a stained glass window. I took a sip of my ale – the bitterness had diminished. My taste buds had adapted. A newspaper lay on the next table and I leaned over to get it. The date at the top told another story. Since yesterday, two monarchs had died – Queen Victoria and Edward VII. I browsed through the newspaper with interest and excitement. After all, an authentic history tutorial ensued. Domestic matters concentrated on the maiden voyage of the Titanic, incidents which involved suffragettes and the Liberals in power with Herbert Asquith as Prime Minister. International topics included the now established Republic of China, the new American President Woodrow Wilson and a dangerous conflict in the Balkans. Due to this insignificant distant skirmish, the face of Europe would change forever. Various articles about advances made with airships, submarines and airplanes, all of which would become relevant tools of the First World War. Sport concentrated on the forthcoming Stockholm summer Olympics. I finished my drink and I was glad to leave another smoky bar. I breathed the fresh air and headed back to my lodgings.

On the way back to the guesthouse, I stopped at the Macmillan solicitor's office. I peeked through the window and observed a lady at a desk. She had short, dark, wavy, hair which was 'trendy' for the period. A bold burgundy jacket and skirt added to her appeal. She spotted me, smiled and waved her hand – a nice, pleasant lady.

In the main street, I started to feel a bit self-conscious. My lack of a moustache or beard no doubt appeared out of sorts. I must have looked unconventional, but I did not sense this in 1896. However, a moustache or beard had now become a male must-have. I also realised it would be advisable to acquire a necktie or a bowtie. My present outfit looked incomplete. Whilst in 1912, I thought I may as well look the part!

When I entered the hallway of my new residence, a woman dressed in a black dress with a white trim approached.

"Sir, a letter has arrived for you." The maid picked it up from the reception desk and gave it to me.

I opened it.

"James, if you seek work then please get in touch. Walter has had to give up his coachman duties, Nancy."

Splendid! This would allow me a return to Docharnea once again. I would vacate my room here the next morning.

I walked briskly from the guesthouse to Docharnea. All this exercise must have been beneficial. I observed three properties being built within close proximity. As I approached the entrance to Docharnea, I anticipated another surreal family moment. The bowtie Sophie Syme gave me matched my jacket, and I perceived myself presentable. I believed that the bowtie belonged to a previous male guest who had left in a hurry. So much, in fact, that he left all of his belongings!

I stood at the pristine white door and pulled the bell handle. It had a loud ring. Then I heard footsteps, which grew louder. One of the double doors opened. A young lady with fair skin and bobbed hair smiled.

"Good morning. I am James Carlisle,"

"Hello, I am Elizabeth Carsell-Brown – please come in."

I stepped into the reception area.

"Come this way." She led me into the drawing room.

The smell of roses and lighter colours made the room desirable. I felt relaxed rather than intimidated on that occasion.

"Do you like the décor?"

"Yes, splendid – fresh."

"The previous owner smoked rather heavily and the rooms became stained. We have had most of the house redone, and it should soon be finished. Please, sit down." She sat near to me on the floral couch with clasped hands on her lap.

She was well groomed, refined and had a lovely warm smile. It should be an enjoyable interview this time.

"Since Walter had to give up his duties, we require the services of a coachman. Nancy mentioned you have worked here on a previous occasion?"

"Yes, I became the coachman sixteen years ago."

"You must have been a young coachman!"

I gave my usual smile.

"Can you start right away?"

"Yes."

"Excellent – you can move into the coach house immediately." She handed me an itinerary of duties and my benefits, plus three keys for various rooms within the coach house. "There is a uniform in your quarters. If you remain unsure about any item on the list, do not hesitate to contact me or my husband." She smiled. "You and Walter have the same extraordinary taste in tweed jackets and trousers with turn ups!"

No comment.

I went straight to the coachman's quarters and to the washroom. I hid my own uniform in a discreet cupboard. It remained intact. Just as well – the one worn by Walter had enjoyed many better days! I therefore disposed of it. I settled in once more to my now-familiar accommodation and prepared my uniform for the next day. I also familiarised myself with the list of duties. The new residents of Docharnea had similar travel routines as their predecessors – take the husband to and from his place of work six days per week, be available for the lady of the household, and to take care of all matters which related to the horses and coach. No Cole or Char – they had moved on to pastures new. Blue and Misty had taken their place.

I went downstairs to check on both horses in the stable. As I walked in, both of them moved towards me in an affectionate head motion. Just as I closed the stable door, a man appeared.

"Good evening, I am James Carsell-Brown." He gave me a warm handshake.

"Glad to meet you." Of average height and build, he had a distinctive dark, wide moustache.

"Do you require any items of furniture for your quarters?"

"No, the quarters are adequate."

"Did my wife tell you she has to visit Lady Beaumont in Ardrishaig tomorrow afternoon?"

"No, she did not mention it. How is her son, Edward?"

"Oh he has a commission in the Army. He is based at Edinburgh Castle. New barracks are being built at Colinton, but they won't be ready for at least a couple of years. From what I have heard, he enjoys Edinburgh a great deal."

"Sixteen years ago, he got a thrill just hearing about it."

"Any problems, get in touch!"

"Thanks." He seemed like a decent chap.

April arrived in the year of 1912. At the start of the month it became a lot warmer than March. To drive the coach became an enjoyable experience. Winter would not have been a pleasant season for this type of role! April brought a climate similar to early summer. It appeared reminiscent of 1976, which was an exceptional year for warm and sunny conditions.

Having been given a loan of cash by Nancy, I could now reimburse her due to my coachman's income. I walked across the courtyard and knocked on the rear door of the main house. The door opened.

"James, come in and sit down. I've just made this." She gave me a cup of mint tea.

I sat down and sipped my cup of tea – perfect timing, and just what I needed to quench my thirst.

"Poor Walter."

"What happened to him?"

She sat down opposite me. "He fell from the coach and broke his leg. He got taken to hospital."

Poor chap, but my saviour!

"Are you aware of Elizabeth's trip to America?"

"No, this is the first time I have heard about it."

"She plans to visit her sister."

"In the summer?"

"No, she is to travel this month. I'm sure Elizabeth departs on the eleventh."

"What ship is she to travel on?"

"I believe it's a new ship – the *Titan*."

"The *Titanic*?"

"Yes, that's it."

I thanked my host for the cup of tea, gave her some money and returned to the coach house. I recalled what Mr Macmillan had said when I asked how Elizabeth Carsell-Brown had died.

"Details are conflicted, but I believe a fatal incident. As a consequence, her husband later passed away due to a broken heart."

The fatal maiden voyage of the *Titanic* must have been the catalyst for events to unfold. This would have a traumatic effect on this line of the family.


In the evening I took Mr Carsell-Brown to the village hall in Ardrishaig. The location catered for gentlemen who would meet on a regular basis within the district. I believed matters were relevant to a fraternal nature.

"James, please return in three hours – say around ten o'clock. The business of the evening should be concluded by then."

Rather than head back to Docharnea, I elected to visit the nearby Royal Hotel. I had been informed that on every Friday evening a musical kilted duo provided excellent entertainment. I walked in and ordered a glass of ale. The bar soon got busy due to an influx of 'weekenders'. I listened to a melody of Scottish songs performed with passion and professionalism. Then a cheery elderly man came forward.

"You may not remember me, sir. I see you 'ad a successful interview for the coachman's job. We met sixteen years ago on the road to Ardrishaig."

I remembered him well. To me, we had met only a short time before. "You gave me a lift on your cart to Docharnea. We discussed various topics – did you go to Russia?"

"You have a good memory, sir. Yes, I went over there. Russia is about to experience change!"

"To what extent?"

"The people have become disenchanted with the Tsar. There's a lot of poverty around the country and people 'ave little or no food."

In five years' time, the Tsar and his family would suffer a terrible fate. I asked if he suspected people would rebel against the Monarchy.

"It would not surprise me. I witnessed much unrest and certain factions demand change."

"Time will tell,"

"Talking of time, sir, did you ever get that clock bracelet fixed?"

"No, just another flawed invention." It was in my trouser pocket.

"I knew it, sir – they invent anything nowadays! Have you heard about this horseless carriage?"

"It could put me out of a job."

He put his hand on my shoulder. "Don't worry, sir, they won't catch on. There'll be too many breakdowns! All the best." He walked towards the bar.

As I left the establishment, the performers had cranked up the calm atmosphere into frenzy. I hoped that the tables could withstand people dancing on them! No doubt the frequent consumption of strong ale played a part.

I arrived at the premises to collect Mr Carsell-Brown. I could still hear a ringing sound in my ears. Whilst I waited, a group of gentlemen exited the main door. It would appear they enjoyed themselves given the loud but polite laughter. Then Mr Carsell-Brown came out with his small case. He missed a step and stumbled.

I looked down from my driver's seat. "Do you want a hand, sir?"

"I hope you haven't been here too long, James. A bit of extra business required my attention." He staggered into the back of the coach.

"No problem, sir – I have just arrived." I could smell the alcohol.

I drove towards Docharnea, looked to my left and admired the coastline of Loch Fyne. Lights shone across the water.

"A beautiful sight, James."

I turned my head. "Yes, superb."

"Elizabeth often comes here to paint. Some of her work is marvellous."

This location would captivate the Carsell-Browns for many years to come. Did I hear snoring? I looked back. *Enjoy your nap!*

The next day I polished the coach. Elizabeth Carsell-Brown came to speak with me. She must have felt warm in her white, ankle-length frock.

"James, I am soon to depart for America."

"When, madam?"

"Next week. I shall visit my sister and niece."

"What part of America, madam?"

"East coast – New York. My sister tells me how delightful the city can be; therefore, I have agreed to take up her offer of a short holiday." Her face beamed.

I could sense her enthusiasm. "How long will you be gone?"

"About four weeks. I want to visit many places in and around the city. To travel there and back could take ten days."

"What ship, madam?"

"The *Titanic*. It is her maiden voyage. The ship departs from Southampton, but passengers also board at Queenstown in Ireland. I will travel there from Ardrishaig."

"What date do you depart?"

"The *Titanic* leaves Queenstown on the eleventh; therefore, I shall depart here on the tenth. A local company provides a service to Ireland."

"Convenient."

"Yes. It sails at eleven thirty in the morning. I want to leave from Docharnea at ten o'clock. I cannot wait, James!"

The thrill of a trip to New York would be an unforgettable experience. However, at what cost? If I revealed what tragedy awaited the 'unsinkable' *Titanic*, who would believe me?

"Before I leave, James, would you pose for me? I would like to paint your portrait."

"Me?"

"Yes, you will be fine."

"Then I agree."

"Marvellous – it should not take too long. The pose will consist of you beside the coach house. Wear your coachman's uniform."

As I headed for Lochgilphead to collect James Carsell-Brown from work, I continued to speculate on how to prevent Elizabeth from taking the trip, or perhaps miss the connection at Queenstown. When I collected her husband, he looked glum and did not speak.

"A busy day, sir?"

No reply. Had he heard me?

"Yes, busy."

Silence followed. "The weather is warm for this time of year."

Again, a pause.

"Yes, it is." He stared at Loch Fyne, then took out a document from his case and looked at it.

A long journey home appeared in store. I recalled what Nancy told me.

"James does not want Elizabeth to go on a journey which would take her such a long distance from home. They got married five years ago and have only been apart for a couple of days."

I tended the horses and cleaned out the dreaded stables – what a smell! It was my least favourite chore and it was concluded in double-quick time. However, whilst in the stable, I had an idea. I would make the coach inoperable on the day of her departure. Elizabeth would then miss the connection from Ardrishaig to Queenstown. But several other properties came into close proximity with Docharnea. This could provide neighbour assistance in terms of substitute transport.

On the penultimate day before her departure, Elizabeth asked if I could take her into Ardrishaig around lunchtime. I prepared the coach and horses accordingly.

We arrived in the main street at twelve twenty five. I had to collect her at around three o'clock. I returned to Docharnea with pensive thoughts. How could I stop events on the tenth? I had a light meal and headed back to the village.

The clock on the church tower showed fifteen minutes to three. I looked at my own watch – the clock was a minute slow! I put it back in my pocket. Rather than hang around, I secured the coach and browsed around the local shops. I ventured into a jeweller's to look at the new style of wristwatch this era had introduced, but they were not digital! In my Victorian experience, gentleman had pocket watches, but this type of new dress accessory would replace them. I observed a wall clock and left the premises at three o'clock precisely. As I approached the coach, I spotted Elizabeth on the opposite side of the street. Her large, colourful, seasonal hat was apparent enough for me to pick out. Before crossing the street, she waited for a coach to pass.

"The village is busy today. The fine weather for this time of year is responsible!"

"The shopkeepers will be delighted."

I opened the door, let her in and closed it, before I got up on my seat, released the brake lever and moved off.

She lowered her head. "James, I have lost a brooch. It must have dropped off in the shop."

I stopped the coach. "Do you want me to come and help you find it?"

"No, I have an idea where it is."

I got down and opened the coach door. She walked back along the street. If only it could have been her ticket for the journey!

A short time later, I saw her cross the street. I then spotted a runaway horse. It galloped in her direction. I shouted but she kept looking in my direction. I rushed towards her. She turned towards the horse. As the horse approached, I pushed her out of its path.

I opened my eyes and ached all over. I gazed around the unfamiliar room. I had been placed in a single ward, no doubt within a hospital. I could only make a slight movement without feeling pain.

A nurse appeared and smiled. "How do you feel?"

"Terrible, I ache all over! Where am I?"

"Lochgilphead General Hospital. A doctor will be here soon to speak with you." She tucked in my bed sheet and left.

A short time later a tall, bald gentleman with a white coat came into my ward. He went to the front of my bed, removed a clipboard and read my medical information. He replaced it and then approached.

"I am Doctor Campbell. You had a lucky escape! Can you remember what happened?"

"I pushed a lady out of the path of a runaway horse. How is she?"

"Thanks to you, just a couple of bruises." He examined my eyes.

"Is she at home?"

"No, on a vacation I believe. She received only minor injuries, and was therefore able to make a trip. Why do you ask?"

"We discussed her trip. How long have I been here?" I tried to sit up.

"Several days. Lie flat – you should be okay to sit up tomorrow."

How could I have been unconscious for such a length of time?

"A lady with a medical background arrived at the scene to assist, otherwise your condition could have been worse."

"Did she leave her name?"

"Miss Murray."

A familiar name, but my memory still could not function.

"Better you rest. I will speak to you later."

As he left, the same nurse came back into the ward with a white pillow under her arm. She put it into a nearby cupboard.

"You have a visitor. This person has called on a previous occasion, but you had not regained consciousness."

"Who is the person?"

"A lady."

"Please show her in."

A well-dressed lady of about my age appeared and stood in front of my bed. I asked her to have a seat.

She sat down in front of me. "In the sixteen years since we last met, your appearance has not changed!"

My goodness – Flora Murray! One of the guests on the evening I collected Mary Carsell-Brown from Lady Beaumont's house. She had at that time just qualified as a medical doctor.

"Do you stay in Ardrishaig?"

"No, I came here for a vacation. I now stay in London."

I anticipated the next question.

"You left Docharnea without even a goodbye!"

"Yes – I apologise, but had to depart."

"Why did you leave so suddenly?"

"It is a long story."

"Did everything work out in the end?"

Not really! "Flora, can you do me a favour?"

"Yes, James, if I can."

"Is this the thirteenth?"

Flora nodded her head. "Yes."

"Elizabeth Carsell-Brown had been scheduled to travel to America on the *Titanic*. I have to know if she is on board."

"Why, James?"

"On the fourteenth, whilst sailing to America, the *Titanic* will hit an iceberg. The ship will sink, with many lives lost."

"How do you know this?"

"Please Flora, trust me!"

A nurse walked into the ward. "Is everything alright?"

Flora turned to the nurse. "He does not feel well."

She then examined me. "His temperature is high."

Flora stood up. "James, I shall come back later. Bye."

At this moment I became frustrated. Being unable to help prevent a disaster. But who would believe someone in a hospital ward who has suffered concussion?

In the morning, I had a breakfast of boiled eggs and toast. Then came my daily examination, and word of another visitor who had come to visit me.

"Hello James, how do you feel today?" Nancy arrived at my bedside with a sympathetic expression.

"I am fine, but I still have a few aches here and there."

"James, you are fortunate not to have suffered serious injuries."

I nodded my head. "Please take a seat."

"Elizabeth felt guilty about what happened and before she left for America asked me to give you this."

"Is today the fourteenth?"

"Yes. Why do you ask?"

"My mind is still confused."

"You have to take things easy. Mr Carsell-Brown made arrangements for your care."

That explained the private ward and visitor privileges.

"He is grateful for what you did."

"Please thank him, although I cannot be certain when I can resume my duties."

"James, you may not need to resume them. Mr Carsell-Brown wants to purchase an automobile. The family who own the nearby property have just received delivery of one."

"Then I have the distinction of being Docharnea's last coachman!"

Nancy got to her feet. "As you have to rest, the nurse said I could only stay for a short time."

"How is Mr Carsell-Brown?"

"He misses Elizabeth already. He comes into the kitchen to chat." Nancy smiled, got up and left the ward.


Two days later, Doctor Campbell came into the ward. He always had a severe expression and did not encourage humour.

"How are you today?"

"A bit tired, but I feel less pain."

"You could be discharged in a couple of days." He picked up my chart. "Yes – three at most."

As the doctor left, I could hear the chatter of nurses in the corridor. A few minutes later, one of them entered my ward. I asked her what the commotion had been about.

"The *Titanic* has sunk! It's a new ship, how could it sink?"

"I am aware of someone on board. Is there any mention of survivors?"

"It is too early for the authorities to know."

I then remembered the letter Nancy gave me from Elizabeth. I took it out of the drawer beside my bed. With apprehension, I opened it.

*'Dearest James,*

*I must first apologise for the accident, which resulted in your admission to hospital. Doctor Campbell has assured me you shall make a full recovery and will soon be fit again. Until an ambulance arrived, a friend of mine helped to assist. I believe she will endeavour to visit you once the doctor deems it suitable. As James and I shall pay all medical expenses incurred, do not worry about hospital fees. I should be back around the middle of May and can then apologise in person for the inconvenience to you. Best wishes, Elizabeth.'*

On the eighteenth of April a nurse informed me that survivors had been rescued. They had been taken by another ship to New York.

I asked, "When are they due to arrive?"

"Maybe in a day or two."

I had been in the hospital for almost a week and was keen to leave. The aches and pains had diminished to allow me a walk around the ward. The warm afternoon sun resulted in a gorgeous day, and therefore I went outside and sat on a bench. The hospital grounds consisted of two large tidy landscaped gardens and appropriate white furniture. With the lovely spring weather, flowers bloomed to enhance the idyllic setting. A variety of blue, red and pink shades had emerged, along with yellow from the dependable daffodils. I sat near a small pond filled with giant goldfish, which proved popular with visitors and patients alike.

Someone had left a newspaper on a seat. I picked up a copy of the *Argyllshire Times* which included headlines and stories about the *Titanic*. Initial reports suggested when it had sunk; not enough lifeboats had been on the ship to cater for crew and passengers. One poignant headline asked if, before *Titanic* entered service, there had been adequate sea trials. In years to come, questions, recriminations and theories would be discussed and lamented.

As a lady's large hat blighted the sun and put me in the shade, I looked up. There stood a lady wearing light clothes and an intriguing smile.

"Hello again, James, I see you are in good health!"

Flora Murray had returned.

She sat down next to me. "How could you have known about the *Titanic*? Also, why have you not aged?"

"You will not believe me."

"James, just tell me. I have to know. Until you do, I won't leave."

I explained my true identity and how Docharnea had become my home, but in the future. How I had found myself back in the nineteenth century and masqueraded as a coachman. Then, how I had been sent to 1912, and my intervention which prevented Elizabeth Carsell-Brown from sustaining a serious injury.

"That is incredible!" She shook her head.

"Elizabeth would not have been on board *Titanic* but for my heroics."

"Yes, but she would have been trampled on by the horse and sustained serious, if not fatal, injuries. As a high percentage of passengers who travelled first class got rescued, she may have survived. This piece of information has just been released to the press."

"How is James coping with the trauma?"

"Not well. I visited him yesterday evening and he looked terrible."

A blessing Nancy was at the house.

Flora checked the time. "James, I depart in a few hours for my home in London. I somehow feel we shall not meet again. You are aware of what the future holds – how will women fare? Will they achieve some sort of recognition and be allowed to vote in elections?"

"I will tell you only this." I revealed a small but significant snapshot of the future.

She smiled warmly, put her hand on my shoulder and kissed my cheek. "Thank you." She got up and departed.

When I returned to my ward, Doctor Campbell appeared. He informed me that I could leave the hospital the next day.


Following a farewell to the staff, I collected my clothes and headed for the exit. When I got there, a lady stopped me. A young boy held her hand.

"Excuse me sir, I am looking for a nurse. My son has injured himself and needs medical attention."

I looked down the corridor. "Here is one coming."

The nurse examined the boy's leg.

"Is it serious?" asked the mother.

"He has sustained only a cut," said the nurse. "I will attend to it right away."

"Thank you," said the mother.

The nurse took the boy to a treatment room.

I turned to the mother. "That type of injury looks worse than it is. I have had my fair share!"

"What sport do you play?"

"Rugby and football in my youth."

"Where did you play?"

"In and around Edinburgh."

She smiled. "We have a house in the Crammond area of Edinburgh. My husband and I work as British Missionaries in China but return home a few times each year. Both of our sons attend boarding school in this country. We return on a regular basis to enable all the family to be together."

"Why did you come to this part of Scotland?"

"The boys love to sail on the lochs; plus, we all admire the scenery."

"Did your son hurt himself on one of the boats?"

"No, playing football. Eric and his brother Robert had been fooling around. Eric came off worse!"

"When he is older, does he want to play for a team?"

"Yes – Scotland!"

The nurse returned with her patient and asked the lady her surname for a standard medical form which required completion.

"Liddell."

It would not be football the young boy represented Scotland with, but rugby and athletics. He would be capped on a number of occasions at rugby and win gold in the 400-metres at the Paris Olympics twelve years from that day.


Thanks to a kind traveller, I got a lift to Docharnea. That two-mile walk from the hospital in Lochgilphead would have seemed like a hike in my condition. As I strolled through the entrance, an unfamiliar sight greeted me. Not one automobile but two! I rang the bell and Nancy appeared.

"James, come in. We have just had news – Elizabeth is safe and well!" She led me into the kitchen.

"Where is she at present?" I stepped into reception.

"In New York. A rescue ship picked up the survivors and took them to a nearby port. Thank goodness!"

"How is her husband?"

Nancy gave a relieved smile. "Happy."

"Who do the motor vehicles belong to?"

"The burgundy vehicle belongs to James and the other is owned by Lady Lambton. She and her son arrived yesterday."

A few moments later a boy came into the kitchen. He had a cheeky grin on his face and approached Nancy.

"Can I please have another piece of ginger cake?"

"Of course you can." Nancy turned towards me. "Alan, this is James Carlisle."

"As in the English town," he said. "Pleased to meet you." He held out his hand.

I shook it. He had a confident manner for a young person.

Alan collected his cake and left the kitchen.

Nancy said, "Lady Lambton is a relative of Elizabeth. After being told of the tragedy, she came to visit James."

Nancy prepared a meal of potatoes and lamb with mint sauce for me. It smelled and tasted delicious – an excellent cook. Fully fed, I retired to my quarters in the coach house. I would miss that exclusive, private hospital ward!

I went into the stables to check on Misty and Blue. They looked at me with a sense of inevitability. "The two of you are not alone. I will also be redundant!"

As I walked upstairs to my quarters, a touch of sadness descended. I had now been confirmed as not just the first, but also the last, coachman of Docharnea.

I put away my clothes for the evening. Where was my watch? I could not find it. When I got taken to hospital, the watch must have somehow fallen out of my trouser pocket. I would call in to the hospital the next day and trace its whereabouts.

# Chapter 6

## *The Approaching Storm*

I awoke to a beautiful April morning – appropriate, as my namesake, James and Elizabeth, would now be reunited. The same day, I had to take Nancy into the village for household supplies and then call into the hospital. Here we were again – my clock bracelet from America! I felt my pocket and addressed myself in the mirror

On this occasion, I suffered only a slight unsteadiness.

Time had no doubt altered once more. My quarters were bare, except for a couple of pictures and the wall mirror. It still hung in an unchanged position. How many years had passed this time? I looked out of the window. The trees had now fully grown. I became aware of a sound of regular traffic from the nearby road. No longer could I see it from the window due to the height of the hedges and trees. I retreated from the window, walked across the room and opened the closet door with curiosity. Empty, apart from a package, sealed envelope and my old cash box. I unwrapped the package. It contained the jacket and trousers I had worn on my previous visit, plus some essential wares. The envelope had been placed on top of my cash box to catch my attention. I opened it and took out a sheet of neat hand-written paper plus a solitary key. I observed the date – the final day of December, 1926.

'*Dear James,*

*I have written this in the hope maybe someday you will return. Since you departed, fourteen years have now passed. Two gentlemen from the Ministry of Defence arrived at Docharnea and wanted to speak with you. I told them you had returned to Edinburgh. Elizabeth and James now live in America. Their home is in Manhattan, which I'm informed can be a vibrant part of New York. I explained to them you had to return home for family reasons. It is with much sadness I have to inform you that Lady Beaumont's son Edward was killed in the war. For his leadership and bravery at the Somme, he received the Victoria Cross. Just after the war, I met Doctor Flora Murray in the village. I got the impression she understood you better than most of us – apart from me! The new owners of Docharnea are Philip and Charlotte Carsell-Brown. They have two sons, William and Geoffrey, aged twelve and ten respectively. They have the distinction of being the first children to live here. The boys have kept me busy on a regular basis, but are well-mannered and good fun. Finally, I leave Docharnea today and look forward to a well-deserved retirement. If you do return, James, please get in touch.*

*With love, Nancy.'*

Could being able to travel in time be interpreted as a method of punishment? Past family members Charles and Mary, Elizabeth and James who I became acquainted with but left them abruptly and without reason. It would be perceived as a betrayal of their warmth and friendship shown towards me. I hoped Nancy will still be in good health. It had been a thoughtful gesture by her to keep contents of the closet intact in case I returned. I sifted through the package. Before being wrapped in paper, the tweed jacket and trousers had been cleaned, pressed and folded. The key resembled that for Docharnea's rear door. Nancy must have had a duplicate made.

I went down the stairs and opened the door. As I walked into the courtyard, once again there had been changes. A layer of grey gravel now covered this area instead of grass. I also noticed another property in close proximity to Docharnea. The place appeared empty – no persons and no car. What became of the horses and that distinguished coach? The key would allow me access to the kitchen where I could get a bite to eat – clever Nancy! Still, I knocked on the door and waited. Since no response came, I turned the key and opened the door. In front of me sat a young black and white cat.

I knelt down. "Are you on guard duty?"

It looked at me, meowed and brushed itself against my leg.

I clapped its head and the little cat started to purr. At least it was a warm welcome! I entered the kitchen with my new friend, who followed in my footsteps. The light wooden furniture had reverted back to dark. I looked in cupboards and other places which could store food. Only a small quantity of meat and a packet of chocolate Digestive biscuits existed.

I stared at the young cat. "You can have the meat, but I insist on the chocolate Digestives."

It tilted its head. "Meow."

"I suspected you would agree!"

We had our snack and then the cat went into its basket and curled up.

My next task – to find out what year I had travelled to. I could not see a newspaper or calendar to reveal the date. By previous experiences, this could be 1940. The next family tragedy had occurred in this year. I wandered around the downstairs rooms and searched for some evidence. The furniture had again changed. Upholstery with rounded-edges, tables and chairs of low quality – not crafted. The rooms appeared sparser than in my two previous visits. I perceived austerity and this gave me an impression of a time where hardship also affected the affluent society, a sharp contrast to the extravagance of 1912.

I locked the door and walked back to the coach house. When I reached it, a young girl approached.

"Are you the coachman who travels through time?"

I had on my coachman's outfit from 1912. It would be difficult to put up an argument! "Yes, it's me."

"I was told you just came here at night time."

I smiled. "I'm afraid of the dark!"

She laughed. "How long have you stayed here?"

"Since 1896. What year is this?"

"The year is 1938. This spring has been like summertime!"

Same as my last visit. "Where do you stay?"

"In the next house." She pointed.

With the several other properties which had been built, this area would develop into a small hamlet.

"Got to go." She waved goodbye.

I speculated on whether she might tell someone about her chat with the coachman. I suspect nobody will believe her.

I re-entered the coach house and went upstairs to the quarters. I changed out of my coachman's outfit into the jacket and trousers. Nancy had also enclosed a pair of shoes – she had been aware that the boots were no good for my feet!

I walked down to the road and gazed at the transformation. The road had been widened and resurfaced in order to cope with a steady flow of traffic. As I trotted along a new pavement, I came across another new property. A lady in a long white dress and hat pottered around at the foot of her large but tidy garden.

"Good day," I said.

She turned around.

"Isn't this weather delightful?" Daffodils bloomed around the borders of her garden lawn.

"It must be the warmest spring weather for a long time."

Possibly 1912!

She held up a trowel. "Ideal for my favourite pastime! Are you a stranger to these parts?"

"Yes. I called to see Philip and Charlotte, but there's nobody around."

"The eldest son William is getting married to Olivia, the granddaughter of Lady Beaumont."

"Also the late Edward Beaumont's daughter?"

She nodded. "Did you know Edward?"

"Many years ago."

We chatted for a short while and then I continued towards Ardrishaig. I couldn't believe how an area had changed due to the automobile boom. Tranquillity had gone!

I reached the village and took accommodation at the now-familiar Grey Gull Inn. The money I had in my cash box should have guaranteed a room for a short period of time, even though the cash had devalued from twenty six years before.

I checked in and went up to my room. I took off my jacket and shoes, then lay on the bed. The next day, I would try to reacquaint myself with Nancy. Many of her years had passed but I hoped she would be in good health. With Ardrishaig being a village, someone must have information on her whereabouts. I felt tired and my eyes became heavy.

I found a general store in the main street, entered it and approached a stocky white-coated male shopkeeper.

"I'm trying to find a lady who once worked at the Docharnea estate, just outside Ardrishaig."

He looked at me over his spectacles. "What did she work as?"

"The housekeeper."

"Nancy?"

"Yes!" An advantage of a village was its close community.

"She is a resident at the local nursing home." He took me to the exit door and pointed. "Over there, the white building."

"Thanks for your help."

I left the shop and walked at a steady pace. I reached the building ten minutes later. In the entrance hall, I looked for assistance. I heard footsteps behind me get louder and turned around. A large woman with a clinical white uniform confronted me.

"Yes?"

"Does Nancy reside here?"

"Nancy? What is her surname?"

"I do not know, but she has lived locally for many years."

"Wait here."

She marched off down the corridor and went into a room. After a few minutes she returned with an unchanged stern expression.

"Is she here?"

"Nancy has been moved to the local hospital in Lochgilphead."

"Thanks for your assistance."

"Don't mention it!"

Too late.

I retraced my steps back along the main street in the direction of Lochgilphead. I stopped to watch all the vehicles. Cars and lorries had now replaced the redundant horse-drawn transport. However, the 'new' vehicles were of the vintage variety. I passed Macmillan Solicitors and had my customary peek through the window. What style for this era? On this occasion I had a restricted view. The window cleaner must have been on extended leave. I could just make out a lady with long brown hair. She wore a sober grey dress with a ruffled collar. She also wore a grim expression – austere times indeed. This would explain why the exterior of the office building had remained unchanged for decades.

When I arrived at the hospital, a nurse explained that Nancy's health had deteriorated but she remained in good spirits. I could see her, but only for a short time. When I entered the private ward, a large smile appeared on her face. I then handed her a bunch of flowers and took a seat beside her.

"My instinct told me you would come back, James. But it has been a long time."

"Yes, it has." Only a day had gone by for me.

"James, it's unfair we all age whilst you remain the same."

I did not reply. "Any news of Charles and Mary, or James and Elizabeth?

"Elizabeth writes regularly."

"She and James enjoy America?"

"Yes, they adore the lifestyle of New York. When Elizabeth describes the city, she becomes enthusiastic. Her letters are never short!"

I calculated that Elizabeth would now be about thirteen years older than myself.

"James, do you have any plans for now?"

"I have still to make up my mind. In the meantime, I am staying at the Grey Gull Inn. I will be able to stop in and visit you on a regular basis."

She smiled.

A nurse came into the ward. "You must leave sir. The lady has to rest."

I said goodbye.

As I left, a sense of sorrow fell upon me. It can be uncomfortable to witness individuals age in such a short period of time. However it must also have been strange for them to see me remain the same.

Before I returned to my lodgings, I stopped off at the Lochside Hotel to have something to eat. The establishment had been built sixteen years before, and had a quality ambience to compliment the maritime location. I sat at a table in the dining room and read the menu. It did not have an abundance of dishes available, but remained appropriate for the current adverse period. The hotel appeared a popular place to congregate, given the amount of customers. In adverse times, people discussed and speculated on events. One such discussion I overheard centred around the then current German Chancellor and his influence on the German people. With the annexation of Austria and an uneasy situation in Czechoslovakia, he would be a frequent topic of conversation.

A young woman at the next table shook he head. "He has made the front cover of *Time* magazine!"

One of her two companions thumped the table. "Hitler is driven by power. He is the type of individual who may start another war!"

"If Germany wants to start a war in Europe then they will have to contend with us, France and Russia," the third companion said. "As Communism and Fascism represent opposite cultures, Stalin will crush Germany if they step out of line!"

Not at the start of the war. A deal 'carved out' between the two extreme cultures takes everyone by surprise. The three young, stylish ladies impressed me. I listened to them with interest. They displayed articulate and knowledgeable grasp of various topical subjects.

A member of the group rose from her seat and put her hand to her mouth. "I almost forgot!" She put her hand over her mouth.

"What's wrong?" another said.

"I have to visit Lady Beaumont at the hospital! What time is it?"

Her friend looked at her watch. "You have fifteen minutes to get there on time!"

"Bye". She dashed from the table.

The third companion shook her head. "Whilst Olivia and William are on honeymoon, Grace promised to visit Lady Beaumont."

Both of the young ladies smiled.

Ah, here came the waitress to take my order. I had to admit that the young ladies had provided me with a wealth of current news and gossip. Qualitative market research!

I would visit Nancy once more and try to get information about my grandfather, namely Geoffrey Carsell-Brown. As he had been killed in the Second World War, I did not meet him. Indeed, my father told me that the details of his death remained vague, much to the distress of our family. When word arrived from the War Office to confirm his death, my father had celebrated only two birthdays.

The delightful weather allowed local people to talk of this as being the driest April they had ever experienced – significant for the district of Argyll!

I arrived at the hospital and met by a nurse outside Nancy's private ward. She informed me that I had to again restrict my visit to a short period of time.

"How long?"

"About ten minutes. Nancy had an uncomfortable night."

I entered the ward and gave her a broad smile.

"Have a seat, James."

I sat down on one of the hard, uncomfortable chairs. I wanted to learn about my family descendants and asked Nancy if she had ever met Olivia Beaumont.

"A nice girl, who shall become an excellent wife to William. Everyone speaks highly of her. William is fortunate to have met someone like Olivia. I got invited to their wedding but was unable to attend."

"What became of William's brother?"

"Geoffrey got married last year to Emily. He met her at Aberdeen University. They moved to Edinburgh, where Geoffrey is employed as an accountant for a ship construction company. I believe they now have a son."

"After graduating from University, I trust they got married?"

"Oh, yes – I would imagine Philip and Charlotte would have preferred Geoffrey to wait for a few years. But he is a determined individual! Once he makes his mind, there is no way to halt him."

*Must be a family trait.*

A nurse entered the ward and nodded in my direction.

I got up. "See you soon, Nancy."

She gave me her usual smile.

After I left the hospital, I reached Ardrishaig's main street. I noticed a poster on the confectioner's shop window. It publicised that the Member of Parliament for this area would be at the village hall on the following Tuesday evening to discuss local issues. I recognised the name of Alan Lambton. Could it be the same person I had met in 1912? It did not surprise me that he had gone into politics, given his family background. I went into the shop to buy a bar of chocolate – the first for a long time! I looked around the small retailer with shelves and trays filled with different types of chocolate. Boxes, bars and assortments of loose flavours secured my undivided attention. The anticipation of my taste buds persuaded me to buy at least two items. I studied the white tablet, pink coconut and various chocolate bars. I chose a Dairy Milk, with its distinctive dark blue wrapper. I lifted two bars from a display and took them to the counter assistant.

"Would you also like to purchase our latest product?"

"What is it?"

"Chocolate Roses. As we have just received a delivery, I've not had time to put them on display. I recommend them."

*Me too. I'd purchase a box sixty one years from now!* "I'll just take the Dairy Milk." I was starving.

"That will be sixpence, sir."

I gave him a sixpence coin. He handed me the bars. "Thank you sir."

I couldn't wait to eat one.

When I got back to the inn, I read a book borrowed from the local library and also finished off my chocolate. *The Coming Democracy in Europe* by Thomas Mann had not long been published, and was not the type of book which would be welcomed in Berlin! I read for a short while, but the clammy weather had given me a thirst. I therefore went downstairs to the bar for a beer. Apart from me, only two other customers were present. In this period, walls had been repainted in olive green and the floor patched up.

"Glad you popped in, sir – not too busy this evenin'."

I ordered a beer and then had a sip. Ah, that was better! It *had* improved over the decades.

The barman smiled. "We serve the best beer in the area, sir."

No argument from me.

"What about magnificent Scotland sir – trounced England at football!"

Impressive! "What was the score?"

"A one goal victory."

How would he react to the nine goals scored by England in 1961! "Who scored the winning goal?"

"Tommy Walker of Hearts."

Tommy Walker would go from elation in the present to dejection in the future. When he stopped playing football, he would become the manager of Hearts. His team would win a series of trophies, but due to a run of poor results, his connection with the club he loved will be severed. Football can be a cruel game.

"Another drink, sir?"

"No thanks, having an early night. Who won this season's Scottish Cup?"

"East Fife, sir. They beat Kilmarnock by four goals to two."

Football can also be an unpredictable game!

The final day of April remained dry, but the long periods of sunshine started to diminish. However, it still made a pleasant change from many of the dull and damp spring seasons I would encounter in the future. I popped into a local newsagent to buy a morning paper. I also purchased a new invention called the ballpoint pen, to fill in the crossword puzzle. Then I proceeded to the popular Lochside Hotel for a spot of lunch.

Afterwards, I retired to the peaceful lounge with its panoramic view of Loch Fyne. The lush green hills against a clear blue sky made me feel content. I settled into a plush dark green leather chair to read my *Daily Herald*.

A waiter with a silver tray appeared. "A drink, sir?"

"No, I'm fine thanks." His Clan Campbell blue, green and black tartan outfit matched the lounge carpet – appropriate, since the hotel lies within the Duke of Argyll's residency.

The newspaper's main headlines highlighted situations which involved Hitler and Germany. The annexation of Austria, discreet rearmament and rumours of Germans being trained as fighter pilots in Russia. Japan's conflict with China over Manchuria also featured. Their soldiers' atrocities on Chinese civilians scandalised. Because of high unemployment and social unrest, the economy received attention – therefore it is not a coincidence that newspaper coverage included Hollywood!

A visit to the cinema gave the British population a temporary relief from constant despondency. Also, it did not cost much – affordable to the masses. 'Snow White and The Seven Dwarfs' plus 'A Star Is Born' still appealed from the previous year. The royal correspondent raised concerns that King George VI restricted public appearances. Strange, given the low morale of the country.

The sports section looked excessive – no doubt another ploy aimed at distraction! A topical boxing article concentrated on the new American heavyweight champion, Joe Louis. It stated a man with great potential to become the heavyweight champion of the world – for years to come! He had to fight Schmeling, the German boxer, in a grudge rematch. The article emphasised if the German boxer defeated Louis, then his winnings would be used to build German tanks. Not the best publicity to endear yourself with the American anti-war brigade! Another main sporting topic was the forthcoming

World Cup in France. Could Italy retain the trophy they won four years earlier? Other articles referred to the aftermath of the British Empire Games held in Sydney, Australia. A lady called Decima Norman had won five gold medals for Australia in track and field events. Australia topped the medal chart, with England in second place and Scotland able to finish eighth. With reference to tennis, Don Budge got mentioned as a possible contender to win the Grand Slam and become the first male to fulfil this achievement. One piece of information which caught my attention featured in a small section of the newspaper dedicated to developing countries. It read, 'oil has just been discovered in Saudi Arabia.'

I put down my newspaper. As I sat beside the window in this peaceful lounge, it became difficult to envisage another upheaval for Britain. In five months, Neville Chamberlain would travel to Munich and meet with Adolf Hitler to avert war in Europe. Certain prominent individuals remained convinced this may be a lost cause. They maintained that appeasement with a dictator does not produce a favourable outcome.

That evening, I went along to the village hall in anticipation of a controversial debate between Alan Lambton and the local citizens. I arrived fifteen minutes early to ensure a seat. By seven-thirty, all the seats had been filled. Alan Lambton shared the stage with another Conservative Party official and two members of the Council. The chairlady stood up and introduced all the guests in a favourable manner. They all got a polite reception by the audience in the packed hall. Of the guest speakers, Alan Lambton spoke last. He proceeded to talk on certain issues about the Argyll constituency. This related to a reduction in unemployment, maintaining an efficient council service and the government's commitment to building more new houses. It sounded familiar.

A lady in the audience stood up. "Is the government also committed to stopping Hitler? If not, he will start another European war!"

I recognised her as one of the young ladies who sat near to me at the Lochside Hotel. There now ensued a murmur of voices in the audience. Sporadic shouts broke out.

A man raised his fist in the air. "What's the government doin' about the situation in Austria and Czechoslovakia?"

Several other controversial questions such as unemployment and poverty were fired at the representatives. The atmosphere now became hostile.

The chairlady got up from her seat and held her hands. "Please, please be quiet, and your questions will be answered."

Alan Lambton remained composed. "The government will monitor the situations in Europe and take action if necessary."

A tall, well-dressed lady stood up. "Why have you not taken any action over the Jewish people being persecuted?"

No response came from Alan Lambton.

"The persecution has been systematically carried out for five years!"

Alan Lambton straightened his tie.

Another man shouted, "Sitting on your backside won't solve the problem!"

Again the chairlady spoke. "Order please, order!"

The peaceful villagers had turned the meeting into a heated and frenzied occasion. One of the Council guest speakers looked horrified. You could have cut the hostile atmosphere with a knife.

The unflappable Alan Lambton fiddled with his tie again. "We remain aware of the situation in Germany. We shall persevere to obtain more hard evidence. As for Austria and Czechoslovakia, the government will pursue a diplomatic solution to the problem."

Clenched fists now got raised from members of the volatile audience. An egg just missed Alan Lambton.

The chairlady stood up once more with a tense expression. "We will take one last question."

I raised my hand and got acknowledged by the chairlady. "Does the Honourable gentleman feel Poland could be a future target for Hitler to invade?"

He gave me a solemn look. "I hope not!"

The public meeting ended thirty minutes early. As war drew closer, the evening had given me an insight to how people really felt on certain issues. The ordinary person in the street could see Hitler's intentions. The public had recent experience of the misery war brings to families. However, diplomacy is a preferred first option for a government rather than mobilisation. After all, Britain did not have the resources or appetite for a prolonged and expensive war.

The month of May brought plenty of persistent rain clouds. On my way to visit Nancy, I stopped at a menswear shop to purchase an umbrella. When I arrived at the hospital, a nurse approached me with a serious expression.

"Mr Carlisle, I have some bad news. Nancy passed away last night."

I remained silent.

"She died peacefully in her sleep." She handed me an envelope. "This is for you. Nancy asked me to make sure you got this should her condition deteriorate."

I opened the envelope and found an address for Elizabeth Carsell-Brown. I looked at the nurse. "Thank you."

She smiled.

I left the hospital and walked along the main street with my umbrella – a good investment, which protected me from the heavy rain. When I started to cross the street a driver tooted his car horn. I stepped back and the car moved off. My thoughts were still with Nancy. I felt it would be one of those days! I noticed a lady huddled inside a shop entrance. Once closer, I recognised her as the outspoken lady on the treatment of Jewish citizens in Germany.

She approached me. "Excuse me."

I stopped and held my umbrella above us.

"I have to meet someone at the Lochside Hotel. Where can I get a cab?"

"They can be scarce around here but the hotel is within a short distance. I'm headed that way. You can shelter under my umbrella."

"How long does it take to walk there?"

"About ten minutes." What an elegant lady. Tall and slim, she wore a small tilted hat, and a stylish pale yellow two-piece outfit was complemented by her long dark hair. Her accent was foreign, but she spoke English in a competent manner. She wore a nice perfume.

It did not take long to reach the hotel and she thanked me for being a gentleman. She admitted to a distaste for damp weather. Me too – however, it could provide certain opportunities!

As I headed towards the Grey Gull Inn, the rain still poured down. Apart from a man who wore a dark hat and raincoat, I did not observe anyone else in the vicinity. The weather had driven people indoors.

The man came up to me. "Excuse me, where can I find the Argyll Arms?"

As I gave him directions, another man appeared in similar attire. "I have a gun pointed at your stomach – come with us! Don't ask any questions – just do what we say. Keep the brolly in the air."

Not again!

They took me to a car, which had been parked in a quiet lane just off a side street. Perfect – no witnesses!

One searched me, pulled out my envelope and got into the driver's side.

The other pointed the gun. "Get in!"

I sat in the rear seat.

Then he sat in the front and turned to me. He clicked the gun.

"What is this about, and who are you people?"

"Why did you meet with that woman today?"

"She required a cab. One did not come, and therefore I walked her to the destination."

"Destination?"

"A local hotel. Why?"

His colleague held up the envelope given to me by a nurse and read it "Is she your contact in America?"

I got anxious. "No, she is a relative. My name is James Carsell-Brown."

His colleague growled. "Oh no, it's not! We have checked. Your surname is Carlisle."

I sighed. "It's a name I made up to avoid confusion."

"Why change your name?"

"It's a long story."

"You're lying!"

The driver started the car.

"May I enquire where you intend to take me?"

"To see someone." He put the gun into his coat pocket.

We left Ardrishaig and travelled on the main road northwards. About thirty minutes later we arrived at Inveraray. The car proceeded up a straight single road. At the end stood a large detached house, which the car drew up alongside. I got ordered out of the car and led inside the house. I found myself in a well-furnished drawing room.

"Wait here."

At least he hadn't pointed his gun at me this time!

A different man came into the room. He wore a dark grey flannel suit and sober necktie. The excessive wide trousers caught my attention – I suppose it *was* the 1930s! He must have been around sixty or sixty five.

" I am Alan Graham Struthers. Please take a seat."

"Why have I been brought here?" I sat down on a couch.

He went behind a desk and pulled the chair forward. "Well Mr… Is it Carlisle?"

"That will suffice."

"I work for the British government. You could say I preserve the security of our country."

"British Secret Service?"

"Yes, something like that. We make up part of an intelligence network which gathers information."

"But why me?"

"You met with a particular lady in Ardrishaig – are you friends?"

"No. As I told your two 'assistants', I took her to a local hotel where she had to meet a friend."

"Did you see the friend?"

I became a bit frustrated. "Who is she? Why the need to bring me here – and at gunpoint?"

"I apologise for the melodrama. The gun is just an imitation."

I looked at the ceiling!

"The lady in question is a Swiss National. Her name is Maya Frielberg, and we believe her friend is a German spy."

"The lady attended a meeting at the village hall in Ardrishaig. She made severe anti-German comments. Why would she have a pro-German friend?"

"If this individual allies himself to her, then it avoids suspicion."

"Do you believe I am a spy?"

"No – you do not strike me as being the type of person would get mixed up in espionage."

"Can I now leave?"

"I would like you to help us."

"Us?" What does he mean?

"Your country, Mr Carlisle. Help your country."

"In what way?"

"All you have to do is shadow Madame Frielberg. Anything suspicious, contact me."

"Why not use the two men I met today?"

"You do not look like a spy, and they would arouse suspicion."

No argument from me. "Apart from being a loyal British subject, why should I get mixed up in all of this?"

"In order to settle your bill at the Grey Gull! I will pay it and give you expenses."

Being stuck with no income, I *did* need cash. "Okay, we have a deal"

"Good show! We have discovered Maya Friellberg and her friend plan to attend the 'British Empire Exhibition' in Glasgow next week. There will be a number of foreign visitors to the event; therefore I expect someone from German Intelligence to make contact. As you have become acquainted with Madame Frielberg, we would like you to meet, gain her trust, and find out what you can."

"Did you not say 'shadow' her?"

"It amounts to the same thing."

"But I just met her!"

He smiled. "Don't worry, you'll be fine – just use your charm! Also, you typify a person who enjoys a challenge – a desire to succeed."

"How can you tell?"

"Before I entered this line of work, my job related to psychology."

Psychology? You mean bribery!

"My two colleagues shall give you a lift back to the Grey Gull Inn. Before you leave, what is your connection with Elizabeth Carsell-Brown?" He handed back the envelope.

"It's personal."

Into the room came my two 'abductors' with a friendlier manner. They looked less sinister without their dark hats and long raincoats.

"Mr Carlisle, this is Peter Lenihan and Harry Creelman. They will be less forthright and more receptive this time. Goodbye for now – I shall be in touch." He put four five pound notes into my palm.

The two tweed-suited, middle-aged men got into the front of the car. I sat in the back and then we departed. The rain had at last stopped. The driver, Harry Creelman, struck me as a strong and silent individual. His partner, Peter Lenihan, was more direct in his manner. I got the impression he would not be slow to show his disapproval for a troublesome issue!

"How long have you chaps been involved in this type of work?"

Peter Lenihan turned round. "Why do you ask?"

"Just curious." *Deja vu*!

"Both of us had previous jobs which allowed us to investigate people."

"As dangerous as this?"

"Worse – we used real guns." He lit his pipe.

"I take it you came across a lot of villains?"

"None we couldn't deal with!" He looked at his colleague. "Isn't that right, Harry?"

Harry nodded.

Peter puffed on his pipe. "Maya Frielberg is a friend of Charlotte Carsell-Brown. She stays just outside Ardrishaig at the Docharnea estate."

"I know."

"We understand they studied at the same University and have remained friends." Peter again lit his pipe. "Maya Frielberg no doubt received an invitation to the recent wedding of Charlotte's son – presumably why she arrived in this country."

"Is she staying with Charlotte Carsell-Brown?"

"Yes."

"Who is this friend she met at the Lochside Hotel?" I was curious.

Harry Creelman looked at me in the car mirror. "He calls himself Karl Jungens, an architect from Dusseldorf. He is a resident at the hotel and has been there for three days. He tends to keep a low profile. Maya Frielberg visits him on a daily basis, either in the afternoon or early evening." Harry Creelman pressed the gas pedal and accelerated past a vehicle. "Tractors!"

"What evidence do you have that Karl Jungens is a spy?"

Peter Lenihan removed the pipe from his mouth. "We've been able to monitor his movements. We've intercepted information which led us to believe he could be an undercover agent."

"A stroke of luck to intercept information."

Harry Creelman smiled in the mirror. "Not really – we got a tip-off from one of our agents in Germany."

Peter Lenihan added, "We also believe Karl Jungens met with another agent in this area."

I was presented with a detailed record of afternoon and evening visits made by Maya Frielberg to the Lochside Hotel.

"As you can see, there is a pattern," said Peter Lenihan. "On the first day, Maya Friedberg visited him that afternoon."

I looked at the information. "Then next day she visited in the evening."

Peter Lenihan nodded. "The following day, back to the afternoon again. If the pattern remains consistent, then she will be at the hotel tomorrow evening. Make sure Karl Jungens does not see you with her. He may become suspicious. Be caution at all times."

"What if I fail to make contact?"

Both replied, "Struthers won't pay you!"

When we reached Ardrishaig, I got dropped off outside the Grey Gull Inn. The black Ford Sedan sped off back towards Inveraray.

The next day I returned to the menswear shop in the high street. With my current attire twenty six years old, I required a new outfit. Mr Struthers had given me an advance, and therefore I would spend it on a new suit. His philosophy could be, 'to gain credibility in a certain type of role; you must dress in the appropriate manner'. I entered the shop and a bell rang. As he attended to another customer, the assistant looked my way.

"Be with you shortly, sir."

The other customer left with a parcel underneath his arm and a bell tinkled. The assistant came over to where I stood.

"Sorry for the delay, sir. The previous gentleman was most particular about his suit. He's from Germany." The tailor removed the tape measure from around his neck.

"Where in Germany?"

"Dusseldorf."

"Could you understand him?"

"His English is impeccable, but he may have struggled with my Scottish accent!"

"What outfits for business and leisure do you have?"

He let me see a selection of jackets, trousers and complete suits. He studied me over his small rounded spectacles. "Do you have a colour preference, sir? How about this one?" He presented me with a navy blue narrow pinstripe suit.

"Perfect."

"Excellent choice, sir – try on the jacket."

He held it up.

The jacket had padded shoulders. I put it on and looked in the wall mirror. The outfit gave a 'square' effect. The trousers appeared too wide and baggy. Still, this was 1938!

He brushed off a hair on my shoulder. "What height are you, sir?"

"Two inches short of six feet."

"The pinstripe gives the impression of being taller. It is a fashionable suit. I would recommend it, sir."

"How much?" I again looked in the mirror.

"Five pounds, two shillings and sixpence sir. Would you like a soft felt hat to compliment the suit?"

"I do not wear one." I gave the sales assistant two five pound notes.

He gave me the change, plus my suit wrapped in paper.

No carrier bags in this era!

"Thank you, sir. See you again."

As I walked out of the shop, the rain started to fall. It might have been the driest April on record but it was a miserable wet start to May. I looked upwards at dull grey skies and took shelter in the menswear shop's doorway. I should have brought my umbrella. I envisaged the sales assistant who had just sold me a suit, eager to further enhance today's revenue.

He popped his head out. "A raincoat, sir?"

"Maybe another time."

"You know where we are, sir!"

I contemplated what to do next. Then I noticed Maya Frielberg walk along my side of the street with a peach coloured umbrella. It coordinated with her dark green raincoat.

She approached with a sweet smile. "My turn to assist! Have you far to walk?"

"I am headed for the Allt-Na-Craig Hotel for lunch. Would you care to join me?"

She looked at her wristwatch. "I do not have much time. Perhaps a cup of coffee."

I lowered my head underneath her umbrella. "I also have to visit the jewellers to buy a replacement wristwatch."

After thirty minutes, we reached the hotel and refuge from the downpour. I now had a watch once more to keep track of the time.

"Why does it rain so heavily in Scotland?"

"Only in May!"

We entered the small quiet dining room and sat at a window table. It looked onto the trim but tidy landscaped hotel garden. A waitress who wore a black frock soon appeared.

"Two coffees, please," I said.

"Coffee?" said the waitress.

"Yes please." I smiled.

"Are you not having lunch?"

"No, not today."

The waitress wrote down the order and left.

"She looked perturbed we did not order lunch," said Maya.

"Establishments like this remain set in their ways. When people come here at this time of day, the staff expect them to have lunch. In the future, everyday habits may change and lunch could disappear from most menus."

She looked intrigued. "Why would they change?"

"Trends, progression – change tends to occur. Compare Germany now to twenty years ago. At the end of the war, Germany became bankrupt, whereas now their economy thrives. With the country's profile and stature being raised, citizens have regained their self-respect."

"German circumstances are different from a lunch menu!"

"Yes, but my point is nothing stands still. Consider air travel. Since the Hindenberg disaster of a year ago, nobody will dare travel in that mode of transport."

"I agree with what you say but there is a negative side to change. Some German citizens are bullied and persecuted because of their race."

I understood what she tried to convey. "I would imagine the situation could become worse if it is ignored?"

"Yes."

The waitress brought our two coffees.

"Do you live in Germany?"

"No, I live in Switzerland but have family in Munich."

"Why did you come to Scotland?" I added two lumps of sugar to my coffee.

"A friend invited me to her son's wedding. She insisted I stay on."

"When do you plan on return home?"

She smiled. "You ask a lot of questions!"

"My apologies – I have an inquisitive mind."

Maya sipped her coffee. "Oh, it is terrible!" She screwed up her face.

"Too strong?"

"No, it is too weak! Tell me, what it is you do?"

"Most of my time gets consumed through travel. It has produced situations of great interest."

"Where have you travelled to?"

"Within Scotland, but I have been to France."

"What part?"

"The Cote d'Azur. I spent most of my time in Nice."

"Why Nice?"

"I worked there, but returned home to Scotland on a family request."

"I have visited Paris on several occasions. The colours in spring can be stunning."

It was my turn to ask a question. "What plans do you have for the remainder of the week?"

"I am undecided. Why?" She sipped her coffee.

"Before you depart, perhaps we could meet again?"

"Do you have a telephone number where I can contact you?"

I wrote down the Grey Gull Inn's telephone number. I picked up my parcel.

"What is that?"

"My new suit. Don't forget your umbrella!" I handed it to her.

"Thank you."

We finished our coffee and after I paid the bill, proceeded to the exit door. The rain had stopped and the sun had at last come out.

She turned towards me. "I do not know your name."

"James Carlisle."

"I am Maya Frielberg." She shook my hand.

As I got to my accommodation, the rain started once more. I got my room key and went upstairs. I then unwrapped my parcel to reveal a new narrow pinstripe suit. I tried it on. Then came three knocks on my door. I opened it.

"Hi."

"Yes, gentlemen – how can I assist you this time?"

Peter Lenihan said, "Did you make any progress with Maya Frielberg?"

"Yes, I did."

"Do you know when she plans to leave Ardrishaig?"

"Not for a couple of days, at least."

"Where's the nearest telephone?"

I pointed downstairs. "Turn first left."

He departed.

I looked at Harry Creelman. "Is he always this persistent?"

He grinned and nodded. "Most of the time!"

Peter Lenihan rushed back up the stairs. "If you learn anything about Karl Jungens, alert us right away. Here is a number to contact." He gave me a card with a number scribbled on it.

"Don't worry, I will get in touch if any developments occur."

As the two of them walked down the stairs, both of them shouted, "Like the suit!"

I then ventured downstairs to the bar for a beer. I found the customer's conversations strange at times. To hear a discussion on the forthcoming World Cup Championship and then the ruthless ambition of Adolf Hitler could be surreal. Someone mentioned the possible threat of Japan, which got dismissed.

"Asia is too far away from us – we don't need to worry about the Japs!" said a customer.

Not us but the United States – at Pearl Harbour in three years!

The telephone at the side of the bar started to ring. The barman had started to wash used glasses in a sink. He lifted the telephone, put it to his ear and looked around the bar.

"Mr Carlisle."

I put up my hand.

"A Miss Frielberg." He handed me the receiver.

We arranged to meet the following day at the Allt-Na-Craig Hotel around one o'clock.


I left the inn at thirty minutes past twelve. I arrived at the hotel in good time for my appointment with Maya. Another overcast day beckoned, but at least I had brought my umbrella – a precaution with my new suit being worn for the first time! I checked my watch – five minutes past one.

A gentleman then approached. "Excuse me, sir, but are you Mr Carlisle?"

"Yes, why?"

"My name is Mr Dodds, the manager of the hotel. The lady you plan to meet has been delayed but should soon be here. She asked me to convey her apologies."

Time passed and I started to imagine she might not appear. From the same window seat as before, I continued to watch two grey rabbits dart around the garden. Then I observed a lady in a two-piece deep-red suit and larger tilted hat.

She came over and took a seat opposite me. "My apologies, James. The suit is perfect but you need a different tie!"

"In the colour of your outfit?"

"Yes, perfect!"

"Let us order something to eat – I'm peckish."

After lunch, our 'resident' waitress brought us coffee. She gave us a courteous smile – maybe because we ordered lunch!

"How does your coffee taste?" I asked.

"Terrible!"

As we chatted, she mentioned the visit to Glasgow.

"When do you leave Ardrishaig?"

"Tomorrow morning."

"After your visit to Glasgow, do you plan to come back here?"

"No, I will travel back to Switzerland."

"Does your friend also come from Switzerland?"

"No, he comes from Dusseldorf. He intends to visit an exhibition in Glasgow. It relates to his job as an architect."

Struthers had got his information spot-on!

Maya added, "His English is terrible, hence the reason why I shall accompany him."

Strange. The sales assistant in the menswear shop commented that he spoke English in a competent manner.

"How much English can he speak?"

"Very little."

"Your English is of a high standard." Not the first time I had encountered this in a foreign lady.

"I studied English and German at University. My native language is French."

"What type of building does your friend design?"

"The company he represents is at present constructing part of the Reich Chancellery in Berlin. Several other cities in Germany are being modernised in which he has been involved."

Busy chap. "Why is he attending the exhibition?"

"You ask a lot of questions, Mr Carlisle! I would suggest getting some fresh ideas!"

Sounds like a credible reason. I felt that I should change the subject. She may have become a bit suspicious. "Did you enjoy the wedding?"

"Oh yes, a wonderful occasion! The groom and his brother are similar in appearance, but have different natures."

"In what way?"

"William is, you would say 'laid-back', whereas his younger brother is the impatient type. Geoffrey and you have similar traits."

*Well, he was my grandfather!*

Maya looked at her gold wristwatch. "I have to go, James. A pleasure to have met you."

How very sudden! She shook my hand with her gentle touch and left.

Nancy's funeral took place after Maya Frielberg left for Glasgow. The lady who had worked as the housekeeper of Docharnea for thirty years was laid to rest at the local cemetery. A large number of people came to pay their last respects on this bright day. After the service, people gathered in the grounds of the church.

A chap came over to me. "Since we last met you haven't changed!"

He looked familiar, but where had I met him?

"I'm Andrew, Angus' son. It's been a long time, I can understand why you may not remember."

Twenty six years had gone by for him, but only days for me. "How is your father?"

An elderly man walked towards us with the aid of a stick.

Andrew turned towards him. "Father, this is James Carlisle."

I remembered Angus being less than half my age in 1896!

"Hello James, it's been a long time. You keepin' well?"

"Yes, so far!"

"You sound well." He peered at me.

A lady walked up to Angus and took his arm.

"You must excuse me, James. I'll see you later."

I looked at Andrew. "Your father is popular!"

"That's Mrs Ferguson. She's one of our customers. We should 'ave tended to her gardens last week, but we've a backlog of work just now."

"Does the firm continue to expand?"

"Yes, thanks to your advice. We now provide a wide range of services other than gardening."

I could not understand why Angus did not react in the same way as his son. However, it would have been impossible to give a credible explanation!

A lady then came into our company. "Excuse me, are you James Carlisle?"

"Yes, I am."

"My name is Charlotte Carsell-Brown. Nancy often mentioned you. How nice to meet at last."

My great grandmother – the first time I had met her.

"Are you all right, James?" said Charlotte. "You look as if you've seen a ghost!"

"I'm fine." *Just!*

Andrew excused himself and went to find his father.

"You have to take care of yourself. You are no longer a teenager."

Teenager? Of course. Since I worked at Docharnea, twenty six years had passed. I felt I should change the subject. "Andrew looks concerned."

"His father has poor eyesight."

That was why he hadn't recognised me.

"Let me introduce you to my husband." She caught his attention.

A well-groomed gentleman arrived.

"Philip, this is James Carlisle."

He shook my hand. This day had turned out into an emotional one in more ways than I could have anticipated.

"Philip, do you notice something familiar about James?"

He moved his head closer.

"Philip, put your spectacles on! His eyes, he has Geoffrey's eyes!"

"My goodness, you are correct Charlotte!"

I pretended ignorance. "Geoffrey?"

Charlotte said, "Geoffrey is our youngest son and lives in Edinburgh."

"Which part?"

"Newhaven. He and his wife have a baby son who is not well, hence their absence today. We also have another son called William, who is on his honeymoon. I am disappointed they could not attend today. Both adored Nancy, and she them."

I understood.

"They would plead for extra cakes and ask her to tell stories about a time traveller." She laughed.

I smiled. "Did she give this individual a name?"

"Just the 'traveller'. William and Geoffrey would then talk to their friends about this person, who appears at our coach house wearing a coachman's outfit."

"Why a coachman's outfit?" I said.

"The previous owners of our property employed a man to chauffeur them. When he carried out his coach duties, he had to wear an outfit."

Philip laughed. "William and Geoffrey found an original version of H.G. Wells' novel *The Time Machine* in the coach house. They became convinced he did exist!"

Charlotte added, "Time traveller or not, he got both of them to start reading books!"

So that was what had happened to my book. Oh well, at least it served a worthwhile purpose!

"Charlotte, where do your son and new daughter-in-law plan to stay?"

"They have a house not far from where her mother lives. Poor lady, she has not recovered from Edward being killed in the war. Olivia did not get to know her father. "

Philip said, "Olivia is a lovely, bright girl. Her father would have been proud."

Charlotte quipped, "Let us hope another war is not forthcoming!"

"Agreed – it disrupts family life," said Philip.

"I had a friend from Switzerland staying with us and she remains adamant Hitler is driven by power. He has invaded Austria. Czechoslovakia will be next."

Philip uttered, "Maybe he just wants to expand the border areas around Germany – reclaim territory taken by the Treaty of Versailles?"

Yes, all the way to Russia! "Has your friend gone back to Switzerland?"

"No. Before returning home, she is going to spend some time in Glasgow. This break is her annual holiday, and therefore she wants to make the most of it."

Andrew came towards me. "James, I have to go. Good to see you again."

I wished him, his family and the firm well.

"My son, Angus, has just started working with me and is a quick learner. All goes well for the future." He shook my hand.

I turned to Philip and Charlotte. "It has been a pleasure to meet you both."

"And you also, James," said Charlotte. "Do you have any arrangements for this week?"

"Not sure yet, but no doubt something will happen. As horse-drawn vehicles have disappeared, what is the coach house used for?"

"We use the old stables for storage, but the rest of the building has been closed for years," said Charlotte.

I left them and the funeral with mixed emotions. I would not see Nancy again, but I had met my great grandparents. I remember being shown old discoloured photographs of them. The day had produced a special moment of realism. Time travel could be surreal.

Later, I browsed through a copy of the *Radio Times*, which had been left in the inn's reception area. The content consisted of comedy shows, drama serials and current affairs programmes. With threat of another European war, the latter had become a topical subject for listeners. No doubt the inclusion of comedy shows was geared to give listeners some light-hearted relief from the austerity which engulfed 1938.

There came a knock on the door. Not the deadly duo again! I put down the *Radio Times* and opened the door.

"You mentioned to the barman that music is one of your main interests. You can borrow this for an evening." Mike, the owner of the inn, gave me a gramophone plus a short pile of 78-rpm records.

My smile grew a lot wider. The gramophone resembled a cumbersome piece of equipment but after all, I was in 1930s Scotland! I thanked him and looked through the records. They consisted of 'One o'clock Jump', 'The Lady is a Tramp' and 'The Moon Got in My Eyes' by Count Basie, Tommy Dorsey and Bing Crosby respectively. However, I did not have 'Begin the Beguine' by Arti Shaw. Pity, as this would become one of the most successful records of the year and was my favourite Cole Porter song. At least I could listen to music again.

Then came three distinctive knocks on my door. I opened it and my suspicions proved correct.

"Did you make any progress with Maya Frielberg?" Peter Lenihan's pipe hung from the side of his mouth.

"Come in, gentlemen."

Peter Lenihan and Harry Creelman each took a chair. They politely removed their hats. As the room only had two chairs, I stood.

"Any progress? Peter relit his pipe.

"I made contact but she has left for Glasgow."

Peter Lenihan looked alarmed. "What, she's gone?"

"Yes, this morning, with Karl Jungens."

Harry Creelman looked at his colleague. "They have departed two days earlier than expected!"

"Maya Frielberg revealed Karl Jungens' plan to attend the British Empire Exhibition because he is an architect. He works for a company in Berlin and seeks new ideas for projects soon to commence."

"And I'm bloody Neville Chamberlain!" said Peter Lenihan. "I will contact Struthers." He dashed out of the room and down the stairs.

His calmer colleague folded his arms. "How did Maya Frielberg react when you spoke to her?"

"A bit defensive. I got the impression she suspected me of probing for information."

Peter Lenihan, with pipe in one hand, stormed back into the room. He took a deep breath. "That's better. Struthers wants you to travel right away!"

"To Glasgow?"

"Yes – follow Maya Frielberg." Peter returned to his chair.

"If I am spotted, she will realise something is afoot!"

"The lady will not be aware of the danger she could find herself in," said Harry Creelman. "We have evidence to suggest Karl Jungens is a spy."

"As a result of her association to him, she could therefore be implicated in whatever plot is being hatched," said Peter Lenihan. "You have to find and warn her of the situation."

As a friend of my great-grandmother, I had to oblige.

"Don't worry – we will get a member of our organisation to contact you in Glasgow," said Harry Creelman.

Peter Lenihan handed me a small package. "This is from Struthers."

I took it.

"The package contains enough money to pay your bills, plus extras. A boat called the *Saint Columba* sails from the harbour at seven o'clock tomorrow morning for Glasgow. It will dock at Govan, then head for the Beresford Hotel in Sauchiehall Street. It has been built for the Empire Exhibition, and therefore rooms may even have a radio for your pleasure."

"Shall I manage to get a room at this busy period?"

Peter Lenihan got up from his chair. "Don't worry – Struthers shall arrange it. After you arrive, someone will be in touch. This person will use 'NOVA' as a codename. Any questions?"

"No."

"Bon voyage," said Peter Lenihan.

Harry just smiled.

# Chapter 7

## *The Document*

I paid my bill and checked out of the Grey Gull Inn early that morning. I headed for the harbour to board the Macbrayne steamer to Glasgow. My trips by boat amounted to only two, and one of them was deemed forgettable due to violent weather conditions. A six hour journey in a choppy sea ensured my stomach's preferred travel option did not involve a sailing craft. However, when the *Saint Columba* departed from Ardrishaig, the sea remained calm.

I stood on the rear deck and admired the view from my rare mariner's position. As the dark blue and white three-funnel steamer sailed between green valleys, I could smell the sea air and feel a breeze on my face. If not for the grey skies, the scene would have been perfect.

I discovered the transportation of mail, supplies and passengers around the West Coast of Scotland had made this type of craft essential for social and economic stability. My perception of sea vessels had changed.

After a 'smooth' sail, the *Saint Columba* docked at Govan in the afternoon. It completed a journey which included stops at Tarbert, Tighnabruaich, Rothesay, Dunoon, Gourock and Greenock. I disembarked and made haste for the main road to catch a tram for Glasgow's city centre.

When I reached the tram stop, I gazed at the overhead mechanism between tenement blocks. Then I noticed a tram come 'gliding' along the rails towards me. As the tram stopped, I stared at it. Until now, I had only seen them in photographs or film clips.

"Not got all day sir," said the conductor, "we've a timetable to keep!"

"Does this tram go to the city centre?

"Which part?"

"Sauchiehall Street."

The conductor nodded. "Near enough, sir."

I boarded the blue number four tram. The conductor pressed the bell. As the tram moved off I sat downstairs on one of the hard and uncomfortable metal seats. A few minutes later the conductor appeared. I gave him a florin to pay the fare. He shook his head.

"Have you nothing smaller?"

I also shook my head. He gave me a ticket and a handful of farthings, halfpennies, pennies, two threepennies and one sixpence. I hoped my pocket had strong stitching. Twenty minutes later, the conductor looked my way.

"This is your stop sir – Hope Street." He pointed. "That way for Sauchiehall Street."

"Thanks." I got off the tram and headed for Sauchiehall Street. During my walk I observed a number of assorted retail outlets. I would not be stuck for a beer.

I reached the Beresford Hotel and entered the impressive, bright and sophisticated new building. I waited at the reception area.

"Can I help you sir?" asked the receptionist.

"Do you have a reservation for a Mr Carlisle?"

The well-presented lady looked through her list. "I am afraid not, sir."

Surely Struthers had not forgotten to arrange a room.

"I can't find any reservation under Carlisle. Who booked the room?"

"A Mr Struthers." I became concerned. All this way and nowhere to stay!

She shook her head. "Nothing for Struthers either." She flicked a hair of her black dress.

"Mr Carsell-Brown, by any chance?"

A smile came forthwith. "Yes sir, we have a recent priority reservation under that name."

Psychologists!

Then an articulate gentleman in a black three-piece suit appeared from the back office. He held a letter in his hand.

"This is for you, sir. It got handed into the hotel early this afternoon." He turned towards the lady receptionist. "Elaine, is everything organised for Mr Carlisle?"

"It is now."

I received the letter, room key and verbal directions to my accommodation. When I entered the white pristine room, my body headed for the bed. The journey from Ardrishaig did not appear long, but unaccustomed sea air must have taken its toll. However, my curiosity prevailed. What could be the contents of the letter? I opened it.

*"Mr Carlisle,*

*Struthers has been in touch and suggested you and I meet to discuss the situation. Make your way to 'Curlers' on Byres Road where there is a small upstairs bar. I shall meet you at eight o'clock.*

*G.C.'*

Following a quick nap, I freshened up and had a bite to eat in the hotel restaurant. I handed my key into reception. The receptionist smiled.

"How do I get to Byres Road from here?"

"Where are you headed for, sir?"

"Curlers."

"You can get a tram just along the road. Take a green number one to the junction of Great Western Road and Byres Road. Walk down Byres Road and Curlers is on your left – next to Hillhead Underground."

I thanked her and crossed the road to the tram stop. I looked upwards – all that overhead equipment – I hoped it had been secured! Five minutes later a tram arrived. That time I had enough change!

I reached my destination at four minutes to eight. I entered the narrow doorway, went upstairs and headed for the bar. The room had red walls, a sanded wooden floor, small dark oak tables and matching chairs. The barman wore a customary white apron, a white collarless shirt and a red waistcoat.

"Can I get you something, sir?"

As I contemplated what to buy, someone came up to me.

"Let me get this, Mr Carlisle." A bald man of stocky build held up a ten-shilling note. "What do you want to drink?"

I looked at the barman. "Do you have any cans of beer?"

"No sir, still waiting for them to arrive from the brewery. Our stock has all been sold."

It must have been the novelty factor. "A bottle of ale, then."

My contact ordered a large glass of ale. We took our drinks and sat at a nearby table. He enquired about cans of beer.

"It is a new product which has arrived on the market. Cans could become more popular than bottles."

He looked at his drink. "I can't envisage them being able to replace cask beer!"

"I agree." I sipped my pale ale. But fads will continue to come around in society. Wait until the latter part of the twentieth century arrives!

He took a gulp of ale – after which only half remained in the large glass.

"How did you recognise me?"

"Struthers gave me an accurate description. Did he give you a codename?"

I revealed it.

He held out his hand. "I am George Cox."

I shook his hand.

"Your accent is unusual – where do you come from?"

"I am from Edinburgh but have also lived in France for a number of years."

"Have you visited Glasgow in the past?"

Only on this occasion in the past, but many in the future, courtesy of Hampden Park! "Whilst on my way to Ardrishaig, I visited Glasgow."

"Why go to Ardrishaig?" He looked intrigued.

"To visit some of my distant relatives." George Cox's manner became serious.

"We have to move fast. Struthers believes Karl Jungens is due to leave Scotland within a few days. This doesn't give us much time to find out what he's involved in."

"An innocent lady is also involved."

"Maya Frielberg?"

"I feel she's unaware he is a spy and could therefore be drawn into any predicament which may arise."

"Is there any other reason?"

"No."

George Cox then swallowed the remainder of his drink. "You should get in touch and make her aware of Karl Jungens."

"I don't have her address."

He grinned. "I do. She and Jungens have rooms at the city's Central Hotel."

"How do you know?"

"Government intelligence, Mr Carlisle! You could arrange to meet her at Willows – it is located not far from here."

"What type of establishment is it?"

"A tea-room. She can reach it by underground train from St. Enoch station and get off at Hillhead station."

"I hope she enjoys tea!"

He laughed. "I'll give you a lift back to your hotel. My car is parked in a lane just around the corner."

George Cox drove a black Ford 40A. As he got into the car, I stared at the empty derelict commercial properties on each side of the cobbled lane. I got into the passenger seat. He stated all of the properties had suffered because of the economic situation. This part of the city had much potential and he hoped astute business entrepreneurs would one day transform this street.

"What is it called?"

"Ashton Lane."


Next morning, I called into the city's Central Hotel. I left a note at reception for Maya to meet me the following day at a particular time and place.

"I will make sure she gets this today, sir," said the receptionist.

"Thank you."

"You're welcome."

I then went to look around the various department stores in Argyle Street and Buchanan Street. Upon reflection, in my future time, consumers can be spoiled for choice given the varied and wide range of goods at their disposal. Whilst in a department store, I came across a similar suit to the one purchased in Ardrishaig. Here, it cost four shillings less. No wonder the sales assistant in Ardrishaig had a smile on his face!

For 1938, I got the impression a popular pastime with Glaswegians would be to browse around the shops rather than to buy. I did not witness many tills ringing. The threat of another war, rations and a recession did not dampen the enthusiasm for this form of behaviour. In fact, it could be therapeutic! I almost forgot that I had intended to purchase some chocolate essentials. Now, where was Woolworths? You could always depend on one of their stores being close at hand.

Thursday brought heavy rain, and therefore I ventured to Willows in the West End of the city with my umbrella. George Cox emphasised the establishment had prestigious status within Glasgow. It portrayed a quality ambience to enthuse the customer. I got a tram to Great Western Road and soon arrived at the rendezvous. I looked at my watch – fifteen minutes early. I entered the premises through glass doors and took a seat at the bay window. The interior had white walls and a high level frieze of coloured, mirrored and leaded glass panels. Against one of the walls stood a dark smoothed-edge fireplace. On a cold day, it made you feel welcome. The soft grey carpet, high-backed chairs, silver tables, crisp white tablecloths and blue willow-patterned crockery lent themselves to a luxurious relaxed atmosphere.

A lady with a smart black and white uniform approached me. "Can I help you, sir?"

"Can I wait? My friend should be here in a few minutes." I hoped that she had got my note.

"Yes, of course you can, sir."

I looked out the window and noticed her approaching. Maya walked into the establishment, spotted me and smiled.

She sat down and gazed around the room. "Exquisite – Charles Rennie Mackintosh." She turned towards me. "Why are you in Glasgow?" She removed her beige raincoat

"A delicate matter required my urgent attention."

"Your note mentioned I could be in danger."

"I will come straight to the point. How long have you known Karl Jungens?"

She hesitated. "Only for a short time. Why do you ask?"

I moved my head forward and whispered. "Are you aware he is a spy?"

"Nonsense! Why do you say that?"

"An organisation which has knowledge of his undercover activities contacted me. After being spotted with you, they thought I was also a spy."

Maya laughed. "Karl is the most timid and disorganised person I know. He cannot speak English. He would make a terrible spy."

"I must advise you to take care."

She placed her hand on mine. "Do not worry, I can look out for myself."

The waitress arrived at our table. "Are you ready to order?"

"A white coffee, please," said Maya.

"We just serve tea, but please hold on." The waitress left and soon returned. "Coffee is available, madam."

"Same for me, please."

"Certainly sir." She departed.

We discussed the various sights of Glasgow and Hitler's aggression in Europe. Both of us finished our coffee and then walked to the nearby underground station. When we reached Hillhead, Maya had a reassuring smile.

"I will be fine." She kissed me on the cheek.

Always a nice smile. Then I felt a warm gust of wind which emanated from the station. As the rain started, we parted and I caught a tram back to Sauchiehall Street.

After dinner, I walked the short distance from the hotel to the Kings Theatre. A play of interest had been highlighted in the media. Allen Boretz and John Murray wrote 'Room Service'. It had opened in New York in 1937. Due to its popularity, RKO turned the play into a film starring The Marx Brothers. Since I was at present in a future European City of Culture, it made good sense to sample the present artistic flavour.

The theatre looked full for this midweek evening performance. This could be a further example for the desire of light-hearted relief in this era. The bright extravagant interior and plush seats made this venue ideal for this type of entertainment. In fact, it made my predicament of being lost in time secondary. This play highlighted the plight of an executive who attempts to avoid paying the hotel bill for his staff. Until the debt is paid, it tells of his subsequent efforts to keep them there.

At the interval, I overheard a group of young ladies discuss forthcoming new films to see. It became a choice between 'The Adventures of Robin Hood' starring Errol Flynn and Olivia de Havilland – a stylish adventure colour movie with romance – and 'Angels With Dirty Faces' starring James Cagney and Humphrey Bogart – a furious violent gangster drama in plain black and white. It resulted in a unanimous decision. The first film became the preferred option amongst this particular section of society. However, one lady looked forward to another Alfred Hitchcock thriller – 'The Lady Vanishes', a film full of suspense and drama with Michael Redgrave and Margaret Lockwood. Those three films would become classics from this year. How may film watchers perceive 'Titanic' and 'The Shawshank Redemption' in the mid-twenty first century?

Loud roars of laughter echoed around the theatre stalls during the first half performance. People in the private boxes remained reserved. Maybe their interval tipple of alcohol courtesy of the theatre cocktail bar could produce a change in behaviour? After the curtain went up I would observe with curiosity. Ah, splendid – the second half.


Maya stood at reception. "Excuse me, I cannot find my friend. We arranged to meet in the hotel bar at eight o'clock."

The receptionist replied, "Is it Mr Jungens you are looking for madam?"

"Yes, it is."

"He earlier met a gentleman at reception and they went into the bar."

"Are you positive?"

"I overheard Mr Jungens' conversation with the other gentleman."

"Do you speak German?"

"No, they spoke in English. Are you alright, madam?"

"Yes, yes. It has been a long day."


As I left the breakfast room, the duty manager came up to me.

"Mr Carlisle, Madame Frielberg telephoned this morning and left a message for you." He gave me a note.

"Thank you." I read the note.


"James, please meet me at Willows around eleven o'clock. It is important. Maya."

I arrived at the specified time and location. I noticed Maya already there, sitting at the same table as on our previous visit.

I sat down. "What is the matter? Your note sounded urgent."

"Yesterday evening, Karl met with a stranger at the hotel."

"Do you know his name?"

"No. They met for about thirty minutes and then Karl joined me in the downstairs lounge. It is not like him to act in this manner. He confides in me about all matters. Also, he has been lying to me about not able to speak English."

"Is he aware you spotted him and this stranger?"

"No, and I did not mention it."

"Did he act normal for the rest of the evening?"

"Yes."

I became intrigued. Should I contact George Cox?

"Karl and I are to attend the Empire Exhibition this afternoon. He has arranged to meet a colleague – what should I do?"

A waitress appeared. "Two white coffees?"

I nodded.

The waitress departed.

I turned to Maya. "Who is the person he met?"

"I am not sure, but they are to meet again at exhibitor number one hundred and nine around three o'clock."

"Attend the event and we can meet here tomorrow morning at the same time. If any problem arises, then contact me at the Beresford Hotel. I can take the call in reception."

"Is it not inconvenient?"

"Not at all. What time do you depart for the Empire Exhibition?"

"About one thirty. I told Karl at breakfast I wanted to look around the shops."

We left Willows just after midday and parted at Hillhead Underground. Whilst I walked to the tram stop, my mind focused on what Maya had said. I therefore had to find out about exhibitor number one hundred and nine and attend the Empire Exhibition. I heard the roar of thunder and looked upwards. As the sky became darker, my casual walk grew faster. The stop in Great Western Road had a shelter and I evaded the downpour. On my tram to Bellahouston Park, the staff wore white-topped caps to signify the destination.

The Empire Exhibition looked a formidable sight. The 'Tower of Empire' stood three hundred feet in the air. Areas for exhibitors, car parks, nursery and the amusement park stretched for just over one hundred and seventy acres. As press reports stated, the number of visitors had exceeded expectations and the wet weather had not dampened public enthusiasm! In a period of austerity and recession, Glasgow City Council must have welcomed this occasion with open arms. More than twelve million people came through the doors from May until October, plus over seven hundred exhibitors who paid rental space. In addition, there were almost nine hundred staff, which included construction, catering, waiting, cleaning, first aid, car park attendants, guides and general helpers hired for the event. A combination of employment, albeit short-term, and visitor revenue helped to enhance the local economic environment.

I paid my entrance fee of one shilling and browsed through the complimentary programme. It contained comprehensive information on the event which included its layout, amenities, seminars and exhibitors. Now, who was number one hundred and nine? Kane and Hogg – Civil Engineers. I studied the layout and proceeded towards the area. When I approached number one hundred and nine, nobody manned the stand.

A nearby exhibitor came over. "They have gone to lunch."

I noticed a catering outlet and went for some refreshments. It soon filled up with school pupils dressed in either blue or black uniforms. It appeared that two secondary education establishments had come to visit the exhibition. I listened to the accents. The pupils did not come from this part of the country, but from the east. I observed the badges on the two different blazers. Those with blue and white uniforms represented Leith Academy, whereas the black and yellow signified Trinity Academy.

A lady sat down next to me. "I hope the pupils do not disturb you."

"Not at all – their conduct is exemplary."

She held out her hand. "I am Morag Mackay, a teacher at Trinity Academy."

She had a strong grip. "I am James Carsell-Brown." I deemed it safe to use my true identity on this occasion.

"Where are you from?"

"Edinburgh, although I now stay in the West of Scotland. In fact, I used to live not far from Trinity."

"Are you related to Geoffrey Carsell-Brown? He and his family stay at Newhaven, not far from our school."

That would teach me – I should have stuck to Carlisle! "No, it is just a coincidence."

"I also stay in Newhaven, not far from their house."

I wanted to change the subject. "Did you get a train direct to this location?"

"Yes. The Leith Academy pupils left from a station in their district, and then we boarded at a station next to our school."

"Convenient."

"Yes, perfect. The train then brought us straight here to a station called Bellahouston Park South. Not bad for five shillings here and back!"

"Splendid." As another matter required my attention, I had to leave.

"Nice to have met you, Mr Carsell-Brown. It is a coincidence, having that rare surname!"

I smiled. "It's a small world."

"Goodbye."

I returned to exhibitor one hundred and nine and spotted Maya in the vicinity. I gathered pace and caught up with her.

"James, you startled me!"

"Are you all right?"

"Yes, yes, I am fine. Karl is about to meet with a contact. Since they plan to discuss business, I have made myself scarce."

"Who is this person?"

"If you look round the corner, he should now be with Karl."

I looked and could not believe my eyes.

"James, that is the same man who was at our hotel."

It was George Cox! What was going on? I asked Maya if she had information on the exhibitors, Kane and Hogg.

"Karl mentioned the two partners come from Ireland but work in Scotland. Also, both of them speak German."

As Maya planned to leave Scotland on Monday, we arranged to meet for a final time. I returned to my hotel. Would the rain never stop?

I had to contact Struthers and make him aware of the current situation. I found his number and went downstairs to one of the telephone booths. They had all been taken but I waited. Oh, for mobile technology! A few minutes later one became vacant. I closed the door, got my money ready and phoned his number.

"Mr Struther's residence."

"Can I speak to Mr Struthers please?"

"What is your name?"

"James Carlisle."

"I will see if he is available."

I heard background chatter and the telephone being handled.

"James, how are you?"

"Very well but I have a concern about your operative in Glasgow."

"George Cox?"

"He met with Karl Jungens yesterday evening at the Central Hotel, and today at the Empire Exhibition."

"Are you positive?"

"Most definitely. What should I do next?" There came a moment's pause.

"Do nothing. I have to attend a meeting in Edinburgh and am just about to leave. I'll be gone for two days and shall contact you on my return."

"What should I do if he contacts me?"

"Stall him."


Saturday brought a rare fresh and sunny morning. As I handed my key into reception, the Duty Manager came forward.

"Mr Carlisle, a message for you."

I read the note. It came from George Cox. I was to contact him at my earliest convenience! I put the note in my trouser pocket and got a tram to Byres Road. Oh, for a theatre seat!

I arrived at the Willows tearoom and took my usual seat beside the bay window. The temperature had become warmer. I took off my jacket and placed it over the back of my chair. Then Maya entered and we ordered our usual beverage.

"Have you enjoyed Scotland?"

"Very much, and being able to see Charlotte again was a joy. She has a beautiful family and is proud of her two sons."

" When in Leith do you plan to visit Geoffrey?"

"I will not have time. The ship sails for Hamburg mid-morning."

The waitress arrived with two coffees. "Here you are." She put them on the table.

"Germany must be a vibrant country at present."

"Vibrant?" She gripped a napkin. "People must now be careful of what they speak about. If a person dares to criticise the government, then they will be dealt with!"

"In what way?"

"It would depend on the crime and their race. Some German citizens have been sent to concentration camps and I have heard of public beatings." She took a sip of coffee. "A war is imminent. Hitler no doubt remains focused on European domination! Britain and France must stand in his way or we will all end up being collaborators. We all have to contribute to prevent such a fate bestowed on us."

The place fell silent and people stared in our direction. Seconds later they started to chat amongst themselves.

"I apologise. I should keep my feelings in check."

"Don't worry – they are probably in discussion about your yellow two-piece outfit!" The one she had worn when we first met.

She looked around. "Everyone wears either grey or black!"

We discussed more European politics and possible outcomes for a short period of time. I got up to pay our bill at the counter.

Maya brought over my jacket.

"Thanks."

When we got to Hillhead Underground, the weather remained fresh and sunny. It seemed appropriate conditions in which to part.

"Nice to have met your acquaintance, James. When the threat of conflict has gone, perhaps we will meet again."

*You would have to wait, Maya – a further seven years.*

She kissed me on the cheek, gripped my arm and went to catch her train.

I got back to the Beresford at one o'clock. As I approached my room, the chambermaid closed my door. She spotted me and smiled.

"Good afternoon, sir."

"Lovely day, isn't it?"

She nodded.

I entered the room and made for the wardrobe. As I put my jacket on the hanger, a brown envelope protruded from the inside pocket. I took it out. How had this gotten there? I opened the envelope with care. It contained three pages of information which related to a sea vessel. This involved diagrams, measurements and technical data for a propulsion system. Maya must have placed this in my jacket at some point in the tearoom. I understood why she had not handed me the document – I would ask too many questions! No doubt Karl Jungens would be an integral part of this. Her situation could now be dangerous. I couldn't contact Struthers – he would still not have returned to Inveraray. Maybe the housekeeper had a number to contact him in an emergency. I went downstairs to a telephone booth.

"Hello, Struthers' residence."

"It is James Carlisle. I have to speak with Mr Struthers."

"He has still not returned."

"It's urgent. Do you have a number I can contact him at?"

"No I am sorry – he did not give me an emergency number. When he returns, I'll tell him you called."

I hung up. Rather than wait for Struthers to return, I would investigate the situation and reassure myself that Maya was safe.


When I got to the Central Hotel, I pushed through the revolving door and walked across the foyer to reception.

A gentleman asked, "Can I be of assistance, sir?"

"I'm looking for Maya Frielberg. Is she in the hotel?"

He checked his board. "Yes, the room key is still here. Her room number is ninety-two and it's on the third floor."

I took the lift, stepped out and walked along the corridor to her room. I knocked on the door and waited. I moved closer to the door but could not hear any sound. Again I knocked, but still no response. Then the lift doors opened. A woman with a German Shepherd dog got out and came towards me. The dog stared at me and growled. The woman pulled it away and walked on. I returned to the reception desk. A lady had replaced the gentleman.

"I have come to visit the lady in room ninety-two but there is no answer."

"The lady has not checked out." The receptionist went into the back office and soon returned. "The lady should be there. Wait here and I will look into the situation."

A short time later she came back with an expression of shock. She went into the office and closed the door. She emerged and asked me to stay at reception. The manager and two other members of staff arrived also with serious expressions.

I asked, "What has happened? Is the lady all right?"

The manager said, "The situation is being attended to, sir."

From the glass door I noticed a police car and an ambulance arrive. Several police officers and a medical crew entered the hotel and rushed upstairs. A small crowd of guests had emerged in the foyer and inquisitive conversations could be heard. Another two police officers appeared and ushered everybody away from the area.

A police officer came towards me. "Excuse me, sir, could you please come this way?"

I was taken into a small room where two men stood side by side. Both wore long dark raincoats and grim expressions.

"I am Detective Albright and this is Detective Smart. Please empty your pockets."

I emptied them. "How is Maya, and what has happened?"

"She has been rushed to hospital," Detective Albright said. "Please take a seat."

I sat down. "What is wrong with her?"

Detective Smart said, "She has a bullet wound."

"Did nobody in the hotel hear a gun being fired?"

"A silencer." said Detective Albright. He looked at the document I had taken out of my jacket pocket. "How did you acquire this?"

"Someone gave it to me."

"Who?" asked Detective Smart.

"Maya Frielberg planted it on me earlier today." I felt tense.

Detective Albright said, "Why come here to see her?"

"I wanted to find out why she gave the document to me."

"Are you a spy?" asked his colleague.

"No, a marketing executive!"

Detective Albright enquired, "Marketing?"

Remember, this was 1938! "Sales."

"What do you sell – secret documents?" said Detective Smart.

"No – it doesn't pay enough!"

Detective Albright barked, "We tell the jokes, not you."

"Why am I being questioned? Surely you do not suspect me?"

"A lady with a dog noticed you acting in a suspicious manner outside the victim's room," said Detective Smart. "She also revealed her dog can perceive dangerous people."

"That's because I am British – it is a German dog! Where is the injured lady's companion, Karl Jungens? He's the one you should be questioning."

The two detectives looked at each other. Detective Smart left the room. His colleague studied the document.

Detective Smart returned and said to his colleague, "He checked out a couple of hours ago."

Detective Albright leaned over to his colleague and whispered. His colleague nodded and again left the room.

"You mentioned this lady is a friend?" said Detective Albright.

"Yes, and also of my family."

"Where is your family located?"

"Ardrishaig."

"Why are you in Glasgow?"

"To visit the Empire Exhibition – to obtain new business contacts."

If only Alan Struthers had left a telephone number where he could be reached. Then I could ask Detective Albright to call him and get the situation rectified. A constable came into the room and muttered to Detective Albright.

Detective Albright turned to me. "Please wait here." He left the room.

I speculated on Maya's condition. I hoped she was not badly wounded. When the two detectives came back, twenty minutes had passed.

Detective Smart said, "Karl Jungens is on his way eastwards. A gentleman in the station booking office sold him a one-way ticket to Leith Central."

"He could catch a ship to Germany from Leith," I said. "I take it he is now a suspect?"

"A couple passed Maya Frielberg's room around one o'clock this afternoon," said Detective Albright, "and they heard an angry male voice."

"Him," I said.

Detective Albright nodded.

"We know what time his train arrives at Leith Central and have contacted the local police station," said his colleague. "They will have officers at the station exits."

"He may get off the train at an earlier stop and then make his way to the port."

Detective Albright grinned. "The area to board is also being watched. If he wants on a ship then he shall have to swim to reach it."

"Is there any further news of Maya Frielberg's condition?"

Detective Smart revealed, "She remains in a serious but stable condition."

I regarded it important that Alan Struthers should be advised of the information at my disposal. "Do any of you gentlemen know of an Alan Graham Struthers?"

"We have just had a conversation with him," said Detective Albright. "He will send two of his agents to Glasgow, and they should be here within the hour."

Detective Smart added, "Because of events in Europe, security has been reinforced and all departments are now interlinked." Both left the room.

I sat alone in the room and gathered my thoughts. I heard voices outside the door and then it opened.

"Well gentlemen, we meet again." I stood up. Peter Lenihan and Harry Creelman – a sight for sore eyes!

"What's the situation?" said Peter Lenihan.

Harry Creelman took of his hat and had a seat.

I briefed them on what had happened – the scene I had witnessed at the Empire Exhibition which involved Karl Jungens and George Cox, and also recent events which related to Maya Frielberg.

Harry Creelman said, "When you arrived in Glasgow, did George Cox make contact?"

"Yes he did, but also with Karl Jungens on two separate occasions."

"Two occasions?" said Peter Lenihan.

"Yes – here at the hotel and at the Empire Exhibition."

Peter Lenihan looked at his colleague in a bewildered fashion.

Harry Creelman asked, "What is the condition of Maya Frielberg?"

"Serious but stable."

Peter Lenihan said, "Where at the exhibition did Karl Jungens and George Cox meet?"

"Exhibitor stand one hundred and nine."

He continued, "What company has rented that stand?"

"Kane and Hogg. They are Civil Engineers from Ireland. Have you been in contact with George Cox?" After all, he was their colleague!

"He reports to Struthers," said Harry Creelman. He looked at his colleague. "Peter, I believe we should pay a visit to the Empire Exhibition."

"Lead the way, Harry."

"What about the document Maya Frielberg gave me?"

Peter Lenihan said, "It is safe."

We arrived at the Empire Exhibition around six o'clock. I took them in the direction of stand one hundred and nine.

Peter Lenihan said, "Wait here, I'll be back in five minutes."

"Have a read of this, Harry." I gave him my programme.

"Interesting." He browsed through it.

"Here is your colleague."

Harry Creelman folded my programme and put it in his pocket.

When we got to their stance, the two exhibitors looked at us with apprehension. They spoke to each other.

Peter Lenihan approached them and produced an official identity card. "We would like to ask you a few questions."

One of them said, "What about?"

Peter Lenihan replied, "Karl Jungens."

The other exhibitor reached inside his jacket and pulled out a small gun.

Behind him appeared Detective Albright. "Don't even think about it!"

Detective Smart, plus another four police officers, now arrived on the scene and the two men got taken away.

"Perfect timing, gentlemen," said Peter Lenihan. "Thanks for your assistance."

People in the vicinity did not appear distracted by the incident – they continued to go about their business.

I said, "What about George Cox?"

"Struthers has dealt with him," said Harry Creelman.

I got a lift back to the Beresford Hotel. Harry Creelman managed to manoeuvre the car into a space outside the entrance.

Peter Lenihan said, "Struthers wants to see you tomorrow afternoon; therefore be available about one o'clock."

"No problem. I'll see both of you then."


The two government agents collected me at the stipulated time. As usual I sat in the rear seat and we drove off. Peter Lenihan's pipe fumes filled the air. Their car needed a scrub.

No doubt the recent persistent rain hadn't helped. I also noticed we travelled eastwards

"Is Inveraray not in the opposite direction?"

Peter Lenihan removed his pipe. "Struthers is still at Tarbrax, near Edinburgh."

"I haven't heard of it."

"Neither have we," said Harry Creelman.

"Why the change of residency?"

"Operational Headquarters have been set up in Edinburgh," replied Peter Lenihan.

We headed into Lanarkshire and through the town of Lanark, then onto a minor road which led to Edinburgh. The landscape looked uninspiring – barren and flat on either side of the road. After half an hour, Peter Lenihan called out.

"Harry, you've just passed it!"

"What? Where?" He slammed his foot on the brake pedal.

Peter Lenihan pointed. "Back there, Harry – a signpost for Tarbrax."

He looked around and drove the car backwards.

We exited the road and continued on a narrower one with frequent bends and inclines. This area displayed rows of distinctive green fir trees. Several miles later a further signpost appeared for Tarbrax. We turned off and onto a single road which led up a hill and beyond. To the left lay fields, and to the right a forest. After a few hundred yards came a clutch of properties.

Peter Lenihan looked at a diagram. "We take the first right and then turn left. It's a large detached property near a church."

"Does the house have a number or name?" asked his colleague.

"No."

We drove around the small village with no success in finding the property. Harry Creelman brought the car to a halt.

"Peter, check the diagram again."

He analysed the piece of paper. A man walked by our stationary car and gave us a curious look. He must have been a local, and therefore would have knowledge of the area. I rolled down the window.

"Excuse me, where is the church?"

"If it's the minister you want, then he's gone off on holiday."

"No, just the church."

"You've passed it. As you come into our village, the church is on your right. Unless you know Tarbrax, the church can be difficult to find – it's hidden by trees." The villager pointed to several large properties. "That way."

We drove off and headed along another single road. I could understand why Harry Creelman was cursing to himself!

Peter Lenihan shouted, "There's Struther's Rover in that driveway, Harry!"

"Thank goodness. You need more than a bloodhound to find this ruddy place!"

As we walked to the entrance of the house, an authoritative gentleman in a black sober suit greeted us.

"Please come this way, Mr Carlisle." He led me into a room. "Mr Struthers will be with you shortly."

Peter Lenihan handed me a document. "Detective Albright asked me to give this back to you." He left the room and closed the door.

I stood for a short time and cast my gaze around the room. I noticed a painting of Edinburgh's Dean Village – Victorian? Somehow that period was not too long ago! I picked up that morning's edition of the *Scotsman* newspaper which had been placed on a nearby table. I sat down on one of the brown leather couches and made myself comfortable. I could smell the rich leather. It felt good to stretch out my legs – those old cars were too cramped! Prominent articles included the prestigious British Empire Exhibition and the demise of Czechoslovakia. The back pages concentrated on sport. The British Open and recent Wimbledon tournament received exclusive coverage. At least this year, Britain had had a finalist in the men's singles final – Henry 'Bunny' Austin. However, he'd been demolished in three straight sets by American starlet

Don Budge. As the door opened, I put down the paper. Alan Struthers came into the room. He looked relaxed in his cardigan, flannels and slippers.

"Good afternoon, James – at least you got here." He put a pipe into his mouth. "The next edition of the *Scotsman* will carry another story which relates to the Empire Exhibition. The true version will have been somewhat distorted."

"Does it refer to the men who got arrested?"

"Yes – one of them tried to escape. He got trapped in a secluded section of the amusement park and took his own life rather than give himself up. Fortunately, none of the public witnessed this incident."

I suggested any adverse publicity would have implications for the event.

"Indeed." He lifted a sheet of paper from the top of his desk. "This is why the story every newspaper will print concerns a man who fell to his death." He put on his horn-rimmed spectacles and read. "'The tragedy happened around ten o'clock in the evening. A man slipped from the big wheel and was then taken to the Southern General Hospital but pronounced dead on arrival.'"

"Convenient."

"Yes, but essential. The public will perceive it as an unfortunate and horrific accident." He removed his spectacles. "I have just received word Maya Frielberg is now out of intensive care and recovering in hospital. If you had not gone to the Central Hotel and alerted the staff, then she would have died. She received medical attention just in time."

"Have the authorities managed to capture Karl Jungens, or is he still at large?"

"Oh yes, he was captured near a football ground in Leith. Just before the train terminated at Leith Central, he got off. Two police officers in plain clothes had boarded the same train. They monitored his movements. When he got off, they followed and later apprehended him. They took him to a local police station."

"Good show."

"Do you have the document Maya Frielberg obtained?"

I took it out my jacket inside pocket and handed it to him.

He reached for his spectacles. "Mm. Are you aware what this refers to?"

"A new propulsion system for a ship?"

"Yes, but a faster and more powerful one ahead of anything we believe exists in Europe. The fact that Germany has tried their utmost to get these details suggests its importance."

I asked if production had already started on the ship.

"It is being built at John Brown's shipyard in Clydebank. The ship is scheduled for launch in late September. It would appear Karl Jungens had been told to collect this classified information and take it back to his superiors in Germany. I would presume Kane and Hogg had obtained the data from a source within the Clydebank-based operation." Struthers looked at me over his spectacles. "Did you know Maya Frielberg worked for the French Secret Service?"

Given my experience in Nice with Michelle Duvallier, I wasn't too surprised!

"That is why she allied herself to Karl Jungens. They met at a charity dinner six months ago in Munich and became friends. The French Secret Service has known about his 'discreet activities' for some time and contacted Maya. When they revealed his involvement with the Nazis, she agreed to help. It turned out to be an uncanny coincidence that she had been invited to a wedding in Scotland. He, of course, had arranged to come over for an illicit deal!"

"I presume when Maya managed to get the document and dispose of it, she put her own life in danger?"

"Yes, the game was up. As with the French Secret Service, we have known of Karl Jungens for some time but not Maya Frielberg. We just found out. When we apprehended you in Ardrishaig, we assumed you were an associate of Karl Jungens."

"Thanks. Why did your organisation not collaborate with their French counterparts on Karl Jungens? It would be advantageous to both parties?"

"I agree, James, but Britain and France have only just begun to collaborate with each other. When Britain signed a treaty with Germany in 1935 to allow them increase the size of their navy, a rift ensued. As you can imagine, the French could not comprehend this act. It broke the Treaty of Versailles Agreement that we signed in 1919. When Germany started to 'acquire' territory from its neighbours, then we cancelled the treaty. This resulted in a fall out with Germany, but closer links with France."

"C'est la vie!"

"Exactly. However, Germany is ahead of everyone in terms of their artillery, tanks and planes. There is an unconfirmed rumour they are experimenting with rocket propulsion. Britain is rearming but is not equipped to mount a campaign. France has still not completed her Maginot Line on the border with Germany. This is vital to their defence strategy. Because of Stalin's purges, the Russian military is in disarray. No country is ready to deal with Hitler; therefore we shall have to appease him and gain some time. Another war will come and all European countries will remain ill-prepared – apart from the aggressor."

"What became of George Cox?"

Struthers gave a wry smile. "Gerhardt Schmidt is on his way back to Germany. He is our contact there and is a double agent. He gives the Germans meaningless information but supplies us with relevant data. He tried to gain Karl Jungens' confidence and get information, but did not succeed."

"What will happen to Karl Jungens and his counterpart from the exhibition?"

"Tried for espionage and other crimes, and used for negotiation purposes in the future. Neville Chamberlain and his advisors will monitor events unfold in Czechoslovakia. A strategy will be in place to resolve any serious problems which may develop. My intuition tells me a war remains inevitable. Hitler wants power and territory. I often speculate on whether Stalin has read *Mein Kampf,* written by Hitler in 1925. The contents of that book alone should alert Russians what lies in store for them and Europe."

Alan Graham Struthers posed a question which many would ask in the future.

He got up. "Well, James, no doubt you want to return home to normality."

It had been a while.

"Peter and Harry shall take you back to your hotel in Glasgow, and then to Ardrishaig. Incidentally, Maya Frielberg is in ward sixteen at the Glasgow Royal Infirmary." He walked to the exit and laughed. "It should be easier to find your way out of Tarbrax."

That would delight Harry. "It's an awkward location."

"Our operation has now been centralised; therefore we work from Edinburgh. It's a long way to Inveraray! I shall remain here for the foreseeable future." He gave me a small package. "Expenses." He walked me to the exit door of his property, shook my hand and finally lit his pipe.

Upon my return to Ardrishaig, I visited Charlotte and Philip to let them know what had happened to their friend. I revealed that Maya had been involved in an accident at her hotel and taken to hospital.

Charlotte asked, "What kind of accident?"

"She tripped on a loose stair carpet and injured her leg."

"How strange – she always takes the elevator to save time!" replied Charlotte.

I explained the elevator might have been out of service.

"Philip, let James see what you have done to part of the coach house. James, I will put your bag in the kitchen"

"Thanks."

We went across the courtyard and Philip opened the door to the disused stables. It had been converted into a wine cellar complete with racks of red, rosé, white and even some champagne.

"James, this is the future. I feel our beer and spirit culture will change to include wine. When that happens, then the price should increase, therefore more profit can be made. I have imported wine from a selection of countries which include Germany, Italy and Spain."

This appeared a good idea, but a war and hardship for everyone would soon engulf the country. I had to try to diminish his enthusiasm in an articulate business manner.

"Philip, do you have customers who wish to buy the wine?"

"Not yet but I'm sure they will!"

"Before you order any more, why not take a consensus of people who want to buy the wine? Also this will give you an indication of how much you need to reorder."

"Good idea James – that is what I shall do."

"Do you have paper and something to write with?"

"Hold on." He came back with both. "What are you writing?"

"When the economy starts to improve, use these techniques to promote your enterprise."

"Techniques?"

I explained the list systematically and he held on to my every word. "Any questions?"

"No James, it all makes sense."

Given the countries which produced his wine stock, there would soon be an anti-fascist backlash. Mind you, wars tended to instigate a 'black market' economy.

"Philip can I look upstairs?"

"Yes of course. I'll get the key."

Sentimentality does not diminish through time.

Philip handed me the key. "When you're finished, James, just lock up.

"Will do."

I unlocked the door and went upstairs to the coachman's quarters. I looked around this familiar room and then out the window. Since 1896, how the scene had changed. I opened the closet door – my coachman's outfit still remained. Next, I stood in front of the wall mirror.

"Philip, did James plan to head back to the village?"

"No, he is still here. He wanted to look around the coach house."

"Over an hour has passed – maybe he has had an accident!"

"I'll check."

"I hope James has not suffered the same fate as Maya!"

Philip headed for the coachman's quarters. "James, are you all right? James?" He looked around and returned to the house.

"Has he gone, Philip?"

"Yes, there is nobody in the coach house. He did not even lock the door."

"He has forgotten to take his belongings with him. He could have at least said goodbye!"

# Chapter 8

## *The Enigmatic Man*

I experienced a warm tingling sensation. Had there been any time fluctuation? I looked around the room and it remained unchanged. Then I walked to the window. It also looked unchanged – the grass and hedges needed cutting. My watch had stopped. I went downstairs and turned the door handle – it had not been locked. As I walked into the courtyard, there remained the now familiar sound of road traffic. I knocked on the rear door of the main house – no answer. The key Nancy had given me was with my belongings. Not even a black and white cat was in the vicinity.

I walked around the property and stood at the foot of the driveway. The sunlight caught my watch – it had started to work again! Perhaps not too much time had passed. I observed the vehicles on the road. Military uniforms worn by most drivers and passengers seemed the order of the day. A lady and a young girl walked towards me. The girl looked familiar and as she got closer, I recognised her. They stopped.

I asked, "I'm looking for Philip and Charlotte Carsell-Brown."

"They have gone to Edinburgh, I believe, to visit their son," said the lady.

"Would that be Geoffrey?"

"Yes. They left two days ago, but are due back soon."

The young girl stared at me, but with a smile.

The lady said, "I live at the next property and when they return could pass on a message."

"I'm at present a resident at a hotel in Ardrishaig. I can call again."

"If I meet Charlotte or Philip, whom should I say called?"

"James."

Whilst I headed in the opposite direction for Ardrishaig, the pleasant lady and the girl continued along the footpath.

"Mummy, that's the coachman who travels through time!"

"Abigail, what do you mean?"

"He arrives here every so often. I spoke to him two years ago."

"Abigail, William and Geoffrey started that rumour to cause mischief amongst their friends!"

"But he is real!"

"There is no such person as a time traveller! Besides, he wore a suit, not a coachman's outfit."

I reached Ardrishaig and went into a newsagent to buy a newspaper. I looked at the date – the tenth of April 1940. Almost two years had passed. Germany would soon invade France. I looked up at the village clock and then at my watch. I had lost half an hour, but not bad over two years! I thought I'd better reset it. There still remained time to have lunch at the Lochside Hotel.

When I got there, the vehicle parking area was full. I entered the dining room and only a few vacant tables remained – no seat beside the window to admire the view on this occasion! A large number of personnel in various military uniforms had descended on the hotel. It made me recall when Alan Struthers spoke of a proposed peace strategy should hostilities increase between Germany, France and Great Britain. He did not have my hindsight. Hitler had already determined Europe's fate. In a short time, the allies would be defeated in a demoralising battle, which will cause misery to many.

The waitress came to my table and I ordered haddock. Due to Ardrishaig's local industry, there should have been no shortage here! However as the war dragged on, this would also be subject to rationing.

Before my meal arrived, I picked up my *Daily Express* for a quick browse. War-orientated content filled the pages but a major conflict did not exist. There had been Hitler's invasion of Poland seven months earlier. After six weeks this had ended when Poland surrendered. A planned British offensive in neutral Norway took place, but this proved unsuccessful. This period became known as the 'phoney war' because people went about their lives with little or no disruption. Current German friction with Britain amounted to attacks on some convoy ships off the English coast.

An important and historic news event started to unfold. After failure to appease Hitler, as Britain's Prime Minister, Neville Chamberlain would soon step down. As to who would be his successor, speculation grew between two possible candidates. Lord Halifax was steady and reliable, whereas the other candidate had a reputation of being a 'risk taker' to his peers. The debate continued over Winston Churchill or Lord Halifax – who should lead the country against Hitler? Due to competitions being suspended, limited sports news appeared. Still, at least favourite teams would remain undefeated – for a while at least! As for entertainment, America dominated the music scene. Artie Shaw and Bing Crosby still retained the top artist's slot, and Glenn Miller and his band introduced their own new distinctive sound. A young, unknown singer appeared with Tommy Dorsey in his act, called Frank Sinatra. Britain's own Vera Lynn continued to serenade the Forces. Leslie Howard, Laurence Olivier, Robert Donat and Vivian Leigh portrayed Britain's main players in the movies. Donat and Leigh both won an Academy Award for Best Actor and Best Actress in 1940.

I put down the newspaper and remembered a school history lesson about British entertainment in 1940. The most notable films made in wartime Britain surrounded the Forces, promotional 'shorts' in order to raise and maintain morale. Because of evening curfews, visits to the cinema would be restricted. However, this did not last long. The 'experience' of the cinema, with comfortable seats and rich interiors, made people forget their current miserable plight. The cinema gave relief – albeit only temporarily. As an alternative, people could listen to a selection of 78 RPM records – if you could afford a gramophone! Most families possessed a radio and they got sole rights to hear the British Home Service. However, the choice of programmes remained scarce.

I left a noisy and smoke-filled dining room with relief. It was good to breathe fresh air again! A smell of tobacco smoke lingered from my suit. I awaited a future non-smoking indoor environment. However, the haddock, peas and potatoes on an empty stomach tasted delicious.

I made my way to the main street and in particular the menswear shop. I had on the suit I had purchased there two 'short' years ago.

"Good afternoon, sir, can I help you? Ah, I recognise that suit!"

"You sold it to me." He also had on the same suit.

"It looks as good as new! You take good care of your suits, sir."

Since I had started to wear this suit, only a few of my weeks had passed. "We all have to in these austere times."

"I agree, sir, but it is not good for business. Could I interest you in a hat to match the suit?"

"No, I don't wear them."

"The reason why you are not bald, sir!" He smiled.

I pointed. "How much is that double-breasted suit?" It had a similar look to one which I would purchase in Aberdeen forty two years from now!

"As a valued customer, I can let you have the suit for six pounds, three shillings and sixpence."

"That sounds reasonable." I felt the material – good quality. I then tried it for size. "I'll take it!"

"Do you have your coupons sir?"

"Coupons?"

"Did you forget them?"

Of course – food and clothes were rationed in 1940. "I will get them and return later."

"Fine, sir – I will put the suit aside for collection."

I departed and soon approached the Macmillan Solicitors' office. The exterior with cracks and faded paintwork looked shabby. Rather than peek through the window, I went inside and waited at reception. I must have been there for five minutes with no acknowledgement, and therefore knocked on the desktop. I could hear a typewriter being used close by. A lady with a plain black outfit and flat shoes came to my assistance.

"Yes, can I help you?"

"I would like to make out a will."

"Mr Macmillan is not in the office today and he is the only person who can advise you. He should be available tomorrow."

"I will come back. Where can I obtain ration coupons?"

"The local government office in Lochgilphead. I am sorry you had to wait. The firm is short of staff."

I sympathised. "You don't have to apologise – there is a war on."

She sighed. "Tell me about it!"

As for accommodation, I called into the Grey Gull Inn. A member of staff passed me in the corridor.

"Back again, Mr Carlisle?"

"Yes, I always sleep well here."

"How long do you require a room for, sir?"

"I'm not sure – perhaps a week."

"No problem." He went behind the desk. I registered.

"We require a deposit, sir."

"Deposit? How much?"

"The equivalent of one night, sir."

An advance payment? It must have been the war – harsh times indeed! I was glad I had some cash. At least my money would not have devalued much over two years, due to the harsh economic period.

In the evening, I ventured downstairs to the bar. Tobacco smoke filled the air, which would influence how long I tolerated this unhealthy environment. All but one of the customers stood near the bar. A distinguished gentleman sat in a corner by himself. He had a dejected look about him. I ordered a malt whisky instead of my usual glass of beer.

"That will be one shilling and tuppence, sir."

I gave the grey-haired barman a florin.

He rang it up on the till and gave me my change. "Thanks, sir."

I commented, "That poor chap looks a bit depressed."

"A lot of men his age are depressed just now. There are rumours Germany will attack France, which will mean another Somme."

A slaughter indeed.

"He got married less than two years ago."

"Does he stay nearby?"

"Yes. He also works locally, in an accountancy firm."

I wandered over to console this poor chap. "Hello, I am told you can help me with a financial problem."

He looked at me with a dazed expression. "I cannot help myself, let alone you!" He slurred his words.

"What's the problem?" I sat down next to him.

"I will soon be called up to fight and do not want to." His eyes were also glazed.

"Nobody enjoys being involved in a war, but it is essential to defeat evil."

"But why? Why do we have to?"

"Would you prefer to be dictated to by others and have no freedom? Your family enslaved and abused?"

He just stared with a blank expression. "My wife's father became a hero in the last war and got decorated. I am afraid she will be disappointed with me."

"Why would she feel that way?"

"Because I can't live up to his reputation."

"His name?"

"Edward Beaumont."

I tried my utmost to console my great-uncle. "But he was a professional soldier. "

He looked at me. "Yes, he was."

"That would be his full-time occupation and therefore experienced in the role. I wager you are the better with calculations!"

"I have to go home. Olivia will be worried."

"I will get you a taxi."

"No need – I have my car."

"You can't drive in that condition."

"I can manage."

*Oh no you won't!* I went to the bar. I asked the barman, "Can you call a taxi?"

"Taxi? There are none!"

I returned to where he lay slumped on his chair. "I will drive you home. If you drive, it won't be a war that kills you."

He raised his head. "Can you drive a car?"

"Yes." Since 1980! I took him to a car parked outside the inn. "Is this your car?"

He managed to nod his head.

There lay a sporty MG TB and it looked new. I shuddered to imagine the consequences if he had attempted to drive.

He went to give me the keys but dropped them. "Sorry."

I picked them up off the ground.

We got inside the trim car and I turned the ignition. This differed from driving the Carsell-Browns around in a coach pulled by horses. The car fired into action. I asked for directions to his house. The smell of alcohol from his breath made me feel light-headed. After ten minutes, we arrived at his home. He had fallen asleep. Whilst I helped my great-uncle along the path and to the main door, the house lights still burned. I pulled the bell ringer.

After a few seconds, the door opened. There, stood an attractive young refined lady with large hazel eyes and long dark hair.

"My goodness!"

"Excuse me – your husband took ill and I brought him home."

"William, you look terrible!"

"Sorry, darling. I am going straight upstairs to bed." He staggered into the hallway.

The lady looked bemused. "Well, I have to thank you."

"Glad to help." I gave her the car keys.

"What is your name?"

"James Carlisle."

"I am Olivia. Do you live nearby, Mr Carlisle?"

"Yes, not far. It will not take long to walk home."

She looked at me with hesitancy. "Have we met before?"

"No, I would have remembered."

"Thank you again, and goodnight."

It turned out a pleasant evening for a walk. I got back to the inn forty minutes later. I reflected on an evening with my great-uncle and Edward Beaumont's daughter. He did not get the opportunity to watch her grow into an adult. He would not have been disappointed.


"Good afternoon. I believe Mr Carlisle resides here?"

"Yes madam, but he went out about two hours ago.

"Do you expect him back soon?"

"Most days he is out all afternoon. Ah, here he is!"

"Good afternoon. Can we have a chat?"

"Why don't we visit the corner tearoom just along the street?"

"Fine."

We managed to find a table and order a pot of tea. This establishment did not have the exclusiveness of a Willows tearoom, but it did possess appeal. The basic furniture, plain white tablecloths and crockery plus three waitresses hard at work appeared to confirm this. Olivia wore a short sleeved floral burgundy dress, black high heels and a matching bag. Her dress had a V neckline and ended just below the knee. It did not seem so long ago that a lady's dress revealed neither.

"Well, Mrs Carsell-Brown, how can I help?"

"William is grateful for your assistance yesterday evening. He has a headache of extreme proportions!"

"The barman mentioned he had consumed much whisky and beer. Not a favourable concoction."

"William assures me it will not happen again."

"Is he at work today?"

"Just! What did you talk about?"

"Very little – he did not appear in the mood for a chat."

"He has been a different person in the last few weeks. Subdued for most of the time."

"I have been told war can make people act in a strange way."

"You have experience of the previous war, Mr Carlisle?"

"Not me – just what I have been told by people who fought in that war."

"What do you think Hitler will do next? Some say he could attack Russia, even though they have a peace agreement. After all, his army is now in an excellent strategic position to launch an attack."

"I believe he will attack Russia, given the different ideology of both countries. It is what happens before that we have to prepare for. Hitler holds a grudge against France because of the last war, hence he will want revenge."

"Then you foresee an attack on France?"

"Yes, I am convinced of it."

She looked into space. "I hope not. I lost my father in the last war and I never got to know him. I don't want to lose my husband as well."

The waitress brought a small pot of tea.

"Where do you come from? Your accent did not originate in Argyll." She sipped her tea.

"From Edinburgh." The tea tasted nice.

"Edinburgh? My grandmother would speak of a gentleman from that part of Scotland. He was the coachman at Docharnea. She told me my father would ask him all about his home city."

"Your father?" I pretended not to know of him.

"Yes. He joined the Army in an officer capacity and got stationed at Edinburgh – much to his delight." Olivia looked straight at me. "The person my grandmother spoke of also got called James. She could never remember his surname. However, you are not that person – he would be much older."

I deviated from the subject. "It is a formidable car William has."

"He bought it last year for well over two hundred pounds. He drives too fast at times."

"Make sure he doesn't use the car if he consumes alcohol. Last night, he or someone else could have suffered a serious injury."

"I promise and shall speak to him tonight."

I paid the polite waitress and we left the spotless friendly tearoom. It was the best tea I had tasted in twenty eight years!

Olivia smiled and shook my hand. "Goodbye, James, and thank you."

"Goodbye Olivia. It's been a pleasure to meet you again." Why did she look at me in that inquisitive way?

Olivia prepared dinner in the kitchen. Her meeting with James Carlisle was still fresh in her mind.

"Is that you, William?" Olivia dried her hands on a towel.

"No, it's the gardener." Her husband walked into the kitchen.

"Very funny! How do you feel?"

"A bit tired, but hungry – I can't wait for dinner."

"I did what you asked and met with James Carlisle to thank him."

"Splendid, darling, and I shall cut down on my intake of alcohol."

"Promise?"

"I promise."

"William, do you recall when your parents told us about Maya Frielberg?"

"Yes. Not long after our wedding she had some sort of accident in a Glasgow hotel."

"Did they by any chance mention James Carlisle being in the vicinity?"

"Yes, they did."

"Why was James in Glasgow?"

"Not sure, but whilst there he visited Maya. When the accident occurred, he alerted the hotel staff and Maya got taken to hospital."

"Before moving to America, which lady member of the family lived at Docharnea?"

"Elizabeth? Yes, Elizabeth."

"Did she not have an accident?"

"I'm not sure."

"Did Nancy not tell Geoffrey and yourself the coachman saved her life? The incident surrounded a runaway horse."

"Now that you mention it, I believe he managed to push her out of its path but he got hurt. Poor chap."

"What happened to him?"

"Oh, he ended up in the local hospital."

"No. What became of him?"

"He left Docharnea. Nancy would speak well of him to Geoffrey and myself. I sensed she believed he would return one day."

"Can you recall his name?"

"James. He also worked as a coachman for the first family. What's all this about, darling?"

"William, I would speculate that an accident also got averted there."

"Olivia, what are you alluding to?"

"Did Nancy ever mention the first family?"

"Let me think. Something did happen. I recall Nancy spoke about a problem which related to the coach."

"The coach?"

"Yes, a problem with a wheel. The coachman took the coach to a firm for repair. If he had ignored the fault, an accident may have occurred. Something to that extent."

"Why would Nancy tell you about that?"

"She didn't! I overheard her conversation with mother. When Mary Carsell-Brown got the bill for fixing the coach, she became annoyed."

"Why?"

"Too expensive. Nancy thought, 'how ungrateful!' Someone could have received a nasty injury if they had not repaired the coach."

"I agree."

"Mother concluded that Mary Carsell-Brown blamed the coachman, and that is why he left."

"William, I feel this is the same person. He appears at the scene of what could prove a fatal situation connected to our family."

"But Maya only tripped on a stair carpet."

"And was taken to hospital!"

"Darling, could these instances not just be a coincidence? Besides, it can't be the same person – he would be at least seventy years old! James is around forty."

"Yes I understand. My conclusion also. What if he is a person who does not age, or can travel through time?"

"Similar to the coachman tale Geoffrey and I made up," William laughed.

"But, have there not been periodic sightings of him throughout the ages?"

"Olivia, your imagination is running amok! Because Geoffrey and I found a book connected to time travel, we declared the former coachman a time traveller. Also, we did not discover any time machine!"

"I spoke to James about my grandmother and father. I got the impression he had known them. It's difficult to explain. William, why do you have a curious look on your face?"

"I have just remembered something from last night. James mentioned your father being a professional soldier. I didn't reveal that information to him."

"There, I told you. How could he have known that?"

"Maybe someone in Ardrishaig told him?"

"You have that look again."

"Just before Nancy retired, she made Geoffrey and I promise not to enter the coachman's quarters."

"Why not?"

"She maintained part of the floor had been damaged and therefore unsafe. We could only play downstairs."

"And did you?"

"Only on one occasion did we go upstairs. The door which led there was kept locked. However, we managed to find the key."

"And?"

"We crept up the creaky staircase and looked around. The only thing that was of any interest was a closet. The door would not budge but Geoffrey used his strength and managed to open it."

"What did you find?"

"A package, cash box and an envelope."

"An envelope?"

"Yes, and guess whose name appeared on it."

"James's! What did you do next?"

"We just left everything in their place. When father found out we had been upstairs in the coach house, he gave us a ticking off. That became the final time we ever ventured there."

"William, could the envelope still be there?"

"Since then, father has no doubt been upstairs. He may have already removed the items."

"Yes, I understand, but there is no reason for him to raid the closet!"

"Olivia, do you mean if the envelope is not there, then James has taken it?"

"Well, it did state his name."

"But we are not sure if it is the same person. You are just speculating. Also, the exterior door which leads upstairs is kept locked – how would he gain entry?"

"When he returns from Edinburgh, we must speak to your father."

"Darling, is there is a way to confirm if James and the coachman are the same person – an eyewitness, perhaps?"

"The one person I know is my grandmother, but she is ill."

"What about her friends?"

"They are also unwell or have passed away."

"The problem is no other person in the village would have met the coachman."

"What about employee records? They must have kept details of those who worked at Docharnea?"

"Not for a coachman. He would be classed as casual labour and paid cash out of the owner's pocket. Wait a minute – what about the original gardener? Angus; that is his name."

"Is he still alive?"

"Mother mentioned he attended Nancy's funeral. His son Andrew now runs the family business. The premises are opposite the canal."

"William, I shall pay a visit there tomorrow. James Carlisle attended the funeral and Angus should be able to confirm my suspicion!"

"And if he does?"

"Then we have uncovered a 'guardian' who travels through time."

"How long until dinner, darling?" William smiled at Olivia.


I arrived at the business premises and from outside I could hear a saw being used. I knocked loudly on the door, which was ajar.

"Just come in."

As I entered, I could smell the sawdust on the workshop floor.

The blue overalled workman stopped using his saw.

"Thought you were someone else, miss."

Olivia looked at the sawn wood.

"Just makin' a garden chair. Customers want them yesterday!" He mopped his brow.

Going by the amount of sawdust, the chap had been hard at work.

"How can I help, miss?" He laid down his saw.

"I would like to speak with Angus. Is he around?"

"He isn't here, miss – he retired two years ago."

"Do you know where I can reach him?"

"He's a patient in the local hospital."

"I am sorry to hear that."

"He got taken into care six weeks ago. Can I help?"

"No, I do not believe so. Thank you."

The workman resumed sawing wood.

I had to speak with Angus and ease my mind about a certain James Carlisle. I walked in anticipation to the hospital.

"Yes, madam, can I help you?"

"Where can I find Angus? I believe he was admitted around six weeks ago."

"Oh yes, hold on," said the lady. She read through a file.

"I am not aware of his surname."

"No problem. Here we are, madam. Ward C – go down the corridor and turn left, then right. You do not have much time – visiting hour is almost up."

"Thank you."

"Madam, this nurse is headed there and can take you."

My high heels echoed within the corridors.

The nurse glanced at her watch. "You only have a few minutes."

"Yes, I understand."

The nurse bent down at the side of the bed. "Angus, there is someone to see you." She turned to me. "He is groggy, madam. What is your name?"

"Olivia Carsell-Brown."

"Angus, Olivia Carsell-Brown is here." The nurse moved closer and turned towards me. "He asks, 'why have you come?'"

"To ask about James Carlisle."

She conveyed the message. "He said to thank him."

I heard footsteps behind me and turned around.

"Andrew, this is Olivia Carsell-Brown," said the nurse.

"I am Angus' son. Can we go outside to talk?"

I sat down on one of the chairs located outside the ward.

"I hope you don't mind me visiting your father."

"Not at all, Mrs Carsell-Brown. Ronnie told me you came to our premises. I have an idea why you may want to talk with my father." He sat down next to me.

"James Carlisle."

"What is it you want to know about him?"

"If the James Carlisle I met is the same person who worked at Docharnea."

He sat back on the chair. "My father met him two years ago. Because of his poor eyesight, could not see James properly. However, I could! We first met in 1912 when I started work with my father. He has not aged in all that time."

"This is strange. He appears to help people and then vanish."

"The original owner of Docharnea dismissed my father. James arranged for another property to employ him. My father embraced another opportunity to work."

"Admirable. It does not surprise me."

"Father mended his ways and then started his own garden business. Our family now has a well-established and profitable company. My son Angus will soon become a part of the workforce."

"It is not just my family he has helped."

"May I suggest you keep this to yourself? Certain occurrences cannot be explained, but both our families have benefitted from this man."

"I agree."

I returned home, content in the knowledge that our time traveller had become a reality. I now had to live with this secret. The prominent question in my mind was whether he had a connection with our family. Perhaps we had been blessed with someone who watched over us.

"Any luck today, darling?"

"They are not the same person." I took off my jacket.

"I told you so – time travel is for the fiction books!"

"I should have known better."

"Mother telephoned – she and father have just got back from Edinburgh."

"How are Geoffrey and Emily?"

"Both are well. Charlie is a bit of a handful."

"He must take after his father."

"Mother would like us to come over for dinner."

"What time?"

"Around seven. I'll give the car a quick wash."

"I had better get ready."


"Hurry up darling, mother can be a stickler for time."

Olivia looked at herself in the hall mirror. "That's me, let's go."

William got into his car and pushed opened the passenger door. He looked at himself in the mirror. "Fine."

"Well done, William – you also cleaned the inside of the car."

He glanced towards me. "Nice dress!"

"It is a warm evening."

"Of course darling." William started the car. "Be there in a jiffy."

"I would like to have been driven along this road in a coach pulled by horses."

"Too slow."

"Yes, William, but grand."

"Still too slow, darling."

"It must have been a different world. My grandmother loved those days."

"Britannia ruled the waves, Olivia."

"Now Germany tries its utmost!"

"Docharnea." William looked at his watch. "Bang on time."

"Look, there's your father waiting to greet us."

"I'll pull in just at the front of the house."

Philip opened the passenger door. "Good evening, Olivia."

"And to you, Philip."

"Hi father, where is mother?"

"Here she is!" Charlotte guided everyone inside. "You look well, Olivia."

"Thank you, Charlotte. It must be my afternoon walks."

"Doesn't she look radiant, Philip?" Charlotte looked at Philip.

"Without question, Charlotte."

"William, you should do more exercise – it can only be good for you."

"I know, Mother, and I will try." William smiled.

"Prior to dinner, you father wants to speak with you on a personal matter. Come, Olivia, let us take a walk outside on this sunny evening."

"The view is splendid from here, Charlotte. I never tire of it."

"Being here and able to gaze at the loch remains a joy. One day, you and William can enjoy this."

"What about Geoffrey?"

"Geoffrey hates gardens. They have a small one and it is a mess! He would not enjoy this place. Besides, he and Emily love Edinburgh."

"I would imagine Geoffrey and Emily like the hustle and bustle of a city."

"Yes, Olivia, I can't envisage them here – no matter how beautiful the scenery!"

"Charlotte, would it be possible to take a look inside the coach house? William has told me so much about it."

"Yes, of course. I shall get the keys." Charlotte went into the house and soon returned. "This way, Olivia."

There was something mystical about the building.

Charlotte opened the nearest door. "This is the horses' stable. Next door is where the coach lay overnight." She turned the key and pushed it open. "The door often sticks."

"What is upstairs?"

"That is where hay got stored for the horses. The coachman's quarters are also up there."

"Can I look around the coachman's quarters?"

"Come this way. I'm afraid there is not much to see. Philip removed the old furniture."

"William told me Geoffrey and he played here." Olivia gazed around the room.

"Yes, as young, mischievous boys! They found some items which belonged to the former coachman and convinced themselves he would return to collect them."

" Charlotte, do you store anything in this closet?"

"No, it's never been used." She opened the door. "My goodness, a coachman's outfit!"

Olivia touched it. "The coat material is of a high quality – it feels smooth. How old would the outfit be?"

"If it is the original, 1896."

"Over forty years. It has a familiar smell."

"Familiar?" Charlotte looked at Olivia.

"Yes, I have encountered that smell." But where? She could not see an envelope, just the cash box. She opened it – empty.

"Since William and Geoffrey, has anyone used this room?"

"No, Olivia, it doesn't get used any more. Now and again Nancy gave it a sweep. She meticulously cleaned this room. Philip would comment that someone must be about to drop in!"

"Maybe a coachman, Charlotte?"

Charlotte laughed. "Yes, perhaps."

"William said Nancy would speak with a fondness for the coachman."

"I gather he helped Andrew's father start the family business. However, he had a habit of disappearing, therefore another coachman would be required. I have just remembered – James Carlisle came up here two years ago. Nice man, we met him at Nancy's funeral. Another one who disappears!"

"What do you mean?"

"He came all the way from Glasgow to let us know about Maya's condition. Before leaving, he wanted to look around the coach house. A short time later, Philip went to look for him but he had left."

"Left?"

"Yes, and without so much as a goodbye!"

"That is strange, Charlotte."

"Our sentiments also, my dear."

"What an unusual mirror."

"Yes – Gothic, I believe."

Olivia moved closer. "Where did you purchase it?"

"We inherited that mirror. Philip decided to leave it when the room got cleared. It hides a nasty crack on the wall."

"It has an endearing quality."

"Come, Olivia – Philip and William will be concerned."

"We can say the infamous coachman wanted a chat with us."

"There you are. Alice phoned a short time ago, Charlotte. A chap called James had stopped by."

"James?"

"The description she gave matched James Carlisle."

"When did he stop by?"

"Alice said two days ago."

"Maybe to pick up the bag he left here from two years ago!"

"Thank you for dinner, Charlotte." Olivia got into the car.

"Our pleasure, Olivia. Give my love to your mother. I spotted her in the village last week – she looked well."

"She keeps active but still gets periodic bouts of depression."

"We shall all be happier when this wretched situation with Germany gets resolved."

"Catch you later," said William.

"Bye," said Philip. He waved.

"Olivia is sharp and bright, Philip. William seems distant."

"It's the possibility of a brutal conflict that's on his mind. I pray that we can negotiate a peaceful solution with Germany and avoid the bloodshed. The cream dress Olivia wore looked nice."

Charlotte turned her head.

"Appropriate for the warm weather, Charlotte."

"Possibly."

"Please drive a bit slower, William."

"Okay darling." His foot eased off the accelerator pedal.

"I'm not sure if we should drink German wine in the current climate!"

"The Sylvaner tasted excellent. Father has still more in stock, hidden away in a discreet place."

"Just as well." She looked at William. "I thought it best not to mention we met James Carlisle."

"Yes, good idea. Mother would have been intrigued and asked a few difficult questions."

"The envelope has been removed from the closet."

"You don't miss much!"

"What did your father and you discuss?"

"The war and Geoffrey. Father believes he could be involved in some kind of secret mission about to take place."

"Well, William, war does involve such activities."

"Yes darling. Here we are – home in one piece!"

"You still drive too fast."

"Do you have the house key, darling?"

Olivia dangled it. "Just as well!" She got out of the car and walked up the path.

William followed and yawned. "I need an early night."

"You ate too much at dinner." She opened the door.

William made for the bathroom.

Olivia got ready for bed, sat at the bedroom dresser and brushed her hair. She put down the brush and stared into the mirror. "Well, Mr James Carlisle, you disappear whilst in the vicinity of the coach house and also reappear there in a future time. Another piece in my jigsaw puzzle."

"'Bye darling, have to dash."

"Have a pleasant day at work. Don't drive fast."

"Will do." William got into his car and sped off.

Olivia picked up the telephone and dialled. "Hello, is that the Grey Gull Inn?"

"Yes, this is the proprietor."

"Can you tell me if James Carlisle is a resident?"

"He left this morning, madam."

"Is he due back?"

"Not in the foreseeable future. He paid his bill and wished me well."

"Thank you."

"'Bye madam."

Olivia replaced the receiver. *Goodbye, James Carlisle, wherever you are.*

Just after six o'clock, William's car pulled up outside the house. Olivia felt tense. She had to give her husband news he had been dreading.

"Did you have a good day at the office, William?"

"Terrible. Mr Blackwell is off sick and we can't get any replacement staff. I hope the situation will not get worse."

"A telegram arrived for you." She handed it to William.

He opened the telegram and paused. "Life has got worse. I have to report to a regiment of the British Expeditionary Force bound for France."

"When?"

"In three days' time."

"Olivia, when are you due to meet Charlotte for lunch?"

"Around one o'clock, Mother. Your house is near the hotel. I'll leave in about ten minutes."

"Could you call into the jeweller's shop in the main street afterwards and collect my bracelet?"

"Yes, but why not join me and Charlotte for lunch?"

"I have to visit your grandmother and may be there for some time."

"Last week she looked tired."

"Your grandmother is in her eighties, Olivia. Give my regards to Charlotte."

"Will do, Mother."

Olivia walked to the Lochside Hotel with a slight guilt conscience. William would be in preparation for a possible imminent battle, whereas she had a lunch appointment at a quiet idyllic location. She entered the dining room – not many spare seats.

"Olivia, Olivia – over here!"

"My goodness, Charlotte, the dining room is busy today."

"The excellent May weather, my dear. But not many have ordered lunch."

Olivia glanced around the room. "There are no food plates – only cups and saucers."

"And plenty of cigarette smoke! Anyway, how is your mother?"

"Just the same."

"Did William have much to say in his last letter?"

"The weather in France is warmer than here, but the food is worse! He will never complain about getting up early for work again. He is wakened at daybreak."

"At least his sense of humour remains intact."

"Yes, even after three weeks in France."

"Splendid – here comes the waitress."

Charlotte and Olivia both settled for fishcakes with herbs. After lunch they left the dining room and stood outside the hotel.

"Olivia, I feel our lives may never be the same again."

"In what way?"

"I am not sure. It's just a feeling I have."

"There is Philip's car."

"Can we take you home?"

"I'm off to the jeweller's shop."

"We'll give you a lift."

Olivia entered the jeweller's shop to the sound of a loud bell. It not only alerted the jeweller but also his two customers who turned their heads.

She stood in the queue.

"Yes madam," said the jeweller. He removed a bit of fluff from his black suit.

"Good afternoon, I have come to collect a bracelet."

"The name, madam?"

"Beaumont. Here is the receipt."

He took it and opened a drawer underneath the counter.

"Here we are." He handed over the gold bracelet. "What's the commotion?" He looked towards the window.

In rushed a lady with a startled expression. "Germany has attacked Holland and Belgium!"

The jeweller said, "When?"

"This morning, at dawn."

"Poor Holland and Belgium," said the jeweller. "They will not stand a chance!"

"Well, the phoney war has now well and truly ended!" quipped a customer.

# Chapter 9

## *Infiltration*

I received a call at the Grey Gull Inn from Alan Graham Struthers. It sounded urgent. He wanted to see me at his location outside Edinburgh. The next day I checked out, and Peter Lenihan and Harry Creelman collected me at the inn.

"Apprehended any more spies, gentlemen?"

Peter Lenihan puffed on his pipe in the front passenger seat. "We try our best!"

We made our way to Tarbrax. After we passed through Lanark, Peter quipped to his colleague.

"Watch out for the signpost, Harry."

I cried, "You've just passed it!"

Harry Creelman put his foot on the brake. "Damn!"

After a short delay, we arrived at the remote location. I must admit, the place had a nice tranquil feel to it.

A lady led me into the room I had sat in two years earlier.

"Would you care for something to drink Mr Carlisle?"

"A cup of coffee, please."

She smiled. "This is Tarbrax, Mr Carlisle, not Texas. We are also on war rations!"

"Tea will be fine."

When Alan Graham Struthers walked into the room, I had just finished my cup of ration tea. I had tasted worse, but also a lot better!

He shook my hand. "I am glad you could come at short notice." He sat at the other side of the brown leather couch. "Since we last met, how are you?"

"Fine, could be worse."

"You haven't changed a bit."

One advantage of time travel. His hair was now more grey than dark.

"We need your help again. It concerns infiltration within our organisation. The reason why I contacted you is, as an outsider, you are unknown."

"What is the problem?"

"George Cox alerted me to an enemy agent who had compromised our organisation. We waited for him to get back to us with a name, but did not do so. We then got word his body had been discovered in a back alley in the centre of Hamburg."

"Someone must have known he had the information."

"Before he could reveal anything, they silenced him."

"To masquerade as a double agent in Germany must be dangerous."

"George accepted the risks. However, we have lost an invaluable source of information about our enemy."

"What do you want me to do?"

"I want you to head for the port at Leith."

"Leith?"

"Yes. Do you recall that situation with the *RMS Queen Elizabeth*?"

I nodded.

"It got built and moved to Leith."

"Why move the ship from Clydebank?"

"Security reasons. It is a state of the art ship with sophisticated technology. That is the reason why the Germans wanted to obtain the designs."

How could I forget?

"As the German Navy does not possess a similar type of sea vessel, they are determined to destroy it. We managed to receive that information from George Cox."

"Do you know when they intend to carry this out?"

"We believe it could be imminent. The maiden voyage of the ship is the fifteenth of May."

"That is only a week from now."

"It should have been the twenty fourth of April, but a problem arose with the propulsion system."

"Do you believe this conspirator may try to blow up the ship?"

"I feel that could be their preferred option."

"Why not send the Luftwaffe to bomb Leith Docks?"

"Too risky, and too far from Germany. There is a squadron of Spitfires based within a short flying distance from Leith."

"The Germans could wait for the maiden voyage and send a U-boat to sink it."

"Our intelligence tells us the U-boats are busy trying to sink the merchant ships. They are deemed more important. If our overseas supplies do not reach our shores then we could lose the war without fighting any battles!"

"You want me to head for Leith Docks?"

"A temporary base exists close to the docks. You will have a role which allows you to work there and board the RMS Elizabeth."

I was curious. "What type of role?"

"A ship's clerk. This type of role can encompass most tasks which relate to a ship. I will issue you with a pass which allows access to most areas."

"Do you want me to depart today?"

"Of course – no time like the present. There is a war on, you know!" He smiled. "Peter and Harry will give you a lift to West Calder railway station. The train terminates at Princes Street station, and from there you can get a connection to Leith. The station is located beside the docks."

"Where shall I stay?"

"On the base." He left the room.

Another adventure loomed!

He returned and gave several items. "These are your identity documents and a generous allowance for expenses."

"Perhaps generous in relation to austere times, Mr Struthers!"

He walked me to the main door and shook my hand. "Good luck." He gave me a card. "Call me on this number if you suspect anything or anyone."

I got a lift to the local railway station at West Calder. I stood at the platform and observed the timetable board. The train due for Edinburgh should have arrived here ten minutes before me. I gazed up the long straight stretch of track and spotted a train approaching. As it came closer, I heard the train's whistle to alert passengers of the arrival. When it stopped, I could smell the steam. I boarded the train bound for Edinburgh and took a seat in one of the carriage compartments. To experience a journey on a steam train again! The red coloured carriages may not have been as comfortable compared to modern Diesel Multiple Units, but the nostalgia remained indefatigable.

The train entered Edinburgh twenty five minutes later. I transferred to a connection for Leith. The timetable stated a journey would take twenty minutes. After stops at Dalry, Murrayfield and Craigleith, the train approached the Northern General Hospital followed by Edinburgh City's football ground. I hope this club made the most of their senior status. After the war, a less prestigious East of Scotland league will beckon! The train then stopped at Granton. There was a steep incline to the station exit, which would test the endurance of rail users. Within ten minutes, the train arrived at Leith North.

I walked out of the terminus station and onto Lindsay Road. Then continued along in the direction of Leith's main dock area. I passed a steady stream of military vehicles. I reached the military base and reported to the dark uniformed Duty Officer.

"Documents please."

I handed over my identity papers.

"This way." He marched me to my quarters.

I put down my bag.

"Report for administration duty at eight o'clock tomorrow morning. Here is your naval uniform"

I hoped it would fit. The Duty Officer marched out.

I looked around my new basic habitat – a bed, chair and cupboard. Not even a view of the sea!

In the evening, I took the short journey along the coast road, parallel to the River Forth. I could feel the fresh sea breeze on my face. I came across the small harbour at Newhaven with several small boats secure in their berths. Then I encountered the Old Chain Pier public house. It held a special prominence for local people. The public house had been built at the water's edge, and was only separated by a short wall. The roof had an abundance of holes and if it rained, you could get soaked. When heavy black clouds appeared, customers soon disappeared. However, it raised the pub's character and ventilated any tobacco smoke. A clear evening engulfed this part of the coast; therefore I entered the single bar establishment. The nicotine-stained interior required a similar remedy to the depressed exterior – a paint makeover. I approached the scratched wooden bar.

"Yes, sir, what can I get you?" asked the barman.

"A pint of lager please."

"What's that?"

Here we go again. "Draught lager?" I raised my eyebrows.

The barman shook his head. "Sorry sir, only heavy or export."

"Export please." I handed over a shilling. I took my drink and sat down beside a window.

I had a view across the River Forth and the Fife coastline. Only two other customers had visited the bar. The two cloth-capped individuals appeared involved in a heated discussion.

"I'm tellin' you, our team will be successful once this war is over. They've a blend of skill, strength and flair. They'll score goals aplenty!"

The other gent replied, "Your team has yet to win a league title."

"I'll bet you they win a league title within four years of football being resumed."

"How much?"

"A ten shilling note."

"Done!"

As Hibs won the Scottish League Title in the second post-war season, the pessimist would be 'out of pocket'.

He continued the discussion. "Since your team won the Scottish Cup, it has been thirty eight years. I'll also wager ten shillings they don't win that either. Hearts have a better chance."

"We'll also win that trophy – no problem. Let us say within three years of resumption."

"Okay."

It appears that both men will win money. As for Hibs to win the Scottish Cup, perhaps the next century would have been a safer bet. Oh, the pain. I had just about finished my drink when the optimist shouted in my direction.

"Do you follow any football team, sir?"

"Yes, Edinburgh City." I finished my beer.

As I left the premises, both punters looked bemused. The white-aproned and white-haired barman bid me a safe journey home. Since it was a fine night, I walked back to the base.

My first days on duty at the base had been harmonious but with a tinge of anxiety. Ten full-time members of staff and two part-time assistants worked in my department. The majority were located in a large room with tiny windows which restricted sunlight and outside activity. How I missed having a panoramic view. The rest of the staff worked in a small confined office. Struthers warned, be wary of everyone and trust none. None of the personnel looked the destructive type. He would advise – don't be fooled by appearances.

On the second day, people went about their business until a telephone slammed down. Everyone in the office turned around.

A secretary announced. "Winston Churchill is rumoured to become the new Prime Minister instead of Lord Halifax."

Britain needs someone strong and passionate to lead the fight against Germany. 'Squeeze the enemy' rather than appease could describe his attitude towards Hitler. At mid-afternoon the same secretary slammed down the same telephone and got our attention.

"Germany has invaded Holland, Luxembourg and Belgium!"

The 'phoney' war had ended and the real one had started. A sudden atmosphere of hysteria emerged, with staff leaving their desks and darting here and there. Until evening, this did not start to abate. The difference a telephone call could make!

With Winston Churchill's appointment, perhaps it was not a coincidence that Germany launched their offensive. A series of developments started to filter through to us. French and British troops moved towards Belgium to engage the Wehrmacht. With the administration centre now a hive of activity, I observed one person who had a calm persona – Karen, one of the first members of staff I met on my arrival. Her articulate manner and composure stood out in a hectic and frantic environment. She carried out her duties in a relaxed manner. In contrast, a colleague called Eric would be the complete opposite. He worked between the centre and certain ships. He appeared like a cat on a hot tin roof!

Sergeant Steele controlled the administration centre and ran it like a military operation. He would appear from his office and bark his commands. On my third day at the centre, he called me into his office

"Carlisle, have you any inventory experience?"

"Yes sir, but a long time ago."

"Don't worry, you'll manage. Before the *Elizabeth* sails in two days' time, I want you to carry out an inventory of the food and drink supplies."

"I'll start now, sir."

"Excellent. The supplies consist of package and tin items to last over the initial journey."

I turned to exit his office.

"Carlisle."

"Sir?"

"There is a party of Sea Scouts and Boys Brigade members due to arrive at one o'clock. They are being shown around certain secure areas of the docks and aboard our new flagship. They may ask some questions about the ship – refer them to the Duty Officer."

"Will do, sir."

I gathered my inventory sheets and headed for the *RMS Queen Elizabeth*. I produced my pass to the guard and made my way to the supply store. After three monotonous hours of recording an assortment of tins, cans and packages, there came the sound of chatter. It grew louder. Before me stood two sets of personnel being given a tour. A moment later, the Officer guide approached me.

"Excuse me, can the party ask a few questions?"

Before I could explain my negative naval expertise, he brought forward a group of Boys Brigade members. I restricted my 'tutorial' to commercial aspects of a ship. The group struck me as being sure and steadfast in their manner and conduct. As the uniformed guests departed, they thanked me for my time. The caps worn signified their company number – sixty four. Thirty years from now, we would meet again. Then I would be the boy pupil.

I presented my pass to the guard on duty and departed the ship at four o'clock. As I left, Eric approached the ship.

"I have to attend a problem on the ship – again!"

"Can I help?"

"No, I can manage. It's a minor mechanical problem."

"Just as well you did not need help – not my forte."

I continued to the administration centre. Whilst at my desk, Sergeant Steele shouted from his office.

"Carlisle."

I stepped into his office. "Yes, sir?"

"Did you manage to complete the inventory?"

"No problem, sir."

"I want you to take your stock documents to Susan. Get her to formalise them into a report. I need it as soon as possible."

Susan worked in another office down the corridor. I made my way to the small room, which could just accommodate one individual – at most! Her wooden desk, black typewriter and dark green filing cabinet gave her office a cluttered appearance. Brash Susan was a petite redhead with shoulder length hair and inquisitive eyes. She had knowledge of what went on in the centre, and with whom.

I knocked on the door and entered. I could smell flowers but could not see any.

"James, Sergeant Steele said you would drop by."

"Yes and here I am – complete with details of the inventory." I handed the documents to her.

She had a browse through them. "Mm. If Sergeant Steele wants this tomorrow morning, he'll be lucky. If he asks, I'll have it by lunchtime."

"Okay." I'd bet he'd want the typed inventory that day.

She smiled, "See you later. Oh James, did you know a member of the tour party got taken to Leith hospital?"

"Sea Scout or Boys Brigade?"

"One of the Sea Scouts. He slipped in a dinghy and damaged his ankle."

Maybe an omen!

Only two days remained until the *RMS Queen Elizabeth* would sail on her maiden voyage. A limited crew would be on board for the exercise. This surprised me given the amount of food supplies in the storeroom – no stipulated rations there!

The main focus of war concentrated on early skirmishes in mainland Europe. The German 'war machine' had invaded Holland and Belgium, this being the first phase of Hitler's offensive strategy. To attack those countries would create an explosion of refugees wanting to head away from the conflict. This would congest the Allies' supply route to their troops at the front. The German Army made their way through the impenetrable Ardennes forest, which would prove decisive in days to follow. When an evacuation is ordered at Dunkirk two weeks from now, I could envisage this place being a busy maritime location. Every available sea-worthy vessel will be required to transport troops back to Britain. This would include the *RMS Queen Elizabeth*. No doubt the Royal Navy had hoped the sea trial would pass without a hitch.

In the centre, regular discussions took place about the situation in France. People speculated on what could happen and what should happen. Only an interruption by Sergeant Steele into our room allowed peace to break out.

"Carlisle!" he ordered.

"Yes, sir?"

"Miss Symington requires your attention." He returned to his office.

"Who is Miss Symington?" I looked at a colleague.

He whispered, "Susan."

I got up from my chair and headed for her office. When I got there, the door had been left wide open. She turned the pages of a magazine.

"Any articles of interest?"

She looked up from her desk. "I did not hear your footsteps."

"I used to work as a cat burglar." I noticed her copy of *Everywoman*.

She placed it at the side of her typewriter. "It is worth the eight pence I paid just for the articles on Clark Gable and the suave Cary Grant. I'm excited about his new film with James Steward."

"'The Philadelphia Story'?"

"Yes, have you been to see it?"

Many times – but I preferred the remake sixteen years from now. "I've only just read about it. Do you like Bing Crosby and Frank Sinatra?"

"Up to a point."

*I hoped she enjoyed the original. 'High Society' would not appeal to her!* What type of music did a twenty-year-old like in 1940? "What artists do you listen to?"

"Glenn Miller is my favourite. I like his new record."

"Is it called 'In the Mood'?"

"Yes, that's the one! I also enjoy music with a faster beat."

"Rock and roll?"

"What is that?" She sat back on her chair.

Oops, wrong decade! "Maybe a new and younger singer will emerge with an upbeat style?"

She gave a long sigh. "I wish they would hurry up."

*No need to despair, Susan! Elvis and Bill Haley would one day arrive. Until then, she just needed to be patient.* "Anyway, why did you want to see me?"

"This inventory report – there are two costings that are out of context."

"Show me." I observed the sheets.

She pointed to them. "This one and that one. What does 'p' stand for?"

I did not change a couple of them back to pounds, shillings and pennies. I had entered amounts of three pounds and sixty five pence and four pounds and twenty four pence.

She looked my way.

"Instead of three pounds and sixty five, enter three pounds and thirteen shillings. For the other, enter four pounds, four shillings and eight pence."

Susan appeared puzzled. "How did you do that?"

"Double the pence amount and you achieve the shillings and pennies value."

"That's interesting!"

*Keep that formula for 1971, Susan.* She altered the calculations. As the report was finalised, I noticed an engagement ring. To my knowledge, her fiancé did not stay in the city.

"That's it, James." She handed the report to me.

"When do you plan to get married?"

"The war has interrupted our plans. Sandy is in France just now with his regiment."

"Who are they?"

"The Seaforth Highlanders. We had planned to marry in September and live in Inverness."

"It's a delightful place with amiable people. I have been there on several occasions, but it can be cold in the winter."

Susan smiled. "Sandy and I will overcome the cold conditions."

*No doubt.* I turned to leave her office.

"James, I almost forgot. Can you give this to Karen? I'm finished with it."

"Karen?"

"Yes – the girl who is dating Corporal Stevens. He is the person on guard duty for the new ship that sails tomorrow."

"Yes, I met him. He scrutinised my pass."

" Not long after she joined the centre, they started to date. About two months ago."

I looked out of Susan's office window.

"Nice view – do you agree?"

"Yes, splendid."

Susan sighed. "Pity the office is tin."

Then I spotted Eric again walk in the direction of the new ship. I could see him search all his jacket pockets, no doubt for his security pass. He managed to find it.

"Eric spends a lot of time on the ship!"

"Between you and me, James, he does not like to work in an office. I believe he finds it too claustrophobic."

*I could sympathise.*

"See you later."

I returned to my office and ploughed through my heavy workload. I thought about the next day, one of anticipation by everyone for the *RMS Queen Elizabeth*'s debut voyage. Although just a sea trial, the ship looked well equipped for a maiden voyage. I picked up a newspaper and made for the canteen. At least I did not have to cook, thanks to this facility on the base.


Just before seven in the evening, I turned on the radio which a kind colleague had loaned me. *No reception – damn!* I persevered but got no joy; therefore I had another read of the morning newspaper. Reports of German successes did not help install optimism for Britain's future. Even though I knew the eventual outcome, it made depressing news. It was time to get out of my room and go for a stroll.

I left the base and travelled once again in the direction of Newhaven. The weather had remained sunny and warm. I welcomed the coastal breeze. On this occasion, I went to the Starbank Inn. Did the establishment sell any lager? After all, a J & R Tennent's sign appeared above the entrance. I entered through a narrow door.

The barman came forward. "Yes, sir?"

"Do you have any lager?"

He hesitated. "We only stock it in bottles, sir, but they're finished. We should get a delivery in two days."

*Oh well.* "I'll have a pint of special." I gave him the money and sat down at a comfortable window seat. That beer tasted bitter.

The barman came over and wiped the table.

This bar also looked onto the River Forth and the Old Chain Pier public house. How that establishment needed an outside lick of paint. The Starbank had a separate 'snug' partition. This catered for female customers – such were those innocent times. The interior consisted of plain white walls and light wooden furniture. The clean-shaven barman cleaned the bar and other table tops.

Two groups of men started to congregate at a particular area – the dartboard. No doubt their custom would be welcome in this period of wartime hardship. The Starbank Inn had a match arranged between the Anchor Inn at nearby Granton. I anticipated a passionate and competitive encounter between the two sets of players. I found a copy of the *Edinburgh Evening News* and whilst the cheers and groans of dart's players echoed, I browsed through this broadsheet. I ignored the war articles and turned to the entertainment section. I looked to see what films had been scheduled at the local Palace and State cinemas. If my radio was still faulty tomorrow evening, then I could head for a nearby picture house. This would also be more desirable than the BBC Home Service. The Palace featured 'Rebecca', a Hitchcock psychological thriller starring Laurence Olivier and Joan Fontaine. The State had a re-run of 'Destry Rides Again' with James Stewart as Tom Destry, the philosophical lawman of a Wild West town. The Embassy at Pilton also featured this film – no doubt a popular one amongst the locals of both districts.

I witnessed a tense, boisterous, but good-natured tussle of a darts contest. It resulted in a close victory for the visitors. It was time to make tracks for the base. As I left the Starbank Inn, the sea air blew in my face. The wind had increased and the sky looked grey rather than its normal blue. Waves appeared on the once calm sea. After weeks of glorious weather, could this have been a storm on the horizon? No walking back to the base on this occasion – I got the tram in case it poured.

When I got back, the evening crept towards dusk. Rather than go to my quarters, I made for the *RMS Queen Elizabeth*. As the ship would depart the dock the next morning, I went to admire the brand new vessel one last time. From a distance, I noticed a person leave the ship carrying a small bag. As I got closer, I expected to find Corporal Stevens or another security guard on duty. No security personnel could be found. I walked back to the gatehouse and spoke to a security officer on duty.

"You have no guard for the *RMS Queen Elizabeth*."

He checked a duty rota and looked at a clock on the wall. "Someone should have reported in twenty minutes ago."

Just at that moment, I could hear quick footsteps from behind. I turned around and Corporal Stevens appeared with a harassed expression.

"Apologies for being late, sir, I lost all track of time."

The Officer glared at him. "Yes you did! We will discuss this later. Take up your duties right away."

I said, "I saw a person leave the ship."

"Leave the ship?" He looked horrified.

"Yes, he carried a bag."

"How long ago?"

"Just minutes ago. He headed in the direction of Salamander Street."

"What did he wear?"

"Dark overalls."

He picked up a telephone. "Intruder alert!" He pressed a red button.

The quiet location came alive with armed military personnel. They headed towards the *RMS Queen Elizabeth*. I got told to leave the scene and return to my quarters. I went to bed but could not get to sleep. I hope my reaction to alert security would not result in a false alarm.

I had an uneasy night and did not get much sleep. When I arrived at work, I looked at my watch – five minutes late. I entered the office and everybody stared in my direction.

Eric said, "James, Sergeant Steele wants to see you right away."

*Oh no!* I walked up to his office door and knocked.

"Come in."

I opened the door. He got up from his chair and walked towards me. He then smiled and put his two hands on my shoulders.

"Well done Carlisle – you may have saved our flagship."

"What happened?"

"The person you reported with the bag was caught. His true identity was that of a German saboteur. After being questioned by naval intelligence officials, he admitted to planting a device on the base. He would not reveal where but thanks to your observation, the 'Elizabeth' was searched. We found the bomb in a cargo bay."

"Thank goodness."

"The device found had a sophisticated time mechanism. After eighteen hours, an explosion would have occurred. The ship had been scheduled to leave Leith at six o'clock the following morning. It would have blown up and sunk out at sea."

"That would have been disastrous." I was glad I'd got the tram back to base. If I had walked, I would have missed the saboteur.

"No doubt about it! On another matter, two gentlemen will be here to collect you at one o'clock. Mr Struthers sent them." Sergeant Steele shook my hand.

As I returned to my desk, I noticed Karen's vacant chair. No paperwork existed on her desk or in either of the grey filing trays.

Eric said, "Off sick."

Too hectic an evening with Corporal Stevens! No wonder he missed guard duty.


Peter Lenihan and Harry Creelman came for me on time and I got into the rear seat of the familiar black Rover. It moved off.

Peter turned to face me. "You earned the expenses this time!"

"Lucky I went to have a final look at the ship before it departed."

"It would have been the final look!" said Harry. "Did Sergeant Steele mention a lady called Karda to you?"

"No, who is Karda?"

"She is known to you as Karen," said Peter. "Karda Hassler co-ordinated the planned sabotage."

"Karen?"

"Yes," added Peter. "She was arrested early this morning."

That came as a shock.

Harry said, "Born in Munich, she came to this country in 1923 at the age of seven."

"The reason why she spoke impeccable English."

"Yes, ideal for a spy," said Harry. "She made sure Corporal Stevens was delayed."

"Poor chap," I said.

"After the previous guard had finished his shift, this allowed her co-conspirator enough time to leave the scene," said Peter. "Just as well you spotted him."

"Why did the guard who finished his shift not wait for Corporal Stevens to take over?"

Peter shrugged his shoulders. "It would make sense."

"Why did the saboteur not dispose of his bag? He could have concealed it somewhere on the ship."

"Maybe in case an official stopped him," said Harry. "Being dressed in overalls, he would look more authentic."

"As if he had been there to carry out maintenance work," said Peter. "He even had tools in the bag."

"Corporal Stevens and Karen had been dating each other on a regular basis."

Peter lit his pipe. "She took advantage of the poor fellow."

The car sped towards Struther's retreat at Tarbrax. No doubt Harry would be aware of the signpost's location by now.

We arrived at the remote, but intriguing destination. As on my last visit, I sat on the leather couch in the same public room and reflected on another adventure. Then the door opened and Alan Struthers entered.

"Well, Mr Carlisle – in the right place at the right time!"

He sat down at his desk, opened a drawer and took out a sheet of printed paper. He laid it down on the desk and lit his pipe.

"Karda Hassler, born on the sixth of April 1917 and was the only child of Werner and Elsa Hassler. Her father got killed at Passchendaele in October 1917 and she, along with her mother, left Germany in 1923. They came to Scotland and lived in Perth with a relative. No doubt they wanted to escape the poverty and political turmoil in Germany. Karda Hassler studied languages at Edinburgh University between 1934 and 1938. After her graduation, she joined the Ministry of Defence. She worked with them in an administrative capacity."

"Why would she jeopardise everything?"

"We believe someone approached her a year ago. We have been monitoring the situation. It is possible the fervour and passion of the New Order has like the majority of German people, influenced her. It could also be to extract revenge for her father's death in the last war."

"It must have been a torrid time in the aftermath of Germany's surrender."

"Yes it would have been but that's not a reason to help blow up a ship. A large number of Navy personnel would have been killed."

"How did the saboteur enter the base and also the ship?"

"He had a security pass and relevant papers, arranged by Karda. When aboard the ship, something must have gone wrong, hence his late departure. All non-Navy personnel must depart a ship by sixteen hundred hours."

"Then it turned out fortunate Corporal Stevens had been late for guard duty."

Struthers puffed on his pipe. "That would be the contingency plan if something had gone wrong. When her co-conspirator was caught and searched, he had in his possession a key. It belonged to an office next to the outside wall which surrounded the restricted area."

"How did he manage to get over the high wall? It must be fifteen feet high!"

"Meticulous planning. There is an upstairs toilet in the office, which overlooks the street below. When his bag got searched, we found a roll of thick wire. This would be tied to a toilet fixture and allow him to climb down onto the pavement.

As he wore dark overalls and at that late time of night, he would have succeeded in not being noticed."

"How did he plan to escape from the area?"

"He had a set of keys for a getaway car parked in a nearby street."

"Amazing!"

"Not so much as amazing but fortunate. When the saboteur made his escape, he would not have expected a 'sight-seer' on the base. Any personnel would either be on the ship or at the gatehouse. However, there is always the unexpected."

"What will happen to Karen?"

"Further interrogation, and then it will be up to the authorities."

"And the *RMS Queen Elizabeth*?"

"A sea trial has been rearranged, and if successful, the ship will continue on a mission of vital importance. By the way, here is a list of the crew members who would have been aboard the *Elizabeth* had it sailed."

I looked at the list. My goodness. The name of Carsell-Brown, Geoffrey.

"You look shocked. I can understand. All those lives could have been lost. We had luck on our side."

*Not luck, Mr Struthers – fate.*

"Thanks for your assistance, James. I can't say if we'll meet again. War is a strange game." He shook my hand.

I got my customary lift back to Ardrishaig from Peter Lenihan and Harry Creelman. Perhaps we would meet again at a future time. I visited the Lochside Hotel for dinner. I could detect an atmosphere of apathy within the establishment. Given the negative news from France, it did not surprise me. The limited dinner menu failed to install enthusiasm and I settled for cottage pie. It tasted terrible. The Navy base canteen food surpassed this meal. Maybe the regular chef had been called up. Even a window seat in the empty dining room failed to elevate this occasion. At least there were no tobacco fumes due to the lack of diners.

I left the hotel around ten o'clock and walked the short distance to Docharnea. As darkness fell, I arrived at the property and sneaked along the side of the ground perimeter. The mature hedge of over forty years made ideal cover. I approached the coach house and tried the door which led upstairs. It had been left unlocked. I went up to the coachman's quarters amidst creaks on the staircase. I searched for a candle to give me some light. I searched the washroom and bumped my head on a shelf!

Ah, there was one, and some matches too. I lit the candle and placed it on the window ledge. I looked in the mirror and composed myself. I must visit a barber, I thought. I closed my eyes, concentrated and opened them again.

I experienced the familiar tingling sensation.

# Chapter 10

## *Evacuation and Occupation*

"William?"

"Yes, Arthur?"

"Have you heard the news?"

"What news?"

"A communication from General Headquarters." He handed it to me.

William read the message. "Take your men and fall back to Dunkirk on the French coast. Operation Dynamo has been implemented."

"All officers are now being issued with new orders," said Lieutenant Bowles.

"Fall back, Arthur?"

"I'm afraid so. The Germans have broken through at Sudan. Both we and the French could soon be cut off. Our armies will be in serious trouble – drastic action is taken."

"But we have only been in the battle for less than a week!"

"From what I have heard, the French Army did not bolster their defence in the Ardennes. The Germans cut through them like butter, and their tanks are about to head for the coast. As we are pinned down here in Belgium, our armies will be trapped."

"What about our planes – can't they attack them?"

"The Luftwaffe have bombed our airfields and what is left has been shot out of the sky."

"Any chance of ground reinforcements?"

"HQ will want to retrieve what army is left to fight at a later date."

"Pretty dismal, may I say, Arthur."

"I have been told whilst the main force evacuates at Dunkirk, there are a couple of brave regiments who will attempt to hold back German forces."

"Brave indeed."

"Good luck, William." He saluted.

"And you too." I shook his hand

"Gather round, men. I have just received new orders. We have to withdraw from our current position and head for the coast at Dunkirk."

"Run from the Germans, sir?" said Sergeant Lawson.

"A retreat, Sergeant – we have our orders. A second German assault has been launched in the south. It has broken through the French defences. The German Army, complete with tanks, will arrive at the coast in a matter of days. A corridor is being kept open by two regiments for Allied soldiers to make haste for safety."

"The coastline remains too shallow for a troop ship, sir!" said Sergeant Lawson.

"Yes, I am aware of that. An armada of small vessels has been dispatched. I believe one of the regiments who defend the thirty mile corridor is Scottish."

"It's the Seaforth Highlanders, sir!" said a soldier.

"For them, let us all get back across the Channel, regroup and return to fight at a later date. Then we'll be better prepared."

"Aye!" cried the squad.

"Sir, here comes an army lorry – maybe we can get a lift!" said Corporal Jackson.

I ran towards it and put out my hand.

"Yes, sir?" said the driver.

"Could you give us a lift to the coast by any chance?"

"Sure, hop aboard."

"A lucky break to get a lift, sir."

"Yes indeed, Corporal."

"Sir, whilst on the beach, will we not be at the mercy of enemy planes?"

"Yes, no doubt, but our own aircraft will do their utmost to protect us."

"We're slowing down, sir."

"Run out of petrol, sir," said the lorry driver. "You'll 'ave to walk the rest of the way."

"Thanks for the lift this far. Men, disembark."

"At least we got a lift part of the way, sir," said Sergeant Lawson.

"Yes, let us be thankful for that."

"Nice day for a walk through the countryside, sir."

I smiled. "Yes Sergeant, a splendid warm sunny day. It could be worse!"

"Corporal, I can hear a plane," said a Private.

"There it is!" said Corporal Jackson. He pointed to a spot in the clear sky. "A Messerschmitt one o'nine."

"Quick men – off the road." I said.

"He's comin' around for an attack sir!" said Corporal Jackson.

I shouted, "Into the ditches!"

The German fighter plane fired a hail of bullets towards the road and then disappeared into the distance.

"Swine! Any casualties, Sergeant?"

He looked around the squad. "Everyone's okay, sir. It may have been on its way back from Dunkirk."

"Hope it meets a Spitfire!" I added, "Let's move on."

We proceeded as fast as possible toward the coast. Vehicles passed us crammed full of soldiers headed for Dunkirk.

"There is a village straight ahead, sir."

"Make sure it is secure, Sergeant. We can stop there for a short while."

"Yes, sir."

The Sergeant took a few men and went into the tranquil village with caution. He returned a short time later.

"All clear, Sergeant?"

"All clear, sir."

We entered the village and stopped to rest. Villagers brought us food and wine – how well both tasted! An elderly gentleman approached.

"You take this, monsieur. I do not want the Germans to get it." He handed me a bottle of fine cognac.

"Merci bien."

"Sir?"

"Yes Corporal?"

"Before the Germans arrive, how long do we have to evacuate?"

"Hard to tell, it depends on how long we can hold the corridor'. HQ states our troops are still able to put up a stiff defence at Cassel and St Valery en Caux."

"When we return home, what will happen, sir?"

"Prepare for an invasion by the Germans – although it could fail."

"Why, sir?"

"Britain is an island and to invade us requires air superiority. This is to protect the troop-carrier vessels. The Spitfire is a fast manoeuvrable plane which prevails against any enemy aircraft."

"Glad to hear it, sir!"

"I am optimistic Hitler may one day fall out with the Russians. This would mean a possible conflict in mainland Europe and divert Hitler's attention from us."

A Private whispered to Corporal Jackson.

"Sir, Private McNair can hear a tank approaching."

"A tank? I can't hear it."

"The reason why we call him Radar, sir!"

"Send someone ahead to find out if the tank is one of ours – be discreet."

"Yes, sir."

A soldier went in the direction off the tank. He returned with a negative look on his face.

"Yes Private?" I said.

"It's German, sir."

"Sergeant, round up the men."

"Right away, sir."

"Since there is just one of them, it may just be a predator. We can ambush it in a specific area of nearby forest. No reason to endanger the villagers."

"Good idea, sir."

"This is what we shall do Sergeant. Fire the bazooka at the front tracks of the tank. When the tank stops, someone jumps aboard at the rear, opens the hatch and drops in a smoke flare. They will soon leave the tank."

"What if the hatch is locked sir?"

"Aim the bazooka at the turret to knock out their guns."

The tank reached the edge of the forest a short time later with its commander poised in the turret. A missile was fired from the bazooka. One of the front tracks took a direct hit. The tank halted. Before the hatch could be closed, Corporal Jackson leapt onto the tank and threw a flare into it. Four German personnel jumped out of the smoke-filled tank and were taken prisoner.

"What shall we do with them sir?" said Sergeant Lawson.

A dilemma. There was no point in taking them with us to Dunkirk. "Tie each of them to a tree. Their own troops should be here soon to release them."

"Watch out sir!" shouted Sergeant Lawson.

"Agh!" I tumbled to the ground.

"Are you hurt bad, sir?"

"It's my leg, Sergeant."

"One of the Germans had a small pistol concealed in his jacket, sir. Private Shaw has just made sure he won't take any further part in this war! Can you move?"

"Help me up, Sergeant."

The Sergeant looked at the wound. "You may need medical attention, sir."

"Damn, of all the bad luck! Take me to the village Sergeant – there may be a doctor."

Sergeant Lawson knocked on the door of a nearby house.

A young woman opened it.

"Excuse me, is there a doctor in the village? Our Lieutenant requires medical attention."

"A moment, please."

A man then came to the door. "What is the matter?"

"Sorry to bother you. Our Lieutenant has been shot in the leg and needs medical attention."

"The doctor is in the next village. Do you have transport?"

"No, we have walked here."

"I can get someone to fetch the doctor, but your office better come inside and rest."

I got taken into the house and laid on a couch. My leg ached and I felt squeamish.

I turned to Sergeant Lawson. "Take the men to Dunkirk and get them home."

"You aren't comin' with us, sir?"

"No, Sergeant. I am not fit enough to travel and would slow you down. The distance to Dunkirk is about twenty miles from here. After twenty minutes I would be in severe pain."

"What about your safety, sir? German soldiers could soon be here."

"Do not worry, Sergeant – we can hide your officer in our loft," said the villager.

Sergeant Lawson smiled and saluted. "Good luck, sir."

The villager bent down. "I am Pierre Deblanc. You will be safe here in the meantime."

"I am grateful to you."

A young woman walked into the room.

"This is my daughter, Dominique."

She had a delightful warm smile – just what I needed!

"Dominique, ask Francois to fetch Doctor Bouillon. Tell him it's an emergency. A British officer has been shot in the leg."

"Yes, father." She left the house.

"The doctor should be here soon. Let me have a look at your wound, Lieutenant." He removed the makeshift dressing.

"It aches."

"I do not imagine you will be able to run for a while!"

"A walk shall suffice."

"Rest for now."


After three hours of searching for Francois and the doctor, Dominique returned to her father's house.

"Did you contact the doctor?"

"Yes, father. How is the young British Officer?"

"He now has a temperature and is in pain. I hope the doctor arrives within the next few hours."

"The doctor may be caught up in the conflict."

"Let us hope not, Dominique."

" Until the doctor arrives, father, I can tend to him."

Pierre glanced out the window. "Ah, here he is."

The doctor chapped on the door.

Pierre opened it. "Thank you for being prompt doctor. This way."

The doctor sat down beside the patient and removed the dressing. "How long has the Officer been like this, Pierre?"

"We believe about twelve hours."

"He has been hallucinating, Doctor," said Dominique.

"Yes my dear, he would be in his condition. The bullet must be removed."

"My daughter can assist you, Doctor."

"We better get started. Let us take him upstairs. "

Two hours later, the doctor and Dominique came downstairs. The doctor put down his black bag and took a deep breath.

"How is he, Doctor?"

"He is calm, Pierre, and should sleep for some time. He must stay here. To move him would aggravate the injury."

"The loft is not used; he can remain there."

"Good. There are German soldiers everywhere."

"What is the latest news?"

"Just bad news! British and French servicemen are on the beach at Dunkirk. They still await rescue. Until the Germans launch an attack to capture Paris, it can only be a matter of days."

"Doctor, how long do you believe France can hold out?"

"A few weeks at best, if we're lucky. The Army must be demoralised at this moment."

"Would you like a glass of wine, Doctor?"

"No, but thank you. I must get back to my village. I will no doubt have more casualties who require my attention."

"Again, Doctor, thank you." Pierre opened the door.

"Goodbye, Pierre."

Dominique waved to the doctor from the front window.

The doctor waved back and walked on.

She continued to look out the window.

"Father, what if any German soldiers come here?"

"I hope not, but if any appear then do not speak. Let me deal with them."

"I can hear the drone of many planes. They appear headed in the direction of the coast."

"The Luftwaffe will attack and finish off the soldiers on the beach. Let us hope the RAF can give them some protection. The evacuation could take time."

"A woman in the village told me many thousands of our own and British troops have been taken prisoner."

"I hope there is enough left of our army to perhaps halt the Germans from reaching Paris."

"Father, I can see German soldiers. They are coming this way."

"Leave the talking to me, Dominique."

A German soldier banged on the door.

Pierre opened it.

"We seek a wounded British Officer," said the soldier. "He has been spotted in this area."

"I have not seen any British Officer."

"Nevertheless, we will search your house. Is anyone else in the property?" He stepped inside.

"Just us."

The grey uniformed soldier looked at Dominique. "How old are you?"

"Why do you ask?" said Pierre

"I ask the questions, not you."

"I am twenty two years old."

"Would you lie to a soldier of the Wermacht?"

"What would be the point?"

"Have you seen any British soldiers around this area?"

"Yes, earlier today. They went in the direction of the coast."

Another German soldier walked into the house. "Sergeant Schultz."

He turned around. "Yes, what is it?"

"Headquarters, sir. We have to move on and join C division at once."

The Sergeant clicked the heels of his black boots. "Heil Hitler." He marched out the door.

"I can imagine the type of medical assistance they would give! God help France if we lose the war. Better check on our patient, Dominique."

She climbed the stairs, stopped and shouted. "Father, come quick!"

Pierre rushed up the stairs. "What is the matter?"

"He is unconscious. He must have heard the German soldiers and panicked!"

"It appears he tried to reach the closet and conceal himself. No doubt in the event of the loft being searched. He must have slipped and hit his head on the bedpost."

"His leg will ache."

"When he regains consciousness, his head may feel worse! Let us lift him back onto the bed."

Dominique touched the Officer's forehead. "His temperature appears fine, father. I shall sit here for a while."

"Where am I? Who are you?"

"My name is Dominique. Do you remember being brought here by your men?"

"My mind is blank! Agh!"

"Do not move. You have been shot. A local doctor has removed a bullet."

"Could I also have been shot in the head? It aches!"

"You fell and hit your skull on the bedpost. Can you not remember what happened?"

"No – I don't remember anything." The Officer looked around the room. "Where is this place?"

"You are in the loft of my father's house. Our village lies near the French coast. Your army is in full retreat at Dunkirk."

"Dunkirk?"

"Rest and I will return later."

"Don't leave."

"I will be back soon. I promise." Dominique went downstairs. "Father, would it be possible to ask the doctor to return? The Officer has lost his memory and does not look well."

"He may be busy at this volatile time, Dominique. Attend to the Officer, and if his condition gets worse then we can try to fetch the doctor."

"What is the latest news on the war?"

"British and our own troops are still being evacuated. The German army has gained much territory on their way to Paris."

"Surely our soldiers will halt their advancement?"

"French morale has collapsed. Even the government and military are in disarray. Certain members have been sacked.

"Britain must be relieved. The country is an island surrounded by sea."

"So much for the Maginot Line to repel any German invasion! What a waste of resources."

Dominique looked out the window. "Francois is headed this way, father. He has a grave expression."

Pierre opened the door. "Come in, Francois; what is the matter?"

"The Germans have launched an assault on Paris. They are just sixty kilometres from the capital."

"We perhaps better pray for a miracle. What news of Dunkirk?" Pierre poured a glass of red wine. "Take this, Francois."

"Thanks." He drank it. "Whilst ships and small boats try to evacuate troops, German Stuka planes bomb the beach."

"Murderers! What about the British Spitfires and Hurricanes?"

"They are in a consistent air battle with the German fighters."

"The situation looks bleak, my friend."

Francois nodded. "I must get back to my home. Take this – you may need it." Francois produced a handgun from inside his jacket and handed it to Pierre, along with bullets.

"Francois, I cannot use this."

"Pierre – you may have to, if only for protection."

"Very well." Pierre put the gun in a drawer. "If you meet the doctor, please ask him to stop by again."

"Okay, old friend."

Pierre opened the door. "Take care."

Francois walked briskly back towards his village.

"Father, you won't use the gun?"

"Not unless it is becomes necessary. However I will hide the gun in a more discreet place, as a precaution in case those German soldiers return."

"Dominique, there is someone at the door, I am busy."

She opened the door.

"Hello Dominique, your father requested I stop by."

"Come in, Doctor. The British Officer fell and injured himself."

He stepped inside. "His leg?"

"No, his head! He has lost his memory."

"How did it happen?"

"A group of German soldiers came to the house. He must have heard them and attempted to hide in the closet."

"And when he got out of bed, the accident happened?"

"Yes, Doctor."

"I will go upstairs and examine him."

"Watch that step, Doctor – it is damaged."

"And it creaks."

I could hear people coming upstairs. They did not sound like German soldiers!

"The doctor wishes to examine you."

"Do you remember me? I came here to attend to your injured leg."

"Vaguely."

"Any headaches?" The doctor sat on the edge of the bed.

"No, they have gone."

"How is your eyesight?"

"Better."

"Smell and taste?"

"Fine."

"How is your memory?"

"I can't remember who I am."

"What about recent events? Fighting the Germans?"

"Nothing."

"How does the leg feel?"

"Painful and stiff." I tried to move my leg.

"I am not surprised!" The doctor removed the dressing. "The wound does not look worse, but you must rest your leg."

"Yes, Doctor, I will."

"I'll try to look in on you later." The doctor left the room. "Those stairs are steep Dominique!"

"I trust also for the Germans, Doctor! Should they return to search the property, it may put them off."

"Yes doctor."

"Pierre, the officer is fine."

"Bon, thank you once more."

"No problem, Pierre. Keep a close watch on the young Officer."

"When will he regain his memory?"

"Difficult to say. He doesn't recall any conflict with the enemy. I treated soldiers in the last war that lost their memory through head injuries. They shut out all knowledge of battles."

"That is understandable."

"Yes. He does not give me the impression of being a professional soldier. Warfare can be a stressful situation."

"What news from the coast?"

"All types of sea vessels have evacuated many British and French soldiers. Since the evacuation began, there have been more than thirty British naval ships put out of action. I have it on good authority more than eighty thousand troops are still at Dunkirk. They have no firepower or supplies."

"If they fall into the hands of the Germans, God help them! I believe our troops now heroically defend the route to Paris."

"Yes Pierre – but if only they had defended Sudan with equal bravery."

"I understand what you mean. We may not be in this desperate situation."

"Dominique, make sure the Officer remains still and try to prompt his memory. Ask questions about his past."

Dominique opened the door. "Yes, Doctor, I will try. Goodbye." She gently closed the door. "Father, will France lose the war?"

"It would appear so. How unfortunate we did not have Russia with us. Their non-aggression pact with Germany scuppered any chance of an alliance with them."

"What will we do? How can we survive?"

"All is not lost, Dominique. Britain will re-arm and return one day. In the meantime, France must not lie down." Pierre put on his jacket.

"Where are you going, father?"

"Off to visit Francois. He has organised a meeting with a group of people."

"What about?"

"I will tell you later, Dominique. How is our patient?"

"When I took up his meal, he appeared well. Prior to being brought here, he still has no recollection of past events."

"What about his identification papers or personal documents?"

"They are missing."

"As the doctor suggested, try to ask him some questions about himself. I should be back in a few hours. If any soldiers come to the door, do not answer. See you later." Pierre closed the door and locked it.

Dominique climbed the stairs to the loft and entered the small room. "How is your leg?"

"It is damn painful – even if I only touch it."

"Is your bed comfortable?" Dominique sat on the edge.

"Yes. What is the situation with us and the Germany?"

"My father tells me the war for France could be lost. The Germans may soon be in Paris."

"I heard someone mention an evacuation at Dunkirk."

"The evacuation has been completed but many British and French troops did not get rescued. Prior to your stay here do you remember anything?"

"Flashbacks of action and some soldiers' faces. I can't put them together."

"Where are you from in Britain?"

"I can't remember, but it feels colder than here. Maybe far north within Britain."

"Do you remember your name? One of your men called you Lieutenant but no name."

"Well, at least I am an Officer!" He stared into space. "I feel frustrated." His hands gripped the bed sheets.

"Yes, you must be."

"What is your name?"

"I am Dominique, Dominique Deblanc."

"Why are you fair? Most French ladies are dark."

"I take after my grandmother. My mother, sister and I resemble her."

"Where is your mother?"

"In the south. My father and she separated five years ago." She started to pull her hair. "I have a younger sister who lives with her."

"Where in the south do they live?"

"Toulouse."

"Your English is good."

"I went to university in Paris to study languages. I completed my course last year. I had arranged to live and work in Italy for a year. The war disrupted my plans."

"You must also be frustrated."

Dominique smiled.

"Why Italy?"

"It is where my father's family originate. I speak fluent Italian. Your eyes are closing."

"I feel tired."

"It must be all those questions you ask! You should rest. Later I will bring you a bowl of soup."

"Dominique, what is the date?"

"Eighth of June."


Dominique gazed out the window. Her father should have returned by now. Here he came. Her father unlocked the front door and entered.

"How is Francois' father?"

"Depressed! As we all are." He took off his jacket and hung it on the coat stand.

"How many attended the meeting?"

"Eleven."

"Only eleven?"

"Yes, Dominique, eleven people who want to take a stand against the Germans. The fighting should soon be over but our resistance shall continue." "

"But father, how can you fight the Germans?"

"We plan to create a network of local units to hit back at them. We discussed it in much detail."

"It will be dangerous."

"I agree, Dominique, but we have to do something."

"You will need guns and ammunition."

"Francois has contacted the British and they have promised to supply us with what we require. However, until communication channels become established, we have to wait."

"Paris radio reports some German units have entered the city and the government is about to leave. Where will they go?"

"Maybe somewhere in the south of the country."

"It all looks bleak and hopeless, father." Dominique wiped a tear from her eye.

"I know, Dominique, but if we establish a resistance movement, then it gives us a purpose to survive. Germany will want revenge for the way we humiliated them in the last war. We removed their territory and handed them excessive reparation payments. I also shudder to imagine what may happen to Jewish citizens who live in France."

"Father, Francois' father is Jewish."

"I am aware, Dominique." Pierre sat down. "How is the British Officer?"

"Inquisitive!"

"Did you not want to ask him questions?"

"Yes. I enjoy our conversations."

Her father smiled. "I can tell."

"How do you feel this morning?" Dominique laid the breakfast tray on one side of the bed.

"A lot better. I slept well for the first time in a long while." The Officer sat up on the bed.

"Since you left Britain?"

"Yes, but I still cannot remember my past."

"Not even your family?"

"Just glimpses of people, but they are unrecognisable. At times I see a coastline."

"It could be you come from a similar place to this location."

"Yes, it is a possibility."

"At least you have some sort of recollection. Perhaps soon, pictures in your mind may become clearer."

"It would be a start. If I could just somehow remember my name."

" Until you do, why don't I select one?"

"All right, choose."

"A British name. How about Charles?"

The officer shook my head.

"Edward?"

He again shook my head.

"Winston?"

He frowned!

"What about Mickey?"

"Mickey?"

"Yes, as in Mickey Mouse. He is famous – even in France. No?"

"Non!"

"I have it! Michael sounds more appropriate. That should be your new name."

The Officer nodded.

"Ah." Dominique gave a sigh of relief and left the room.

"How is the Officer this morning?"

"Much better, father. He slept well last night. You look concerned again. What is wrong?"

"The government has left Paris. The radio also mentioned Italy has declared war on Britain and us. How much worse can the situation get?"

"What about Paris?"

"It has been declared an 'open' city."

"How much longer can France survive, father?"

"I fear not long. Tonight there is another meeting and a government agent will be there."

"Why?"

"To advise on tactics in our fight with the Germans. Francois said the government want all similar groups organised and coordinated."

"It would appear certain officials are not going to lie down."

"We have to do something, Dominique."

"Can I attend the meeting?"

"No, it is too dangerous. Besides, you have to attend to the Officer. We do not want him to suffer another mishap."

"He can now stand with a support for a short time."

Pierre raised his grey eyebrows. "That is an improvement."

"He should soon be able to walk down the stairs."

"The result of excellent care and attention he has received."

"I know, father."

Later that evening Dominique rushed into the kitchen. "How did you get down the stairs?"

"I used this brush as a support. I had to get out of that claustrophobic loft." The officer sat down on a kitchen chair.

Dominique laughed. "You look funny in my father's baggy shirt and trousers."

He looked at himself and then at Dominique. "I could not manage into my military clothes."

She continued laughing. "The German soldiers would also be amused!"

The Officer smiled. "To more serious matters, what news on the war?"

"The government has left Paris and are now located in Bordeaux. The Italians have declared war on Britain and France."

"Any good news?"

"I am afraid not."

"Where is your father?"

"He has gone to a meeting with people from the local community."

"Are they forming a resistance movement?"

"I am not sure, but a government agent is to attend."

"It would appear your government is not lying down."

"The final Paris radio broadcast stated there had been many changes in government personnel. One change includes a person called Charles de Gaulle who is young, passionate and patriotic. If only other similar officials had been part of our government."

"I see your point. Your country may not be in the desperate position it finds itself."

Dominique lowered her head.

"How long will your father be?"

She looked up and smiled. "Long enough."


"You arrived home late, father." Dominique set the table for breakfast.

"The meeting went on later than I expected." Pierre sat down at the table. "A woman turned up as the government agent – much to the delight of Francois and his colleagues!"

"What age is she?"

"About mid-forties, and feisty. I am glad to have her on our side! She told us the British would supply the Resistance with weapons through various channels. We will be notified later."

"Does she know what the situation with our Government is?"

"Marshal Petain has been put in charge of the government. An armistice will be announced on the twenty-second. The South is to administer North and West regions."

"Is the South about to collaborate with the Germans?"

"Yes, it's unfortunate. The North and West will be occupied."

"It is a betrayal."

"As a reactivist, Marshal Petain will not want the war to result in any more bloodshed. He may feel France has suffered enough. He led the army at the battle of Verdun in the last war and experienced the carnage, which resulted. As leader of the new government, to sign an armistice could be the best option for France."

"A sad time for France." Dominique held her father.

"That bacon smells delicious – let us have breakfast."

Dominique dried her eyes.

"Afterwards, you can take some food up to the young Officer."

She smiled.

Pierre looked at the clock on the kitchen wall. "Is that the correct time Dominique?"

"Why, father?"

"The terms of the armistice are being broadcast by the new regime at ten o'clock."

"Not long to go. I hope they are favourable, father."

"Yes, let us hope so for all our sakes."

"I can hear Michael manoeuvring down the stairs."

"Michael? Has he remembered his name?"

"No, we chose a name for the present."

"Good morning, Monsieur Deblanc."

"Good morning – you feel better?"

"Yes, thank you. It is a joy to walk again."

"I can tell Dominique has taken good care of you."

"Yes she has – an excellent nurse."

"I have maintained she should enter a care profession."

"I agree." The Officer looked at her.

"But father, my qualifications are in languages. Those are my strengths."

"Michael, she would like to become a secret agent."

"A bit too dangerous, but there *is* a demand for them at this moment!"

"Father, the armistice terms are being announced on the radio."

"Quick, Dominique, turn up the volume."

A solemn French voice spoke. "Here are the main points of the French-German Armistice. German and Italian troops will occupy the north and west of the country. The south and east are to remain neutral. All areas will be administered by the south in Vichy. The Army, Navy and Air Force will demobilise. Weapons, facilities and hardware will be handed over to German Reich forces. The French Channel and ports in the country and abroad will fall under German Reich control.

"All French prisoners of war are to remain in captivity. The French government will give details of German personnel held in captivity. A minimal French army will be allowed to maintain control and police the country. The French government has to pay the cost of the German forces which occupy the country. No unauthorised flight will pass over occupied air space. Also, when the surrender comes into force, all French wireless transmissions will terminate."

"Scandalous, ridiculous! We, liable for the occupation of our country?" Pierre thumped his hand on the living room table.

"Calm down father, calm down."

"Also we have to give them all our ships, planes and artillery." He shook his head.

Dominique looked at Michael. "Those armistice terms leave France weak and demoralised."

"At least the south and east of the country will not be occupied – yet!" Pierre again shook his head.

"Where are you off to, father?"

"To chat with Francois and get drunk." Pierre put on his jacket, opened the door and stormed out.

Dominique closed the door.

"How long will your father be gone this time?"

"Until he feels sober enough to return home." She gazed out the window. "I will now have to put my career aspirations on hold."

"Everyone will have to – not just in France but also in my country."

"At least my mother and sister will not have much disruption being in the south."

"Such a large country – no wonder the Germans only occupy the north and west. Dominique, what does your father do apart from attend his meetings?"

"He has a small restaurant in the village. Francois' brother is the chef."

"Does your father not cook?"

"Not really. Can you cook?"

"Not really."

"How do you know?"

"I just do."

"Has your memory started to function?"

"I feel puzzled but also hungry."

"I will prepare something. but you can assist, monsieur!"

Michael devoured a cooked meal of eggs, ham and tomatoes. His leg may not have been tip-top, but he had no problem being able to consume food.

Dominique washed the dishes.

"Can I help?"

She shook her head. "I can manage."

"You are not just proficient in languages, but can also prepare delicious food."

"Your taste buds appear in order. My mother remains the best cook in our family. When she left, father could not hide his disappointment."

"Did she work in the restaurant?"

"Yes. They got on better there than at home!" She pulled her hair.

"Can I turn on your father's radio?"

"There is no point. Wireless transmissions are now prohibited."

"Of course, the Armistice agreement. There could soon be curfews."

"You have a pensive look on your face."

"Dominique, I have to somehow re-join my unit in Britain. I can't stay here."

"Then we have to come up with a solution. One which allows you to return across the channel."

"It is dangerous for me to stay here. I don't want to get you and your father into trouble."

" When father returns, I will speak to him. Someone in the resistance may be able to help."

Dominique put the clean dishes in a cupboard.

"Finished?"

"Yes, I am all yours."


"Are you still hung over from yesterday, father?"

"Yes I am Dominique. It is not often France loses a war!" Pierre slumped into a living room chair.

"Did many people frequent the restaurant?"

"Yes, about thirty."

"Father, Michael feels it is risky to stay here. He has to re-join his unit."

Pierre looked at his daughter.

"Would it be possible to arrange for him to escape back to Britain?"

"Do you want him to leave? The journey would be a perilous one. The Germans monitor the towns and villages for infiltrators."

"Yes father, I am aware of such methods."

"There will be other difficulties. I will speak to Francois. He can get in touch with his contact in the resistance. Is Michael resting?"

"No, reading. He wants to improve his French language skills."

"It may prove beneficial to include German in the event of being captured. How is his memory?"

"Well, he did remember he cannot cook."

"I suppose it's a start. It must frustrate him not able to remember his past."

"Yes, and being confined to the house – now he can walk again. Would it be safe to venture outside for a brief spell?"

"No, Dominique, it is too dangerous. There may be German collaborators in the village and a stranger could cause suspicion! Francois told me German soldiers have stopped people in the next village and interrogated them."

"Why?"

"They did not say, but the 'vulnerable' were picked upon."

"Bullies!" Dominique banged a cup on the table.

"Be careful and do not give the soldiers a reason to assert themselves. They will take pleasure in their efforts to humiliate us."

The following days brought more misery for villagers with regular patrols of German soldiers. They did their utmost to act superior, much to the distaste of older residents. People such as Pierre had to curb their temper or suffer the consequences. This made Dominique anxious. She did not often leave the house because of possible harassment. Whenever she returned from the village, I could sense another instance of intimidation had taken place. Not being able to go outside made me feel frustrated. Also I had still not regained my memory which accentuated the situation.

Early one evening, I heard people come to the house. I put down my book and stood at the top of the stairs. As they appeared friends of Pierre, I breathed a sigh of relief.

"Good evening, Francois."

"Pierre, this is Colette."

"Good evening." Pierre shook her hand. He turned to Dominique. "This is my daughter, Dominique. Would you like a glass of wine?"

"Due to the curfew we do not have much time, Pierre. Colette has joined our movement."

"Good." Pierre smiled.

"I have come here because of the British Officer." Francois removed his dark blue beret.

"A problem, Francois?"

"No Dominique, our government contact in the resistance has a plan to get him out of the country. Colette's uncle has a small fishing boat. It can take him over the channel but the

Germans have regular patrols along the coast. We may have to create a diversion which could allow the Officer to escape."

"It sounds daring, my friend."

"When the details get finalised Pierre, I will inform you."

Pierre moved towards the door. "Safe journey to you both."

"And to you, my friend."

Pierre opened and then closed the door.

"Father, why did Francois bring Colette?"

"For security, Dominique. When a couple are out prior to the curfew, it appears less suspicious to the Germans."

"I will go upstairs and tell Michael of the situation." Dominique climbed the steep stairs.

"I heard a number of voices downstairs."

"Francois and a colleague came over to give us some news."

"About the war?"

"No – the resistance may be able to arrange safe passage for you across the channel."

"My goodness! I did not expect an escape this quickly."

"Francois will contact father with details. Perhaps within a few days."

"We only have another few days together?"

"It appears so." She touched his hand.


"How are you today?"

"I am fine, father."

"You are a bit subdued – but I understand why. You can all meet up again once this dreaded war is over. The British will one day return with the Americans and defeat the enemy."

"But when, father?"

"I hope in the near future. There is also the threat of Russia once they become equipped and ready for a war."

"What about the peace treaty with Germany?"

"Take it with a pinch of salt."

"It does appear bizarre. Two arch-enemies who sign a non-aggression pact."

"Your aunt asked me why you haven't visited her for some time."

"You are correct, father." Dominique looked at the clock. "There is still time before the curfew starts. I'll go now." She grabbed her jacket and dashed out the house.

Pierre stood at the foot of the stairs. "Michael," he shouted.

"Yes, Pierre?"

"Do you want to come downstairs? I am preparing a meal."

"Be down in a few minutes."

"I hope you enjoy this. I do not possess Dominique's expertise." Pierre poured two glasses of wine.

"Where is she?"

"Dominique has gone to visit her aunt who does not keep good health. She should not be long." Pierre sat down at the table. "You will be glad to return home?"

"I am still not sure where home is located! However when I return to Britain, no doubt the government will enlighten me." I started my meal. "This stew tastes delicious."

"The doctor mentioned your memory could return at any time. It requires something to create a spark."

"It is strange, not being aware of who you are and where you come from." I stared into empty space.

"It could not have been too negative – you are a British Officer."

"Yes, I suppose. What is the latest news on the war?"

"As the radio transmissions have stopped, we now have to rely on gossip. It would appear the Germans are in and around Paris, with Hitler sightseeing and Goering shopping!"

"They perhaps do not plan to invade Britain just yet?"

Pierre laughed. "The German Chancellor prefers a summer vacation rather than an invasion."

"It is good for us, and long may the vacation continue. Britain has to organise their defences for an invasion. The longer Hitler stalls, the more time we have to get ready for the German offensive."

"Let us hope this will be a long summer. Let us also have a toast, Michael – to a peaceful summer."

"I will drink to that." I clinked my glass against Pierre's and finished my red wine.

Pierre refilled it and then his own. He looked at the clock on the kitchen wall. "It will soon be curfew time. Dominique must have been delayed – her aunt is a chatterbox! She also finds it difficult to prise herself away."

"I hope she is all right."

"There are many locals around at this time of the day to protect her in case any German soldier gets any ideas. Pierre looked towards the door.

"That must be her now Pierre. She must have forgotten to take her key."

"No, it is Francois' knock." He got up and headed towards the door and opened it.

"Good evening, Pierre."

"Come in, what is the matter?"

"Ah, the British officer. Bonsoir, monsieur. We have to move fast! It may be possible to get you out tonight. The patrols get relaxed on Sundays. We just found out – now is the best opportunity for an escape."

"I'll get ready."

"As we have a strict deadline, please hurry."

I dashed upstairs.

"Make sure he gets to the boat in one piece, Francois."

"I will, Pierre, do not worry."

I walked down the stairs with care. I didn't want any mishap.

"I'm ready." I turned to Pierre. "Thank you for everything. I am disappointed Dominique is not here. Upon my return, I will write to her."

"I will, and bon chance." He opened the door and gave me a warm handshake.

"See you later, Pierre," said Francois.

Pierre returned to the kitchen and opened a drawer. It contained medals he had been decorated with in the previous war. After our victory of just twenty one years ago, how could this humiliating defeat have happened? He sat down and poured another glass of red wine.

"Is that you, Dominique?"

"Yes." She closed the door and took off her jacket.

"How is your aunt?"

"Fine. She told me mother is also well."

"And your sister?"

"The same." Dominique sniffed the air. "Has Michael had his evening meal?"

Pierre got up out of his chair. "Michael has gone, Dominique. He left with Francois a short time ago."

"Is the escape not tomorrow?"

"A change of plan. Tonight is safer."

"Did he say anything?"

"He wanted to say goodbye in person. When back home, he promises to write. He had to leave at some time."

Her head tilted. "I know." She looked up. "Which route did they take to the coast?"

"They headed for the dense woods – it is secluded."

"Thank goodness. German units patrol the coastal road. I hope he reaches Britain safely."

"With Francois and his men, he is in good hands."


"This way, monsieur – watch for the traps."

"The traps, Francois?"

"We spotted the Germans laying mines."

"Why in the woods?"

"To injure British and French soldiers who made their way towards Dunkirk for the evacuation. Many were killed."

"Monstrous!"

"Do not worry – we know this area and can bypass the obstacles. If you happen to step on something solid, do not move your foot."

"Then what?"

"Pray, monsieur!"

"Will do. Does this route take us straight to the coast?"

"We are headed for a safe house on the way to the coast."

"Why not go straight there?"

"Another two British soldiers are also making their escape on the boat. They should already be at the safe house."

"Good for them."

Francois pointed. "There it is, monsieur."

"You would have to know the exact location to find this place." I could just distinguish the outline of a cottage surrounded by large bushes and trees.

"The reason we use it to hide people, monsieur!"

We approached with caution the secluded wooden building shrouded in darkness. Our dark clothes would blend in well. I stepped on a large twig. Francois looked my way and put a finger to his mouth. Everyone crouched down. One of the men moved forward and peered in the corner of a window.

He nodded and Francois took up a position beside the door. He knocked twice then once. No answer. He then gave a distinctive whistle. The door opened. I could see a young woman with a lamp.

"You are late, Francois!"

He turned towards me. "This is Colette, monsieur. She is a stickler for time."

We entered the cottage and another woman greeted Francois. She then looked at me and came closer.

"William, is it you?" She looked surprised.

"William?"

She smiled. "Yes, William Carsell-Brown, it is you."

The lady appeared familiar, someone from my past. Maya.

"You are Maya, Maya Frielberg!"

"Yes, of course I am. Why did you not recognise me?"

Francois interrupted. "Maya, the Officer got injured and lost his memory."

"William, do you not remember me at your wedding?"

I started to recollect images; the tank, an ambush, my arrival in France and Olivia.

"You look shocked, monsieur," said Francois.

Maya led me to a chair and I sat down. "Colette, is there any cognac left?"

Colette handed me a glass. I took a sip.

"Better?"

I stared at Maya. "A bit."

"There are two of your countrymen here, William. You can all escape through the same route."

"Are the two men from my regiment?"

"No, they belong to the regiment which fought at Saint Valery."

"The Seaforth Highlanders?"

"Yes, they managed to avoid capture and we hid them."

"I remember one of my men told of their heroics."

"They put up a shield to hold back the Germans for the evacuation."

My memory was returning.

"As the coast is a three hour trek from here, you must leave soon. Are you up to it ,William?"

"Yes, Maya, I feel better. It is fine cognac!"

She smiled.

Colette brought two men into the room.

"Ah, here are your two companions for the journey," said Maya. "This is Sandy Jarvis and Donald Watt."

I shook both their hands. I then turned to Maya. "Are you coming with us?"

"No, William – Francois and his men will take you to the boat. Colette and I shall remain here."

"I have much to speak to you about. When I return home, mother will want to know everything!"

"Yes I am certain. Tell her I am fine and when this war is over, we must all meet up." She gave me a hug. "Bon chance."

We proceeded with care through the dense woods. It would not be too long until we reach the coast and the small fishing boat, which would take us to England.

"Are you okay, sir?" said a Seaforth Highlander.

He spotted my slight limp. "Yes, but call me William. Why do you address me as sir?"

"Well, you are an Officer. Ian and I are just Privates."

"We are out of uniform – William is fine."

"Okay, sir."

"Is Donald not your colleague's name?"

"He prefers his middle name."

"I understand."

"Do you have a middle name, sir?"

"Yes but I prefer William."

"Do you have a middle name, Francois?" I asked.

"Like you, monsieur, I also do not prefer it."

"Until we reach the coast, how long, Francois?"

"At least another hour, monsieur."

"Where do you come from, sir?" asked Ian.

"A village in Argyll called Ardrishaig."

"I once went sailing there with my grandfather. It's on Loch Fyne?"

"Yes, I'll be glad to get back. How about you, Sandy, where are you from?"

"I'm from Nairn sir. Not far from Inverness."

"What about you, Ian?"

"Inverness sir."

"My mother and father visit Inverness on a regular basis at holiday time."

"They don't want to visit in January sir – it's freezing!"

"I can imagine! What is the name of the public house across from the railway station? When my mother wants to go around the shops, my father makes himself scarce and ends up there."

"The Academy Bar, sir. The best beer served in the town."

"My father would no doubt agree."

"Allez monsieurs, we have to hurry."

I smiled. "D'accord Francois, keep your beret on! Just Scottish chit-chat."

One of Francois' men held up his hand. We stopped. The man retreated from his position and spoke to Francois.

Francois turned to me. "Henri has spotted a German vehicle in the distance."

"What type of vehicle?"

"It resembles a small, armoured vehicle."

"A tank?"

"No, monsieur – I believe a type of truck for surveillance."

All of us settled ourselves within a safe distance, where we could observe. A faint light came from inside. Francois tapped Henri on the shoulder and pointed to the truck. He moved with caution towards it and stopped. He went in closer and remained there. A few moments later, he made his way back to us. He spoke to Francois.

"Monsieur, Henri said there could be at least three in the truck. They are in discussion about various local landmarks. There are also – how you would say – clicking noises."

"Clicking noises?"

"Yes, like a typewriter."

"They wouldn't type a letter at this early time of the morning. I wonder what they are up to?"

"Monsieur, the Germans can observe the coastline from their position. Perhaps they monitor the area for sea vessels which bring supplies for the resistance?"

"That's possible – they could spot our boat!"

Francois looked at his watch. "It should be here in just under fifty minutes."

I turned to my Seaforth colleagues. "What do you think?"

"Let's take them, sir," said Sandy. "If they catch sight of the boat, their headquarters will be notified."

"Then it is settled." I turned to Sandy and Ian. "You cover the front of the truck. We will confront them at the rear."

Francois looked at me.

I pointed to his watch. "What is the time?"

He looked at it. "Twenty minutes after two. The boat should be here at three o'clock." Francois handed me a gun.

We moved at a slow and quiet pace towards the vehicle. When we approached, I could hear the occupants chatter. The rear of the truck had a sheet which covered the exit. I signalled to Francois – 'When we aim our guns at it, pull back the sheet.' He nodded in understanding.

Three German soldiers sat around a machine – they stared at us. They stared at our guns pointed at them.

"Guten morgen herren – hands up!" I ordered.

We removed their pistols. As the three Germans put their hands on their heads, Francois and his men took them into the woods.

Ian said, "No problem sir!"

"The advent of surprise." I went inside the vehicle and examined the mechanism.

Sandy followed. "It's only a typewriter sir."

"All the same, let's take this with us. It may prove worthwhile."

He pointed. "And those manuals sir?"

"Yes, they could be relevant."

We heard three muffled shots. Francois and his men appeared from the woods. I asked, "Why the gunfire?"

"We had to shoot them, monsieur. We cannot take them prisoner. If we let them go, it would jeopardise our security."

With no further obstacles, we reached the rendezvous and waited. It would not be long now. I took a deep breath and smelled the sea.

"He should be here soon, monsieur," said Francois.

I again asked Francois the time.

"Almost three o'clock."

Sandy Jarvis pointed, "There he is, I can just make out the boat."

"Everyone take cover," said Francois. "It's a German patrol boat!"

As it approached, each of us darted into the nearby bushes and watched. The patrol boat came to a halt and lay motionless in the calm water. After an anxious period, it moved off. The boat continued on its way along the coast. Only a few minutes went by, but it appeared much longer.

I said, "Well spotted, Francois – and in the dark!"

"Not my eyesight monsieur, my ears. The German patrol boats have a distinctive motor sound."

Just as well.

"Sir, another boat is headed this way." said Ian.

"Well, Francois, is it our chap?" I held my breath.

He hesitated for a minute. "Yes, monsieur – it is he."

The boat came in our direction and stopped about two hundred yards from our position. Then a light flashed on and off three times. After a few moments, this signal got repeated. Henri repeated the signal and the boat moved towards us. It stopped a short distance from the shore.

"You will have to get your feet wet monsieur, but worth it n'est ce pas!"

"It sure is, Francois. Thanks to you and your men for helping us." I shook his hand.

"Bon chance, monsieur."

Sandy, Ian and I waded out to the boat. We got lifted aboard and the boat made its way through the darkness. I had heard the Germans had planted mines in the channel to thwart an evacuation. I mentioned this to a member of the crew.

"Do not worry, monsieur – there is a mine-free passage to Dover. Before the evacuation, your navy made certain."

"That's a relief."

As we left France, I thought about Dominique and the time we spent in each other's company. I had to forget what happened but it would not be easy. She was a warm, affectionate and intelligent person. I hoped that after the war she would meet someone of fine quality – like herself. My leg started to ache, so I rested it on a stool. Thank goodness we were nearly home.

Just before daybreak, we arrived at Dover. My two colleagues and I grateful for a safe return to British soil. We got taken to the local military headquarters for a hot meal and some rest.

I had to appear at Military Intelligence for a debriefing. After two days of recuperation, I still felt fatigued. I got taken into a well-lit room and before me stood two Officers.

"I am Captain Fuller and this is Major Dow."

"At ease, Lieutenant, please sit down," said Major Dow.

I removed my hat. Both sat opposite me, similar to an interview.

Major Dow rolled his grey moustache. "Recovered from recent exertions, Lieutenant?"

"Just about, sir."

"How is your leg?"

"Fine, sir." Damn painful.

"How did you obtain the machine brought back from France?"

"We acquired it from a German unit situated on the French coast sir."

"Acquired?"

"Yes, sir."

"Did they give it up without a fight?"

"We took them by surprise, sir. They didn't get the chance to put up a fight."

"Are you aware what the machine is used for, Lieutenant?"

"We could not decide, sir. One of the men suggested it could be some sort of typewriter."

He raised his bushy eyebrows. "Did he?"

"It does resemble one, sir," said Captain Fuller.

"We understand the machine may be used to send and receive codes."

"Codes, sir? My goodness!"

"Yes. The machine is being taken to a special unit, which has been established to intercept German communications to its military. If this device is what we believe it may be then our military could learn of planned enemy movements."

"A strategic advantage, sir." *Thank goodness we'd decided to take it!*

"Correct, Lieutenant." Major Dow sat back on his chair. "After what happened at Dunkirk, this would give us a welcome boost." He looked at Captain Fuller.

"Definitely, sir," said Captain Fuller.

"That is all for now, Lieutenant."

The Major got to his feet. I stood up and put on my hat and turned to Major Dow.

"Sir, could someone find out if the men in my unit got back?"

Captain Fuller stood up. "We'll look into it, Lieutenant."

I returned to my temporary quarters for some rest. Even though the base doctor had treated my leg, it felt uncomfortable. After my trek to the coast I should not have been surprised.

"Sorry to bother you, sir, but Colonel Armstrong-Smyth would like a word with you."

"Right now?"

"Within the next ten minutes, sir."

"I'll come now."

The corporal escorted me to the Colonel's office. He knocked on the door.

"Yes?" A distinguished voice came from inside the room.

The corporal entered and saluted "Lieutenant Carsell-Brown is waiting outside, sir."

"Thank you – show him in."

I entered and saluted.

"At ease, Lieutenant. Thank you for being prompt."

I removed my hat. "No problem, sir."

"Please, sit down." Colonel Armstrong-Smyth sat down in a large black leather chair – extravagant for this austere time.

He looked at me over his gold horn-rimmed spectacles. "You leave tomorrow morning?"

"Yes sir – early. I catch the train to London then a connection to Glasgow."

"Telephoned your wife?"

"Yes sir, yesterday morning."

"Splendid." He clasped his hands on the metal desk. "The reason why I wanted to speak with you is because we believe the Luftwaffe could be about to launch an attack on Britain."

"Which part, sir?"

"The south of the country, in preparation for an invasion."

"How can I help, sir?"

"Did you spot any German activity along the coast?"

"No – in fact, apart from three German soldiers and a patrol boat, it remained peaceful."

"Due to its close proximity, our Ministry of Defence believes the Germans will launch attacks from the coast. It would not take their aircraft long to fly from France to here. The Royal Air Force has sent certain planes to spy on the area but could not find any evidence."

"What about the resistance, sir?"

"They will keep us informed if there are developments."

"Perhaps Hitler is still on holiday, sir."

He laughed. "Yes, the longer the better. It gives us a chance to rearm and prepare for an invasion."

"Sir, could it be the German unit we encountered had been placed there to monitor RAF activity?"

"It's possible. If we located their airfields, then a series of night raids with Wellington bombers would dent any plans to invade. For a successful invasion, the Germans must have air superiority over Britain."

"Most definitely."

He got out of his chair and stepped forward. "Nevertheless, have a good break and thanks for retrieving an important piece of German hardware."

"My pleasure, sir." I put on my hat and left the room.

"Corporal?" said the Colonel.

He entered. "Yes, sir?"

"Can you ask Captain Cunnington to come in?"

The corporal left the room. "Colonel Armstrong-Smyth will see you now, sir."

"Afternoon, sir." He sat down.

"Alex, I have just spoken with Lieutenant Carsell-Brown. There did not appear to be any activity which involved the Germans on the coast."

"Sir, maybe they will launch an air attack from further inland or even Germany."

"I'm not sure. That would mean more flying time and fuel consumption."

"They would have the advantage of surprise, sir."

"Perhaps, but I can't envisage Goering doing the unexpected."

"We could send out another Lysander to take some more aerial shots."

"Good idea. Just to make sure."

"Sir, the Luftwaffe may wait until Hitler completes his summer vacation!"

"Yes – also Lieutenant Carsell-Brown's view."

"Extraordinary stroke of luck to get our hands on a German decoder, sir."

"Yes, and also a code book. They could prove invaluable. A team of specialists have been assembled to try and find out how the machine operates."

"Military Intelligence didn't waste any time!"

"High priority, Alex – the sooner the better to help the war effort. However, when the Germans realise their machine is missing then they will change all codes."

"Still, it's something to work on, sir."

"Yes, indeed."

"I'll get those photographs taken right away."

"Thanks, Alex."

Captain Cunnington left the room.

"Corporal?"

"Yes, sir?"

"Could you get me the Special Forces section?"

"Major Hart, sir?"

"Yes."

"He won't be back for another two days, sir – on vacation."

"Oh well. No rush – yet!"


As Olivia gazed out of her lounge window, the evening sun had not yet diminished. The weather remained bright, and also the Carsell-Brown family's future. The weight of uncertainty had been lifted from her mind. William, safe and well, soon to return home. Then her trance-like state ended with Philip and Charlotte's arrival.

"Good evening, Charlotte, Philip."

Charlotte gave me a warm hug. "You must be relieved Olivia. The length of time to wait for some news about William."

"It has been difficult and glad it is over. Let me take your jacket and hat, Charlotte."

Philip handed Olivia his hat. Olivia returned to the lounge.

"How did he sound on the telephone?"

"In good spirits, Philip. He can't wait to get home."

"When is he due back, Olivia?" asked Charlotte.

"He departs the Army base tomorrow and will travel to Glasgow by train. I will drive there and collect him at Central Station."

"Did he explain what had happened in France?"

"Yes, Philip. He said a German soldier shot him in the leg, and therefore he could not manage the journey to Dunkirk. Until he became fit enough to escape, a French family gave him refuge."

"How did he escape, Olivia?" asked Charlotte.

"The French Resistance, Charlotte – they assisted him."

"Good for them! I like the French – they stay passionate for a just cause."

"I look forward with anticipation to hear the full story!"

Charlotte looked at her husband. "Philip, I am certain Olivia has told us all we need to know."

"Yes, Charlotte." Philip cleared his throat.

Charlotte put her hand on Olivia's arm. "It is a blessing he got home safe and well."

"As you know, my mother lost father in the last war and she has not recovered from the trauma. I prayed it would not happen to me."

"Olivia, we felt the same way," said Charlotte. "When William returns, it will be a delight for us to reunite."

"I can't wait. Let us go into the garden and have some tea. It is a fine evening."


"Have you used all the petrol rations, Philip? I would like to visit Martha tomorrow."

"Just about – that is why I have to drive home at a slow speed. It consumes less fuel. We could drive to Inverary next week, Charlotte?"

"Fine."

Philip glanced towards Charlotte. "Something on your mind, dear?"

"This war gets me down. Poor Olivia – what she has gone through."

"She has much fortitude, Charlotte."

"Just as well. We all need fortitude given the current situation."

"I suppose if William had been at Dunkirk, he may have been rescued by his own brother!"

Charlotte looked at Philip. "I just feel relieved both William and Geoffrey are still alive. War only serves to disrupt and ruin family life."

"Yes Charlotte, they do. Ah, Docharnea."

"We must get those hedges at each side of the driveway trimmed."

"I'll contact the gardener tomorrow."

Philip drove up the driveway and parked the car beside the coach house.

"Philip, did you put those old items of furniture in the coach house?"

"Yes, even the old ringer. I put it in the upstairs wash closet. I noticed a burnt-out candle on the window ledge."

"Really? When were you previously in the room?"

"Let me think – about five or six weeks ago."

# Chapter 11

## *Family Visit*

"At last, Debbie. We want to get there today if possible!"

"Charlie Carsell-Brown, you are too impatient. Besides, I want to look my best for your aunt."

"Is it far to her house, father?"

"I'm afraid so, son." Charlie started the car and drove off. "This Ford Corsair is a better car to drive than the Anglia."

"Charlie, as long as the car gets us from Granton to Ardrishaig and back. Mind you, I do like the light blue shade of the Corsair."

"Don't worry, Debbie, it's a reliable car." Charlie tapped the dashboard.

"Stop at Graham's newsagent. I'll get something for James to read on the journey." Debbie glanced back. "What comics do you want, James?"

"The *Hotspur* and *Victor* please. Can you also get the *Eagle* and *Valiant*?"

"Anything else?"

"A packet of Mintolas, please."

Charlie stopped the car. "No time for a chat, Debbie!"

"If you insist. Won't be long." She got out and closed the door.

"Why did you get another car, father?"

"This is a faster car, James. It can get us to Ardrishaig in less time than the Anglia."

"Good."

Debbie got into the passenger seat.

"That was quick!"

"I'll be longer next time!"

Charlie smiled.

"Charlie, what route have you decided to take?"

"Head for Glasgow then Crianlarich and on to Inveraray. Ardrishaig is only a short distance from there. It should take us about three and a half hours." He opened the glove compartment. "Where is the AA road map?"

"Here it is father." James held it up.

"Let me have a look at it, James." Charlie studied the road map. "Yes, that appears the best route. I'll leave the map here on the dashboard in case we get lost."

Debbie looked at her husband.

Charlie laughed and turned the ignition. "Only joking!"

Debbie glanced to the left. "James, there is the old Granton railway station."

"Where?" He gazed around.

Debbie pointed. "Back there – we've just passed it."

"It should not have been closed. With more people buying cars, Edinburgh's roads will become congested. The local train service would have been an ideal alternative. It works for Glasgow."

"Charlie, I suppose they also should have kept the trams in operation!"

"Debbie, you never know what the future holds. Trams may become popular again."

She grinned. "Like mens' double-breasted jackets and wide ties?"

"Don't exaggerate, Debbie – they won't return."

"Could we have got the train today, father?"

"The train doesn't go to Ardrishaig, James." Charlie glanced at Debbie. "What magazines did you buy?"

"*Vogue* and *Rolling Stone*."

"Let's have music from my new fitted radio." Charlie leaned forward and turned the left-hand knob.

"Charlie, why did the manufacturers not have one already installed?"

"It would make sense rather than the purchaser arranging the installation. The Americans have a phrase – build a solid customer relationship. Increase product potential and the user will re-buy."

"True." Debbie browsed through her magazine.

"Debbie, did you also get a newspaper?"

"As it has a fashion supplement I bought the *Express*."

"Father, 'The Saint' is on tonight. Will we get back in time to watch it?"

"Maybe. What is the television schedule for tonight, Debbie?"

"Hold on, let me have a look." She put down her magazine, picked up the newspaper and turned a page. "Roger Moore is on at seven o'clock, followed by 'The Prisoner' with Patrick McGoohan. 'The Fugitive' starts at nine and on BBC2, it's a repeat of 'The Forsythe Saga'. Oh, 'Z Cars' is on BBC1 at seven thirty."

"Will David Jansen ever get captured, or the one-armed man found?"

"Charlie, only if the ratings start to drop!"

"You may miss 'The Saint', James, but 'Man in a Suitcase' is on tomorrow night."

"I prefer 'Time Tunnel', father." James turned a page of his comic.

Debbie stared at the radio. "What radio station is that?"

"One of the pirate stations. It could be Radio Caroline? The reception isn't good, but at least we can listen to pop music."

"Will 'The Monkees' be on, father?"

"I'll let you know – just sit back and read your comics."

"That's the first time I have heard this song, Charlie." Debbie turned up the volume.

"Me too! This show is a selection of new releases. Anita Harris sang it – 'Just Loving You'. The previous song also sounded good."

"Who sang it?"

"A group called Procol Harum. The song had a catchy melody."

"And so did 'Puppet on a String' by Sandie Shaw – winning the Eurovision Song Contest last month."

"The Procol Harum song is just as good, if not better. Anything of interest in your *Rolling Stone* magazine?"

"They highlight the forthcoming marriage of Elvis and Priscilla. The Beatles' new album, 'Sergeant Pepper's Lonely Hearts Club Band', is due for release early next month."

"When Englebert kept them off top spot in the charts last month, it must have been a shock to their record company."

"Charlie, there is the unexpected! Can we stop at Crianlarich? I wouldn't mind a cup of tea."

"And a coke please, mother."

Debbie looked at James. "Are you thirsty?"

"Yes."

"What time is Ann expecting us, Charlie?"

"When I spoke to her yesterday, she mentioned between twelve and one o'clock."

Debbie looked at her watch. "Plenty of time."

"We must go to see the new 'Bond' movie; 'You Only Live Twice'. July is the release date. What say you, James?"

"Yes, father."

"Charlie, what about 'In the Heat of the Night'? I have read Rod Steiger is excellent in the film."

"He also gave a good performance in 'Doctor Zhivago', although Omar Sharif received the plaudits."

"What does plaudits mean, father?"

"More money, son."

"In this edition of *Vogue*, it also states he could get an Oscar nomination for his role as a racist law officer."

"Racist?"

"Yes Charlie – he plays the sheriff of a small town in America's Deep South."

"Father?"

"I'll explain later, James."

"The magazine gives a lot of coverage to someone called Dustin Hoffman in a film called 'The Graduate'. This film centres around a younger man and an older woman."

"Interesting. Here we are, Crianlarich."

"That looks like a nice place, Charlie." Debbie pointed.

"It resembles a log cabin."

"It's a tearoom – let's stop."

"A quaint establishment, Charlie."

"And clean. As car ownership increases, it should attract more visitors. The future could prove a blessing for small towns similar to this."

"Did you like that place, James?"

"Yes, the cakes tasted nice."

"What time is it, Charlie?"

"Ten minutes past eleven. We should arrive at Ardrishaig at about twelve thirty."

"At this speed we may get there sooner!"

Charlie smiled.

"Since your uncle passed away, how does Ann spend her time?"

"She runs a charity shop in Ardrishaig. Also the gardens require constant attention."

"The size of that property must be a handful!"

"My aunt has a gardener to take care of the grounds. She just potters around."

"What does 'potter' mean, father?"

Charlie glanced to the back seat. "To move about in an unstressful way."

"What does…?"

"I'll explain later."

"At your uncle's funeral, she looked well, considering the circumstances."

"She is a strong-willed and positive lady. As a young child, she lost her father in the First World War and did not get to know him. Perhaps that made her more independent."

"She also remains a likeable person."

"Must be a family trait, Debbie."

"Together with modesty!" Debbie looked behind. "How are you, young sir?"

"Almost finished my comics."

"Good for you – we shall soon be there."

"James tends to travel well. Given the length of the journey, he hasn't been restless. When my father and mother took me on a journey, I could not sit still."

Debbie smiled. "No comment!"

"Mother, I feel sick."

"Your father spoke too soon."

"I'll stop at this lay-by."

"Do you feel better now James?"

"Yes, mother."

"The sea air from the loch must have helped."

Debbie gazed out the car window. "The view from the road is a joy."

"When we come back it will be on my side!"

Debbie looked at James. "Not be long now. He is as white as a sheet, Charlie."

"Here we are – Dochar."

"Father, is it not Ardrishaig we are going to?"

"Your great-aunt lives a mile from the village."

"Docharnea is on the left – somewhere."

"There, Charlie!" Debbie pointed. "The name of the house is on the gatepost."

Charlie drove the car up the driveway.

"She must have an excellent gardener Charlie. The gardens look impressive. There is Ann! She must have heard the car."

Charlie parked the car and got out. "Good afternoon."

"It's good to see you again, Charlie." His aunt walked towards him.

Debbie came to meet Ann with her son.

"And you too, Deborah."

"Ann, this is James." Debbie put her hands on his shoulders.

Ann bent down. "Hello, young man, how are you?"

"Fine, thank you."

"How old are you now?"

"Eight – nine in December."

Ann turned to Debbie. "Informative and polite."

"Yes, Ann, he can be that!"

"Come inside. Pearl can serve us tea in the lounge – you too, young man."

Debbie looked around the room. "It is stunning! Traditional – the cornice is exceptional."

"The house is now over seventy years old and I like to keep it in the Victorian mould. I must admit it takes a lot of upkeep, but it's worth the time and expense. I will let you see other parts of the house later if you wish, Deborah?"

"I would like that. This property is a complete change from our house. How I adore character. I tell Charlie there is not much to surpass an old traditional house."

Ann smiled. "Wait until the maintenance bills appear Deborah – then you may change your mind!"

"It's a nice house, isn't it? Debbie turned to James.

He nodded.

"Come, let us have a seat." Ann turned to Charlie. "How are your mother and father?"

"They are both well. Father has started to play bowls at a local club. He has tried to get mother interested, but without much success."

"Your mother is the creative indoor type, Charlie. Does she still paint?"

"Yes, she has painted a scene of the Fife coastline. It hangs above the wooden fireplace in our living room"

"She is a talented lady. I advised her twenty years ago to rent a studio and sell her paintings. She can have my coach house for free."

"Too far from Newhaven, Ann."

"Yes – pity though, Charlie. I cannot envisage your parents moving from their home. They have lived in the same house all of their married life."

"They adore that house and it is close to father's office. He has worked there all his life."

"Charlie, loyalty is an invaluable trait."

"Do you use the coach house, Ann?"

"No, Deborah – it has lain dormant for many years. Charlie's grandfather used it to store old furniture. When we moved here, the items got sent to a charity shop – coincidentally, the one I now run!"

James turned to Debbie. "What is a coach house, mother?"

"In Victorian times, many years ago, this property had a person who stayed in the coach house. They did not have cars in those days and the coachman drove a coach with horses."

"How fast would it travel?"

"Adequate for the Victorians, but not for us!" said Charlie.

Ann leaned towards James. "Would you like to look around the coach house?"

"Yes please."

"After tea, I will let James see inside the coach house Deborah. Pearl can take Charlie and yourself around the rest of Docharnea at your leisure. Then we shall go for a bite to eat."

"This is a beautiful setting with the view of Loch Fyne." Debbie looked out of the reception window. "A perfect location."

"When this place opened, Deborah, it was called the Lochside Hotel. I'm not keen on the Seaview Lodge Hotel, but then my sentiments are influenced by the past."

"It is busy – I just managed to get the car parked!"

"Take a brochure, Charlie, we can pass it on to our friends."

Charlie lifted one from a table. "Only one left, it must be a popular place!"

"It is Charlie – even though the prices have been increased. Ah, here comes a waitress."

"Can I help you sir?" The black-outfitted waitress smiled.

"A table for three adults and one child, please."

"Smoking or non-smoking, sir?"

"Non-smoking." Charlie looked at Debbie. "Impressive!"

"Please come this way." The waitress took them to a table in the dining room. She distributed menus. "I will be back soon to take your orders."

"This is a lovely room – comfortable and plush. I like the mint green colour scheme and velvet upholstery." Debbie turned to Charlie. "What do you think?"

"It's a bit different from our local hotel. However, it is also close to the seafront."

"I would imagine it must be picturesque, Charlie."

Debbie laughed. "It could be – if a railway embankment didn't block the view!"

Ann smiled. "Ah, here is the waitress to take our orders." She turned to James. "The strawberry ice cream is delicious!"

His smile became wider.

"An excellent meal, Ann."

"The hotel has a reputation for quality cuisine, Deborah."

"I can tell James enjoyed the food – he ate everything! It is a good idea to have a portion for children."

"Yes Deborah, I agree. Children do not require large portions – it could lead to obesity."

"Father?"

"Tell you later."

"Does the hotel get busy in the evening, Ann?"

"Yes Deborah, especially at weekends. Couples like Charlie and you come here on a regular basis. The hotel uses local and area advertising to promote itself. They adopt a competitive pricing strategy for customers. Hotels have a life cycle and they must re-invent themselves to remain ahead of any rival. The current owners seem to have succeeded. If I am being honest, the Lochside had reached the end of its life cycle."

Charlie looked at Debbie.

"However, I still have a fondness for the Lochside. William proposed to me here in 1936. He asked me to marry him on Christmas Eve."

"How romantic. Charlie proposed to me at Crammond. We had gone for a stroll along the coast. I speculated if he would ever ask!"

Charlie smiled. "Better late than not at all, Debbie!"

"Mm."

"Can I pay at reception?"

"Don't bother, Charlie. I have an account here. Let us return to Docharnea and enjoy the sunshine."

Debbie rolled down her car window. "Phew. It's warmer inside the car than outside!"

"Soon be at Docharnea Deborah."

"It's ideal, the hotel being on your doorstep!"

"I've walked to it on a fine day Charlie. Ah, home. Let us go into the main garden and enjoy the glorious weather."

"Ann, James would like permission to play with his football."

"Of course, Charlie, there is enough space!"

Debbie placed her hand above her eyes. "The view from here is marvellous, Ann. You can see the other side of the loch."

"And on a warm, sunny afternoon like this." Ann glanced at the other side of the garden. "I trust Charlie will manage to keep up with James."

"He should be okay." Debbie cast her gaze around the area. "How many properties are there in Docharnea?"

"There are now eight. I believe Docharnea became the second property built, in 1896. Over time, others followed and the last one being that villa to our left." She pointed. "William's mother and father sold part of the estate to a couple who got a local builder to construct their dream house. Docharnea now consists of three acres."

"It must take a lot of effort to maintain the grounds."

"A local firm carries out any work which requires attention. They just charge a nominal fee for the work undertaken. I believe it is a practice which has been on-going prior to the First World War."

"Do you know why?"

"It has to do with a long-standing goodwill gesture and I am grateful!"

"They have done an excellent job."

"James enjoys being out in the open."

"Charlie struggles to keep up with him! Last month James watched his first football match on television and has wanted to play with a ball ever since."

"The England versus Scotland game at Wembley?"

"Yes, Scotland won by three goals to two."

"I overheard the gardeners discuss the game. They sounded ecstatic!"

Pearl entered the garden and approached Debbie. "Would you like some tea, madam?"

"No thanks."

"And the two footballers?"

"They are fine."

"I am also fine, Pearl, thank you. That is a stylish cream trouser suit, Deborah."

"Charlie accompanied me to Princes Street last month and paid the penalty."

"Your hair is shorter."

"Yes, it's the style for this year. I managed to persuade Charlie to get a new style."

"Combed to the side rather than straight back?"

"Yes. He doesn't need to use hair oil now. However, styles can change."

"The way of life in today's society. When I reached your age, I dressed similar to my mother! Now people like you have distinctive styles – thank goodness for progressive times. Mind you, I am not keen on some television programmes."

"What sort of programmes?"

"Oh, 'Peyton Place' and 'Coronation Street'. I cannot imagine why viewers would want to find out what happens in a street! I feel those type of programmes will one day disappear."

"Unlike transistor radios."

"The couple who stay in the house to our left have a teenage daughter. She carries her transistor everywhere."

"Do you have any holidays planned for this summer?"

"One of my old University friends has invited me down to London in August. Alison hints at how vibrant the city can be and worth a visit. She is also from Ardrishaig and has kept in touch. Her husband is American. When based in England prior to D-Day, she met him in London. He is not an admirer of President Johnson and the war in Vietnam. I suppose being a Republican does not help!"

"Charlie can't envisage an end in sight for that conflict."

"Since the 1950s, it has been in progress. The French fought there with no success and now it is America's turn to try and prevail."

"According to Charlie, the Vietnamese only want their independence – they aren't colonialists."

"My dear, it is the same with Scotland. Some want independence with the discovery of North Sea gas. This could lead to gas and oil production which would result in many jobs being created."

"That should help the economy!"

"It may not be long until the Scottish National Party makes themselves known. Harold Wilson and other members of the government will no doubt monitor developments with eager anticipation." Ann looked towards Charlie. "I believe your husband is in need of a break."

Charlie came across the lawn and sat beside Debbie.

"What is wrong, Charlie?"

"I need a break – I'm tired out!"

Debbie smiled. "Until our vacation – only two months to go."

Charlie shook his head. "Where does he get his energy from? I will need to visit the gym."

Debbie nodded. "Agreed."

"What holiday do you have booked, Deborah?"

"A Spanish holiday. We have booked a package holiday through a travel agency and will fly to the destination. The journey would take too long by car."

"The climate shall be warm."

"Debbie has already started to stock up on sun creams!"

"All of you have fair skin – you will need them. How long for, Deborah?"

"Two weeks. It is a small resort near Barcelona and that is the airport we fly to. In the future, it could be similar to television sets. The price should come down."

"I agree, Charlie. Your grandfather would state that competition is terrific for the consumer. Pricing strategies become customer-focused and goods become affordable which creates more sales. Everybody wins – manufacturer, producer, seller and customer."

Debbie raised her eyebrows. "That philosophy sounds ahead of its time!"

"About thirty years ago, Philip met a businessman who had knowledge about commerce. He gave Philip advice which sounded worthy. Philip recorded the details and I found the document amongst his old possessions. However, the passage of time has made it illegible."

"Fascinating! What do you think, Debbie?"

"The concept makes sense."

"Companies like to have slogans and terminology Debbie – what would they call this?"

"Ingenious!"

"Deborah, I believe James has used all of his energy."

"He may sleep all the way home to Edinburgh!"

James came over to the table.

Debbie smiled. "Finished?"

"Yes, mother." James sat down.

"Ah, here comes Pearl with cold orange drinks."

She placed the four drinks on the white metal table.

Charlie picked up one and drank it. "Ah, that's better!" He shook the glass and the ice clinked.

His aunt smiled. "How long will it take to drive home, Charlie?"

"We should be back between six and seven o'clock."

"It's been delightful to see you all and you must come again soon."

Debbie looked at Charlie. "Our son is about to fall asleep."

Charlie wound down the car window.

Ann stood next to the Corsair. "It has been good to see both of you again." She looked towards the back seat. "And a pleasure to meet you James. He is well behaved, Deborah. I hope to see you in the future, James."

James smiled.

"Safe journey home." Ann waved.

Charlie turned the ignition key and drove off.

"Did you enjoy your visit, James?"

"Yes, mother."

"It is a gorgeous house, Charlie."

"Yes, and also the grounds which surround it. The gardeners will be kept busy."

"Did you like the coach house, James?" Debbie turned around. "Charlie, James has fallen asleep!"

"I'm not surprised – too much football."

He looks peaceful in his white ladybird top and shorts."

"Ideal for today."

Debbie looked over to Charlie. "I am curious. Why do you call your aunt 'Ann'? Your mother and father call her Olivia."

"When I first met her as a toddler, I could not pronounce Olivia properly, therefore she asked me to call her Ann. That is her middle name. It has just stuck with me."

"As your aunt discussed those business terms, I became intrigued."

"Competitive pricing strategies, a product life cycle and being customer-focused."

"She also mentioned to me the process of market segmentation, target marketing and product positioning."

"Debbie, you and I are sales people – have you heard of those concepts? I understand what a product and a market is, but the others are unknown to me! My boss' interpretation of being customer-focused is – get within close proximity of the person you sell to."

"Likewise – maybe your grandfather met a foreigner all those years ago."

"I'll bet he and my grandmother would have a tale to tell about that certain individual."

"Pick his brains, impress our Heads of Department and get promoted!"

"If only. Is James still fast asleep?"

Debbie looked back. "Yes, lying across the rear seat."

"We should be home in about a couple of hours. Not as many cars tended to travel east today."

"Charlie, it is a pity James did not meet your uncle."

"I know."

"As your uncle and aunt had no children, James may have been a welcome distraction! I observed how Ann warmed to him."

"She doesn't have to play football with him!"

"You know what I mean."

Charlie nodded.

"You did not tell me why your uncle got decorated in the last war."

"Nobody in the family ever mentioned why! I asked father, but all he would say is that it was for gallantry."

"That's a bit vague! I would have presumed your father knew."

"Me also. I believe his award had been associated with a secret type of operation. It happened at the start of the war. He received a leg injury which prevented him from further active service."

"Do you think that contributed to his fatal illness?"

"After that injury, he could not even manage a brisk walk! In fact, father revealed my uncle's ability to walk became impaired."

"He could have lost his leg. In the war, a lot of soldiers got killed in France. My friend Janie lost her father and uncle."

"My aunt confided with mother that she felt my uncle had received an extension on his life. Instead of losing him in the war, they shared many years together. Also Debbie, they had not long been married."

"Look Charlie!" Debbie pointed. "That chap's car has broken down."

"I'll pull into the side of the road and ask if he requires any assistance."

"Charlie, he looks similar to Paul McCartney!"

"Paul McCartney would not drive the same type of car as me, Debbie! His car would be a bit more exclusive. Won't be long." Charlie got out of his car. "Hi, do you need any help?"

"Hi there, it's the wheel. I had a puncture and lost one of the nuts for the spare."

"I can give you a nut from my spare wheel."

"Won't you need it for your car?"

"I'll get a replacement from my car dealer. We can work it out."

"Thanks mate."

Charlie opened the boot of his car and got the spare part. He handed it over. "Here you are. I'll give you a hand."

"Thanks."

"Are you on holiday?"

"I viewed a property down at the Mull of Kintyre. I came up from London yesterday and now on my way back to the airport, near Glasgow."

"That must have been a long and eventful journey driving around the Mull of Kintyre?"

"It's been like a magical mystery tour – here, there and everywhere!"

Charlie tightened the last nut. "That's it, you'll get back to the airport now."

"Thanks mate, we'll just let it be."

Debbie got out the car. "Is everything all right?"

"This is Debbie, my wife."

"Hello, pleased to meet you. I'm James."

"That is our son's name."

"Thanks for the assistance. I'll now be able to catch my flight." He got into his car, waved and drove away

"Well Debbie, back to this long and winding road! Told you it could not be Paul McCartney."

"He did speak with a Liverpudlian accent. Did he say why he came to visit Argyll?"

"Viewing a property at the Mull of Kintyre."

Debbie got into the car. "Oh, you have awakened, young sir!"

"I heard voices."

Charlie got in and started the car. "Mother believes she spotted one of the 'Beatles' at the side of the road."

"He did look and talk the same, Charlie." Debbie started to read a magazine. "Wait a minute, this article in *Rolling Stone* refers to a James Paul McCartney – look, it's him!" She pointed to a photograph.

"I suppose his Corsair may have been a rented car."

"Just another day tripper, Charlie. It was a quick hello, goodbye."

"Just another day."

"Father, will we get back before eight o'clock?"

"Yes, no problem."

"Good. I'll be able to watch 'The Prisoner' after all."

"Hold on young sir, 'The Forsythe Saga' is also on! Debbie looked at Charlie. "Did you mow your parent's lawn yesterday?"

"No, I didn't have time. I should have known better than make a promise. I'll drop James and you off, and then visit mother and father. I should manage to get their lawn cut before dusk."

"Father, can you turn on the radio?"

Charlie switched it on. "There."

"Charlie, there is that song again."

"The one by Anita Harris?"

Debbie nodded. "It hasn't been discussed on Juke Box Jury."

"Perhaps the song did not appeal to David Jacobs. Do you like this song James?"

"Yes."

Charlie sighed. "Edinburgh at last."

"It appears quicker on the return journey, Charlie."

"I shouldn't be too long." Charlie stopped the car.

"See you later." Debbie got out the car.

"Bye, father." James jumped out.

"James, no disagreements over what television programme to watch!"

"Yes father." James closed the door.


"Hi mother, we got back early from Ardrishaig. Before it gets dark, I'll cut the grass."

"Will you have enough time?"

"Yes, no problem. Where is father?"

"Across at the bowling club."

"I thought he had a sore back."

"He has gone to watch, not play."

"Well, it is a fine evening." Charlie took the mower into the garden and cut the grass.

Emily came into the garden. "Finished already, Charlie?"

"The grass had not grown as quick this time." He emptied the lawn mower bucket into a black refuse bag.

"Charlie, you have a stain on your shirt."

He wiped his brow. "I got it changing a car wheel on the way home. Debbie's soap powder will remove the stain."

Emily stood on the lawn and took a deep breath. "Ah, the smell of freshly cut grass. Come inside, Charlie, I have made herbal tea."

Charlie sat on the couch.

Emily handed him a full cup. "You look thirsty!" She sat on a chair.

"Thanks mother."

"How is Olivia?"

"She looks well."

"Does she still run a charity shop?"

Charlie took a drink of tea. "Yes, she receives a lot of donations from near and far afield. She also strikes me as being a shrewd businesswoman!"

"Oh, why?" Emily laid down a plate of blueberry cookies onto a glass table.

"She discussed some impressive business techniques with me and Debbie."

"Olivia could have learned them from your grandfather. Philip became knowledgeable in business practices. He met a stranger and this person passed on his expertise."

Charlie picked up a cookie. "Mother, did grandfather talk about him – who he was, where he came from?" Charlie bit the cookie.

"He came from Edinburgh of all places! Do you like my homemade cookies?"

Charlie nodded. "Edinburgh? Why would he go to Ardrishaig? It is on the other side of the country and just a small village."

"Your father and I did not meet him but could have."

"What happened?"

"When your father lived at Docharnea, a woman called Nancy carried out housekeeping duties. Not long before the outbreak of the last war she passed away. Just prior to the funeral you became unwell, and therefore we did not go. The stranger attended the funeral."

"Did he know Nancy?"

"I presume so – maybe your father can enlighten you." Emily looked out the window. "Speak of the devil, he is walking up the garden path."

Geoffrey opened the door and took off his jacket.

"Hello father."

"Well done, the lawn looks perfect."

"Thanks."

"Did you all enjoy your trip to Docharnea?"

"Yes, very much, father."

"How is Olivia?"

"Very well. She sends her best wishes."

"Where are Deborah and James?"

Charlie glanced at his watch. "In discussion over what television programme to watch!"

Geoffrey sighed and sat on his armchair. "How did families ever survive without television?"

Emily smiled. "They attended bowling clubs, Geoffrey!"

"Emily, there is not much enjoyment in watching – I would rather dig up the garden weeds!"

"Charlie and I were discussing when he became ill just prior to Nancy's funeral."

"Just after William and Olivia got married?"

"Yes. Can you remember the name of the person your father and mother met from Edinburgh?"

Geoffrey touched his chin.

"When we visited them the following Christmas, I seem to recall they spoke about him."

"His name, James – James Carlisle. Same as the town."

"Father, how did he know Nancy?"

"I'm uncertain of his connection. Maybe he could have been the coachman who travelled through time!"

Charlie stared. "Who?"

"Your father is being mischievous, Charlie."

"Tell me more, father – this intrigues me."

"Nancy told me and William of a coachman who once lived at Docharnea. When families started to use cars, a coachman no longer had a role and his services dispersed with. As boys, your uncle and I played in the disused coach house. We found a book by H.G. Wells."

"Don't tell me, father – *The Time Machine*?"

Geoffrey nodded. "We said to our friends, the coachman travels through time and periodically returns to the coach house."

Emily tutted. "Geoffrey!"

"On a serious note, Nancy would often talk about the original coachman who worked at Docharnea but left after a short time. He came back years later but soon departed once more."

"He doesn't sound the dependable type."

Geoffrey smiled. "I agree, Charlie. However I got the impression Nancy hoped one day he would again return. But it can't be the same person who attended her funeral."

"Why not, father?"

"The coachman in 1896 would be around thirty years old."

"Why that age?" Charlie drank his cup of herbal tea.

"In those times, a coachman had to accumulate an abundance of experience with horses, coach maintenance and other relevant duties. When my mother and father met James Carlisle in 1938, he was aged around forty. I recall him being described by mother."

"You are correct – it can't be the same person. The coachman would have been around seventy years old." Charlie placed the white cup into the matching saucer.

"Besides, a Victorian coachman would be unaware of advanced business practices."

"That's true, father."

Emily sat back on her chair. "Unless, of course, he *was* a time traveller."

# Chapter 12

## *The Summer of Love*

I opened my eyes and looked around the room. Items of furniture from 1940 had gone. As the sun shone through the window, the room got brighter. I noticed a bag in a corner – the one I had left behind in 1938! Maybe the current owner of Docharnea could find a use for the bag's contents of old clothes.

I walked towards the window and looked out to see if the view had altered. There now stood three small fruit trees in front of the coach house. The dark plums and green apples added character to the garden. Some plums had already fallen onto the short grass therefore this time of year could be late summer. The cars, which passed by on the road, had light colours and streamlined chassis.

I opened the closet to find out if there had been anything added, finding only one difference – my coachman's outfit had been cleaned and pressed. I walked down the stairs and found the door locked. I unlocked it with my own key and ventured into a different courtyard. It had now been covered with small white stone chippings. Those previous large, grey stones ensured regular aches on my feet! There appeared to be no activity and I speculated on who now lived there. I turned and gazed at the loch. Whilst I moved through time, this view never changed. On this occasion, the clear blue sky and bright sun enhanced the green hills and crystal water. The trees and hedges around the property had fully matured and complimented the scenic outlook.

"Can I help you?"

My tranquil state of mind was shattered. I turned around. There stood a small, but imposing woman with a stern face and her arms folded.

"Lost your tongue?"

"Is Mrs Carsell-Brown at home?"

"Why?"

"I have an appointment with her."

"Strange, she did not mention it to me. Who are you?" She moved closer.

"I am James Carlisle."

"How did you get into the property?"

This could be interpreted as an interrogation, and in my future home! "I walked up the driveway."

"I did not see you."

"I'm a quick walker." The look on her face conveyed to me a feeling of suspicion. "Mrs Carsell-Brown is a distant relative. I found myself in this part of the country and wanted to pay a visit. I called her. "

"When?"

"Last week." This woman did not appear convinced.

"Mrs Carlisle, Mrs Carsell-Brown must have forgotten. She is on holiday."

"That is a pity. Who are you, if I may ask?"

"You may."

"Are you the maid?"

"No, the housekeeper – I'm in charge."

Déjà vu again – 'rule the roost' sprung to mind! "I'll be off then. Nice to have met you."

"Goodbye."

I walked down the driveway, looked round and gave her a polite wave. No response. I turned onto the main road. My goodness – a bus stop! I stood in amazement. Then a red, single-decker bus approached and slowed down. It had changed some from 1940. I hope this period of time would be prior to 1971. Decimalisation came into force in this year and I only had old coinage. I got on the bus and took a window seat. The dark, uniformed lady conductor appeared.

"Yes sir, to where?"

"A single to Ardrishaig, please."

"Two pennies, sir."

I gave her a three penny piece. "How often does the bus travel to Ardrishaig?"

She handed me a penny and a ticket. "Once every hour sir – here is a copy of the timetable."

Well, customer service was alive in this era, but what year? I looked at the timetable – 1967. The bus soon arrived in the village, and I got off at the main street.

I went into a newsagent to get a newspaper and checked the date – the third of August, 1967. From my youth I remembered that this year had a traditional summer. But why had I travelled to this particular time? My parents and I had visited Olivia only a few months earlier. The street looked brighter and vibrant. People smiled – a welcome change from my previous visitation! Another observation concerned the appearance of branded carrier bags advertising particular local outlets. I sensed from some glances that my current suit may now be out of fashion. I headed for the same tailor's shop frequented in the past.

The shop remained in its same location but now had a classic burgundy facade with two large windows. This allowed passers-by to gaze at clothes displayed inside the shop. As I entered, a gentleman left with a large branded carrier bag. The interior consisted of light décor and bright ceiling spotlights. I browsed around the various displays. My perception of this establishment was one of quality and freshness.

"Can I help you, sir?"

A lady sales assistant in a menswear retailer? That *was* progressive for Ardrishaig in 1967! Around thirty and well-groomed, she wore a smart, but casual red top with black trousers. "I require a new suit."

"Something with thinner lapels and trousers not as wide, sir?"

I nodded in agreement.

She presented to me a selection of materials, which contrasted in colour and quality.

I turned to her. "Which of these would you suggest?" I showed her four samples.

She pointed with her long red fingernail. "That one, sir – it will look perfect." She touched it.

"Excellent quality."

"When could the suit be ready?" In the sixties, made to measure suits prevailed.

"About sixteen days, but there is a similar one already made up."

"That is a coincidence!"

"We keep a collection of ready-made suits for customers who do not wish to wait."

"How astute." I tried on a light blue suit and looked in the mirror.

"A perfect fit, sir." She stood back.

"How much?"

"As the suit had been ready-made, I will discount the price twenty per cent. It will cost you seven pounds and ten shillings."

"Fine, I'll take it."

"Would you like a shirt and tie to complement that lovely suit?"

Definitely an astute sales person. "Any suggestions?"

She led me to another part of the shop with a shirt and tie display. "How about this, sir?"

What, a matching floral tie and shirt – no chance! She noted my negative expression.

"This is the latest trend in shirt and tie fashion."

"I don't care."

"Something more conservative, sir? How about this?"

"Better. I like that." I elected for a crisp white shirt and an appropriate tie which matched my suit.

The sales lady then took me past the footwear section. I could smell the leather. I stopped and looked at my shoes, which had been worn since 1896!

She held a shoe in her hand. "This style has become fashionable and popular with gentlemen like yourself."

I studied it, sat down and tried on the pair for suitability.

"I hope the shoes feel as good as they look. They are today's special promotion."

"Promotion?"

"A price discount of ten per cent, sir."

"I will also take them." I accompanied her to the counter.

"Cash or cheque, sir?"

"Cash." I gave her two ten pound notes.

She looked at them for several seconds.

Yes, they were old – twenty seven years! I received four pounds and eighteen shillings in change.

"Thank you, sir – please accept this promotional voucher. When you visit us again it entitles you to a discount of fifteen per cent. Please can you also fill in this customer research questionnaire – I would appreciate your comments. You can return it at your convenience." She put my purchases, cash receipt and questionnaire inside the branded carrier bag with the shop logo.

As I left the shop, another customer entered. I had a near-full carrier bag and a near-empty wallet! The lady displayed business acumen ahead of this time. I would not be surprised if a customer credit facility would be soon introduced – special rates for loyal customers.

I looked down the main street and recalled when horses and coaches rumbled over a disjointed, muddy surface. Now cars, vans and an occasional bus motor on a smooth grey tarmac road. At least there should not be any runaway cars! Still, the horse and coach had portrayed a certain sophistication and style in that bygone era.

After a few minutes I approached the office of Macmillan Solicitors. The exterior had at last changed, with gold sign writing on a dark blue background. The stonework had been cleaned, and a bright but sober fascia emerged. I looked through a window and spotted two young ladies at their typewriters. Both had short, dark hair and pastel coloured blouses. The younger of the two got up and walked towards a tray which contained cups, ingredients and a kettle. No doubt in a few years, a beverage-making machine might appear.

Further along the street appeared a new outlet. This stood where the grocer's shop had once been located. I entered and found an enlarged self-service supermarket. Inside, I found a wide variety of tinned, packaged and frozen food products on display. An in-store tasting of a new exclusive pate was proving popular, given the large number of customers wishing to try it. The buy one and get another for free added to the appeal. I tried a piece – the pate tasted delicious. I sampled another and then made for the confectionery section where I spotted a Tiffin chocolate raisin biscuit bar. I had not purchased one for years. I grabbed a bar and then joined the checkout queue. Whilst there, I overheard a sales assistant put forward a question to a customer.

"Would you be interested in a loyalty membership, madam?"

After she explained many benefits, the shopper agreed and another member of the dark green uniformed staff completed the process.

"That will be sixpence, sir."

I handed over a sixpenny piece.

"Would you like a small carrier bag, sir?"

"No thanks." Carrier bags matched the logo and colour of staff uniforms. I picked up the chocolate bar with its white and red wrapper.

"Your receipt, sir." She smiled and handed it to me.

As I left, a group of teenagers walked past me in their light summer shirts and blue jeans. One of them carried a transistor radio in a brown case. A song about going to San Francisco could be heard. Following my journeys, it can seem 'topsy-turvy' to observe guys with longer hair and girls with shorter hair! How hairstyles tend to alter over seventy years. But then, I had witnessed this in a matter of months.

I next came across a hairdresser's salon. The clean and bright façade looked smart; thus I elected to try their service. Also, I needed a trim. Inside, I observed a male and female member of staff at work. All the staff wore black compatible outfits. I could hear current pop music over the client chatter and hair dryers.

A young blonde female came up to me. "Do you have an appointment, sir?"

"I've just arrived in the village on holiday."

"Can you wait for a short while?"

I observed three other waiting customers, but nodded in agreement.

"Please take a seat. I'll put your carrier bag in a safe place."

"Thanks." I handed it to her.

"Would you like a tea or coffee, a magazine to read?"

"White coffee would be fine."

I soon got taken and shampooed, and the female stylist went to work on my hair. Before she was finished, I managed to hear one side of 'Sergeant Pepper'. The stylist brushed of loose cuttings and helped me put on my jacket. I could still smell the apple concentrate shampoo. I paid my five shillings to the receptionist and was handed a voucher.

"If you recommend a friend to our salon then you shall receive a twenty five per cent discount on your next visit."

"Splendid!" I handed over a tip and departed the busy salon. Someone had injected the business community in this remote village with a marketing philosophy. The tailor, grocer and now the barber. I hoped the midges didn't like apples!

I noticed a charity shop on the other side of the street. I presumed this could be the shop run by Olivia. I crossed over and went into the shop. A variety of people browsed around the displays, young, old, male and female. The bric-a-brac, items of furniture and various articles of clothes had been sectioned and well presented. Clothes had been put on appropriate hangers with separate gents and ladies rails. I spotted a nice sky blue casual shirt. Bric-a-brac and furniture had individual displays. I also observed a selection of jewellery and books. The confectionery counter which sold jars of toffee, tablet bars and chocolate cakes, had personal appeal. My taste buds began to ignite.

"Can I help you?"

I turned around. "Your confectionery display entices me."

"Thank you. The lady responsible for display design is not here just now. Can I give you one of our business cards?"

I took the card. "Do you receive many donations?"

"Oh, yes. The manageress is a member of the local Rotary Club and also visits companies within the district. We have our own newsletter distributed by the staff and volunteers. You can take one from this pile on the counter. We keep a supply in the shop."

I wanted to ask if they had considered a website. "How many work here?"

"Five – the manageress, myself and three volunteers. I am a neighbour of the lady who runs the shop."

I have met this lady. "Do you have a daughter?"

"Yes – Abigail."

"You may have met one of my relatives many years ago. He often paid a visit to Charlotte and Philip Carsell-Brown."

"Yes, I remember. I thought you looked familiar. Was it your father who visited?"

"No, a close relative. Anyway, I must dash."

"Are you here on vacation?"

"Yes, for a short time. The summer weather here has been superb."

"When Olivia returns, I will tell her you called. What is your name?"

"James. Before I go, how much for a gents' shirt?"

"Which one?"

I took a shirt off the rail.

"To you, five shillings."

"Splendid." I paid the 'bargain' amount.

The lady folded the shirt and popped it into a white carrier bag. She handed it to me. "Have a pleasant day."

On the opposite street corner, another new establishment had been put in place, an authentic milk bar with neon signs. The downtrodden shoe repair shop had been turned into a trendy outlet for young people. I walked up to it. The glass windows from floor to ceiling did not allow customer privacy! From the pavement I could see a list of milk-orientated soft drinks. I now felt thirsty. I could hear music from a jukebox. Live for the present, and make the most of this facility – McDonalds was a long way off.

I then arrived at a familiar place visited by me over the decades. The Grey Gull Inn still had the same name and traditional exterior. I entered the doorway and found myself in a spacious reception area. A longer reception desk, additional seating arrangements and a brighter hallway now greeted guests. A lady arrived with a nice smile.

"Good afternoon, sir, may I help you?"

"I would like a room for a few days."

She looked at a register book and turned the pages back then forward. "Can't find a vacant room, sir – we are busy in the holiday season."

"I have been a customer for a number of years."

The lady looked up. "How long?"

More than half a century! "A while."

She smiled and scrutinised the register book. "Ah, here we are – a single room on the second floor."

"Splendid."

"Just sign the register, sir, and here is your room key."

I signed my name. "Thanks."

"You're welcome, sir."

I proceeded up to the second floor and entered my room. It had dark wooden furniture and cream soft furnishings. The modern white private bathroom sparkled. A small colour television sat on a stand in a corner of the room. A fresh bowl of fruit had been placed on a small table. I would have the orange later. The window looked onto the rear-landscaped garden of the hotel. I opened it and listened to the birds tweet in harmony. I went over to the wardrobe and hung up my new garments. Time for refreshment.

I handed in my key at reception and went through to the bar, a place I had first experienced a lifetime ago! It now had a polished wooden floor and leather upholstery compatible with the dark coloured furniture. The bar portrayed a traditional ambience. On the counter stood well-polished brass beer fonts, and behind it lay glass cabinets for chilled products. The male and female bar personnel wore similar black and white attire. I noticed a selection of foreign beers on display from America, Germany and Sweden. I waited at the congested bar for service.

A bar person eventually came forward. "Sorry for the delay, sir – what will it be?"

"A glass of lager please."

"Which type would you prefer – foreign or Scottish?"

I pointed to my usual Scottish beer.

"Certainly sir." The bar person reached for a glass and filled it.

I looked at my watch and noted the time – three o'clock. Bars in the sixties and seventies would have had their doors closed thirty minutes ago!

The bar person put my drink on the counter. "The inn is open from eleven in the morning until eleven at night. We have an all-day license." He pointed to a sign on a wall.

*That explained it.* I paid for my drink and found a spare seat. I marvelled at the 'metamorphoses of this Argyll village. Businesses had gone from austerity to prosperity and well ahead of the times. However, the prices appeared higher for this era than normal but customers would not complain if the service was comparable. With regard to customers, I could hear a mix of foreign accents in my vicinity. The cool lager quenched my thirst on this hot summer's day and it did not take long to consume. As I took my empty glass to the counter, I realised the usual smell of tobacco smoke did not exist.

"Is there a ban on smoking?"

"A trial period, sir," said the bar person. "Smoking is prohibited inside the majority of the district's licensed premises."

"And the exception?"

"Hotels. They have introduced a part ban."

"Part?"

"Smoking and non-smoking areas exist within dining rooms. Otherwise the ban applies."

That was advancement for this era! "The ban has not affected business?"

"Look around you, sir – we're busy." The bar person served another customer.

I went to reception for my key. As nobody appeared, I had a seat and browsed through one of the hotel's brochures on display. This particular one highlighted local attractions and businesses within the village.

"Mr Carlisle?"

I looked up. At last, the receptionist.

"Since I met you twenty seven years ago, you haven't changed." She smiled. "Apart from your hair – it looks shorter."

She would have been in her mid-thirties; therefore, when I met her, the lady must have been a child.

"I am Abbie Anderson. I was with my mother. You spoke to her outside one of the properties in Dochar."

She had a good memory. "That is correct – I remember you." To me, this had happened in the last few weeks. It had been a strange, but pleasant,, experience to meet her – that of a nice mature lady.

"You must reveal to me the secret of how not to age."

"It's a long story. If I tell you it must remain a secret," I smiled.

"You have my word."

"Do you have any plans for this evening?"

"Yes I do, but I can cancel them."

"I'll meet you at the Lochside Hotel around seven."

"Fine, but it has now been renamed the Seaview Lodge Hotel."

"Has it? See you later."

She gave me my room key.

I walked upstairs. Lochside sounded better.

I waited inside the Seaview Lodge Hotel entrance. This 'arrangement' gave me an opportunity to wear my new suit. At a nearby information desk lay brochures for weekend breaks, business facilities and accommodation. The hotel looked modern and affluent due to its makeover. The exterior had been redesigned and cleaned with spotlights around the perimeter. When darkness arrived it must have looked impressive. I peeked into the dining room, lounge and cocktail bars. The new interior decor, furniture, fixtures and fittings elevated the establishment to an exclusive status.

A member of staff walked past and then stopped. "Can I help you, sir?"

"I am waiting for someone." I glanced at the reception wall clock. "Is it correct?"

"I believe it could be five minutes fast, sir." He walked on.

That made it ten past seven. I heard a car pull into the car park and looked through the glass doors. At last! Abigail looked stylish and attractive in a short black dress. I opened the door.

"Have you been here long?"

"No, I have just arrived." Twenty five minutes ago.

We went into the cocktail bar and ordered drinks. We took a seat, and the waiter brought over our order on a silver tray.

"Are you having something to eat, sir?"

I nodded.

"Smoking or non-smoking area, sir?"

"Non-smoking."

"I will bring you menus."

"Thanks."

"Tell me, Mr Carlisle, what period are you from?"

I smiled and sipped my liqueur brandy.

"I know you have an ability to move through time. No pretences!"

I put down my glass on the table. "Take a guess." I would play along.

"I suspect the future, but I am not sure of what date – later this century?" She sipped her tonic water.

I moved my head forward. "I travelled back from springtime in the new Millennium."

She lowered her glass. "Do you have a machine?"

I gave her a wide smile. "Similar to H.G. Wells'?"

"No need to smile – you know what I mean! How does it happen? How do you travel?"

I looked around the vicinity. "I promise to explain later."

"Don't worry, Mr Time Traveller, I won't tell."

"Being able to travel in time can only happen at a particular place."

"And where is that?"

"Can't we discuss this after dinner?"

"No!"

"Inside the Docharnea coach house. I stand in a certain part of the coachman's quarters, close my eyes and then arrive in another time."

"What, just like that?" She sat back on her seat.

"I didn't think you would believe me."

"What is your connection with Docharnea?"

"In the future, I own the property."

"Are you aware of what time period you will arrive at?"

"No – I have no control of when I will end up." I took another sip of my drink. Surely she doesn't believe me.

"How far have you travelled back?"

"1896 – the year Docharnea was built. Then 1912, 1938 and 1940."

"Is there a connection between all of those dates?"

*She was persistent!* "I believe so. Any family who stayed at Docharnea in those dates suffered trauma through the loss of a loved one. My existence in those years alters events and prevents any tragedy."

"A guardian angel – how extraordinary! Why have you arrived in 1967?"

"I am not sure."

Abbie appeared nonchalant.

"You don't seem surprised with regard to my revelation."

"I can tell you are being truthful. I perceive an honest person – why would you make up a story like that? Nobody would believe it!"

That's true.

She consumed most of her drink. "Besides, I've met you twice in the distant past."

The waiter appeared "Your table is ready, sir."


"A delicious meal, far better than twenty seven years ago!"

Abbie smiled. "There are many other questions I want to ask you, about the past and the future."

"There are some questions I also want to ask, Ms Anderson. What has happened to Ardrishaig? The commercial transformation is an economic model for society! Businesses promote their goods and services with effectiveness. Retail outlets are busy and the area represents a prosperous location."

"An excellent local community spirit exists. The local bank and building society have made funds available to develop enterprise."

"They should be applauded! I have noticed the techniques used in the shops are unique for this period in time."

"Unusual?"

"Promotional methods, customer service, environmental aspects, shop layouts and décor."

"That could be the reason why members from other Chambers of Commerce have visited our village."

"When did this change occur?"

"The late fifties."

I cried, "The late fifties!" I sat back on my chair.

"Yes. Since then all the businesses in the main street have been in place. Some were upgraded, similar to Ally's place."

"Ally? Who is he?"

"Alison! The person who sold you that nice suit!"

*Interesting.*

"The record shop at the end of the street became the last business to start up."

"In what year did it open?"

"1960. Adam Faith performed the ceremony. Whilst on a tour of Scotland with his band in 1964, Billy J. Kramer made a personal appearance."

"Who is next – the Beatles?"

"Well, one of our guests said they had seen Paul McCartney in Argyll a few months ago."

"I'm intrigued by what has happened with the local business community. When and how did this 'revolution' start?"

"1958. Philip Carsell-Brown contacted local businesses to start a member's club. This would serve the purpose to help each other and generate additional income. He also put forward ideas on how to develop a business. Until a certain level of standard had been achieved, he would persevere with each of them. When he became ill, his son William took over and carried on Philip's good work. When William had to stop working, his wife Olivia carried on the role."

"My goodness."

"We have a lot to thank them for. You've gone pale!"

"I'll be fine." I looked at my watch. "Does this establishment also remain open until eleven?"

"All local establishments which serve food now have a special license for a six month trial period."

The waiter arrived with our coffees.

"Thank you." I took a sip. "Do you stay with your mother?"

"For the time being. My husband and I separated ten months ago. My mother's house is large enough for both of us." She smiled.

"Splendid. What kind of music do you listen to?"

"Most types. As a teenager, Bing Crosby, Perry Como, Vic Damone or Doris Day. I like the Beatles, Rolling Stones and Manfred Mann – but their lead singer has left the band."

"Paul Jones?"

"Yes. Oh I also like Tom Jones – he's cool."

Cool? Even the terminology was ahead of its time!

"Any American artists?"

"The Beach Boys – I enjoy their distinctive type of music. Jimi Hendrix is also unique."

I agree. "The Monkees?"

"Not particularly."

"Tamla Motown?" That got a reaction.

"Yes – why?"

"There is a concert at the Apollo in Glasgow this weekend. A portfolio of their artists will perform hit records."

"Which ones?"

"I wrote them down." I took out a piece of paper from my inside pocket. "The Supremes, Little Stevie Wonder, the Four Tops and Martha with her Vandellas."

"Do you have tickets?"

"It's pay at the door. I may even tell you what becomes of them in the future!"

She smiled and drank her coffee. I finished mine.

"Can I give you a lift back to the inn?"

"It's a fine evening – I will just walk back."

Abbie got up. "I'll get you in reception."

I settled the bill and waited. After a while she emerged from the ladies room. Her long hair had been brushed back. I walked her to a small red Mini.

She kissed me on the cheek, got into her car and wound down the window. "Thanks for a nice evening. See you later, Mr Time Traveller. Don't vanish until after the concert!" She waved and drove off.

As I walked back to the inn, it surprised me that this lady believed my story. After all, it was a far-fetched one! However, what had happened to retailers I visited could not be judged as fiction. In 1938, I had advised Philip on the concept of marketing and its techniques. He asked me to write them down and elaborate. After those discussions, he now had the fundamentals, practices and strategic aims of marketing at his disposal. It would appear my great-grandfather got his timing right for their introduction and subsequent regeneration of Ardrishaig's local economy – the late fifties.

Prime Minister Harold Macmillan said at the time, "you have never had it so good!" As I say, marketing makes success.


At midday, I ventured to the record shop. An opportunity to hear original music from this generation beckoned. Most record outlets in the sixties and seventies had booths which let customers listen to records at their leisure. If the customer liked what they heard, then a purchase could ensue. I hoped this facility would exist in this Ardrishaig retailer. I entered the shop and did not experience disappointment. It contained two booths on one side of the outlet. However, both of them had a prospective purchaser. I gazed at the photographs of current pop artists on the walls. Interesting – since 1964, Billy J. Kramer and the Dakotas had not been taken down.

I approached the shop counter. The young sales assistant came forward. I looked at the booths.

"You will have to wait, sir – should be just a few minutes."

"Excellent."

"What artist do you want to hear?"

"The Bee Gees."

"Are they British?"

"I believe they are."

"I've not heard of them. The B – jeans?"

"The Bee Gees – they are a group."

"The record could be among the new released records which arrived on Monday. I'll just check."

She looked through a pile of records on the counter. "Here we are – 'Massachusetts' by the Bee Gees. Booth number one is now available."

I entered the booth and put on the headphones. I sniffed the air – the previous occupant must have splashed on too much Old Spice. I listened to the new release several times and then vacated the booth. *Ah, fresh air!* I returned to the counter.

"Thanks."

"Do you want to buy the record, sir?" The sales assistant held it in her hand.

"Undecided – I may come back later."

"See you, then."

In another five weeks, that record would top the charts. It would become one of many in a successful career which spanned four decades.

Whilst on my way back to the inn, I heard an assortment of foreign accents. Those voices originated from the continent. I felt this enhanced the village holiday atmosphere and added style to the summer scene. I entered the reception area.

"There is a letter for you, Mr Carlisle," said the owner. He handed it to me.

I opened the letter.

*'James, I shall meet you here on Saturday at three o'clock. Abbie.'*

Saturday soon arrived and I looked forward to seeing the Motown stars perform live – one distinct benefit of travelling back in time! To pass the early afternoon, I watched

'Grandstand' in my room. At a quarter to three, I went downstairs and handed my key into reception. It was another sunny and warm day; therefore I waited outside. A small bright red car drew up close to where I stood.

"Get in, then!"

I smiled, opened the passenger door and got in. "You're five minutes late." I pointed to my watch and rolled down the window.

She glanced my way. "That's an old watch."

Correct – three decades! "Quality lasts."

"Did you purchase it on your travels?"

I nodded.

She raised her eyebrows. "Nice shirt, though."

*The one I had purchased in the charity shop!*

"Glasgow, here we come."

I was whisked away by my dark blonde driver. She looked casual, but smart, in a lilac top and trousers.

I looked around the compact Mini.

"Do you like the car?"

"Yes – I learned to drive in one."

"When?"

"Eleven years from now."

"Of course – Mr Time Traveller! You have a sense of humour."

"It helps with my predicament!"

"Are you still impressed with what you have seen?"

"Yes." I looked at Abbie and smiled.

"I meant the village."

I kept a straight face. "That's what I was referring to."

She glanced my way.

"I've become aware of many foreign visitors in the village."

"Representatives from the business community attend overseas Trade Fairs to promote the area. Because of cheaper air travel, being close to an airport and accessible by water makes our location a desirable option for tourists."

"Without doubt. The proof is in the pudding!"

"I hope my car is fast enough for you."

"Does it go any slower than seventy?"

"On occasion." She smiled.

"That's a relief!"

"Does time travel affect you in any way?"

"Not as much as this journey! I'm not sure, but I have only travelled for a short time. My hair still grows – I had to pop into the local hairdressers."

"Hair salon, James. Do you know where the Apollo is located in Glasgow?"

"Yes – close to the city centre."

"When we reach Glasgow, could you take over and drive us to the concert hall? I'm not used to cities – just villages and small towns."

"Okay and then before the concert a bite to eat." I looked at my watch. "My antique mechanism signifies we have enough time."

"Terrific."

"No need to ask if you enjoyed the concert, Abbie. I can tell by your expression."

"All the artists performed to a high standard – especially Little Stevie Wonder. But he is not much shorter than the other performers!"

"His record company will no doubt soon drop the 'little' in his name. As a pop star, his stature will grow."

"Now, where did you park my car?"

"Round the next corner." I pointed. "There it is. Do you want me to drive?"

"No, I will manage."

We reached the parked Mini and then got on our way towards Ardrishaig. As we left Glasgow, the daylight had also departed. A trail of car taillights stretched along the main route westwards.

"Well, James, what does the future have in store for those artists we watched tonight?"

"The Four Tops carry on for at least another twenty-one years. After that, the line-up changes but they still perform.

Martha and her Vandellas will disappear within two years and Diana Ross will leave the Supremes."

"Why would she leave them?"

"Personal situations within the record company."

"You mean she has influence?"

"Spot on!"

"What of Stevie Wonder?"

"He will go on to become one of the biggest pop artists of all time."

"That does not surprise me – he has talent. A terrifically soulful voice."

"Yes, he has."

"Tell me, what happens to The Beatles in the future? Don't worry – I shall keep it a secret."

I looked at Abbie. "Promise?"

"Yes, I promise."

"They go their separate ways two years from now. This won't be announced until May 1970."

Abbie looked my way. "Are you kidding me?"

"In 1969, John Lennon remarries and Paul McCartney ties the knot with a photographer called Linda Eastman."

"Is he not going steady with Jane Asher?"

"At present – but circumstances change."

"Who does John Lennon marry?"

"Yoko Ono."

"Who?"

"She is Japanese – they have already met. Don't tell his wife!"

"As you say…"

"I know. Guess which of the four is first to release a solo record and top the singles charts?"

"John Lennon?"

"Try again."

"Paul McCartney?"

"Try again."

"George Harrison?"

"Nine months after the official split he has a top selling single in the charts. Ringo and Paul followed."

"What about John Lennon?"

"Until December 1980, he did not top the singles chart. However, another two of his songs repeat this at the start of 1981."

"Any particular reason?"

"Yes, but you will have to wait and find out why."

"Then tell me this – does pop music improve in the future?"

"Well, it does develop. In the early seventies, certain pop artists dress in glamorous bright glittery costumes and dye their long hair! This will be labelled 'glam rock'. In 1976, young people form groups and appear unglamorous. Some groups behave terribly and go out of their way to shock – this is 'punk rock'. The 'electronic' age appears four years later."

"Electronic?"

"Music made by keyboard instruments. Even drum sounds are replicated by a machine!"

"Are technicians part of the group?"

"It would help if the equipment malfunctions. Other various phases come and go. The terms 'boy' and 'girl bands' become prominent in the nineties."

"The Rolling Stones – a boy band?"

I raised my eyebrows. "Good point."

"James, how do you rate music in the future?"

"A quality song shall always prevail. We are fortunate to experience an era of not just quality songs, but also formidable people who sing them. However, some talented musicians and singers emerge in the future."

"Any other exclusives you can reveal to me, apart from music?"

"People will become more aware of a healthy lifestyle. Smoking will diminish in public places."

"Similar to the Seaview Hotel and the inn?"

"Yes, and people will drink less alcohol."

"Why?"

"As an issue detrimental to good health, alcohol will be highlighted. Also, as more people own cars, they will use them to frequent places – similar to us. To consume alcohol and driving will be frowned upon."

"When driving my car, I do not drink alcohol."

"Others do."

"Any nice changes which happen?"

"More equality amongst the population."

"That sounds better – tell me more."

"Salaries for ladies increase."

"More money and more holidays?"

"Yes, and even maternity leave. Also, more choice for consumers in many aspects of life – cheaper prices."

"This future which you come from has appeal."

"There is, however, more unemployment."

"What is the cause?"

"Progress brings technological advances, therefore machines replace the workforce – men and women."

"I suppose change is inevitable."

"I wonder what Lady Lydia Beaumont would make of the time where I come from?"

"Lady Beaumont?"

"Yes, Olivia Carsell-Brown's grandmother. I met her in 1896. After a gathering at her house, I collected Mary Carsell-Brown."

"A gathering?"

"Lady Beaumont had a number of women present at her house – a meeting of some sort."

"She would have welcomed the equality you mentioned – she became a Suffragette. As a friend, my grandmother often visited her house."

I hit my hand on the dashboard. "I knew it! Incidentally, what was your grandmother's name?"

"Martha Reid. I suppose Lady Beaumont and I have something in common."

I looked at Abbie.

"Both of us have seen you in a coachman's uniform!"

I smiled.

"We should be at Ardrishaig soon."

"Already? Abbie, something else about the future."

"Yes James?"

"Cameras monitor the speed of a vehicle on the road!"

"Be home in about an hour – at normal speed!"

"Have a seat James. Tea or coffee?"

"Coffee please."

"Sugar?"

"Two please."

"Won't be long." Abbie departed the sitting room.

I sank down into a beige couch and looked around the dimly lit room. She returned with two coffees, placed them on a table and sat next to me.

"This is a tasteful room – makes you feel relaxed."

"Mother leaves all the décor ideas to me."

"Where is your mother?" I sipped my coffee.

"At my aunt's. Mother stays over and returns home the next day. How is your coffee?"

"Fine." Despite my words, it tasted too sweet.

"You really are a time traveller, aren't you?"

I smiled and nodded. "Yes, I am."

"I have more questions to ask."

"You can ask but I shall only tell you certain bits of information. For example, in the year 2000, coffee in Scotland becomes more popular than tea."

"Really?"

"Yes – also wine consumption increases dramatically. No doubt due to the continental influence. We become part of the European Community in the seventies."

"So, they accepted us?"

"Yes, they believed we would be a welcome addition. Oh, remind me later to tell you about mobile phones."

She looked intrigued. "When you travelled back to 1896, how strange that must have been! After all, over a hundred years had gone by. What about the clothes you had on? Not the style for that time – they must have looked odd!"

"I had on my coachman's outfit."

"For what reason?"

"I found it in a closet within the coach house. I tried the outfit on, looked in a mirror and then materialised in the past. Mary Carsell-Brown spotted me and assumed I had come about the vacant coachman's position."

"How fortunate."

"Yes, very much. Whilst employed as the coachman, I could blend in and acquaint myself with the era. I even got a replacement outfit!"

"Did nobody suspect anything?"

"Maybe when I vanished and then reappeared in 1912."

"But did Docharnea not have a new owner?"

"Yes, but Nancy the housekeeper still worked there. However, I got the impression she knew of my situation."

"It's incredible how the legend of the coachman started and carried on throughout the years."

"You have William and Geoffrey to thank for that!"

"They would tell my friends and I stories of how you would appear at night near the coach house."

"But when we first met in 1938, you were not afraid."

Abbie touched my arm. "James, as the coachman you did not get portrayed in a bad way."

I smiled.

"Also, when you spoke to me, I sensed only good vibes."

I finished my coffee.

"However, I am not a child any more."

"I can see that. You have grown into an attractive lady – and in all the right places."

She now smiled. "Did you meet any nice ladies on your travels?"

I paused. "Why do you ask?"

"Just curious." She drank her coffee.

"Only one." I moved closer.

Abbie put her cup on the table and then mine. "It could be too late for going back to the inn."

"What a coincidence, my sentiment also!"

She moved closer and kissed my cheek. "It would make perfect sense for you to stay here tonight."

"I believe sensible ladies are wonderful."

She whispered in my ear. "Let us go upstairs."

"Abbie?"

"Don't worry, a precaution has been taken." She led me upstairs to the landing, turned and put her arms gently on my shoulders. "I should, however, make you aware of something."

"Yes?"

Abbie looked into my eyes and glanced at an open door. "You will sleep in the guest room!" She gave me a warm, tender kiss. "Goodnight, see you in the morning." She smiled and went into her bedroom.

I entered my 'designated' room and closed the door. A lady with dignity *and* humour – terrific!

Just before midday, I arrived back at the inn. I wrote a letter to Olivia Carsell-Brown. If anything happened to me, then the contents could prevent a tragedy in the future.

I visited Docharnea that afternoon. Maybe the housekeeper would be more receptive on this occasion. I walked up to the main door and rang the bell. Seconds later I heard approaching footsteps and the door creaked open.

"Hello again."

Phew! "Has Olivia returned from her vacation?"

"No, but I expect her here at any time."

"Could you give her this letter?"

She took it. "Before you go, would you do me a favour?"

"Yes, of course."

"Someone left a large painting for the charity shop. Could you put it in the coach house?"

"No problem."

"This way." She took me to the rectangular shape with a white sheet spread over it. "Be careful."

"I used to do this many years ago." I lifted the large object. "In what room?"

"The old coachman's quarters. That is where all the charity items get stored. I'll make us some tea."

As I took it upstairs, the sheet slid off. When I reached the coachman's quarters, I placed the uncovered painting against a wall. With curiosity, I stood back to look at it. *My goodness!* I became light-headed.


*That sounded like Olivia's car.* Pearl opened the rear entrance door.

Olivia got out of her white Hillman Imp. "Hi Pearl." She stepped into the house.

"You timed that well, Olivia – I have made tea. Did you have an enjoyable time?"

"Yes, thanks." Olivia put down her brown suitcase.

"You have a visitor."

"Oh – who?"

"A James Carlisle."

Olivia paused.

"Olivia, are you all right? You've gone pale!"

"Is he in the lounge?"

"No, he is in the coach house. Somebody left a painting for you. I asked him to put it in one of the rooms."

"I must speak to him." Olivia walked across to the coach house. "James, James – where are you?" She climbed the stairs to the coachman's quarters.

Pearl entered the coachman's quarters a few minutes later.

"Pearl, he is not here. I've looked in all the rooms "

"Not here? He must have left!" She pointed. "Olivia, the painting."

"Now you look shocked, Pearl!"

"The portrait – it's him!"

Olivia stared at the painting.

"Olivia, observe the name of the artist – E. Carsell-Brown. A relative?"

"Who brought it to the house?"

"I'm not sure. I found it at the back entrance this morning, wrapped in a sheet."

"This?" Olivia picked up a crumpled piece of white linen.

"Yes."

"I shall phone Emily, my sister-in -law. She paints, but she would have contacted me if a delivery had been arranged."

"Does this belong to you?" Pearl picked up a key from the wooden floor.

Olivia examined it. "No, it's not mine."

"It looks similar to a closet key. Pearl turned towards the closet. "Maybe that one over there."

Olivia put the key into the lock, turned it and the door opened. "My goodness, a coachman's outfit!" She looked at Pearl. "Was the key missing?"

"There has not been one. Since I have worked here, that closet has remained closed."

"James must have dropped this key, but why would he have it? Also why suddenly leave? It is not the first time Mr Carlisle has vanished without even a goodbye!" Olivia locked the closet door. "Let us go back into the house and have some tea. After my journey I'm parched."

Pearl gazed at the painting. "Olivia?"

"Yes?"

"The coachman is wearing an outfit similar to that in the closet."

"That tea tasted good!" Olivia sat back on the wooden chair and put her cup on the kitchen table.

Pearl handed her a letter.

"For me?"

"Our visitor asked me to give you this upon your return from holiday."

Olivia looked at it. "'Only open on the first day of August 1989.' What a strange phrase to write on the front."

"That is twenty-two years from now!"

"I know Pearl – it's sinister. Did he appear all right?"

"Yes. Are you going to open the letter?"

"No. There must be a good reason for him to do this. I will put the letter in a safe place."

"What about the closet key?"

"I will also put that in a safe place. He may reappear to ask for it!"

Pearl washed the blue and white crockery.

"How old would you say James Carlisle looked?"

"Younger than you, Olivia."

She raised her black pencil-thin eyebrows. "Younger?"

"Around forty."

"He does not age."

"Did you say something, Olivia?"

"Just thinking out loud, Pearl. I will phone my sister-in-law later this evening. I want to clear up this mystery."

Olivia went through to the hall, picked up the cream handset and dialled Emily.

"Hello?"

"Emily, it is Olivia."

"Olivia – how are you? Did you enjoy London?"

"I had a superb time – or, should I say, swinging!"

Emily laughed. "Yes, exactly."

"Emily, did you send a painting to me for the shop?"

"No."

"The signature of the artist is E. Carsell-Brown."

"E. Carsell-Brown? Wait a minute – oh yes. Before the Great War, an Elizabeth Carsell-Brown lived at Docharnea."

"Of course! I forgot all about her. I did not realise she painted."

"I recall Charlotte talked about her. Philip found a couple of paintings in the coach house which had her signature."

"Why would she leave them in the coach house?"

"Maybe they were earmarked for a future charity shop?"

Olivia laughed. "Yes, over half a century later! Give my regards to Geoffrey."

"Shall do. Bye."

Olivia replaced the handset into the cradle. She returned to the kitchen.

"Any luck?"

"No Pearl, it's still a mystery." Olivia sat down. "Was that the doorbell, Pearl?"

"I'm covered in flour, Olivia."

Olivia went to the front entrance and opened the door. "Abigail! Come in – nice to see you."

She stepped inside. "Olivia, where can I find James Carlisle? My mother spotted him at Docharnea."

"Yes, he came here."

"He did not return to his room at the Grey Gull Inn."

"My dear, I have a long story to tell you. Perhaps a 'tall' one but nevertheless, I believe it could be true."

# Chapter 13

## *Circle of Time*

'Olivia,

*I trust twenty-two years have passed and you are well. I will now explain the reason why I wanted you to wait this length of time.*

*As a result of mistaken identity, an innocent young woman will shortly be murdered. Since I have not been in contact, I am unable to prevent this incident and need your assistance. The enclosed letter addressed to a Detective Claude Laurant could avert a loss of life. Please send this immediately.*

*I apologise for my disappearance, but had no control over a sudden and untimely departure. You will no doubt have suspected my ability to travel is not natural, but fate works in mysterious ways. This gift has allowed me the privilege to meet past family members whom I had only heard about. It does not seem so long ago when, in 1896, I met your father. In relation to my home city of Edinburgh, he would ask countless questions. It did not come as a surprise that he chose to serve there in the Army. I observed commendable traits he possessed within you. Please give my love to Abbie Anderson, and I hope that one day we can all somehow meet again.*

*Finally, I must reveal my true identity – your great-nephew, James Carsell-Brown. As an infant, thank you for the time I spent at Docharnea. It still remains a special childhood memory.'*

Olivia put down the letter. "My goodness, James! I am aware he recently moved from Aberdeen to Nice. Whilst there, he must have known of the circumstances which led to a murder being committed. However, this letter was written in 1967! It would appear he may indeed be from the future, given his knowledge of an event about to happen – foretold twenty-two years ago! My instinct had been correct. James possessed the ability to move through time but I did not suspect him of being a family member. If only William was still alive and I could recall our conversation about a certain James Carlisle. Now I had an explanation for a number of unanswered questions from the past."

Pearl entered the drawing room. "Is something wrong, Olivia? I heard your voice."

"I'm fine, Pearl." Olivia got up from the cream patterned couch.

"Did the letter contain bad news?"

"I must go to the Post Office. I have to send a letter overseas to Nice."

"Good morning, Detective."

"Morning, Estelle." Detective Laurant hung up his light-coloured jacket on the wooden coat stand.

"A letter from Scotland has arrived for your urgent attention."

"Scotland?" He raised his black eyebrows. "Let me have a look at it." He sat behind his desk.

Estelle handed over the letter.

Detective Laurant cast his eyes over it. "Mm. When does the ninth day of September fall?"

Estelle looked at her diary. "A week from Saturday."

"This looks intriguing. Is Sergeant Perez in today?"

Estelle glanced at the clock on the wall. "He passed here about ten minutes ago, headed for his office."

"Good, I shall give him a call." He picked up the handset and pressed three digits. "Bruno, it is Detective Laurant. Are you busy?"

"No, not at present. Is there a problem?"

"Information of an impending crime has come to my attention."

"I'll come over right away."

Detective Laurant replaced the handset into the cradle. "Good."

"Coffee, Detective?"

"Thank you, Estelle. Incidentally, order a calendar for the office."

"Will do." She turned around. "Detective, here is Sergeant Perez."

"Come in Bruno, have a seat."

Sergeant Perez sat opposite Detective Laurant.

"What do you make of this letter?" He moved it forward over the desk towards his colleague. "It is from Scotland."

Sergeant Perez read the letter.

"Well?"

"No signature – it may not be genuine."

"Nevertheless, the letter mentions Zoren Diaz. That is enough to get my interest."

"Who is Monique Duvallier?"

"I have no idea. The letter gives a description and adds she lives in Montpellier. Perhaps this would be a good place to start."

"Start?"

"Yes, Bruno, find out what you can about her."

"D'accord." Sergeant Perez held the letter. "The writer of this must be proficient in French."

"Yes, I noticed. Maybe a person who has studied or taught French in Scotland. Find out what you can. Meanwhile, I will contact Colonel Fontaine."

"Secret Service?"

"Yes – he will be interested in any information relevant to Zoren Diaz. You could say they remain arch-enemies!"

"See you later."

"Bruno?"

"Yes?"

"I'll hold on to the letter."

"I will take a photocopy and bring back the original." He left the room.

Detective Laurant smiled.

Estelle laid a cup of coffee on Detective Laurant's desk.

"Thanks Estelle." He continued to browse through a newspaper.

"Any important articles in the *Nice Matin* this morning?"

"Not really, Estelle. This edition does however mention the long-awaited upgrade of the approach road into Nice." He sipped his black coffee.

"About time – my boyfriend just about left the road at one of the bends last night."

"Which one?"

"Didier."

Detective Laurant smiled. "I meant which part of the road?"

"Oh, the last one – at the bottom of the hill."

"But he drives fast, does he not?"

"Some of the time." She laughed. "In fact, most of the time!"


"Detective, Sergeant Perez is on line two."

Detective Laurant picked up the handset and sat back on his brown leather chair. "Yes, Bruno?"

"I have traced three females who fit or closely resemble the description and called Monique Duvallier."

"Three?"

"Yes. One is in Quebec, Canada. She has gone to visit her parents. Another is about to leave for Italy on honeymoon. The third lives in an apartment near the centre of Montpellier. She has a sister who stays in Nice. It appears person number three could be the candidate."

"I agree, Bruno. Monitor her movements and contact me of any developments. Until Saturday, five more days remain. She could be about to spend the weekend with her sister. Maybe a possible departure on Thursday or Friday."

"I shall keep you informed."

"D'accord, Bruno."

"Detective, Colonel Fontaine is on line three."

"Put him through." Detective Laurant paused. "Colonel, how are you?"

"Just back from a diplomatic trip."

"I understand, Colonel. Did it go well?"

"As well as can be expected. I got your message about Diaz. What does this relate to?"

"I received a letter last week. It named Diaz being responsible for the death of an innocent woman."

"What is her name?"

"Monique Duvallier."

"Did you say Monique?"

"Yes, Colonel."

"At what location did this incident take place?"

"Close to the Nice seafront."

"Who sent this letter?"

Detective Laurant held the letter in front of him. "No signature appears on the letter."

"Can it be genuine?"

"I had my doubts, Colonel. However, there is such a person in Montpellier and she has a sister in Nice. Colonel, are you still there?"

"Yes, Claude, still here. Keep me informed of any developments."

"I will, Colonel."

"'Bye, Claude."

Detective Laurant put the handset into the cradle and turned to his secretary. "Estelle, do we have a timetable in the office for trains from Montpellier to Nice?"

"We do, but it is now out of date. I will be in the vicinity of the station at lunchtime. I could call in and get a new timetable."

"Excellent, thank you."

She smiled. "But I shall require an extended lunch period!"

"Naturellement!"


"Detective Laurant, Colonel Fontaine is on line two."

He picked up the handset. "Good afternoon, Colonel."

"Good afternoon, Claude. Has there been any developments concerning Monique Duvallier?"

"Not yet, Colonel. One of my men is in Montpellier. He will contact me if anything transpires. I expect to hear from him soon. If Madame Duvallier travels to Nice, her departure should be imminent. Only two days remains until Saturday."

"When the murder is supposed to take place?"

"Yes, Colonel."

"Keep me informed."

"Will do." Detective Laurant replaced the handset. Strange, the Colonel does not act in an impatient manner.

"Did you say something, Detective?"

"I could do with a coffee, Estelle."

She brought a coffee to his desk. "Detective?"

"Yes, Estelle?"

"Would it be possible to leave earlier tonight?"

He sipped his coffee. "Ah. How early?"

"Only an hour. I have arranged to meet someone at the station. My friend Lori from Cannes has come to visit me."

"For the holiday weekend?"

"Yes. I'm going to take her around the city."

"Any particular places?"

"She enjoys cultural venues; therefore we'll frequent the museums and art galleries."

"If she prefers modern art, then the Musée Massena should impress her."

"Yes, I've been there on several occasions."

"I'm sure she may also enjoy the market in the old part of Nice."

"Of course – plus the newly opened nearby Ascenseu nightspot! Lori enjoys dance music, and this club plays it non-stop."

"I believe the rival Ambassade serve free champagne for one hour up till midnight."

"Do they?" Estelle smiled. "That could sway our decision!"

"Have a good time, wherever you go!"

"Goodnight Detective – see you Monday."

A police officer knocked on Detective Laurant's door. "Morning, Detective."

"Morning, Alain, come in. Any serious incidents last night?"

The officer held a report in his hand. "Three arrests for alcohol over-indulgence, two for theft and another two for breach of the peace."

"Not bad for a Friday night."

"Excuse me, Alain, I'll answer this call." He picked up the handset. "Yes?"

"Detective, it is Marie on the main switchboard. I have Sergeant Perez on the line."

"Put him through."

"Detective, Bruno here."

"I can just hear you."

"I am at Montpellier Airport. Monique Duvallier has booked a seat on the one o'clock flight to Nice."

"Follow her, Bruno. Can you get a seat on the flight?"

"I have already done so. We are due to arrive in Nice at twenty five minutes after one."

"I will send Alain Boyer to meet you at Nice Airport. He will be just outside the terminal building – the car pick-up area. When she gets off the plane, stay close to her."

"D'accord."

Detective Laurant replaced the handset. "Alain, I want you to meet Bruno at the airport. He will board a flight from Montpellier in one hour. He should be out of Nice Airport at around thirty minutes past one."

"That is a short flight!"

"Yes, the distance can't be more than two hundred miles."

"Is it not convenient to drive or take the train?"

"Yes, but Bruno has to follow one Monique Duvallier. Here is her description."

The officer took the piece of paper. "One and three quarter metres tall, twenty four years old, slim and with shoulder-length blonde hair."

"Do not lose sight of her."

"I would not want to! You have my assurance, Detective." He turned to leave Detective Laurant's office.

"Alain?"

He turned around.

"Change into plain clothes."

"Will do, Detective."

"Bruno, over here!" cried Alain as he sat in the navy blue Peugeot.

Bruno looked around

Alain waved his hand in the air through the open window.

His colleague walked over. "Well timed, Alain." He pointed. "There she is – just about to get into that yellow taxi. Let's go!" He opened the passenger door and jumped in.

Alain started the car and they drove off. "Did you enjoy Montpellier?"

Bruno shook his head. "Comme-ci, comme-ca."

"Why have we to follow this person? Detective Laurant did not reveal much to me."

"This young woman could be connected to a murder crime. Detective Laurant does not have evidence, but he is concerned she may be the victim."

"When does this happen?"

"According to Detective Laurant's source, in about five hours!"

He glanced at his colleague. "Is his source a fortune-teller?"

"I agree, Alain – however, we shall soon find out."

"The taxi is headed for the old part of the city."

"Yes, and within the speed limit!"

"Look, Bruno, he has begun to slow down."

"Pull in here."

Bruno pointed to a space by the roadside.

His colleague brought the car to a halt.

"There she goes – into that apartment block."

"Do you want me to park the car closer? I've spotted a space just opposite the building."

"No, here is fine." Bruno looked at his watch. "Drat – my watch has stopped! What is the time?"

Alain looked at his watch. "Almost fifteen minutes past two."

"No doubt the reason why I am hungry! Since my breakfast in the hotel, my food intake has registered zero."

"There is a café just around the next corner."

"Good – I'll get a pack of sandwiches. Do you want anything?"

"No, I'm fine, Bruno."

"Back soon." He got out of the car and made his way towards the café.

"That was quick!"

Bruno closed the passenger door. "I'm a quick eater. The chicken tasted delicious. I feel better now."

"There are two men standing in a doorway opposite the apartment block."

"When did they arrive?"

"Not long after you left."

"Let us wait and see what they do next."

"Do you recognise either of them?"

"No, they are not familiar. Both do not look the amiable type!" He nudged his colleague. "Look, there is Monique Duvallier!"

"Yes, and those men have started to follow her."

"Alain, did you bring a gun?"

"Detective Laurant issued me with two, just in case." He handed one over.

"Good." He checked the gun and put it inside his jacket. "Allez!"

Alain locked his door. "Bruno?"

"What?"

"Do you have change for the parking meter?"

"To heck with the meter!"

"She is a fast walker."

"No doubt the other two will be of the same opinion. This young woman will test all of our stamina."

"She has entered Nico's Bar and Diner."

"Thank goodness – this forty year old is out of breath! Our two 'stalkers' have taken up a position nearby."

"Bruno, I could do with something to drink."

"Okay. Let's go inside – we can monitor her from inside."

"What is the time now Alain?"

He looked at his watch. "Almost five o'clock."

Bruno nudged his colleague. "It looks as though someone could be about to leave. She is going to pay her bill. Quick, Alain – pay ours! I'll see you outside." Bruno exited the café.

Alain paid the waiter and rushed outside.

Bruno looked onwards. "She's headed for the beach. The fortune-teller may be genuine after all! As in the letter to Detective Laurant, events have started to unfold."

"And those two still remain in attendance, Bruno."

"As we do also, Alain."

"Look, she has wandered onto the beach."

"Maybe for a stroll? There is a secluded section of the beach further on. I will wager our two stalkers make for that area. There they go! Let us pursue with caution."

"The young woman seems unaware of the situation. She is walking along the beach and casually looking out to sea."

"They are not amateurs given their discretion. The only way we would suspect them is because of information from a source. She will soon approach the secluded area."

"They are closing in on her!"

"Alain, contact the station on your communication device. Detective Laurant awaits our call. Tell him we will move into position."

His colleague brought out the device from an inside pocket and called Detective Laurant. "Impelle."

Bruno stared at him.

Alain smiled. "A code word." He replaced the device into his pocket.

"Have your gun ready."

Alain held it in his hand. He moved towards the area with his colleague.

"I hear voices," Bruno whispered. "Wait here behind this wall." He pulled out a small tape recorder from his side pocket, adjusted for maximum clarity and pushed the start button. After a few minutes, Bruno nodded.

The two men emerged from their secluded position. Alain circled round the back and Bruno confronted the two men.

"Hands up, gentlemen – now!" He pointed his gun at both of them. "Search them, Constable!"

Alain searched the two men. "Two handguns, Sergeant." He emptied out the bullets and threw the guns aside.

"I trust you have a licence for those?"

"Who are you?" said the stout villain.

"My name is Sergeant Perez of Nice Counter-Espionage, and this is my colleague, Constable Boyer."

Bruno looked towards Monique Duvallier. "Are you all right, Madame?"

"Yes, I think so." She picked up her bag.

"Gentlemen, we will give you an escort back to the centre of Nice – Police HQ!"

"We have not committed any crime," said the bald villain.

"Oh, yes you have! Observe this small accessory I have in my possession. This has recorded your conversation with this young woman. Also, we will check your gun licences. Ah, I hear our colleagues." Sergeant Perez looked towards the promenade. "They have arrived, *bon*!"

A plain-clothes officer approached Monique Duvallier. "Madame, I am Detective Laurant. How do you feel?"

"I'll be fine. Your men came just at the right time." She looked towards the two men being led away by several police officers. "They took my bag and searched it. They referred to me as Michelle."

"Michelle?"

"Yes, my sister."

"We can give you a lift home. Where do you stay?"

"Eight Rue De La Loge. It is not far from here – I can walk."

"It is no problem. Two of my officers shall escort you home. Can you call into Police HQ to make a statement?"

"Would Monday suffice?"

"Yes, Madame – here is my card. If you have any problems, do not hesitate to get in touch. Oh, Madame, is your sister at home?"

"No, I do not know where she is."

"Did she expect you?"

"Yes."

Detective Laurant took Monique to a police car and opened the door. "Please, have a seat."

"Thank you, Detective."

Detective Laurant closed the door and walked over to Sergeant Perez. "Bruno, you and Alain each take a shift to watch the apartment block."

"Do you believe there is more to this?"

"Yes, something does not equate! Those two 'gentlemen' could be professional hit-men. Someone may try again. Also her sister is missing. I shall endeavour to trace her whereabouts."

"Hello?"

"Michelle, it is James."

"James?"

"Yes – we met last night."

"Michelle is not here. I am Monique, her sister."

"Do you know where Michelle is?"

"I arrived at the apartment yesterday afternoon but she was not here to greet me. I do not know where she has gone."

"How did you gain access?"

"She had previously given me passkeys to enter the building and the apartment in case of an emergency. It's not like her to just disappear! When she returns, I will ask her to give you a call."

"Merci bien."

"Je vous en prie."

James set the handset back into the cradle. *Strange – why would she just leave?*

"Can I help you, Madame?"

"I have come to see Detective Laurant."

"Your name?"

"Monique Duvallier."

"Please have a seat, I will contact him."

"Thank you." Monique sat on a firm wooden chair adjacent to the reception desk.

The officer picked up a black handset and pressed three digits. "Detective Laurant?"

"Yes."

" Monique Duvallier is here."

"I will speak with her now."

"D'accord." The officer turned towards Monique. "Madame, Detective Laurant will see you now."

"Where do I go?"

He pointed. "Down the corridor and first door on the left."

"Thanks."

Detective Laurant opened his office door. "Madame Duvallier, please come in. Take a seat. Coffee?"

"No thanks." She sat down on a softer chair and looked around the room.

Detective Laurant sat down behind his desk and smiled. "It is due for redecoration later this year."

Monique smiled.

"After Saturday's experience, how are you?"

"Better – but my sister has vanished! Michelle always tells me in advance if she is about to go on vacation or a short trip."

"The two of you had made an arrangement for last Saturday?"

"Yes, we had."

"I shall look into the matter. One of my officers will take a statement from you about the incident. Also give him information about your sister. The minute I hear anything, I will contact you."

"Thank you." Monique stood up. "Oh, Detective, a foreign gentleman telephoned the apartment yesterday. He wanted to speak with Michelle."

"A foreign gentleman?"

"Yes, he may have been English."

"Why did he call your sister?"

"It may have been connected to her job."

"Her job?"

"She deals with foreign business contacts."

"Who does she work for?"

"The government; research and development."

"In Nice?"

"I believe she travels around the region."

Detective Laurant got out of his seat and approached his visitor. "What do you intend to do now?"

"This afternoon I leave for Montpellier. I have to return back at work tomorrow."

"Do you also work for the government?"

"No, I work as an account manager for a sports firm in Montpellier."

Detective Laurant escorted his visitor to reception. "Bon voyage, Madame." He shook her hand.

"Thank you, Detective, and goodbye."

Detective Laurant returned to his room and sniffed the air. It was a nice scent. Estelle came into the room. She also sniffed the air. Soft, light, citrusy. Detective Laurant looked at her and smiled.

"Monique Duvallier!"

"Indeed!"

"Estelle, can you get me Colonel Fontaine?"

She lifted her desk handset and tapped three buttons with her long rouge fingernails. "Detective, the voicemail states he is not in his office today and won't be back until Thursday."

"No doubt another business trip!"

A plain-clothes officer entered the room. "Detective, here is Madame Duvallier's statement." He handed it to him.

"Thank you, Edgar." Detective Laurant read it. "The English gentleman called himself James."

"He did not give a surname. Do you believe he could be connected to the incident?"

"I am not sure. I believe the Colonel knows more about this situation than any of us. Until Thursday, we will just have to wait."

Estelle put down her handset. "Detective, a call from reception. A gentleman wants to report a missing person."

"Can nobody else deal with it?"

"It concerns Michelle Duvallier."

Detective Laurant organised his desk papers and then went to reception. "Monsieur, my name is Detective Laurant – can I help you?"

The gentleman stood up. "I hope so. It relates to a lady who has vanished."

"Please come this way." Detective Laurant led the gentleman to his office. He held out his hand. "Have a seat."

The gentleman sat down.

Detective Laurant sat down behind his desk and reached for a pen and paper. "Her name, monsieur?"

"Michelle Duvallier."

"Can you describe her?"

"About one and three quarter metres tall; late twenties, slim, and blonde hair."

"Short or long?"

"Shoulder-length."

"When did you last see her?"

"A week ago. We went for a drink in the evening."

"Have you known her for some time?"

"A week."

Detective Laurant laid down his pen. "Why do you think she has disappeared?"

"Since last Saturday I have tried to contact her, but without success."

"Maybe she has gone on a business trip or a vacation?"

"No – I feel something could be wrong. As we were having a drink, a man entered the establishment and she panicked. We had to leave."

"Did she give his identity?"

"An acquaintance of her ex-partner."

"Maybe a possible explanation why she wanted to leave?"

"When I arrived home, my apartment had been searched."

"Did you report this?"

"No – nothing got taken and no damage occurred." The gentleman moved forward on his seat. "I called Michelle on Sunday. Her sister answered – even she does not know where Michelle is."

"Are you from England?"

"No, Scotland."

"Monsieur, what is your name?"

"Carsell-Brown."

"How do you spell your first name?"

"J-a-m-e-s."

"Did you not say Carsell is your first name?"

"No, that is my surname."

"What about Brown?"

"That is also my surname."

"You have two surnames?"

"Yes, with a hyphen in between."

"D'accord. Excuse me, I'll answer this call." Detective Laurant picked up the handset.

"Claude, sorry for the delay in getting back to you. Michelle Duvallier is safe and well. I will explain the situation to you in private. Can you be at my office this evening – say, seven o'clock?"

"Yes, that should be fine, Colonel."

"Claude, Michelle Duvallier met a man from Scotland."

"Yes, Colonel – what about him?" Detective Laurant glanced across his desk.

"I would like to meet this person."

"Why, Colonel?"

"He could be useful to us."

"Useful?"

"One of Zoren Diaz's men spotted him. I have devised a way to catch Diaz with his assistance."

"Diaz is involved?"

"Yes – it was two of his men confronted Monique Duvallier."

"Colonel, I have the person you wish to meet with me. He called into Police HQ to report the disappearance of Michelle Duvallier."

"Is he available to meet with us tomorrow morning?"

"I will ask him." Detective Laurant put his hand over the receiver. "Monsieur, Michelle Duvallier is safe and well. I am speaking to a Colonel Fontaine of our Secret Service and he wants to meet you."

"Why me?"

"All shall be explained. Are you available tomorrow morning at nine o'clock?"

"Fine."

Detective Laurant removed his hand from the receiver. "That will be suitable, Colonel."

"Claude, has he ever acted?"

"As in, being an actor?"

James Carsell-Brown had a curious expression.

"Yes, Claude – ask him."

"Monsieur, have you any acting experience?"

"A small part in a primary school play."

"Colonel, you may have a problem."

"We can discuss the situation tomorrow morning."

"Okay, Colonel." Detective Laurant put his handset into the cradle.

"At least I know that Michelle Duvallier is not in any danger."

"Everything shall be explained tomorrow, monsieur. Be here at nine o'clock to meet the Colonel."

"I'll be here."

"I will see you out, monsieur." He led his visitor to the exit and grinned. "I witnessed your national rugby team beaten in Paris last March."

"I witnessed your national football team beaten at Hampden Park, Glasgow in the same month!"

"Touché monsieur. See you tomorrow." Detective Laurant smiled and shook his visitor's hand.

"Au revoir, Detective."


"Madame Duvallier?"

"Yes, this is her." She sat down at her desk.

"It is Detective Laurant." He doodled on a piece of office paper.

"Good afternoon, Detective. You have just caught me – I was about to go for lunch."

"I will not delay you, Madame. I have good news which concerns your sister – she is not in any danger."

"Where is she?"

"On a work-related government assignment."

"Assignment?"

"Yes. An urgent one therefore she had to immediately leave her apartment."

"Thanks for your call."

"No problem, Madame – goodbye, and have a nice lunch."

"Good morning Monsieur Carsell-Brown. Come this way. Colonel Fontaine should be here shortly." Detective Laurant took his visitor from reception to an interview room. "Please, make yourself comfortable.

"Thanks." The room was pretty basic; plain walls, three chairs and a table.

Detective Laurant returned to his office. He glanced towards the door.

Colonel Fontaine entered with Michelle Duvallier. "Good morning, Claude – is Monsieur Carsell-Brown here?"

"Yes, Colonel, next door."

"Reunite him with Michelle and we will chat to him later."

"Madame Duvallier, this way please." He led her to the entrance of the interview room and then walked in alone. "Monsieur, I have someone who wishes to speak with you."

"Michelle!" James cried.

"Hello James, how are you?"

"I will leave the two of you. No doubt you have much to discuss." Detective Laurant left the room and returned to his office.

"Did he appear glad to see her, Claude?"

"Yes, Colonel, he was."

"I want him to meet with Diaz and return the documents Michelle obtained."

"The documents Diaz originally stole from our government?"

"That is what spies do! When the exchange is made, my men will arrest Diaz."

"Caught red-handed!"

"Yes, Claude. Do you believe he can carry this out?"

"Well, Colonel, he may not be James Bond – but he is British!"

The Colonel looked at his watch. "We will give him another ten minutes with Michelle."

Detective Laurant entered the interview room. "Monsieur Carsell-Brown, may I present Colonel Fontaine of the French Secret Service?"

The Colonel walked forward.

James Carsell-Brown stood up.

"I am pleased to meet you, Monsieur Carsell-Brown. Michelle has spoken to me about you." He gave a firm handshake.

"In a positive way I trust, Colonel?"

"Most definitely – that is why I wanted to meet you. When one of my top operatives makes a recommendation, then I listen."

"Recommendation?" He raised his fair eyebrows.

The Colonel twirled his grey moustache. "We have a situation, monsieur. The only way to resolve it may be the capture of a certain person and his gang."

"Michelle told me about what happened to her sister."

"If that gang is not apprehended, then other people shall be in danger and lives could be lost."

"What can I do, Colonel?"

"Sit down, monsieur, and I will explain."


Detective Laurant glanced at his watch. "Almost nine o'clock. It should not be long now, Colonel."

"I hope so, Claude. Having to sit around makes me nervous."

"If he pulls this off, will he get a commendation?"

Colonel Fontaine laughed. "And all the French champagne he desires!"

"I believe he enjoys beer, Colonel."

"He can have that as well! It could be said Monsieur Carsell-Brown had the misfortune to meet Michelle Duvallier given her circumstances. However, it has turned out fortunate for us. We have an opportunity to capture Diaz."

Detective Laurant checked his watch again.

"This type of situation always tends to drag on." Colonel Fontaine glanced across at the second car. "No doubt Bruno and the others feel the same way."

"Colonel, the communicator is flashing." Detective Laurant lifted it off the dashboard. "Lucas has sent the code word."

"Advancez, Andre! Start the car and head towards the underpass."

The agent turned the ignition, roared the car into action and sped off.

Detective Laurent pointed. "Colonel – there is Diaz!"

On a barren piece of land, the two vehicles screeched to a halt alongside Diaz and his silver BMW. Armed government agents got out.

Colonel Fontaine aimed his gun at Diaz. "Hands in the air! Any false move and I will not hesitate to shoot. I'll take that file." The Colonel grabbed it. "Bruno, get the others."

"My pleasure, Colonel." Bruno pointed a shotgun at Diaz's car. "You three – out!"

The Colonel stared at Diaz. "You won't sneak out of this."

Diaz had a stunned look on his face.

"Caught at last – and with the assistance of an amateur!" The Colonel glanced at Detective Laurant. "Put him in my car, Claude."

"Yes, Colonel." He led Diaz away.

Colonel Fontaine walked up to James Carsell-Brown and shook his hand. "Bravo monsieur – bravo." He took the suitcase full of money and got into his car. He rolled down the window and raised a clenched fist.

The two navy blue, unmarked government cars moved off, engulfed in a storm of dust. A lone agent followed them in Diaz's car back to HQ.

James Carsell-Brown returned to Lucas's car.

"Where to, monsieur?"

"Just drop me at my apartment, Lucas. I'm drained!"

"Pas de problem, monsieur."

"Can I have another look at the device you operated?"

"Here you are, monsieur." He handed it over.

"Ingenious, and compact. The device no doubt has potential for a future commercial market."

"Diaz thought so!"

Detective Laurant lifted his desk handset. He looked through his office telephone notebook. Carsell-Brown, there it was. "I hope he does not mind a call on a Saturday morning!"

Detective Laurant pressed the digits and waited. No answer – perhaps he had gone out to do some early chores.

"Hello?"

"Monsieur Carsell-Brown, it is Detective Laurant."

"Who?"

"Detective Laurant."

"What time is it?"

"Eight o'clock, monsieur."

"Why are you calling?"

"Can you let me have a written statement of the incident with Diaz last week? We require this for our records."

"When do you need it for?"

"At your leisure, monsieur."

"How about Monday evening? I can call into Police HQ around seven o'clock."

"Perfect, monsieur! See you then."

"'Bye."

Detective Laurant smiled. "I apologise monsieur – c'est le weekend, la long lain!"

"Detective Laurant, Monsieur Carsell-Brown has arrived."

"I will see him now."

The Duty Officer put down the telephone. "This way, please." He took the visitor to a now-familiar office and knocked on the door.

Detective Laurant appeared. "Punctual as ever, monsieur. Come in and have a seat."

"Thanks." He handed over an envelope. "This contains the statement you requested."

Detective Laurant opened the envelope, took out the written piece of paper and read it. "Bon." He popped the statement into a yellow folder. "I will be back soon, monsieur – make yourself comfortable."

Detective Laurant left the office, complete with folder.

His visitor got up and walked towards the window. *The birds are in good voice! Autumn will soon be here – glad I don't have to pick up all those leaves from the park trees.* He looked at his watch. Detective Laurant had been gone for half an hour. *Ah, footsteps.*

"Sorry for the delay, monsieur." He sat behind his desk, put down the folder and took out the contents.

"Anything wrong, Detective?"

"Not so much wrong, monsieur, but strange."

"In what way?"

Detective Laurant held up a sheet of writing paper. "This is the statement you gave me which relates to recent events with Diaz." He laid it in the centre of his desk.

"Yes?"

"Here is a letter I received several weeks ago." He placed it next to the statement. "The handwriting is a near-perfect match! See for yourself."

The visitor picked up the letter and studied it. "My goodness! Who wrote this?"

"We do not know."

"No name or address on the reverse of the envelope?"

"Nothing, monsieur – all we have is a postmark from the country of origin."

"Which country?"

"Scotland."

"I did not write this."

"Our handwriting expert has confirmed it must be the same person."

"This letter describes the murder of Monique Duvallier, along with another incident which will happen."

"Yes, and because of this information, certain tragedies have been avoided."

"Extraordinary!"

"As you will notice from the letter, it makes reference to Guerrin, Diaz's bodyguard, who escaped from our custody. He did complain of severe stomach pains and was taken to the local hospital. He managed to elude one guard but not the additional officers deployed to watch all possible getaway exits."

"He would have come after me."

"Without a doubt."

"Monique Duvallier and I owe the person who wrote this letter a debt of gratitude. But how did this individual know what events would take place?"

"Our forensic specialist is of the opinion the letter had been written between twenty and twenty three years ago."

"That rules me out – I had not long started school and could barely write!"

"An intriguing mystery, monsieur, but one with a beneficial outcome – even though we are unaware of the source."

"It's uncanny how similar this handwriting is to mine. Even the letter 't' has been crossed in a diagonal slant."

Detective Laurant sat back on his chair and clasped his hands. "Maybe you have still to write the letter, monsieur."

"The future has not yet happened, Detective." He laid the letter back on the desk.

"Perhaps not, but at least Monique Duvallier now has one." Detective Laurant eased out of his chair. "I'll see you out." He led his visitor to the main exit door and gave him a warm handshake. "Thank you, monsieur."

"My pleasure, Detective Laurant."


As darkness descended that evening, I stood on the balcony of my apartment and gazed down onto the empty street below. Could it be that certain individuals fulfil a destiny to act as a protector against wrongful misfortune? Was this fate; someone or something which shapes our existence?

Maybe events have already been pre-ordained and, in particular instances, the wrong is put right.

Only time may reveal the answer.